TWELVE SUMMER ROMANCES

Leigh Bardugo

Jennifer E. Smith

Francesc

Libba Bray

Jon Skovron

Cassandra Clare

Veronica Roth

SUMMER DAYS & SUMMER NIGHTS

Brandy Colbert

Stephanie Perkins

Tim Federle

Nina LaCour

Lev Grossman

Edited by STEPHANIE PERKINS

MACMILLAN

First published in the US 2016 by St. Martin's Press

First published in the UK 2016 by Macmillan Children's Books
an imprint of Pan Macmillan
20 New Wharf Road, London N1 9RR
Associated companies throughout the world
www.panmacmillan.com

ISBN 978-1-5098-0989-9

FOR JARROD, BEST FRIEND AND TRUE LOVE

CONTENTS

HEAD, SCALES, TONGUE, TAIL

LEIGH BARDUGO

HEAD

There were a lot of stories about Annalee Saperstein and why she came to Little Spindle, but Gracie's favorite was the heat wave.

In 1986, New York endured a summer so miserable that anyone who could afford to leave the city did. The pavement went soft with the heat, a man was found dead in his bathtub with an electric fan half-submerged in the water next to his hairy knees, and the power grid flickered on and off like a bug light rattling with moths. On the Upper West Side, above the bakeries and delicatessens, the Woolworth's and the Red Apple market, people slept on top of their sheets, sucked on handkerchiefs full of crushed ice, and opened their windows wide, praying for a breeze. That was why, when the Hudson leaped its banks and went looking for trouble on a hot July night, the river found Ruth Blonksy's window wedged open with a dented Candie's shoe box.

Earlier that day, Ruth had been in Riverside Park with her friends, eating lemon pucker ices and wearing a persimmon-colored shift that was really a vintage nightgown she'd dyed with two boxes of Rit and mixed success. Rain had been promised for days, but the sky hung heavy over the city, a distended gray belly of cloud that refused to split. Sweat beading over her skin, Ruth had leaned against the park railing to look down at the swaying surface of the river, opaque and nearly black beneath the overcast sky, and had the eerie sense that the water was looking back at her.

Then a drop of lemon ice trickled from the little pink spoon in her hand, startling as a cold tongue lapping at her pulse point, and Marva Allsburg shouted, "We're going to Jaybee's to look at records."

Ruth licked the lemon ice from her wrist and thought no more of the river.

But later that night, when she woke—her sheets soaked through with sweat, a tangle of reeds at the foot of her bed—that sticky trail of sugar was what came first to mind. She'd fallen asleep in her clothes, and her persimmon shift clung wetly to her stomach. Beneath it, her body burned feverish with half-remembered dreams of the river god, a muscular shape that moved through the deep current of sleep, his gray skin speckled blue and green. Her lips felt just kissed, and her head was clouded as if she'd risen too fast from some great depth. It took a long moment for her ears to clear, for her to recognize the moss-and-metal smell of wet concrete, and then to make sense of the sound coming through her open window—rain falling in a steady patter onto the predawn streets below. The heat had broken at last.

Nine months later, Ruth gave birth to a baby with kelp-green eyes and ropes of seaweed hair. When Ruth's father kicked her out of their walk-up, calling her names in Polish and English and making angry noises about the Puerto Rican boy who had taken Ruth to her junior prom, Annalee Saperstein took her in, ignoring the neighborhood whispers and clucking. Annalee worked at the twenty-four-hour coin laundry on West Seventy-Ninth. No one was sure when she slept, because whenever you walked past, she always seemed to be sitting at the counter doing her crossword beneath the fluorescent lights, the machines humming and rattling, no matter the hour. Joey Pastan had mouthed off to her once when he ran out of quarters, and he swore the dryers had actually growled at him, so nobody was entirely surprised that Annalee believed Ruth Blonksy. And when, waiting in line at Gitlitz Delicatessen, Annalee smacked Ruth's father in the chest with the half pound of thinly sliced corned beef she'd just purchased and snapped that river spirits were not to be trusted, no one dared to argue.

Ruth's daughter refused milk. She would only drink salt water and eat pound after pound of oysters, clams, and tiny crayfish, which had to be delivered in crates to Annalee's cramped apartment. But the diet must have agreed with her, because the green-eyed baby grew into a beautiful girl who was spotted by a talent scout while crossing Amsterdam Avenue. She became a famous model, renowned for her full lips and liquid walk, and bought her mother a penthouse on Park Avenue that they decorated with paintings of desert flowers and dry creek beds. They gave Annalee Saperstein a tidy sum that allowed her to quit her job at the coin laundry and move out of the city to Little Spindle, where she opened her Dairy Queen franchise.

At least, that was one of the stories about how Annalee Saperstein came to Little Spindle, and Gracie liked it because she felt it made a kind of sense. Why else would Annalee get copies of French and Italian *Vogue* when all she ever wore were polyester housedresses and Birkenstock sandals with socks?

People said Annalee *knew* things. It was why Donna Bakewell came to see her the summer her terrier got hit by a car and she couldn't seem to stop crying—not even to sleep, or to buy a can of green beans at the Price Chopper, or to answer the phone. People would call her up and just hear her sobbing and hiccupping on the other end. But somehow a chat with Annalee managed what no doctor or pill could and dried Donna's tears right up. It was why, when Jason Mylo couldn't shake the idea that his ex-wife had put a curse on his new Chevy truck, he paid a late-night visit to the DQ to see Annalee. And it was also why, when Gracie Michaux saw something that looked very much like a sea monster breach the waters of Little Spindle Lake, she went looking for Annalee Saperstein.

Gracie had been sitting on the bank of what she considered *her* cove, a rocky crescent on the south side of the lake that no one else seemed to know or care about. It was too shady for sunbathers and devoid of the picnic tables and rope swings that drew vacationers like beacons during the tourist season. She'd been skipping stones, telling herself not to pick the scab on her knee, because she wanted to look good in the jean shorts she'd cut even shorter on her fourteenth birthday, and then doing it anyway, when she heard a splash. One, two, three humps breached the blue surface of the water, a glittering little mountain range, there and then gone, followed by the slap of—Gracie's mind refused to accept it, and at the same time clamored—a *tail*.

Gracie scrabbled backward up the banks to the pines and dragged herself to her feet, heart jackrabbiting in her chest, waiting for the water to part again or for something huge and scaly to haul itself onto the sand, but nothing happened. Her mouth was salty with the taste of blood. She'd bitten her tongue. She spat once, leaped onto her bicycle, and pedaled as hard as she could down the bumpy dirt path to the smooth pavement of the main road, thighs burning as she hurtled through town.

It wasn't much of a hurtle, because Little Spindle wasn't much of a town. There was a mini-mart, a gas station with the town's lone ATM, a veterinary clinic, a string of souvenir shops, and the old Rotary hall, which had become the public library after the library in Greater Spindle flooded ten years before. Little Spindle had never gotten the traffic or the clusters of condos and fancy homes that crowded around Greater Spindle, just a smattering of rental cottages and the Spindrift Inn. Despite the fact that the lake was nearly as big as Greater Spindle and surrounded by perfectly good land, there was something about Little Spindle Lake that put people off.

The lake looked pleasant enough from a distance, glimpsed

through the pines in vibrant blue flashes, sunlight spiking off its surface in jewel-bright shards. But as you got closer you started to feel your spirits sink, and by the time you were at its shore, you felt positively mournful. You'd convince yourself to walk down to the beach anyway, maybe swing out on the old tire, but as you let go of the rope, you'd hang for the briefest second above the water and you'd know with absolute certainty that you'd made a horrible mistake, that once you vanished beneath the surface, you would never be seen again, that the lake was not a lake but a mouth—hungry, blue, and sullen. Some people seemed impervious to the effects of Little Spindle, but others refused to even put a toe in the water.

The only place that did real business year round was the Dairy Queen, despite the Stewart's only a few miles away. But why Annalee had chosen to set up shop in Little Spindle instead of Greater Spindle was a mystery to everyone but her.

Gracie didn't head straight for the DQ that day—not at first. In fact, she got all the way home, tossed her bike down in the yard, and had her hand on the screen door before she caught herself. Eric and her mom liked to spend Saturdays in the backyard, just lying next to each other on plastic lounge chairs, snoozing, hands clasped like a couple of otters. They both worked long hours at the hospital in Greater Spindle and hoarded sleep like it was a hobby.

Gracie hovered there at the door, hand outstretched. What could she really say to her mother? Her weary mother who never stopped looking worried, even in sleep? For a moment, at the edge of the lake, Gracie had been a kid again, but she was fourteen. She should know better.

She got back on her bike and pedaled slowly, meditatively, in no direction at all, belief seeping away as if the sun was sweating it out of her. What had she actually seen? A fish maybe? A few fish? But some deeper sense must have been guiding her, because when she got to the Dairy Queen she turned into the half-full parking lot.

Annalee Saperstein was at a table by the window, as she always was, doing her crossword, a Peanut Buster Parfait melting in front of her. Gracie mostly knew Annalee because she liked listening to the stories about her, and because her mom was always sending Gracie to ask Annalee over for dinner.

"She's old and alone," Gracie's mother would say.

"She seems to like it."

Her mom would wave her finger in the air like she was conducting an invisible orchestra. "No one likes being alone."

Gracie tried not to roll her eyes. She tried.

Now she slid into the hard red seat across from Annalee and said, "Do you know anything about Idgy Pidgy?"

"Good afternoon to you, too," Annalee grumped, without looking up from her crossword.

"Sorry," Gracie said. She thought of explaining that she'd had a strange start to her day, but instead opted for "How are you?"

"Not dead yet. It would kill you to use a comb?"

"No point." Gracie tried to rope her slick black hair back into its ponytail. "My hair doesn't take well to instruction." She waited then said, "So . . . the monster in the lake?"

She knew she wasn't the first person to claim she'd seen something in the waters of Little Spindle. There had been a bunch of sightings in the sixties and seventies, though Gracie's mom claimed that was because everyone was on drugs. The town council had even tried to turn it into a tourist draw by dubbing it the Idgy Pidgy—"Little Spindle's Little Monster"—and painting the image of a friendly-looking sea serpent with googly eyes on the WELCOME TO LITTLE SPINDLE sign. It hadn't caught on, but you could still see its outline on the sign, and a few winters back someone had spray painted a huge phallus onto it. For the three days it took the town council to notice and get someone to paint over it, the sign looked like the Idgy Pidgy was trying to have sex with the *E* at the end of LITTLE SPINDLE.

"You mean like Loch Ness?" Annalee asked, glancing up through her thick glasses. "You got a sunburn."

Gracie shrugged. She was always getting a sunburn, getting over a sunburn, or about to get a sunburn. "I mean like *our* lake monster." It hadn't been like Loch Ness. The shape had been completely different. Kind of like the goofy serpent on the town sign, actually.

"Ask that kid."

"Which kid?"

"I don't know his name. Summer kid. Comes in here every day at four for a cherry dip."

Gracie gagged. "Cherry dip is vile."

Annalee jabbed her pen at Gracie. "Cherry dip sells cones."

"What does he look like?"

"Skinny. Big purple backpack. White hair."

Gracie slid down in the booth, body going limp with disappointment. "Eli?"

Gracie knew most of the summer kids who had been coming to Little Spindle for a while. They pretty much kept to themselves. Their parents invited each other to barbecues, and they moved in rowdy cliques on their dirt bikes, taking over the lakes, making lines at Rottie's Red Hot and the DQ, coming into Youvenirs right before Labor Day to buy a hat or a key chain. But Eli was always on his own. His family's rental had to be somewhere near the north side of the lake, because every May he'd show up walking south on the main road, wearing too-big madras shorts and lugging a purple backpack. He'd slap his way to the library in a pair of faded Vans and spend the entire afternoon there by himself, then pick up his big backpack and trundle back home like some kind of weird blond pill bug, but not before he stopped at the DQ—apparently to order a cherry dip.

"What's wrong with him?" asked Annalee.

It was too hard to explain. Gracie shrugged. "He's a little bit the worst."

"The cherry dip of humans?"

Gracie laughed, then felt bad for laughing when Annalee peered at her over those thick plastic frames and said, "Because you're the town sweetheart? You could use some more friends."

Gracie tugged at the frayed end of her newly cut shorts. She had friends. Mosey Allen was all right. And Lila Brightman. She had people to eat lunch with, people who waited for her before first bell.

But they lived in Greater Spindle, with most of the kids from her school.

"What would Eli Cuddy know about Idgy Pidgy, anyway?" Gracie asked.

"Spends all his time in the library, doesn't he?"

Annalee had a point. Gracie tapped her fingers on the table, scraped more of the chipped lilac polish from her thumbnail. She thought of the story of the green-eyed baby and the river god. "So you've never seen anything like Idgy Pidgy?"

"I can barely see the pen in my hand," Annalee said sourly.

"But if a person saw a monster, a real one, not like . . . not a metaphor, that person's probably crazy, right?"

Annalee pushed her glasses up her nose with one gnarled finger. Behind them, her brown eyes had a soft, rheumy sheen. "There are monsters everywhere, *tsigele*," she said. "It's always good to know their names." She took a bite of the puddle that was left of her sundae and smacked her lips. "Your friend is here."

Eli Cuddy was standing at the counter, backpack weighting his shoulders, placing his order. The problem with Eli wasn't just that he liked to be indoors more than outdoors. Gracie was okay with that. It was that he never talked to anyone. And he always looked a little—damp. Like his clothes were clinging to his skinny chest. Like if you touched his skin, he might be *moist*.

Eli planted himself in a two-seater booth and propped a book open on the slope of his backpack so he could read while he ate.

Who eats an ice cream cone like that? Gracie wondered as she watched him take weird, tidy little bites. Then she remembered those shapes moving in the lake. *Sunlight on the water,* her mind protested. *Scales,* her heart insisted.

"What's *tsigele* mean?" she asked Annalee.

"'Little goat,'" said Annalee. "Bleat bleat, little goat. Go on with you."

Why not? Gracie wiped her palms on her shorts and ambled up to the booth. She felt bolder than usual. Maybe because nothing she said to Eli Cuddy mattered. It wasn't like, if she made a fool of herself, he'd have anyone to tell.

"Hey," she said. He blinked up at her. She had no idea what to do with her hands, so she planted them on her hips, then worried she looked like she was about to start a pep routine and dropped them. "You're Eli, right?"

"Yeah."

"I'm Gracie."

"I know. You work at Youvenirs."

"Oh," she said. "Right." Gracie worked summer mornings there, mostly because Henny had taken pity on her and let her show up to dust things for a few dollars an hour. Had Eli come in before?

He was waiting. Gracie wished she'd planned this out better. Saying she believed in monsters felt sort of like showing someone the collection of stuffed animals she kept on her bed, like she was announcing, *I'm still a little kid. I'm still afraid of things that can curl around your leg and drag you under.*

"You know the Loch Ness monster?" she blurted.

Eli's brow creased. "Not personally."

Gracie plunged ahead. "You think it could be real?"

Eli closed his book carefully and studied her with very serious, very blue eyes, the furrow between his eyebrows deepening. His lashes were so blond they were almost silver. "Did you look through my library record?" he asked. "Because that's a federal crime."

"What?" It was Gracie's turn to scrutinize Eli. "No, I didn't spy on you. I just asked you a question."

"Oh. Well. Good. Because I'm not totally sure it's a crime anyway."

"What are you looking at that you're so worried people will see? Porn?"

"Volumes of it," he said, in that same serious voice. "As much porn as I can get. The Little Spindle Library's collection is small but thoughtfully curated."

Gracie snorted, and Eli's mouth tugged up a little.

"Okay, perv. Annalee said you might know something about Idgy Pidgy and that kind of stuff."

"Annalee?"

Gracie bobbed her chin over to the booth by the window, where a nervous-looking man in a Hawaiian shirt had seated himself across from Annalee and was whispering something to her as he tore up a napkin. "This is her place."

"I like cryptozoology," Eli said. Off her blank look, he continued, "Bigfoot. The Loch Ness Monster. Ogopogo."

Gracie hesitated. "You think all of those are real?"

"Not all of them. Statistically. But no one was sure the giant squid was real until they started washing up on beaches in New Zealand."

"Really?"

Eli gave her a businesslike nod. "There's a specimen at the Natural History Museum in London that's twenty-eight feet long. They think that's a small one."

"No shit," Gracie breathed.

Another precise nod. "No. Shit."

This time Gracie laughed outright. "Hold up," she said, "I want a Blizzard. Don't go anywhere."

He didn't.

That summer took on a wavy, loopy, lazing shape for Gracie. Mornings she "worked" at Youvenirs, rearranging knickknacks in the windows and pointing the rare customer toward the register. At noon she'd meet up with Eli and they'd go to the library or ride bikes to her cove, though Eli thought another sighting there was unlikely.

"Why would it come back here?" he asked as they stared out at the sun-dappled water.

"It was here before. Maybe it likes the shade."

"Or maybe it was just passing through."

Most of the time they talked about Idgy Pidgy. Or at least that was where their conversations always started.

"You could have just seen fish," Eli said as they flipped through a book on North American myths, beneath an umbrella at Rottie's Red Hot.

"That would have to be some really big fish."

"Carp can grow to be over forty pounds."

She shook her head. "No. The scales were different." Like jewels. Like a fan of abalone shells. Like clouds moving over water.

"You know, every culture has its own set of megafauna. A giant blue crow has been spotted in Brazil."

"This wasn't a blue crow. And 'megafauna' sounds like a band."

"Not a good band."

"I'd go see them." Then Gracie shook her head. "Why do you eat that way?"

Eli paused. "What way?"

"Like you're going to write an essay about every bite. You're eating a cheeseburger, not defusing a bomb."

But Eli did everything that way—slowly, thoughtfully. He rode his bike that way. He wrote things down in his blue spiral notebook that way. He took what seemed like an hour to pick out something to eat at Rottie's Red Hot when there were only five things on the menu, which never changed. It was weird, no doubt, and Gracie was glad her friends from school spent most of their summers around Greater Spindle so she didn't have to try to explain any of it. But there was also something kind of nice about the way Eli took things so seriously, like he really gave everything his full attention.

They compiled lists of Idgy Pidgy sightings. There had been less than twenty in the town's history, dating back to the 1920s.

"We should cross reference them with Loch Ness and Ogopogo sightings," said Eli. "See if there's a pattern. Then we can figure out when we should survcil the lake."

"Surveil," Gracie said, doodling a sea serpent in the margin of Eli's list. "Like police. We can set up a perimeter."

"Why would we do that?"

"It's what they do on cop shows. Set up a perimeter. Lock down the perp."

"No TV, remember?" Eli's parents had a "no screens" policy. He used the computers at the library, but at home it was no Internet, no cell phone, no television. Apparently, they were vegetarians, too, and Eli liked to eat all the meat he could when they left him to his own devices. The closest he got to vegetables was french fries.

Gracie sometimes wondered if he was poor in a way that she wasn't. He never seemed short of money for the arcade or hot pretzels, but he always wore the same clothes and always seemed hungry. People with money didn't summer in Little Spindle. But people without money didn't summer at all. Gracie wasn't really sure she wanted to know. She liked that they didn't talk about their parents or school.

Now she picked up Eli's notebook and asked, "How can we surveil if you don't know proper police procedure?"

"All the good detectives are in books."

"Sherlock Holmes?"

"Conan Doyle is too dry. I like Raymond Carver, Ross Macdonald, Walter Mosley. I read every paperback they have here, during my noir phase."

Gracie drew bubbles coming out of Idgy Pidgy's nose. "Eli," she said, without looking at him, "do you actually think I saw something in the lake?"

"Possibly."

She pushed on. "Or are you just humoring me so you have someone to hang out with?" It came out meaner than she'd meant it to, maybe because the answer mattered.

Eli cocked his head to one side, thinking, seeking an honest answer, like he was solving for x. "Maybe a little," he said at last.

Gracie nodded. She liked that he hadn't pretended something different. "I'm okay with that." She hopped down off the table. "You can be the stodgy veteran with a drinking problem, and I'm the loose cannon."

"Can I wear a cheap suit?"

"Do you have a cheap suit?"

"No."

"Then you can wear the same dumb madras shorts you always do."

They rode their bicycles to every place there had ever been an Idgy Pidgy sighting, all the way up to Greater Spindle. Some spots were sunny, some shady, some off beaches, others off narrow spits of rock and sand. There was no pattern. When they got sick of Idgy Pidgy, they'd head over to the Fun Spot to play skee ball or mini golf. Eli was terrible at both, but he seemed perfectly happy to lose to Gracie regularly and to tidily record his miserable scores.

On the Friday before Labor Day, they ate lunch in front of the library—tomato sandwiches and cold corn on the cob that Gracie's mother had made earlier that week. A map of the US and Canada was spread out on the picnic table before them. The sun was heavy on their shoulders and Gracie felt sweaty and dull. She wanted to go to the lake, just to swim, not to look for Idgy Pidgy, but Eli claimed it was too hot to move.

"There's probably a barbecue somewhere," she said, lying on the bench, toes digging in the dead grass beneath the table. "You really want to waste your last school-free Friday just looking at maps in the middle of town?"

"Yeah," he said. "I really do."

Gracie felt herself smiling. Her mother seemed to want to spend all of her time with Eric. Mosey and Lila lived practically next door to each other and had been best friends since they were five. It was nice to have someone prefer her company, even if it was Eli Cuddy.

She covered her eyes with her arm to block the sun. "Do we have anything to read?"

"I returned all my books."

"Read me town names off the map."

"Why?"

"You won't go swimming, and I like being read to."

Eli cleared his throat. "Burgheim. Furdale. Saskatoon . . ."

Strung together, they sounded almost like a story.

Gracie thought about inviting Eli when she went to see the end-of-season fireworks up at Ohneka Beach the next night, with Lila and Mosey, but she wasn't quite sure how to explain all the time she'd been spending with him, and she thought she should sleep over at Mosey's place. She didn't want to feel completely left out when classes started. It was an investment in the school year. But when Monday came and there was no Eli walking the main road or at the DQ, she felt a little hollow.

"That kid gone?" Annalee asked as Gracie poked at the upended cone in her dish. She'd decided to try a cherry dip. It was just as disgusting as she remembered.

"Eli? Yeah. He went back to the city."

"He seems all right," said Annalee, taking the cup of ice cream from Gracie and tossing it in the trash.

"Mom wants you to come for dinner on Friday night," Gracie said.

But she could admit that maybe Eli Cuddy was better than all right.

The next May, right before Memorial Day, Gracie went down to her cove at Little Spindle. She'd been, plenty of times, over the school year. She'd done her homework there until the air turned too cold for sitting still, then watched ice form on the edges of the water as winter set in. She'd nearly jumped out of her skin when a black birch snapped beneath the weight of the frost on its branches and fell into the shallows with a resigned groan. And on that last Friday in May, she made sure she was on the shore, skipping stones, just in case there was magic in the date or the Idgy Pidgy had a clock keeping time in its heart. Nothing happened.

She went by Youvenirs, but she'd been in the previous day to help Henny get ready for summer, so there was nothing left to do, and eventually she ended up at the Dairy Queen with an order of curly fries she didn't really want.

"Waiting for your friend?" Annalee asked, as she sifted through her newspaper for the crossword.

"I'm just eating my fries."

When she saw Eli, Gracie felt an embarrassing rush of relief. He was taller, a lot taller, but just as skinny, and damp, and serious looking as ever. Gracie didn't budge, her insides knotted up. Maybe he wouldn't want to hang out again. *That's fine,* she told herself.

But he scanned the seats even before he went to the counter, and when he saw her, his pale face lit up like silver sparklers.

Annalee's laugh sounded suspiciously like a cackle.

"Hey!" he said, striding over. His legs seemed to reach all the way to his chin now. "I found something amazing. You want a Blizzard?"

And just like that, it was summer all over again.

SCALES

The something amazing was a dusty room in the basement of the library, packed with old vinyl record albums, a turntable, and a pile of headphones tucked into a nest of curly black cords.

"I'm so glad it's still here," Eli said. "I found it right before Labor Day, and I was afraid someone would finally get around to clearing it out over the winter."

Gracie felt a pang of guilt over not spending that last weekend with Eli, but she was also pleased he'd been waiting to show her this. "Does that thing work?" she asked, pointing to the column of stereo gear.

Eli flipped a couple of switches and red lights blinked on. "We are go."

Gracie slid a record from the shelves and read the title: *Jackie Gleason: Music, Martinis, and Memories.* "What if I only want the music?"

"We could just listen to a third of it."

They made a stack of records, competing to find the one with the weirdest cover—flying toasters, men on fire, barbarian princesses in metal bikinis—and listened to all of them, lying on the floor, big black headphones hugging their ears. Most of the music was awful, but a few albums were really good. *Bella Donna* had Stevie Nicks on the cover dressed like an angel tree-topper and holding a cockatoo, but they listened to it all the way through, twice, and when "Edge of Seventeen" came on, Gracie imagined herself rising out of the lake in a long white dress, flying through the woods, hair like a black banner behind her.

It wasn't until she was pedaling home, stomach growling for dinner, singing *Ooh baby ooh baby ooh,* that Gracie realized she and Eli hadn't talked about Idgy Pidgy once.

Though Gracie hadn't exactly been keeping Eli a secret from Mosey and Lila, she hadn't mentioned him, either. She just wasn't sure they'd get him. But one afternoon, when she and Eli were eating at Rottie's Red Hot, a horn blared from the lot, and when Gracie looked around, there was Mosey in her dad's Corolla, with Lila in the passenger seat.

"Don't you only have a learner's permit?" she asked, as Mosey and Lila squeezed in on the round benches.

"My parents don't care, if I'm just coming down to Little Spindle. And it means they don't have to drive me. Where have you been, anyway?" Mosey glanced pointedly at Eli.

"Nowhere. Youvenirs. The usual."

Eli said nothing, just carefully parceled out ketchup into a lopsided steeple by his fries.

They ate. They talked about taking the train into the city to see a concert.

"How come your family doesn't stay at Greater Spindle?" Mosey asked.

Eli cocked his head to one side, giving the question his full consideration. "We've just always come here. I think they like the quiet."

"I like it, too," said Lila. "Not the lake so much, but it's nice in the summer, when Greater Spindle gets so crazy."

Mosey popped a fry in her mouth. "The lake is haunted."

"By what?" asked Eli, leaning forward.

"Some lady drowned her kids there."

Lila rolled her eyes. "That's a complete lie."

"*La Llorona,*" said Eli. "The weeping woman. There's legends like that all over the place."

Great, thought Gracie. *We can all start hunting ghosts together.*

She tried to ignore the squirmy feeling in her gut. She'd told herself that she hadn't wanted to introduce Eli to Mosey and Lila because he was so odd, but now she wasn't sure. She loved Mosey and Lila, but she always felt a little alone around them, even when they were sitting together at a bonfire or huddled in the back row of the Spotlight watching a matinee. She didn't want to feel that way around Eli.

When Mosey and Lila headed back to Greater Spindle, Eli gathered up their plastic baskets on a tray and said, "That was fun."

"Yeah," Gracie agreed, a bit too enthusiastically.

"Let's take bikes to Robin Ridge tomorrow."

"Everyone?"

The furrow between Eli's brows appeared. "Well, yeah," he said. "You and me."

Everyone.

TEETH

Gracie couldn't pinpoint the moment Eli dried out, only the moment she noticed. They were lying on the floor of Mosey's bedroom, rain lashing at the windows.

She'd gotten her driver's license that summer, and her mom's boyfriend didn't mind loaning Gracie his truck once in a while so she could drive up to Greater Spindle. Gas money was harder to come by. There were better jobs in Greater Spindle, but none that were guaranteed to correspond with Gracie's mother's shifts, so Gracie was still working at Youvenirs, since she could get there on her bike.

It felt like Little Spindle was closing in on her, like she was standing on a shore that got narrower and narrower as the tide came in. People were talking about SATs and college applications and summer internships. Everything seemed to be speeding up, and everyone seemed to be gathering momentum, ready to go shooting off into the future on carefully plotted trajectories, while Gracie was still struggling to get her bearings.

When Gracie started to get that panicked feeling, she'd find Eli at the Dairy Queen or the library, and they'd go down to the "Hall of Records" and line up all of the Bowie albums, so they could look at his fragile, mysterious face, or they'd listen to *Emmett Otter's Jug-Band Christmas* while they tried to decipher all the clues on the cover of *Sgt. Pepper's*. She didn't know what she was going to do when the school year started.

They'd driven up to Greater Spindle in Eric's truck without much of a plan, radio up, windows down to save gas on air-conditioning, sweating against the plastic seats, but when the storm had rolled in they'd holed up at Mosey's to watch movies.

Lila and Mosey were up on the bed painting their toes and picking songs to play for each other, and Gracie was sprawled out on the carpet with Eli, listening to him read from some boring book about waterways. Gracie wasn't paying much attention. She was on her stomach, head on her arms, listening to the rain on the roof and the murmur of Eli's voice, and feeling okay for the first time in a while, as if someone had taken the hot knot of tension she always seemed to be carrying beneath her ribs and dunked it in cool water.

The thunder had been a near continuous rumble, and the air felt thick and electrical outside. Inside, the air-conditioning had raised goose bumps on Gracie's arms, but she was too lazy to get up to turn it down, or to ask for a sweater.

"Gracie," Eli said, nudging her shoulder with his bare foot.

"Mmm?"

"Gracie." She heard him move around, and when he spoke again, he had his head near hers and was whispering. "That cove you like doesn't have a name."

"So?"

"All the little beaches and inlets have names, but not your cove."

"So let's name it," she mumbled.

"Stone . . . Crescent?"

She flopped on her back and looked up at the smattering of yellow stars stuck to Mosey's ceiling. "That's awful. It sounds like a housing development or a breakfast roll. How about Gracie's Archipelago?"

"It's not an archipelago."

"Then something good. Something about Idgy Pidgy. Dragon Scale Cove, or the Serpentine."

"It's not shaped like a serpent."

"Beast Mouth Cove," she said.

"*Beast Mouth?* Are you trying to keep people away?"

"Of course. Always. Silverback Beach."

"Silverbacks are gorillas."

"Silver Scales . . . Something that starts with an *s*."

"Shoal," he said.

"Perfect."

"But it's not a shoal."

"We can call it Eli's Last Stand when I drown you there. You're making this impossible." She flipped back on her stomach and looked up at him. He was propped on his elbows, the book open before him. She'd had another suggestion on her lips, but it vanished like a fish slipping free of the line.

Mosey and Lila were talking in low murmurs, tinny music coming out of Lila's phone. Eli's T-shirt was stretched taut across his shoulders, and the light from the lamp by Mosey's bed had caught around his hair in a halo. She could smell the storm on him, like the lightning had followed him home, like he was made of the same dense rain clouds. His skin didn't look damp. It seemed to gleam. He had one finger on the page, holding his place, and Gracie had the urge to slide her fingers over his knuckles, his wrist, the fine blond hair on his forearm. She reared back slightly, trying to shake the thought from her head.

Eli was looking at her expectantly.

"The name should be accurate," he said, his face serious and determined as always. It was a lovely face, all of that thoughtfulness pushing his jaw forward, making that stern divot between his brows.

Gracie said the first thing that came into her head. "Let's call the cove Chuck."

"Because . . . ?"

"Because you throw things into it." Was she making any sense at all?

He nodded, considering, then broke into a ridiculous, light-filled, hideously beautiful smile. "Perfect."

The ride home was like a kind of punishment—cool air rushing through the windows, the radio turned down low, this strange, unwanted feeling beating a new rhythm in her chest. The dark road spooled out in front of them. She wished she were home. She wished they would never stop driving.

Eli's transformation was a betrayal, a bait and switch. Eli Cuddy was supposed to be safe, and now he felt dangerous. She cast around for someone else to want. She'd had a crush on Mason Lee in the ninth grade, and she made Lila take her up to Okhena Beach, where he was lifeguarding, in the hope that seeing him might jolt some sense into her. Unfortunately, the only amazing thing about Mason was the way he looked with his shirt off. He was like a golden retriever. She understood the appeal, but that didn't mean she wanted to take him home.

Mornings when she knew she was going to see Eli felt suddenly breathless and full of possibility. She bought a new shirt in lush, just-dusk purple, picked out slender silver earrings in the shape of feathers, bought apple blossom lip gloss because it looked like something magical in its pink and gold tin, and when she touched her fingers to her mouth it felt like an incantation. *See me. See me the way I see you.*

Gracie knew she was being stupid. If Eli liked her as more than a friend, he'd never given her any clue. He might even have a girlfriend in the city who he wrote long letters to and made out with between classes. He'd never said he did, but she'd never asked him. It had never mattered before. She didn't want it to matter now.

The summer took on a different shape—a desperate, jagged shape, the rise and fall of a dragon's back. The world felt full of hazards. Every song on every album bristled with portent. She found herself trying to communicate through the records she chose, and interpreting the ones that he chose as code. She forced herself to spend more time with Mosey and Lila, and at Youvenirs, cleaning things that didn't need to be cleaned, battling her new greed for Eli's company. But was it new? From the first, her hours with Eli had been warm sand islands, the refuge that had made the murky swim through the rest of the year bearable.

She was torn between the need to say something, to speak this thing inside her before summer ended, and the conviction that she had to avoid that disastrous course of action at all costs. For the first time, she found herself counting down the days until September. If she could just make it to Labor Day without letting her heart spill out of her lips, she'd have the whole school year to get over this wretched, ridiculous thing that had taken her over.

On the Saturday before Labor Day, Gracie and Eli watched the closing fireworks above Greater Spindle. They sat next to each other on the edge of the truck, knees almost touching, shoulders brushing.

"I wish you had a phone," she said, without meaning to.

"Me too. Sort of."

"Only sort of?"

"I like saving up all of the things I want to tell you."

That has to be enough, Gracie told herself, as blue and silver light washed over the sharp gleam of his features. *That should be better than enough.*

It got easier. She missed summer. She missed Eli, but it was a relief to be free of the prospect of seeing him. She went to junior prom with Ned Minnery, who was funny and played trumpet. He loved puns. He wore suspenders and striped pants, and did magic tricks. He was the anti-Eli. There was nothing serious about him. It was a fun night, but Gracie wondered if maybe she wasn't any good at fun. She drank enough peach schnapps to talk herself into kissing Ned, and then got sick by the side of the road.

When Memorial Day came around, she felt ready to see Eli, but she didn't let herself go to the Dairy Queen. She couldn't have that kind of summer again. She wouldn't. She went to Okhena Beach instead, planted herself next to Mosey and Lila on the sand, and stayed there as the sun sank low and the opening weekend bonfire began. When someone brought out a guitar, she found a spot atop a picnic table a little way off, bare feet on the bench, shivering in her sweatshirt. *I'm fine,* she thought, telling herself she'd rejoin the others by the flames in just a minute. *I'm good.* But when she saw Eli walking toward her with those long, loping strides, his hair bright in the firelight, face eager, carrying that stupid backpack, all those months of hard work vanished. How had he even gotten to Greater Spindle? Were his parents letting him use the car now? Longing unfurled inside of her, as if it had just been waiting for the warm weather to be aired out.

He sat down beside her and said, "You're not going to believe what I found today. The Hall of Records has a whole collection of spoken-word albums behind the Christmas section. It's amazing."

Gracie made herself laugh. "Can't wait." *Did you miss me? Did you kiss anyone? I did, and it was terrible.*

She couldn't do it. She couldn't spend another summer this way. It would drive her insane. She would make up some excuse— emergency hours at Youvenirs, a cholera outbreak. Whatever it took. She pulled the pot of apple lip balm from her pocket. It was nearly empty, but she hadn't bothered to buy more. It was too embarrassing to remember the things she'd let herself think when she'd paid for it.

Eli snatched it from her palm and hurled it into the darkness, into the lake.

"Hey!" Gracie protested. "Why would you do that?"

He took a deep breath. His shoulders lifted, fell. "Because I've spent nine months thinking of apples."

Silence dropped around them like a curtain. In the distance, Gracie could hear people talking, the lazy strum of guitar chords, but it was all another country, another planet. Eli Cuddy was looking at her with all of his focus, his blue eyes nearly black in the firelight. That hopeless thing in her chest fluttered, became something else, dared to bloom.

Eli's long fingers cupped her face, traced the nape of her neck, kept her still, as if he needed to give her every bit of his attention, as if he could learn her like a language, plot her like a course. Eli kissed Gracie like she was a song and he was determined to hear every note. He kissed her the way he did everything else—seriously.

Now summer was round and full, fruit ready to burst, a sun emerging fat, yellow, and happy from the sea. They kissed behind Youvenirs, in the red velvet seats of the Spotlight, on the floor of the record room—the sound of static filling the headphones around their necks as some song or other reached its end.

"We could go to your house," she suggested.

"We could go to yours."

They stayed where they were.

On afternoons, when they left the DQ, Eli's lips were cold and tasted like cherry. On balmy evenings, when they lay on the banks of the cove named Chuck, his hands were warm and restless. Gracie floated in her sandals. She felt covered in jewels. Her bicycle was a winged horse.

But sometime around the end of July, Gracie heard the drone of the insects turn sorrowful. Despite the heat and the sunburned backs of her thighs and the neon still lit on the main road, she felt summer begin to go.

At night she'd hear her mom and Eric laughing in the living room, the television like gray music, and she'd curl up on her side, that narrow panic settling in. With Eli she could forget she was seventeen. She could forget Little Spindle and what came next. A page out of her mother's life, if she was lucky. A car loan so she could go to community college. Watching the kids from her school leave for other places, better places. She wished Eli had a phone. She wished she could reach out to him in the dark. *We could write letters. I could take the train to New York on the weekends.* At night, she thought these things, but by the next afternoon, Eli was bright as a coin in the sunlight and all she wanted was to kiss his studious mouth.

Days and nights dissolved, and it wasn't until the Saturday before Labor Day that Gracie said, "Mosey's talking about applying to NYU."

Eli leaned back on his elbows. They were lying on a blanket at the cove named Chuck, the sun making jagged stars through the branches of the oaks and birches. "Will she?" he asked.

"Probably. She's smart enough to get in." Eli said nothing, and Gracie added, "It might be fun to work in the city."

The furrow appeared between Eli's brows. "Sure," he said. "That's a big change, though."

Don't say anything, she told herself. *Leave it be.* But the knife was right there. She had to walk into it. "Do you not want me there?"

Eli shifted forward and tossed a pebble into the lake. "You should go wherever you want."

The hurt that bloomed in her chest was a living thing, a plant out of a science fiction movie, all waving tendrils and stinging nettles.

"Sure," she said lightly.

There was nothing wrong with what he'd said. This was a summer thing. Besides, he was right. She should go where she wanted. She didn't need Eli waiting for her to move to the city. She could crash on Mosey's couch until she found a job. Did dorm rooms have couches?

"Gracie—" Eli said, reaching for her hand.

She hopped up. "I've got to go meet Mosey and Lila."

He stood then. Sunlight clung to his hair, his skin. He was almost too bright to look at.

"Let's meet early tomorrow," he said. "I only have one more day to—"

"Yup."

She had her bag on her shoulders and she was on her bike, determined to get away from him before he could see her pride go rolling down her face in big fat tears. She pedaled hard, afraid he'd come after her. Hoping so hard that he would.

She didn't go to work the next day. It wasn't a decision. She just let the minutes drain away. Eli wouldn't come to her house. He'd never seen her room or watched TV on their sofa, just hovered outside in the driveway with his bike while Gracie went to grab a sweater or change her shoes. She'd never even met his parents. Because that was real life and they were something else.

You're being stupid, she told herself. *He'll be gone in two days. Enjoy it while it lasts. Let it be fun.* But Gracie wasn't good at fun, not the kind of fun that other people had. The person she liked best didn't like her enough to want more of her, and she didn't want to pretend that wasn't awful. She was cherry dip cones, all those old paperbacks, records stacked on dusty shelves—something to hold Eli's interest, maybe even something he really liked, but a summer thing, not quite real when the weather turned.

She read. She watched TV. Then the weekend was gone, and she knew Eli was gone with it. That was okay. Next summer she wouldn't be waiting at the Dairy Queen or working at Youvenirs. She'd graduate, and she'd go to New York or Canada or wherever. But she wouldn't be in Little Spindle.

TAIL

A week after school started, Gracie went to see Annalee. She hadn't known that she meant to, but she ended up in the fluorescent lights of the Dairy Queen just the same.

She didn't order. She wasn't hungry. She slid into the booth and said, "How do I get better? How do I make this stop hurting?"

Annalee set down her crossword. "You should say good-bye."

"It's too late. He's gone."

"Sometimes it helps to say it anyway."

"Can you tell me . . . Did he ever feel the way I did?"

"Ah, *tsigele*." Annalee tapped her pen gently on Gracie's hand. "Some of us wear our hearts. Some of us carry them."

Gracie sighed. Had she really expected Annalee could make her feel better? This town was full of sham monsters, fake witches, stories that were just stories. But anything was worth a try.

Though the weather was still warm, the main road was quiet, and as she turned onto the narrow dirt path that led to her cove, the woods seemed almost forlorn, as if they were keeping the last watch of summer. She felt guilty. This had been her cove, nameless and comforting before Eli. *Where have you been?* the pine needles whispered.

She leaned her bike against a tree at the clearing and walked down to the shore. It didn't feel like sanctuary anymore. Hadn't Mosey said the lake was haunted? The cove felt full of ghosts she wished she could banish. She had so many good memories with Eli. Did she have to lose all of those, too?

That was when Gracie heard it: a single, soft exhalation that might have been a breeze. Then another—a rasping breath. She peered past the shady banks. A body lay slumped in the shallows.

She didn't remember moving, only that one moment she was standing, stunned on the shore, and the next she was on her knees in the water.

"Eli," she cried.

"You came."

"What happened? What is this?" He was so pale he was nearly blue, his veins too close to the surface of his skin.

"I shouldn't have waited. I get three months. That's the rule."

"What rule?"

"I wanted to say good-bye."

"Eli—"

"I was selfish. I didn't want you to go to the city. I needed you to look forward to. I'm sorry. I'm sorry, Gracie. The winters get so long."

"Eli, I have my phone. I can call—"

"I'm dying now, so I can tell you—"

"*You're not dying,*" Gracie shouted. "You're dehydrated, or you have hypothermia." But even as she said it, she realized the water was warmer than it should be.

"It was me that day. You were skipping stones. You'd skinned

your knee. I saw you just for a second. It was the last day of May."
His eyelids stuttered open, shut. "I shouldn't have kissed you, but
I wanted to for so long. It was better than ice cream. It was better
than books."

She was crying now. "Eli, please, let me—"

"It's too late."

"Who says? *Who says?*"

He gave the barest shrug. It became a shudder. "The lake. Three
months to walk the land. But always I must return to her."

Gracie's mind flew back to that day at the cove, the creature in
the water. It was impossible.

"There are no books, below," he said. "No words or language."

No Dairy Queen. No bicycles. No music. It couldn't be.

Gracie blinked, and Eli's form seemed to flicker, ghostly almost,
part boy and part something else. She remembered Annalee tapping her hand with the pen. *Some of us wear our hearts. Some of us
carry them.*

Gracie's eyes scanned the beach, the tangle of brambles where
the woods began. There, a dark little hump in the leaves. She'd never
seen him without it—that ugly purple backpack—and in that moment, she knew.

She scrambled for it, fell, righted herself, grabbed it open, and
split the zipper wide. It gaped like a mouth. It was full of junk. Skee
ball tickets, mini golf score cards, a pink and gold lip gloss tin. But
there, at the bottom, glinting like a hidden moon . . .

She pulled it from the bag, a long, papery cape of scales that
seemed to go on and on, glittering and sharp beneath her fingers,
surprising in its weight. She dragged it toward Eli, trailing it behind
her, stumbling through the shallows. She pulled his body close and
wrapped it around him.

"Here," she sobbed. "Here."

"Three months," he said. "No more."

"It was only a few days—"

"Leave Little Spindle, Gracie. Get free of this place."

"No," she shouted at the lake, at no one at all. "We can make
a trade."

Eli's hand gripped her wrist. "Stop."

"You can have me, too!"

"Gracie, don't."

The water lapped against her thighs with its own slow pulse, warm as blood, warm as a womb, and she knew what to do. She curled herself into the cloak of scales beside Eli, letting its edges slice into her arms, letting her own blood drip into the water.

"Take me too," she whispered.

"Too late," said Eli. His eyes closed. He smiled. "It was worth it."

Then the hand around her wrist flexed tight, retracted. Gracie watched it stretch and lengthen—a talon, razor sharp.

Eli's eyes flew open. The smell of rain clouds reached her, then the rumble of thunder, the roar of a river unleashed. The rush of water filled her ears as Eli's body shifted, blurred, shimmered in the fading light. He rose above her, reeling back on the muscular coils of his body, a great snake, a serpent of gleaming white scales, his head like a nodding dragon, his back split by iridescent fins that spread like wings behind him.

"Eli . . ." she tried to say, but the sound that left her mouth wasn't human.

She raised a hand to her throat, but her arms were too short, the wrong shape. She turned and felt her body, strange and strong, thrash through the shallows, as her back arched.

In the sunlit water, she glimpsed her reflection, her scales deep gray and alive with rainbows, her fins the bruised violet of twilight, a veil of starlight cast against the darkening sky. She was monstrous. She was lovely.

It was her last human thought. She was diving into the water. She was curled around . . . who was this? Eli. The dim echo of a name, something more ancient and unpronounceable, lived at the base of her brain. It didn't matter. She could feel the slide of his scales over hers as they slipped deeper into the lake, into the pull of the current, together.

HEART

W hen they found her bicycle leaning against a pine near Little Spindle, Annalee did her best to explain to Gracie's mother.

Of course, her mother still called the police. They even sent divers into the lake. The search was fruitless, though one of them claimed that something far too big to be a fish had brushed up against his leg.

Gracie and Eli had summers, three perfect months every year, to feel the grass beneath their feet and the sun on their bare human shoulders. They picked a new city each summer, but they returned most often to Manhattan, where they'd visit with Annalee and Gracie's flummoxed mother in a penthouse on the Upper East Side, and try not to stare at their beautiful host with her running-water skin and river-green eyes.

When fall came, they shed their names with their bodies and traveled the waters of the world. The lake hated to give them up. She threatened to freeze solid and bind them there, but they were two now—sinewy and gleaming—monsters of the deep, with lashing tales and glittering eyes, and the force they created between them smashed old rules and new arguments. They slipped down the Mohawk to the Hudson, past the river god with his sloped gray shoulders, and out into the Atlantic. They met polar bears in the Arctic, frightened manatees near the Florida Keys. They curled together in a knot, watching the dream lights of jellyfish off the coast of Australia.

Sometimes, if they spotted a passenger leaning on the rails of a freighter by himself, they might even let themselves be seen. They'd breach the waves, let the moonlight catch their hides, and the stranger would stand for a moment—mouth agape, heart alive, his loneliness forgotten.

THE END OF LOVE

NINA LaCOUR

don't realize how early I am until I open the door. The rows of desks and chairs are empty, the room is silent, and Mr. Trout peers at me from behind the podium.

"It's been a few years," he says. "I got a note that you're auditing this class?"

"Yeah. I want to brush up."

"For what?"

"I don't know. My future?"

He laughs. "I'm not supposed to say this, but you don't really need this stuff for your future. You need it for high school. It's a box to check, and you've already checked it. *Perfectly,* if I'm remembering correctly."

"Maybe I just want to feel really good at something." I cross the room and claim a front-row desk. "Maybe I just happen to love geometry."

"All right. Whatever floats your boat, Flora. But I have never in my career had a student repeat a class for fun. And during *summer*."

He turns to the window, the bright morning light streaming in as if to prove my foolishness. But I look instead to the stacks of geometry textbooks on his desk, and I swear, the sight of them sends beams of light straight to my heart.

"I can pass these out," I offer.

"Sure," he says.

As I'm centering them at each desk, placing the bright yellow textbook checkout slips inside each cover, I send silent thank yous to Jessica for letting me do this. It was the last week of school, and the impending summer at home with my parents—with both of my best friends away the whole time (Rachel working at a summer camp in Tahoe, Tara in Barcelona with her cousins)—was closing in on me. It was like a creeping fog. So much heaviness. "What do you need?" Jessica asked me. Even she wouldn't be here for me over the summer break, and my weekly visits to her office had become the best part of school. I was going to miss the way she touched her fingertips together when she asked me questions, and her plants by her window, and even her tissue box, perched next to me like a suggestion to cry. I told her I didn't know what I needed.

And then I said, "Actually, maybe I need summer school. A reason to get out of the house every day. Homework, so I can stay in my room whenever I'm home."

"I don't know what we're offering this summer . . ." she said, opening her laptop and pulling up the schedule. "Too bad there isn't art or theater."

"What about geometry?" I asked.

She cocked her head. "Aren't you in trig?"

"Maybe I could audit."

Her fingers tapped the keyboard. "Tim—Mr. Trout—he's teaching it on the Potrero campus."

I smiled. Even better. He was my teacher the first time I took it, my freshman year. He's the one who first talked about axes and symmetry.

"Perfect," I said, and she enrolled me right then. She made it so easy, even though it wouldn't have made sense to any other adult.

I finish passing out the books, and Mr. Trout and I make small talk for a few minutes, until he tells me, "Okay, go take a lap. I need a few minutes to plan the first lesson."

I leave my backpack on a front row desk and head to the corridor. For a week or two, when I was a freshman, I rode the bus here after school to hang out in the front quad with Blake. He liked to stand with his arm around me. I liked being mysterious, the girl from Baker High. All these random kids would come up to me and ask if I knew their cousins or exes or friends, and I would say yes and yes and yes, and Blake's arm would be there around my waist the whole time, and I usually liked having it there.

I never got past the front quad then, so I give myself a tour now. The main buildings are squat, a faded blue, and behind them are rolling hills, golden with summer. I trace the campus's edges, along the basketball court and the pool and the administration wing, and the morning is so bright, and I'm glad to be here, about to learn something I already know. I reach the parking lot. Heading toward the stairs to the campus entrance is a group of three kids, and my breath catches.

They're taller now. A little wilder. Louder.

Travis stops walking and squints at me.

"Hey," Mimi says. Her hair is the same length as it was then, but now part of one side is buzzed short. Her cutoff overalls are only clasped on the right, the left buckle dangling. I feel my face get hot at the sight of her. "It's you. Blake's ex-girlfriend."

I force a laugh. "I didn't realize that month of my life would define me forever."

Hope, still kind, says, "Our long lost Flora!"

"Hi, you guys," I say.

"Please tell us you're here for geometry," Travis says.

I nod because I can't speak. Sharing a class with them was the furthest thing from what I imagined when I thought about what summer school would offer me. When I chose this class, I was choosing shapes and logic, angles and numbers, strangers and anonymity. Not this gang of three who I never thought I'd see again. Not this girl whose presence makes my head tingle and my hands shake. Even though I'm trying to look anywhere else, I can't help but stare at the bare skin of Mimi's hip, between where her overalls end and her tank top begins, as I follow the three of them up the stairs.

When I was a freshman and stood in this same quad with Blake, I knew that it would never last between us. Even when I was enjoying the feeling of his arm around me. Even when I liked the way he looked at me, liked being his girlfriend. Because, even then, certain truths about myself were floating up from the depths of my heart. Standing right here, now, in the corridor outside of a class I don't need to take, those truths flare up again. Because Mimi Park was what dislodged them in the first place.

Back then she always had at least one earbud in, and often she'd be looking into the distance, and her head would bob so slightly it would have been imperceptible to anyone who wasn't riveted by her. Once she asked me if I'd heard a certain song, and I said no, and she took the right side out and fit it, gently, in my ear. It was Nirvana, "Come as You Are." Kurt Cobain had been dead for almost twenty years, and I'd heard of him but never *heard* him, and now he was singing to both of us at the same time. *Only* us. His voice in her left ear, my right one. We listened through the whole song, right there in the quad, and I smiled and nodded early on so that she wouldn't take it away, but after that I couldn't look at her face anymore. Too much happened when our eyes met. I looked at my Converse and a gum wrapper. I looked at her Vans and a yellow flower growing through the concrete. The guitar sounded like it was being played underwater. The lyrics were confusing and contradictory, a lot like standing with your boyfriend's arm around you while sharing earbuds with a girl you wished you were kissing.

When the song was over, she reached to my ear and took it out.

"What do you think?" she asked.

"It was good," I said.

And now it's the summer after junior year, and I'm remembering what it was like to be chosen out of a quad swarming with people to listen to a song. I'm remembering asking her if she'd be at homecoming, and how she'd said something about going camping. I'm remembering how hard I cried when I broke up with Blake, and how so much of the sadness was about losing those afternoons on the Potrero High campus and the riot of light that filled me each time I saw Mimi in the distance.

We've reached the classroom door. They cross the threshold ahead of me and head toward the back. If I had my bag still slung over my shoulder, I would stay in their group and sit back there, too, but my stuff is at the desk in the front, where I left it. I would have to cross the room, gather my things, and then go back to see if a desk next to them was still empty. I don't know if they want me there, adding a fourth member to their group, so I sit where my stuff is. Maybe tomorrow can be different.

Mr. Trout stands at the whiteboard. I thought he needed to prepare for his lesson, but instead he used the time to draw a giant fish on the board, covered in scales. When he has everyone's attention, he writes a "Mr." right before the tip of the fish's nose.

"Welcome to summer school," he says, but the rush of calm I imagined from being here doesn't come, because Mimi is also here, sitting five rows behind me.

No one is home when I walk inside. I go to hang my bag on the coatrack but stop when I see a Post-it stuck to it that says *Leave*. The coatrack is brass, each hook in the shape of an animal. I touch the rhino's horn, the elephant's trunk. I put my bag back on my shoulder and head into the living room, but everywhere I look are more Post-its. The clock on the mantle says *Craigslist*. The portrait of Granny has a question mark. The side table, its surface covered in faded rings from mugs of coffee and tea, says *Goodwill*.

I turn my face to the floor, step around more Post-its safety pinned to the rugs, and walk through the house and up the stairs to my room. I drop my bag. I step out of my sandals. I pull back my sheets and climb into my bed. I make myself small. I make myself sleep.

It's Monday again. Mimi and Hope and Travis are standing by the open classroom door as I approach it, and I try to work up the courage to talk to them. I think I messed it up. I should have joined them on the first day, or at least on the second. Now too much time has passed, and they haven't asked me to sit with them, and our conversations have consisted solely of heys and good-byes.

But I don't need to find the courage, because Hope spots me and says, "Flora, come see Mimi's tattoo!"

So I join them. It's a life-size California poppy on the inside of her right forearm.

"I can't believe your mom let you get it," Travis says.

"What can I say? I'm the daughter of a rebel."

"It's gorgeous," I say. "The petals—they're so perfect."

And I feel myself flush while I say it, because it's so close to saying that *she's* gorgeous. The truth is that the tattoo is beautiful, but even that vivid orange and green are no match for her face or her knees or the way she's posed now, with her arm extended toward us, no hint of self-consciousness.

"I want to get a tattoo," I say. "I have it planned out."

I show them where, up the inside of my bicep.

"What of?" Travis asks.

"Words. A phrase. 'The end of love.'"

Mimi squints. "What's it from?"

"It's just something in my head."

It's something that hurts, that I can't seem to get out, that keeps me up in the early morning. I think that maybe if I could *do* something with it, write it on my body forever, I could get it out of my heart.

"It sounds like a song," Hope says. "Or a book, maybe. I can't really picture it as a tattoo."

"It'd be like a warning sign to chicks, though," Travis says. "All the girls would know to stay far, far away."

My blush returns. I didn't think I was significant enough to be gossiped about at Potrero High, but turns out that I am. I glance up, see Mimi watching me.

"You *guys*," Mr. Trout calls from the classroom. "This may blow your precocious young minds, but class is held *inside* the classroom."

I almost follow them to the last row, but before I do, I see that there are only three open desks back there, so I take my usual spot at the front.

Today Mr. Trout is introducing polygons, though he hasn't announced that yet. I can see it from the shapes he's drawn on the board. I know all of their names. Triangle, quadrilateral, pentagon, hexagon, heptagon, octagon, nonagon, decagon . . .

"What do all of these have in common?" he asks us.

"They're all shapes?" people murmur. "They have straight lines?"

"Yes," Mr. Trout says. "What else?"

I write down everything I know about polygons in my notebook. How they are bound by a finite chain of line segments. About all of their edges, and the points where two edges meet. How the space inside is called the body.

I write about convexity and nonconvexity, about simple polygons and star polygons. I write about equality and symmetry, and each word steadies my heart. Mr. Trout is talking about all of these things I know already. Most of the time he sounds a little bored, but it doesn't matter. His words leave his mouth, carry across this room, and I'm filled with wonder because *she's* listening to them, too.

My parents are in the dining room when I get home, stationed in front of the china hutch with their Post-its.

"Look at this," Mom scoffs, holding up the serving platter. "What were we thinking?"

It's the platter they've used my whole life. I don't see anything wrong with it, but Dad scoffs along with her and throws up his hands.

"What can I say?" he says. "It was the nineties."

"Goodwill pile? Unless you want it."

"Oh, Goodwill for *sure*," he says.

He carries it to the dining table, where there are three Post-its labeling the piles. *Hers, His,* and *Goodwill.* The Goodwill pile has expanded, taking up the entire table.

"You guys aren't keeping anything?" I ask.

"Oh," Dad says. "Hi, Flora."

Mom waves from across the room. "I didn't even know you were here!" she says.

In my room, I open the textbook and begin the homework that, as an auditor, I don't technically need to do. Mr. Trout assigned only the odd-numbered problems, but I decide to do them all. Halfway through, just as I'm drawing a perfect cyclic with my protractor, a knock comes at my door.

It creaks open, even though I haven't said to come in.

"How's it going?" Mom asks.

"Fine. Just doing homework."

"Is the class challenging?"

I shrug.

"What is it again?"

"Geometry."

She nods, cocks her head. "For some reason I thought you already took geometry."

I don't respond, but it doesn't seem to matter. She's already scanning my room. My chest constricts, and my stomach clenches, and I can practically hear Jessica telling me to give these feelings a voice.

"Any thoughts yet on what you want to keep?"

"Everything," I say.

"We could get you a nicer desk. Something more modern."

"I only have a year left at home anyway."

"Well. Let's see how it looks in your new room, and we can decide then."

"I was just getting into this," I say, pointing at my textbook.

"Oops! I'll leave you alone. I'm looking forward to Saturday. A friend told me about a new shop in Berkeley that I thought we could check out."

"Are you sure you want to go curtain shopping before you know where we're living?"

"I already know the style I want. Turkish-inspired. We can see what's out there."

"Okay," I say.

"Fantastic. Back to work for you. Dad and I are tackling the hall closet next. You know, we're having a really good time through all of this." She flashes me a smile as though to prove it. "Closure is so important, and we keep reminiscing and laughing. We're getting rid of so much stuff, and it just feels *great*."

My vision tilts and then rights itself. There's a beehive in my body, swarming and dangerous, but I tamp it down and say, "That's great for you. I really need to get back to this."

I turn back to the book, but I can't even see what I'm looking at anymore. I sit very still until I hear the door close. Mom's footsteps fade down the hallway. I turn to a new page in my notebook and pick up the protractor, but I press too hard on the curve and the lead breaks.

I set my homework aside and open my laptop. I search for Turkish textiles and start a new Pinterest board. I collect patterns and colors, pictures of Turkish tiles for inspiration. I learn about the different traditional motifs—animals and flowers and trees—until I get very tired and give in to the comfort of my bed.

In the midst of a lecture on the Pythagorean theorem, Mr. Trout sees something out the window. His whole face transforms; a smile takes over. I turn to find out what he's seeing. It's a woman, carrying a picnic basket.

"Flora," he says. "Do me a favor and finish this proof, will you? And then move on to the next one." On his way out the door, he turns. "And then the one after that."

So I go up to the whiteboard and take the marker. I turn back around to see Mr. Trout embracing the woman. When they let go, she takes a picnic blanket from where it was tucked under her arm and spreads it out, right there on the grass outside the classroom.

I finish Mr. Trout's drawing and explain what I'm doing, and then I turn back. Everyone is watching as the woman removes two sandwiches from the picnic basket, both wrapped in parchment paper and tied up in bows. Next comes a dish of strawberries and two champagne flutes. She reveals a bottle of sparkling water with a flourish, says something, and they both laugh, their heads thrown back.

I feel awkward standing here, not doing anything, so I check his notes for what I'm supposed to be working on next, erase the drawing I just did, and start the next one.

"Okay, so this is the algebraic proof," I say. "A squared plus b squared equals c squared."

I draw the big square with a smaller square tilted inside of it and label all the parts. I don't even turn around, because I know no one is paying any attention. When I'm finished, I set down the marker and look out the window. Mr. Trout and the woman are relaxed on the blanket, eating and talking as though they are in the middle of a park on a Saturday afternoon. Everyone in the room is turned toward the window, taking in the sight.

Everyone except Mimi, who is looking at me.

All at once, it comes back: the first time I saw her, when I was waiting for Blake by the oak tree, and she was passing out flyers for the Gay-Straight Alliance. "Do you go here?" she asked. I shook my head no. "I didn't think so," she said. "Too bad." And then she handed me a flyer anyway.

A couple weeks later, under that same tree, my heart beating hard at the sight of her. "How's the club going?" I asked.

She shrugged. "It isn't, really. Too much Straight, too little Gay, which kind of defeats the purpose."

Travis and Hope were there, beside her.

"Don't blame us," Travis said. "We're just being supportive."

"I don't think I'm really a club person anyway," Mimi said.

Now, almost three years later, with our teacher picnicking outside and the rest of the class engrossed in it, she raises her hand.

"Yes?" I say.

"Why are you taking this class?"

And maybe it's because of the bizarreness of the moment. Or because, in the midst of the twenty other students facing away from us, it feels like Mimi and I are alone in this classroom. Whatever the reason, I decide to answer honestly.

"I needed to get out of the house."

"We're going camping," Mimi says, two hours later. "Want to come?"

We're in the spot where Mr. Trout and his lady friend had their picnic, but the evidence has been cleared away. He came back into the room as though nothing had happened and told us all to head to lunch.

"When?" I ask her.

"Tomorrow morning, just up to Muir Beach for a couple of nights."

"I don't think I can," I say. "I want to, but I have plans."

"Fourth of July party?"

"Not quite. It's, like, a decorating thing. With my mom."

"That's too bad, because we could all use some help with geometry."

"Oh," I say. "You're just in the market for some free tutoring?"

"Not *just*," Mimi says.

"Break's over!" Mr. Trout calls from the classroom. "I shouldn't have to be telling you this! You all have cell phones with the time!"

"Pretty bold for someone who just had a picnic during their workday," Travis calls back.

"That's fair," Mr. Trout says. "But I'm still in charge."

I pivot and head back to the classroom.

At the end of the day, on her way out of class, Mimi hands me a note. Across the span of our history, it's the second piece of paper she's given me. This one is bigger than the GSA flyer, on graph paper, folded into a little square. *In case your plans fall through,* it says. Then, under it, a drawing of a tent, a couple trees, the moon and stars, and a fire. Beneath, she's written, *Muir Beach, site 12.*

"Lattes first," Mom says. "Then the curtain shop!"

She wants to drive separately because she has more errands to run afterward. While she's ordering at our usual café, I choose a table and open up my laptop to show her the board I've created.

"This is so fun," she says when she sits. "Look at this one! I love that color."

"I do, too," I say, and scroll down so she can see more like it. "I was thinking maybe it isn't crazy to get the curtains first, before we know what the space is like. It could help us commit to the decorating scheme."

"You're so smart. I think the barista just called our names," Mom says. "Let's go."

We drive to the textile store and finish our lattes outside. I can see from the front window that there will be lots of choices, and I tell myself that the excited feeling is good, not a betrayal of myself. Feelings can be complicated, Jessica always tells me. They can contradict each other. They don't need to make sense.

I peer into the window and catch sight of a pattern featured on a wall.

"I think I see one," I tell her.

"Where?" she asks.

"Next to that window, the third one in."

Mom's face, next to mine at the window, the feeling of showing her something . . . It sparks something forgotten in me, from before *the end of love* appeared and began repeating itself, even in my sleep. We throw our cups away and step into the shop.

"Hi there!" the woman behind the counter says. "I have your order in the back."

"What order?" I say.

Mom shrugs like it's cute. "You caught me! I couldn't resist taking a quick look. I popped in a couple days ago and fell head over heels for a print."

"Why am I here then?"

"We'll need more than one set of drapes. Now, show me the ones you were looking at."

I lead her to the wall I spotted through the window, but up close they aren't what I thought they would be.

"Great colors," she says. "Come see what I chose—you're going to love them."

The saleswoman lays a panel on the counter for my mom to inspect. They're blue and white Ikat, not Turkish at all, not the warm colors we've been looking at.

"Isn't it beautiful? Maybe with a rustic coffee table and leather sofas . . ." Her eyebrows are raised, she's smiling in expectancy.

"Sounds nice," I muster.

"Okay," she says. "I have a surprise for you. One more stop. Follow me!"

I follow her onto the freeway and through the tunnel, into our cluster of tiny suburban towns. She turns onto a residential street and I turn after her. We park in front of a new condo complex. She's holding a key in one hand and the bag with the curtains over her arm.

"What's happening?" I say.

"Come and see," she singsongs. And then she leads me up some concrete steps to a red door. She turns the key, and there's an empty living room. "Surprise! Welcome home, Flora."

The beehive is back, all buzzing and beating wings inside me. My vision blurs with it. "Are you fucking *kidding* me?"

Confusion flashes across her face.

"You don't like it?"

"*Surprise, welcome home? Help me choose curtains?*"

"Flora . . ."

But I've already turned away. I'm already back down the stairs, and inside my car, and I don't even look at her as I drive away. I don't know where I'm going, and soon I have to pull over because I'm crying too hard.

I thought when you got divorced you were supposed to fight over all the stuff. The house and the cars and the furniture. The wedding gifts that are still around. The art collection, if you're the type of people who collect art, which my parents happen to be. I thought you were supposed to want to hold on to the pieces of your life. I thought the years that came before were still supposed to matter.

I want the love seat. I want the daisy mugs. I want the eggcups. I want the welcome mat, and the portrait of Granny, and the rocking horse, and the wallpaper off the walls. I want the piano and the Navajo rug. I want my room and I want my dad and I want, I want, I *want*.

"So you *do* like us!" Travis says when I get out of my car and step from gravel to grass.

"Of course I like you."

"You don't sit with us in class," Hope says. "It hurts our feelings."

All three of them are perched on folding chairs in different bright colors. Mimi is resting her bright-red sandaled feet on a tree stump. She's twisting the loose strap of her cutoff overalls and smiling at me. I blush, and it's like I'm a freshman again. But we're both older now and more able to say what we want.

"I was hoping you'd show up," she says.

I open my mouth to say something flirtatious and light, but instead a cry comes out. Tears fall. I didn't see this coming. I put my hands over my face.

"Oh my God," I say. "This is so embarrassing." But thankfully I'm laughing now, and the crying has stopped.

"Are you okay?" Hope asks.

"It's just been a rough . . . day? Month? Last couple of years?"

"We've been wondering what's wrong. You sit in the front, and you never talk to anyone unless we, like, *force* you to talk to us."

"You space out a lot," Travis says.

"You look sad," Mimi says. "I remember you smiling a lot more."

"My parents are getting divorced," I say. I never really speak the words, unless I'm talking to Jessica. Divorce is so common, such a privileged problem to have when some people are faced with truly horrible things. But once I say it, I say it all. "They've been on and off for two years. Trial separations. For a long time, they seemed to truly hate each other—like viciously—but now it's permanent, and the hate is gone. They're fucking *cheerful*. My dad has started *whistling*."

"So you signed up for geometry, even though you could teach the class," Mimi says. "And what happened with your decorating plans?"

I shake my head. "Disaster."

"Well," Travis says, "if you have to run away, at least you are now finding yourself in paradise."

It's true. We're in the woods, but I can smell the ocean. Redwood trees tower above us; a flock of blue birds takes to the air from a branch near us. I watch them move through the sky, dipping and spreading apart and coming back together, until they are out of sight. I turn back to the camp and take all of it in. There are two tents pitched, a neat row of backpacks lined up between them. Their chairs circle a fire pit, and next to it is a giant cooler covered in California state park stickers.

They are clearly pros at this.

"You guys," I say. "I am so unprepared. I stopped at Walgreens on the way, but all I got was a toothbrush."

"My tent sleeps two," Hope says.

"I have an extra blanket," Mimi says.

Travis gestures to the old Volvo parked in front. "In my car I have enough hoodies to clothe a small village."

It feels so good to laugh.

"So what compelled you to come camping with the misfits?" Travis asks.

"What makes you misfits?"

"Well, to begin," Mimi says, "we're all terrible at math."

"And we're all mixed," Travis says. "Mimi's half Korean American and half white, I'm half Mexican and half white, and Hope? Well, Hope's got it rougher than anyone."

Hope nods in mock solemnity and says, "Half French, half Dutch."

"Besides all that," Mimi says, "we're, like, the only group of friends in the history of high school that has never had a fight, never fallen in love with each other, and never made out with another one's significant other."

"We feel more at home at campsites than we do in our houses," Hope says.

"We've encountered four bears over the last three years and we have never been eaten."

"And," Mimi concludes, "we have never—not once—attended a high school dance."

"Why not?" I ask.

"We camp instead," Hope says. "It was established homecoming of freshman year. Our parents wouldn't let us camp alone, though, so Travis's parents set up their tent a few sites away and came to check on us every few hours."

"That's sweet," I say.

Mimi says, "Once, sophomore year, we camped in Hope's backyard."

"Desperation," Hope says. "None of our parents were willing to camp in December."

"Do you like fish?" Travis asks. "We got a trout in our teacher's honor."

"Seriously?"

"Well, we always grill a trout, but this time it has special significance."

"Bad news on the booze front," Hope says, unzipping one of the backpacks. "I was only able to get my hands on the dregs of a bottle."

Travis examines the label. "Bourbon."

"I prefer tea when camping anyway," Mimi says, holding up her mug.

"Did you bring tea?" Travis asks.

"There's mint growing everywhere around here," Mimi says.

"So you just picked it and dropped it into your cup?"

"Yeah."

"Gross."

"I have no idea what you are even talking about," Mimi says. "I do this every time. And how is mint tea gross?"

"But is it really *tea*," Travis says. "Because my understanding is that tea is *dried* stuff."

Mimi shakes her head, opens her eyes wide, and stares into her mug.

"We can't even look it up," Hope says.

"It's possible we'll never know," Travis says.

"I want to try it," I say. "The tea."

Mimi looks at me. "So you're with me on this one?"

I smile at her and shrug. "I guess I need to taste it to find out."

She stands. Sets her mug down where she was sitting. She has all these little marks on her thighs from the texture of the rock she was sitting on. She walks along the path to the patch of mint, and I watch her break off a stem.

She pours water from the bottle into the tin pot and sets it over the flame.

"Did you bring a mug?" she asks me.

I shake my head.

She steps into her tent and emerges a few seconds later with a green mug, and I can't help thinking about how her mouth has probably been pressed to it so many times, and soon mine will be, too. She drops in the mint that she picked for me. She pours the hot water and places the mug into my hands.

"Let it steep for a few minutes," she says.

"I was thinking," Hope says after dinner. "About your tattoo. If you get it, you should also get one on your other arm, and that one should say *the beginning of love*. That way, depending on whether you choose to read them left to right or right to left, it could be that love began and now it's ending, or that love ended and is now beginning again."

The fire they built is going strong, lighting up their faces.

"But I thought love was supposed to be eternal," I say.

Travis sighs. "Just another lie they feed us when we're children. At least they're happy about it, though."

"They're *not* happy," I say. "They've just obliterated themselves."

There was a night last January, a night that Mom and I pretend never happened. The holidays had been full of stress and traffic and travel. The whole ride up to Portland, where we always spent Christmas, my heart had raced with the anticipation of coming out to my cousins and aunt and uncle and grandmother. Someone was bound to ask me if I had a boyfriend—they did every year—and I didn't want to just say no. I was so swept up in it that I barely noticed that my parents were more hostile than usual, until the drive home, when my mind was clearer. They stayed together for most of January, but the house may as well have been a trap—one misstep and blades would plummet from the ceiling, or the living room would fill with poisonous gas.

By the end of the month, Dad was staying with his friend a few towns away. One night I was up late with homework, trying to concentrate, and I thought a snack might help me through it.

My mother was down there, alone at the kitchen table.

"It didn't make things easier on us," she said out of nowhere, "that you had to tell the family when you did. I'm not saying you caused it, but there was tension between us before that, and to have that added stress . . . And at *Christmas*."

I tell them about it.

Mimi says, "And I hope you said, 'That's fucked up, Mom.'"

"No," I say. "I didn't say that."

"Well, I hope you do." She sips her tea. I sip mine. "I hope you tell her in the near future."

"The nearest future," Hope says.

"Like, tomorrow night," Travis says. "Like, the first thing you say when you walk through the door."

"Wait," Hope says. "What about now?"

And she stands on her tiptoes and waves her phone in the air, searching for a signal, until I say, "Not now, not now, not tonight."

The fire is burning down, still hot, but not as grand as before. Mimi pours simmering water into my mug.

"So, how is it?" Travis asks me.

"What?"

"The tea."

"Be honest," Mimi says.

"It tastes exactly like mint tea."

Travis's eyebrows shoot up in surprise. "Well okay then."

It's too cold to stay up any longer. I take my new toothbrush out of its packaging, untwist the lid of the travel-size toothpaste. I spot Travis coming out of Hope's tent with a sleeping bag and pillow. "Oh no," I say. "I'm taking your place?"

"Nah," he says. "It's better this way. She's always trying to get with me."

"Oh, please," Hope says. "You're like my brother."

He climbs into his bag.

Mimi says, "I'd invite you to stay in my tent, but you'd basically have to sleep on top of me."

"Girl," Travis says, "you know I don't want to listen to you snore all night."

He zips his bag higher, until only his eyes show.

"Don't suffocate," Mimi says. "We'd be lost without you."

"I promise," Travis says, and then even his eyes disappear.

"Do you have everything you need?" Mimi asks me.

She's given me two blankets, and Travis let me scavenge through his car for extra layers. Lucky for me, he's the kind of boy who smells nice.

I nod.

She says, "I'm so glad I drew you that picture."

"Me, too," I say.

"I'll see you in the morning, right? You aren't going to change your mind and leave us once we're all sleeping?"

"No way."

She touches my wrist. "Well, good night, then."

We close ourselves into the tent. Once Hope's in her sleeping bag and I'm in layers of sweaters, the rustle of our movement dies down and all I hear is the night. Wind and crickets. The faraway laughter from another site.

Hope whispers, "My parents got divorced when I was twelve."

"Oh," I say. "I'm sorry."

"It was like the ground was dropping out. It was terrible. I got used to it, but 'home' has never felt the same since."

The top of her tent is clear. I can see the moon and the stars, and her words feel just as vast and true. As much as people want to look on the bright side, skip straight to the future when everything will be okay, the truth is that there is *this* time, where you sometimes have trouble breathing, and you feel powerless. Like you're screaming and no one hears you, and the myth of the happy future is nothing you can count on, and the only word that makes sense is *escape*.

The end of love. The end of family. The end of being a daughter to people who wake up together in bed, leave their toothbrushes in the same little cup, roll their eyes and sigh and maybe hate each other but still come home to the same place each evening and sit at the same table.

"We only have a year," Hope says. "And then we get new homes that we make for ourselves."

"Yeah," I say.

"And, until then, we can camp."

Hope falls asleep. I lie very still and listen for Mimi's snores. Her tent is so close, but no sound escapes it. So much time passes that I worry it will get light soon and I won't have slept at all.

I breathe in.

She drew me a picture.

I breathe out.

She wanted me here.

"There's a magic tree," Mimi says in the morning. "I want to take you there. After breakfast, of course."

From out of nowhere come sausages and potatoes and eggs, somehow all hot on our plates at the same time, despite having only one pan and an open flame. We eat in silence, sip the coffee Hope makes cup by cup. Morning light streams through the redwoods. The air smells like campfire and earth and ocean, and I don't have a word for how I feel except maybe *alive*.

And then Mimi and I are walking to her car and climbing in, just her and me, and I'm touching the crystals she has on her dash: one clear, one pink, one yellow.

"What are these for?" I ask.

"My mom makes me have them in the car at all times. She believes they'll protect me."

I don't have words for this. I can't imagine having a mother who believes in something like that.

"Good thing they're pretty, right?" Mimi says, and I nod.

She drives slowly down the dirt road that leads away from camp, stopping to let a small group of children cross. She waits a moment after they're gone, and soon a little boy comes darting after them. She smiles.

"Had a feeling," she says. "There's always a straggler or two."

When she pulls over ten minutes later, it's into a turnabout that appears to be completely random. There's no trailhead, no sign, nothing to indicate that we are anywhere anyone is meant to be. I expect her to say she missed our turn, but instead she turns off the car and looks at me.

"Ready?" she asks, and then we're darting across the narrow street. She's leading me up a hill, through trees and ferns, tall grasses and wildflowers. We duck under branches and sidestep blackberry bushes, and then the land levels out into a clearing, and beyond the clearing, right under us, is the ocean.

"This," Mimi says, "is my favorite place in the entire world."

She leads me to the magic tree. It's not a redwood or an oak or a pine or a maple. I've never seen anything like it before. It's old—I can tell—but it isn't majestic like the redwoods. It's wider than it is tall, with thick branches that spread far on either side, its trunk covered with knots.

She jumps up onto a welcoming branch, climbs a little higher. I touch the bark and find a place where a tiny green shoot is beginning.

"I have a story to tell you," I say.

Mimi nods.

She reminds me of Alice in the tree, before she goes to Wonderland. I climb onto a branch and sit with my legs dangling. We could hurl ourselves into the ocean with just one push of our limbs, but it also feels safer, more peaceful, than any place has felt for a very long time.

It feels the way I thought summer school might feel.

"It's about me and my mom and our house."

"I want to hear it," Mimi says.

I feel like I do in Jessica's office when I'm starting to tell a story and already wondering why I'm telling it. But, as Jessica always says, I have to start somewhere.

"We bought the house when I was in seventh grade," I say. "And it was something that my mom had wanted really badly for a really long time. We lived in a fine house before that, but it wasn't a beautiful house, and my mom wanted all of these things, like a front porch and natural light. Room for a garden and nooks and crannies. She loves nooks and crannies. I do, too."

Mimi smiles. "I'll remember that."

"My dad works a lot of weekends, so my mom and I were the ones who went to all the open houses. We looked for months for the right house, and then we found it. It had everything we wanted, and it was on a pretty street lined with oak trees, and it was just a tiny bit more than my parents had wanted to spend. They put a bid on the house, and they got it, and that's when my mom and I really got started."

A breeze picks up, and I take a moment to look at the branches sway above us. I try to remember what it felt like back then, back when every day was a day I wanted to spend with my mother.

"We made plans for each room—the paint colors, the furniture arrangements. We held up all the paintings to all of the walls to find the perfect spots for each of them. We made long wish lists of things to buy. We chose wallpaper for the nooks and crannies. I got to pick the paper for under the stairs. I chose this retro pattern, dandelions against a pink background. We put a little chair and reading table there, and it was my favorite spot in the house for a long time.

"We went to thrift stores to hunt for antiques. We went to auctions to bid on more art. We went to galleries and chain stores and showrooms. I learned about colors and how to mix patterns. I learned about layering textures and caring for houseplants. Every time someone complimented my mother on the house, she said, 'Flora and I decorated it together.'"

Now they're just throwing it all away. *All* of it. As though it never mattered. But I can't find the words to explain what it means to me. There are tears on my face, and I didn't even know that I was crying. The end of love. The end of love.

Mimi slides off her branch and climbs up to mine. She takes my hands in her hands, but the gesture isn't consoling. It's more than that. "I remember when I first saw you," she says. "You were this happy, confident girl. And I wished I could yank Blake's arm away from you, put mine around you instead."

"I would have liked that."

"Even then?"

"Couldn't you tell? I feel so obvious around you. I always have."

"I knew you felt something." She lets go of one of my hands and touches my cheek.

I lean my face into her hand. I want her to keep it there forever.

"I wanted to kiss you then, when you were happy. And I want to kiss you now, while you're sad."

She just keeps looking at me, though. She doesn't move.

"I want that, too," I say. "A lot."

And then we tilt our faces, lean toward each other.

I am kissing Mimi Park, two years after I met her. I am kissing her even though I often told myself that I would probably never see her again. At night, sometimes, when I was awake and thinking of her, I told myself that maybe we weren't supposed to be together. Maybe, somehow, I got confused. Just because a person reveals something to you about yourself doesn't mean they're meant to do more than that. So just because catching a glimpse of Mimi that first time—and then each time after—made every part of me glow, made me want to press against her, didn't mean she was the one for me. Maybe all it meant was that I needed something different from what I was getting. I needed a *girl*.

But I'm three years older than I was then. I've kissed a few girls by now. I think I've even been in love. But nothing has ever felt like this.

I'm up against the trunk now, her hands on my face, in my hair, along my ribs, and then on the small of my back. I'm holding on to a smaller branch, afraid to let go.

"We're gonna fall out of this tree," I murmur, her mouth on my neck.

She pulls away. I want her back. She drops onto the grass, and I drop down after her. The ocean glitters below us. The sky is blue and clear. The tree is still magic. She pulls me down to the earth, and she kisses me again, and again, and I shift my body until she's under me, her hair against the moss, her eyes open wide, her lips still wet and smiling.

"I don't feel sad," I say.

She laughs and says, "Good. That's good. I don't, either."

"It's Flora and Mimi," Travis calls out when we get back, and just that sentence—just our names, joined by *and*—it floods me with happiness all over again.

"It's hiking time," Hope says.

Mimi kicks up her foot. "I only brought my sandals!"

"Oh, please," Travis says. "It's not that kind of hike."

We walk into redwood groves, where it's almost as dark as night, where the air is so much cooler, and then out of them again, into the sun. We walk cliffside with the ocean crashing below us, wild-flowers growing between rocks, and into the tiniest meadow I've ever seen, where we sit in a circle to rest.

I discover a cluster of California poppies next to me.

"I would pick you one," I tell Mimi, "if it wasn't illegal."

"Laws are for breaking." She leans over my lap and snaps a stem, weaves the poppy into my hair.

She looks at me.

"Perfect," she says, and Hope agrees, but Travis squints and shakes his head.

"She needs a second one for symmetry."

He plucks another and hands it to Mimi, and I don't know how I got so lucky, to be here with the three of them. It makes no sense that we would meet again the way we did, in a summer school class, us the only rising seniors in a classroom full of fifteen-year-olds.

"I have a question," I say.

"Tell us," Hope says.

"Why—*how*—are you *all* in geometry?"

"We're doomed when it comes to math," Hope says. "We've always been behind."

Mimi says, "It was the only class we had together last semester. First the teacher separated us because we couldn't stop talking to each other—"

"No exaggeration," Travis says. "It was, like, physically impossible for us to stop talking."

"And then we spent the whole time texting."

Hope shakes her head. "It was terrible. I tried to ignore my phone, but they kept shooting me meaningful looks. We all got Ds! And now here we are in summer school and we're all together *again*."

Travis says, "It's our second time through, and none of us are learning anything."

"You guys," I say. "What you need to understand is that geometry is the best math."

Hope laughs. Travis says, "*Best* and *math,* used in the same sentence . . . You've lost me." Mimi runs her hand along her tattoo and smiles.

"It's the most personal. It relates to our bodies." I stand up and hold my arms out. "Symmetry. Proportion. You guys know that Leonardo da Vinci drawing, where the man stands like this, and then you also see his limbs like this?" I widen my stance and raise my arms higher.

"Yeah, the naked dude," Travis says.

"I'm pretty sure most of his dudes were naked," Mimi says.

"But this one has a circle around him, right?" Hope asks.

"Yes! And a square, too. That drawing is all about geometry. And then there's all this other natural stuff—like when you throw a rock into water, and the ripples spread out, getting bigger and bigger? And the veins on a leaf. And the pattern of scales on fish. The way you can look at a tree trunk and see how it's grown. Beehives! Succulents!"

"What I don't get," Travis says, "is why they don't teach us *that* stuff. It's like they *want* us to fail."

"What *I* don't get," I say, "is that I signed up to take geometry because I thought it would be completely familiar and mundane, but I ended up here instead."

"That sounds like a compliment," Mimi says.

"It is." I sit down again and kiss her, quick and light, right at the corner of her mouth.

"Looks like some new dynamics have been established," Travis says, raising his eyebrows. "When we get back, I'm gonna go ahead and move my sleeping bag back into Hope's tent. Last night was fucking *freezing*."

Night is falling again. Hope comes back from her car with a ukulele. Travis disappears into the brush and returns with two fistfuls of leaves.

"I'm making tea," he says. "A very special blend. Mint and some other stuff."

"Is it going to kill us?" Mimi asks.

"Oh, come *on*," he says. "Nobody has ever died from tea."

I don't take a single sip, but it warms my hands as the air grows cooler.

"In honor of you, Flora, I'm singing exclusively love songs tonight," Hope says.

Mimi heats up minestrone over the campfire and divides it among four bowls. Every move she makes is enchanting. A drop of soup splashes on her thumb, and she sucks it off. She hands me a bowl, and our fingers touch.

She doesn't say much, but she's still telling me things. She's saying that yes, there are Januarys, and the terrible things people do to each other when they are no longer in love. She's telling me that *the end of love* is a fine phrase to ponder, but it's a poor choice for a tattoo. Because just as there are Post-its and red condominium doors, there are also tree branches and coastlines. There are sleeping bags and tents and pinpricks of stars, there are people like her, there is the person I'm becoming.

I'm going to have to drive home tomorrow. Maybe my parents will yell at me for going away like this. Maybe they'll smile and ask if it was fun. Either way will hurt.

In two weeks, our house will be empty. And then the stagers will descend with the trucks full of no one's furniture and art and try to make it look like a different family lived there, an imaginary family with no photographs or mail or food in their refrigerator. In real life, we were sometimes messy. We didn't always do the dishes. We left pots soaking. We let the papers pile up, and left too many pairs of shoes by the door, and didn't vacuum as much as we should have.

We were not always happy, but we were always us.

Tomorrow I'll walk in and we won't be us anymore, we'll be different people; we won't belong in the way we did before. I don't know what to do with that yet, but I know that it's true.

Hope's singing another love song, though, just as she promised. She strums a little clumsily, but her voice is clear and sweet, and she knows all the songs by heart. When she finishes, she announces that she's going to bed, and soon after, she and Travis disappear.

Mimi leans in close. I can smell mint on her breath—not like toothpaste or gum, like something real that's from the earth—and then her lips are on my ear and she's whispering, "I don't really snore."

I'm smiling.

Our heads pivot, until it's my mouth against her ear, and I say, "I know."

We're alone by the fire now, and the wind is picking up, and she takes my hand, and we walk together to her tent. I can hear everything: The pounding of my pulse. The crunch underneath our feet. The rustle of her clothes when she bends over to reach the tent's zipper. And then it begins: the sound of unzipping, from the ground on one side, and up, and up, and down again. I close my eyes even though it's already dark, because of this *sound*. It's like my life opening up.

And then it stops.

And we climb in.

Last Stand at the Cinegore

Libba Bray

O n the last night of the Cinegore, the sky looked like it needed
to call in sick, all yellow-green going dark around the
edges like an infected cut, a summer storm heading in hard.
Across the highway, bulldozers sat waiting like an army that had
the advantage. Come Monday morning, they'd advance to pulver-
ize the old Cinegore Theater into dust, and in its place would be
new condos, a phone store, and a Starbucks. Oh, yay.

"Kevin! Just in time."

As I shimmied under the concessions counter, my best friend,
Dave, reached over and dragged me to him into selfie position, his
phone held high above our faces.

I sighed. "Don't do this."

"C'mon, dude. We should record this moment."

"Can't the moment just be a moment?"

"Sh-h-h. Try to look pretty." Dave pursed his lips coyly. I wore my usual expression, something between resignation and disdain—resigdain. The camera blinked, and Dave released me so he could type. "Hashtag: LastNightAtTheCinegore."

"Yeah," I said, checking the pressure in the soda jets. "Going out with a bang."

"Exactly. *Last night,*" Dave said meaningfully. He jerked his head in the direction of the lobby's far end, where the object of my unrequited affections, Dani García, had positioned the yellow DO NOT FALL ON YOUR ASS AND SUE US cone in front of the ladies' lounge while she mopped. Her aqua-dyed hair had been cut into a Bettie Page do, then shaved on one side, above an ear that sported an array of earrings stacked like tiny silver vertebrae. For months, I'd been making a movie in my head starring the two of us. In that movie, we fought off a variety of monsters and saved the free world. Then we had celebratory sex. Which meant that there was a narrative in which we had also had a date. Which we hadn't. Not even close.

"You do the deed yet?" Dave asked around a mouthful of half-chewed gummi bears. Rainbow spit dribbled down his chin.

I grimaced and handed him a napkin.

Dave moaned, "Aw, you pussied out, didn't you?"

"'Pussied out' is sexist. I prefer 'made a strong choice for cowardice.'"

"Keva-a-a-an—"

"Dude. Shut up." I glanced over at the bathroom. Dani had moved inside with her mop. The door was closed. "I'm gonna do it," I said quietly, pushing my glasses up on my nose. "Just . . . not tonight."

Dave tossed two gummi bears at me in rapid succession. "Why? Not?"

"Ow?"

Dave threatened a third attack-gummi. I put up my hand. "It's . . . just not the right moment."

"Dude. Did Lincoln wait for the right moment to make the Gettysburg Address?"

"Yeah, Dave. He waited for Gettysburg to happen."

"Whatever." The third gummi bear bounced off my cheek and landed in the Sartresque territory beneath the ice bin. "The point is, you *make* it the right moment. Tonight's the last night you're gonna see her up close and personal. You've got two months of summer left, and then she's off to college, and then you'll be kicking yourself at our high school reunion because she'll be married to some heavily tattooed, Bentley-driving rock star and she won't even remember your name. She'll be all, 'Oh, hey, Kyle, right? Didn't we work together or something? Wait, you're that lame ginger dude who *didn't have the stones to ask me out!*'"

I yanked my skinny, freckled arms through the sleeves of my regulation red Cinegore usher's jacket, the one that made me look like a deranged Michael Jackson tribute band member. "Thanks for the encouragement, Dave. You always know just the right thing to say."

Dave ignored my sarcasm. "I'm here to save you from yourself. And from a life of perpetual masturbation."

"Dave."

"Yes, Pookie Bear?"

"Die in a fire."

"You're so pretty when you're angry," Dave said, and kissed me on the cheek. "Ask her."

"Ask her what?" Dani had emerged from the bathrooms. She wiped her hands on a paper towel, wadded it into a tight ball, and arced it toward the trash can, pumping her fist when it landed inside, a perfect two-pointer.

"Oh, um. We were talking about *I Walk This Earth*," I said quickly, pouring the artificial butter mixture—the I Can't Believe It's Not Going to Kill Me—into the popcorn hopper.

Dani snorted. I found it devastatingly attractive. In the movie in my head, she did that a lot. It was an audience pleaser. She grabbed the tongs and poked with disinterest at the overcooked hot dogs sweating under the heat lamps. "Ri-i-ight. The movie that's supposed to be cursed. Ooh!"

"Have you never seen *Showgirls*? Movies can be cursed." Dave raised his right hand. "Truth."

Dani rolled her eyes. "I didn't say *bad*. I said *cursed*. As in, not supposed to be seen by human eyes. Ever. How did Scratsche get his hands on a copy of it, anyway? I thought it was in some lead-lined safe deposit box somewhere."

I broke open a carton of straws and started shoving handfuls of them into the pop-up dispenser on the counter. "Beats me. As for the curse: according to that paragon of journalistic integrity, the *Deadwood Daily Herald*—circulation eight hundred and two, unless somebody died this afternoon—*I Walk This Earth* allegedly opens a gateway to hell as it's played. Kinda like when you sync up *The Wizard of Oz* and *Dark Side of the Moon*, but minus the drugs and plus demons."

Dani smiled big, and it kick-started my own movie montage.

```
SCENE 12: Dani and Kevin run through
a meadow of bluebonnets while a
sensitive rock-folk band on a nearby
hill plays an acerbic but heartfelt
love song. Dani wears a white sundress
that exposes the cool Japanese cherry
tree tattoo with her little brother's
name under it that decorates her
upper arm.
     "Take this mug I made for you in
Ironic Ceramics class," she says, and
hands me a cup that's completely
solid, no hole.
     "Thanks. I love ironic coffee most
of all," I answer, and the camera
catches the sexy stubble that lines
my action-hero jaw.
     Our faces move in for a kiss. We
never notice the zombie horde
advancing toward the emo folk singers.
```

I snapped out of my reverie to see Dani looking at me, eyebrows raised.

"Anyway," I said, blushing. "What with this being the end of the Cinegore, you'd think Scratsche would show up tonight."

Dani grabbed two straws and shoved them over her incisors like fangs. "He's probably home roasting children in his oven."

Dave shrugged and double dipped in the nacho cheese sauce. "Just more grist for the Scratsche rumor mill."

For several decades, Mr. Scratsche had been Deadwood, Texas's, favorite urban legend. He'd moved to town in 1963, when the nation was still mourning its beautiful promise of a president, and promptly bought Deadwood's run-down 1920s movie palace, the Cinemore Theater. Within a year, he'd turned it into a horror movie palace nicknamed "the Cinegore," due to its bloody slate of films. The Cinegore featured state-of-the-art details like Smell-O-Vision, Tingler shocker seats, skeletons that zoomed above the audience's heads on an invisible wire, and the only screen outfitted for 3-D in a forty-mile radius. People used to come from as far away as Abilene to see a first run. Personally, I can't imagine why anybody would want to build anything in Deadwood, Texas, which is true to its name. Leaving Deadwood is pretty much the best option out there. If you're somebody who has options.

Anyway.

No one had seen old Scratsche in years, not even us. When the Cinegore staff was hired, we'd each had to fill out a short, weird questionnaire about our hopes, dreams, and fears. Afterward, I'd gotten a brief note in the mail, written in very formal script, that said, *Congratulations. You are a good fit for the Cinegore, Mr. Grant. Sincerely, Mr. Nicholas Scratsche.*

His reclusiveness fed the appetite for speculation: He was from Transylvania. He was from a circus town in Florida. He was tall. He was short. He was a defrocked priest specializing in off-book exorcisms. He'd killed the son of a nobleman back in the old country and was hiding out here. There were dozens of rumors but only three pieces of tangible evidence that Mr. Scratsche had ever existed at all. One was the Cinegore. Two was his signature on our paychecks. And three was a framed black-and-white photo that hung on the badly lit wall of the staircase leading up to the projection room, a photo of Scratsche cutting the ribbon at the opening of the Cinegore, October 31, 1964.

I'd never much liked that picture. In it, Mr. Scratsche has on this shiny, sharkskin suit, the kind of thing that looked like it would go up with one match. But it wasn't Scratsche's questionable fashion choices that gave me the creeps; it was his eyes. They were dead-of-night black. You could look into them and see nothing but yourself staring back. Every time I passed that picture, those eyes found me, judged me. They made the hair on the back of my neck whisper dread to my insides. They made me *look*.

Overhead, the Gothic chandelier bulbs flickered and dimmed—a power surge, one of the Cinegore's infamous quirks. A few seconds later, they blazed back up to full wattage. We let out a collective exhale.

"Dodged that one," Dani said and high-fived me.

I enjoyed the momentary feel of her skin against mine, even if it was just some palm-to-palm action. Fact: When most of your nights are spent threading old horror movies through an artifact of a projector, any human contact is exciting. Which sounds kind of pathetic. That's probably because I *am* a little pathetic. In life as in film, find your niche and work it.

John-O, our resident freshman, signaled urgently from outside that he was ready to release the velvet rope barrier keeping the ticket holders in line. John-O was a short spark plug of a kid with a learner's permit and a habit of telling us the plot of every movie we'd still like to see. In an act of petty revenge for this, Dave, Dani, and I all pretended not to understand his wild gestures. We added some of our own, turning it into a dance, until finally, in frustration, John-O opened the door and yelled in, "Uh, you guys? I'm gonna let people in now, okay?"

"Do it, pumpkin! Be *you!*" Dave finger-gunned at John-O, who stiffened and ran over to the rope, fiddling nervously with the brass release hook. Dave sighed. "God bless freshmen."

"Here we go. Last stand at the Cinegore," I said as people

swarmed in through the doors. "We who are about to die salute you."

Maybe a third of the seats were filled. Even on our last night, with a supposedly haunted movie, we couldn't draw a crowd. No wonder they were bulldozing us. Dave reminded everyone about turning off cell phones just before he snapped pics of the audience, who were, in turn, memorializing themselves and uploading it all.

Then I went into my bit. "Welcome to the last night of the Cinegore Theater, your premier vintage horror movie experience."

"Shut up and start the movie!" Bryan Jenks called from the back row. There was a reason we called him Bryan Jerks.

I took a deep breath. "As you know, *I Walk This Earth* is cursed—"

"Mo-vie! Mo-vie! Mo-vie!" Bryan and his pals chanted. A couple of the hipsters tried to shut them down with an apathetic "Dude, c'mon" chorus, but that only made Bryan try harder.

"Hey, Jerks—your mother still cut the crusts off your sandwiches?" Dani was suddenly beside me, shining her usher's flashlight right in Bryan's eyes.

He held up a hand. "Damn, girl. Don't blind me."

"Don't piss me off, and I won't," she said. "Got your back, vato," she whispered in my ear. Her breath sent a shiver down my neck.

"All the people who worked on this movie died in mysterious ways," I continued. "The lead actress, Natalia Marcova, hung herself in a cheap motel room. Teen heartthrob Jimmy Reynolds was beheaded when he crashed his car into a tree. The mileage on his odometer? Six hundred sixty-six miles."

"Ohmigod," a girl in the front row said, giggling nervously with her friends. The booze on their breath was eye-wateringly potent.

"Lead actor, Alistair Findlay-Cushing—"

"That was his actual name, not a stage name," one of the local college hipsters said smugly.

Dani mouthed, "Wikipediot."

Fighting a grin, I said, louder, *"Alistair was found facedown on his bed*, a pentagram scrawled on the floor, his heart nailed to the center of it." I stopped to enjoy the audience's squirms. "But the creepiest part? When director Rudolph Van Hesse was on his death-bed, he confessed that he'd sold his soul to the devil to make the film, and that it had the power to corrupt anyone who watched it. 'There is evil woven into this film. A powerful darkness shines out from each frame. It must not be seen *by human eyes!*'"

"How can darkness 'shine out'?" Hipster Dick said.

In my movie, he would die slowly and painfully, thanks to sentient, malevolent facial hair. I ignored him. "Van Hesse may have spent the last ten years of his life in a mental institution, but it didn't stop him from having every print of his film destroyed . . . except for one copy kept under lock and key for the past fifty-five years. That single existing copy is the one you're about to watch."

"Ooh," the audience said.

"So put on your special DemonVision 3-D glasses and enjoy the show. We'll see you at the end—if you survive."

The theater went dark, and I stumbled into Dani on the way out. "Sorry! You okay? Jeez, I'm so . . . sorry."

The smell of her vanilla perfume made me want to bury my face in the crook of her neck. She quirked an eyebrow, and I realized I was still holding on to her. I sprang back. "Sorry."

"It's okay," Dani said, and pushed through the theater doors into the bright lobby. I hung behind for a second to get my shit together.

"Sorry," I said again to the dark. But really I was just sorry I had to let go.

I met Dani halfway through our junior year, when she moved to Deadwood from San Antonio and landed in my alphabetically appointed homeroom class (A–G, Dani García, Kevin Grant). She had pink pigtails and the air of somebody from the Big City. Plus, she wore a Bikini Kill T-shirt. I was toast.

"Hey. Nice shirt," I'd said, pointing.

"Oh my gosh," Lana French had shouted. "Kevin just pointed to the new girl's boobs!"

For two weeks solid, I was known as McBoobster. After that, my exchanges with Dani were on a strictly "Heyhowareyou/Wellseeyalater" basis. I'd watched from the sidelines as she cycled through short-term-parking romantic partners: Paul Peterson (he of the any-surface-can-be-skateboarded fame), Ignacio Aguilar (a strange, mostly texting-based relationship), Martha Dixon (the brief bi-curious period, documented through a variety of Hot Topic T-shirts), and the true horror show, Mike Everett, who had broken up with Dani three days before the Valentine's dance so he could go with Talisha Graham instead, which was just wrong—like, adult-diaper-party wrong.

And then, by some spring miracle, Dani had taken a shift at the Cinegore. "Thought I'd see what all the fuss is about," she'd said. "Besides, it beats working the fry baskets at Whataburger."

For the past four months, we'd been toiling side by side, our Saturday nights playing out like a montage from every bad teen romance ever filmed: Wayward fingers briefly touching in the vast fields of popcorn. Heads bending in sympathy as we restocked the Raisinets. Eyes glancing while we talked smack with Dave about which Richard Matheson movie adaptation was the best: *The Last Man on Earth* (me), *The Omega Man* (Dani), or *I Am Legend* (Dave, who was a sucker for both Will Smith and German shepherds). When our shifts ended, we'd stagger down the road to IHOP at two a.m. for plates of spongy pancakes and endless cups of burned coffee. Sitting there with my best friend in the world and the girl I secretly loved, I would feel like a vampire, staring out through night-painted windows at the lonely semis crying down the interstate, willing the dawn to stay tucked in for just a few hours more so I could suck up all the living I could get.

When the first streaks of pink lit up the West Texas scrub, we'd wobble out to our cars. "Later. Unless we're killed in our sleep by malevolent forces," I'd say. Dani would laugh and give me a half-wave, and for the entire ride home I'd obsess about the meaning of that one gesture, reading hope into every flutter of her fingers. I'd let myself into the house, stepping carefully over my mom's empty vodka bottles. Then I'd crawl into bed and let the Dani–Kevin horror movie in my head spool out toward its inevitable victorious-romantic conclusion.

"And we . . . are . . . go," I said, as the dramatic score blared from the Cinegore's speakers. Through the projection booth window, I could just make out the grainy opening credits before I walked away.

"Aren't you going to watch this marvel of cinematic art?" Dave taunted from the floor, where he sat hunched over his bag of weed.

"Maybe later." I glanced pointedly at Dani, but Dave was already engrossed in his Olympic-caliber spliff-rolling skills.

"I wish we'd at least go out with something good, like *Final Destination 12: We Really Mean It This Time*. Now *that* is a rad movie," he said.

Unlike me, Dave thought that vintage horror films were crap. He couldn't see the beauty in blood splatters made from chocolate syrup and werewolf transformations achieved via painstaking stop-motion. If it didn't feature multimillion-dollar explosions and a heavy body count, Dave wasn't interested.

"Like, why would you come here and pay twelve bucks and eat stale corn and get gum on your new kicks," Dave said, his voice tight with held smoke, "when you could stream that shit on your phone from your toilet?"

I rolled my eyes. "Classy."

"Dude, that's the future. This . . ." Dave gestured to the small confines of the projection room as he exhaled a gust of weed fumes. "This is a graveyard."

He offered the joint to me. I shook my head, and he offered it to Dani.

"No, thanks. I'll just enjoy the inevitable contact high."

Dave shrugged and took another hit.

"Yeah, but what about the ritual of getting your ticket and your snacks, finding the perfect seat," I countered. "All those strangers watching the movie with you, they change how you see it, you know? You should hear their gasps and laughter and sniffling. It's a communal experience. You can't get that on your laptop or phone. That sharing, it's the foundation of storytelling. It reminds us that we're . . ."

"What?"

"Human. Humans who need other humans," I said, glancing quickly at Dani.

"That was so beautiful, Kevin." Dave pulled me into a crushing hug and kissed the top of my head. "Mother, our little Kevey's all grown up."

I pushed Dave away hard. "Not everything is mockable."

"Then you're not trying hard enough," Dave shot back, and even though I loved him, I wanted to punch him, too. Because I was gutted about the Cinegore closing down. I loved the old place like crazy—the sneaker-flattened, rose-patterned carpets; the ratty projection room that always smelled vaguely of weed and BO; the gaudy chandeliers with their fluttering, unpredictable lights; the popcorn-littered rows of red leather seats; the billboard-sized marquee out front with the letters frequently rearranged by drunken pranksters to say rude things. After my dad took off and my mom's drinking got worse, the Cinegore had been my safe place. It had become more home than home.

"I get it," Dani said, surprising me. "When you watch one of these old movies in a place like this, you're connected to everybody else who's ever watched it. You can practically feel them around you."

"I hope you brought condoms, then," Dave said, pinching the end of the joint to put it out. "Safety first, kids."

"Oh my God." Dani's eye roll was a thing of beauty.

"Dave," I said, a little sharply. "Make yourself useful. Take out the trash. It smells like a bag of your farts."

"Kev, how do you expect me to get my curse on if I can't watch the movie? Why can't *you* take out the trash?"

"Because I'm the manager, that's why."

Dave sighed dramatically as he staggered to his feet and headed for the door. "Absolute power corrupts absolutely. Discuss. Oh, and one more thing." He turned his ass to us, farted loudly, and shut the door. I heard him shouting "Victory for the proletariat!" on his way down the hall.

"Admit it: He's your community service project," Dani said, waving her hand in front of her nose.

"Sadly, I get no points for befriending David Wilson. Just a lifetime of painful stories to tell my children someday."

In her flimsy Misfits tank top, Dani shivered from the Cinegore's icy AC. She steadfastly refused to wear the beribboned usher's jacket, citing her reasons, alternately, as "I don't do butt ugly," "Dress codes are basically fascism," or "It's not like the boss is around to fire me."

She offered me an apologetic smile that made my stomach tingle. "Sorry. Forgot my sweater again. Can I . . . ?"

Automatically, I peeled off my jacket and draped it around her shoulders, as I did practically every shift.

"Thanks." Dani threaded her arms through the sleeves and gave my jacket a surreptitious sniff. I hoped it didn't smell bad, but she smiled, so I figured it was okay. She picked up a Cthulhu plush figurine from the elaborate horror diorama she'd been adding to over the months. In his current incarnation, Cthulhu wore a Strawberry Shortcake dress. "Is it weird that I'm gonna miss this place so much?"

"No. It's not weird at all." I couldn't help hoping that I was included in the things she'd miss. "Maybe we'll have to get together on Friday nights and dress up in our uniforms and throw Coke on the floor just to relive the experience." I tried to make it sound like a joke, in case she wasn't interested.

"I'll spray some Scorched Popcorn air freshener so we can have that feeling of being nauseated but strangely hungry at the same time."

"For sure," I added, my hope making me a little dizzy. "And then one of us can shout, 'Please deposit all trash in the receptacles. Thank you. Good night.'"

My imaginary movie cranked up again. This time, we drove a vintage Mustang through the desert like a couple of badass outlaws.

"Do it, Kevin," Dani says, sliding
behind the wheel while I jump up
through the sunroof, my sawed-off
shotgun trained on the semi full of
undead trying to force us off the
road. "How do a pack of revenants know
so much about driving?" It's a legit
question. Dani's a smart girl.

"I don't know, baby. I'll work it out
in post," I say, and toss a hand
grenade behind us, where it explodes
in a fireball of zombie-infused glory.
"That's for remaking <u>Psycho</u> with Vince
Vaughn!" I shout.

Dani was playing nervously with Cthulhu Shortcake's dress.
"Hey, um. I've never really said thank you."

"For what?"

She used Cthulhu to gesture toward her diorama. "You were the
first person to ever take my art seriously."

I shrugged, embarrassed. "That's because it's awesome. You're
awesome. I mean, an awesome, awesome artist. Your art is . . .
awesome." *Jesus.*

"Still, it meant a lot," Dani said, thankfully ignoring my babble.
"You're the reason I applied to UT and got that art scholarship."

I was the reason she was leaving Deadwood. Great.

"You should let me draw you sometime."

My face went hot at the idea of posing for Dani, maybe on her
bed. Shit. I did not want to get sprung now. "Um. Like in *Titanic*?"
I splayed my hand against the wall. "Jack! *Ja-a-ack!*"

Dani laughed. "Just for that, I'm never giving back your jacket.
It's mine now." She pulled it tight around her. Her eyes shone with
challenge. The inside of my chest was a cage match between heart
and breath, and both were losing.

"Moot point now," I said. "Keep it."

Dani nodded, but her smile faded. "It's sad that all this history can be gone just like that." And I knew she didn't mean the Cine-gore.

Six months before Dani had landed in my homeroom, her mom and her little brother had been flying to a family wedding in Mexico City. The weather had been shitty, thunderstorms up and down the Gulf. They'd just cleared Corpus Christi when lightning struck an engine. The plane had floated, powerless, and then plunged. The wreckage had been scattered for a mile along the pretty spring break beaches of South Padre. Up in the dunes, somebody found the wedding present Dani's mom had been carrying. It had washed ashore, perfectly intact.

I rifled through the dusty cardboard box for a pair of black-framed 3-D glasses. "So, um, apparently? These help you see things that are invisible otherwise," I said, hoping to bring her back from the brink of sad. "Supposedly, there's a special effect where it looks like demons are coming out through the screen—that's how the whole gateway to hell rumor got started. The effect was a huge deal. And nobody knows how they did it."

"Really?" Dani spun a pair of glasses around by the temple piece. "Should we give DemonVision a try?"

"On three," I said. "One."

"Two."

"Three," we said, and slid them on.

On-screen, it was just an early 1960s take on an old mansion. Lots of wood paneling, framed oil paintings, and taxidermied animal heads. The James Dean–like Jimmy Reynolds leaned against a fireplace in full angst-rebellious mode, even though he wore an early nineteenth-century suit with a cravat. Fact: Nobody looks bad-ass in a cravat. Beautiful Natalia Marcova lounged on a divan, her raven mane curled over the shoulders of her ball gown. Beside her, square-jawed Alistair Findlay-Cushing gulped what I supposed was a manly Scotch from a crystal tumbler and delivered his lines in a world-weary Mid-Atlantic accent: "I've heard the rumors about your family. Madness is in the blood. You're originally from the Carpathian Mountains, if I'm not mistaken."

Lightning flashed, revealing waxwork-like creatures with

hideous mouths peering in through the mansion's windows. And then, suddenly, Jimmy Reynolds raced toward the screen in a panic: "Please, get out while you can! Take off your glasses and leave this theater at once. You're in great danger!"

"Whoa. Super meta," Dani muttered.

"Yeah. Very *Invasion of the Body Snatchers.*" My shoulder touched hers, and I wanted there to be a word for the current that shot up my arm, a word like *ShoulderSplosion!* or *AlmostSex.*

"Please, you must believe me," Jimmy Reynolds continued. "They'll come for you, soon. I've seen it before. You won't survive. Turn it off now, I beg you! That's the only way!"

Natalia Marcova glanced nervously toward the audience and back to Jimmy Reynolds. "Now, Thomas, what are you saying? You're not yourself."

"Man, this is so-o-o bad. Still. It's oddly . . . compelling," Dani said, her words a bit dreamy.

"I love how inventive they were with the special effects back then, you know? All those models, double exposures, split screens, and stop-motion. They used foam latex to make the outfit for *Creature from the Black Lagoon.* And all those stabbing sounds? That's just guys dropping fruits and letting them splat."

"Yeah? Cool," Dani said.

For the first time ever, I didn't care about the movie. I just wanted to be with Dani, talking about stupid shit that eventually became meaningful shit, and then, if everything went well, we could stay up all night and watch dawn creep over the flat grassland, turning everything a golden pink as we shared our first kiss.

Sweat slickened my palms, and I rubbed them against my jeans. "Hey, um, are you, like, sticking around this summer?"

Dani was still engrossed in the movie, so I tapped her arm.

"Huh? Oh. Sorry." She turned to me. The oversize 3-D glasses gave her a mutant bug creature quality. I dug it. "Yeah. Yeah, I am. I've got a job nannying for the Cooper twins. They're total booger-eating firestarters. But the money's decent."

Lame dialogue drifted up from inside the theater: "You know this old house has its secrets . . ." "Why are we continuing this pantomime? We know how it ends. I want out of my contract. I want to leave!" "Sh-h-h, Jimmy. He'll hear you."

"Well, this summer, when you're not, like, tending to the children of the damned . . ." It was like I was trying to swallow an air egg. "I was just wondering if maybe you'd want . . ."

The door to the projection room swung open and Dave burst in, cradling three giant Cokes and several boxes of no doubt stolen candy. "Refreshments!"

"Awesome." Dani removed her glasses. She pocketed a box of Milk Duds, then took a sweating paper cup from Dave and punched a straw through its plastic top.

"Yeah. Thanks. Great timing," I snarked, grabbing my Coke.

Dave dropped onto the stool by the projector and slipped Dani's abandoned glasses over his eyes. "Whoa. You guys are green. No, red! Green *and* red. Why, you're *three-dimensional!*"

Dani snorted. "At least some of us are."

"Harsh, García!" Dave pushed the big black frames up on the top of his head like a starlet. "You know what? Alastair Findlay-Cushing is kinda hot. I'd do him."

"Your list of men you'd do isn't exactly discriminating. You have a crush on Coach Pelson," I said.

"Coach Pelson is a hottie. In a former-wrestler-going-to-seed kind of way. I'll bet he talks dirty."

"A-a-ah, stop!" Dani laughed. "You are ruining my beautiful, sepia-toned memories of gym class."

That was the thing about Dave—everybody liked him. Even his obnoxiousness had a certain charm to it, like the time he'd scarfed down my red Jell-O in the cafeteria and pretended to "vomit Ebola" on a screaming Lyla Sparks, who was mean-girling Jennifer Trujillo for having a "starter mustache, just like a baby lesbo." Junior year, when Dave had come out, he'd actually gotten a bump in popularity. He'd been my best friend since seventh-grade science class. In two months, he'd leave for Stanford, and I wasn't sure how I'd cope with the loss of him.

Downstairs, the movie continued, unconcerned with my fate: "It's the cloven foot—the calling card of the one who must not be named. Lucifer himself."

"Dude, he just said he should not be named, and then he's all, 'Oh, yeah, let me just say *Lucifer* right now.' Hey. You know about old Alastair, don't you?" His thick eyebrows drawbridged up and down. Dave was practically a walking Google search of salacious Hollywood gossip. "Total Team Dorothy. He tried to kill himself once."

I raised my soda in toast. "That's a big party upper. Thanks, Dave."

"Slow your roll, holmes. He didn't try to kill himself in some tired, tragic gay-hatred moment. No. Before his attempt, Alastair begged a priest to perform an exorcism and cleanse his soul. He claimed that he'd made a deal with the devil for fame, and he hadn't had a moment's peace since. He claimed that *I Walk This Earth* wasn't a movie; it was a living thing that demanded souls and a willing sacrifice. Don't you think it's weird that the only two times they showed the movie, the theaters burned down?"

"Yeah. That's pretty freaky, all right," Dani said, dangling Cthulhu Shortcake by its string. "But this is not a night for the tragedies of the past. This is about avoiding the tragedies of the future." She looked me right in the eyes. It made me want to be a better man. "The old gods demand an answer to last week's burning question."

The week before, Dani had agreed to be Creepy Balloon Girl in *Zombie Ennui,* the fourth opus in my series of six-minute horror films. Honestly, it wasn't much of a script, just something I'd come up with on the fly as an excuse to spend more time with her. Halfway through filming, we got chased out of the cemetery by some kind of tweaker squirrel, and then we couldn't stop laughing long enough to get back on track. Punch-drunk and sweaty, we'd retreated with a couple of Big Gulps to the town park, taking refuge from the Texas heat under the measly shade of a drab brown live oak.

Dani sucked up helium from one of the drooping balloons. "It is I, your guidance counselor, Titus Androgynous. What are your future plans, Kevin?" she'd asked in her Minnie Mouse voice. Then she pressed the edge of the balloon to my lips, her fingers warm and soft against my face.

I hesitated for as long as I could, greedy for the feel of those fingers. At last, I inhaled. "I will be on my home planet of Totally-fuckedtopia, aka working at the Deadwood Froyo shop." I was grateful that the helium made it sound funny instead of painful.

Dani wiped at eyes still smudgy with stage makeup. "How come?"

I had wanted to reach for the familiar rip cord of an emergency joke. Instead, I told her the truth. "Money, for one. Unimpressive grades, for two. And three . . ." I sipped some Dr Pepper. "I gotta look after my mom. She's got some . . . health issues."

"What about your dad? Can't he help out?"

"My dad's in Arizona," I said.

Every Christmas, we got a fancy holiday card featuring a smiling photo of him and his New and Improved Family 2.0 in matching shirts and smiles, hugging it out in front of a big-ass, professionally decorated tree. It was a far cry from the cigarette-stained walls of the crappy apartment that my mom and I shared, where she spent most of her time passed out in her bedroom or hungover on the couch watching daytime TV. The booze had wreaked havoc on her diabetes, and now she was drinking down the disability checks as fast as they came in. In rare sober moments, she'd kiss my forehead and murmur, "I don't deserve you. You should get out." But I didn't want to be a bailer like my dad.

"Well, as your guidance counselor, I feel obligated to remind you that you have options," Dani had said, and the way she'd looked at me, so full of hope, I wanted to believe her. The only thing I was solid about were my feelings for Dani. When I dared to imagine a future that didn't totally suck, somehow, it always started with the two of us—her painting and me making indie horror films. But breaking into the film industry would be impossible, stuck here in Deadwood. And there was no way Dani would want to waste her time with a nowhere dude like me, anyway. The truth was, *Dani* had options, and I was pretty sure I wasn't one of them.

"Kev?" Dani prompted. "Plans?"

I snatched away Cthulhu Shortcake, avoiding Dani's gaze. "I hear there's a future in contract killing."

"My man Kev's going to direct the first hipster horror movie," Dave said, throwing me a bone.

"Totally." I slurped more soda to ease the ache in my throat. "The thing is, you won't be able to tell who's a zombie and who's not, because who can tell the difference between the terminally ironic and the undead? It will be called—wait for it—*The Undudes*. It'll be all 'Narghhhzzmnnnn,' and then the other undudes standing in line outside the concert venue in bloodstained, sardonic beer caps will be like 'Mnnngggggrrrr,' which translates to 'That flesh was too mainstream.'"

Dani nodded. "Got it. So, the *Undudes* plot: what happens?"

I shrugged. "Nothing."

Dave grinned. "Which is why it's the perfect Kevin movie!"

He was kidding. I knew he was. But it lodged in my chest like a piece of truth shrapnel. I shoved Cthulhu Shortcake deep into my pocket. "Not cool, Dave."

He looked at me, hard, and that was almost worse. "Dani's right. Not too late to be a part of the future. It's coming, pal. Ready or not."

"Yeah," I said. "And I hear it's gonna have a Starbucks."

The lights started doing their taunting flicker-dance. The voices on screen slowed to a drunken crawl, and then the film stopped altogether. We were plunged into darkness. Power surge. A real one this time.

"Shit," I said to the dark.

A chorus of protests erupted down below in the theater. People were actually screaming. Jesus. Fucking entitled wankers. In that moment, I hated them all.

Dave shook his head. "Dude, I went last time."

I sighed. "I'm on it." Maybe I'd just stay down there in the basement for the rest of my shift.

Dani grabbed the flashlight from its perch on a two-by-four beside the door. "I'll go with you. You know, in case Scratsche keeps his coffin down there and you need backup."

And, just like that, my hopes for the night came back online.

We felt our way toward the stairs to the lobby. The small emergency bulbs that lined the sides of the floor had come on, turning the carpet dark as blood. When I got to the photograph, I stopped. Even in the near dark, those eyes taunted: *Look at me, Kevin. I see into your heart. I know you.* I took the last four steps in a leap, my heart pounding.

Outside, lightning crackled in the dark sky as heavy rain pounded the Cinegore's nearly empty parking lot. As we followed Dani's flashlight beam, John-O fell in behind us like a hyperactive puppy. "Hey, what happened to the movie? It was just getting good. It's weird, but I was actually starting to feel like I was part of it."

"Wow. Cool story, bro." I brushed past him, pulled open the door of the theater, and yelled in, "Sorry, folks. There's been a power surge. We'll have the movie up and running in just a few minutes. Thanks for your patience." I readied myself for the usual litany of complaints, but it was mostly strange moaning, and I hoped I wouldn't have to break up a heavy make-out session in the back row.

"It was kinda spooky," John-O continued. "I thought I saw—"

"Dude, we gotta fix the lights. Back in five," I said.

Dani and I opened the door behind the concessions stand and trundled down the steps to the rank, damp basement. There was no AC down there, and the summer heat had baked into the walls, giving the room the high warmth of a kitchen after a full day's work. It was a sharp contrast to the frigid temps upstairs, but it wasn't unpleasant.

"Where's the fuse box?" Dani's flashlight bounced around the cinder block walls in George Romero circles of light.

"On the right," I said. "Higher."

She raised the beam, and I pried open the metal cover. I toggled the master switch until I heard the familiar *glurg-kachunk* of the generator wheezing back to life, along with the muffled slur of bad movie dialogue as *I Walk This Earth* got back up to speed. Above our heads, long fluorescent tubes blinked like children startled awake and then, all at once, they caught, and a sickly bluish glare flooded the basement. I knew we should go back up, but I wanted more alone time with Dani.

"Wow." I walked deeper into the basement. "This is like an episode of *Hoarders: Horror Show Edition*."

Metal shelves stuffed with crumbling *Fangoria* magazines lined one wall. A six-foot-tall swamp monster replica rotted in a forgotten corner behind stacks of busted theater seats. On the floor was a box of dusty promotional giveaways—red-eyed rubber rats and fake-guillotine cigar cutters. Dani leafed through water-stained, foam board–mounted placards for movies in Glorious Technicolor! "*Satan's Nuns. The Diabolical Mr. Lamphrey*," she read. "*The Five Fingers of Dr. Killing Time*."

"Check this one." I pulled out a 1970s-era poster of a leisure-suited vampire karate chopping the necks of two drug dealers. Behind him, a werewolf angled his hairy torso out the window of a gold Cadillac, his giant canine teeth bared like he meant drug dealer–eating business. I read the tagline aloud as if I were a movie announcer: "'Dr. Drac and Mr. Wolf: They're here to put a bite on crime.' Okay, seriously. How is this even a horror movie?"

"It's Dracula and the Wolfman. Doesn't get more old school than that," Dani said and shoulder-checked me, and I swear I felt it everywhere at once.

I grinned like a doofus. "No. Huh-uh. This is an abomination. It's, like, *Law and Order: Transylvania*. The Wolfman has a *gun*. By all the horror gods, how is that possible? *He doesn't even have thumbs!*"

Dani laughed, and I'm not gonna lie, I just wanted to keep telling jokes so I could hear her laugh more.

"Nice swag." Dani picked up a realistic-looking bow-and-arrow set, a special giveaway from *Robin Hood: Prince of Darkness*. "You could do some damage with this. Seriously, they let kids have these?" She pressed the arrow against the bow's string, aiming it playfully at my heart.

I put up my hands. "Careful with that."

"Don't worry." Dani lowered it again. "I only took one semester of archery. My biggest score was impaling Coach Pelson in the ass."

"Whoa, that was you? You could be in the inevitable remake of

Hippolyta Rises from the Grave, Pinewood Studios, 1966."

Dani perched carefully on top of a replica tombstone. "You really love these old movies, don't you?"

"Yeah. True horror is based in all that deeply human stuff— sorrow, fear, doubt, anxiety. Desire." I swallowed awkwardly. "But the new movies? Five minutes in, somebody's getting cut up by a chain saw or sewn into a skin suit. There are no emotional stakes. It's completely impersonal, like Internet porn."

Shit. Why did I say "porn"?

"Did I ever tell you that my parents' first date was a horror movie?" Dani said, and I shook my head. "Yeah. My grandmother is mad Catholic, and she wouldn't let my mom go on a date without my aunt Yoli tagging along. My dad said that Yoli screamed so much the manager made her wait it out in the lobby. And then my dad was all, 'Middle fingers, we out!' He slipped through the fire door with my mom and they went dancing in a club down the street. So, in a weird way, I owe my existence to a horror movie." She smiled at me, and my heart started playing a punk beat.

"Wow. Cool," I barely managed. The heat was starting to catch up to me. I wiped a thin layer of sweat from the back of my neck.

Dani looked me right in the eyes again. "UT has a great film school, you know. You wouldn't be that far from Deadwood. No— wait! Don't make that face! I'm serious."

"Yeah, yeah . . ."

"Kevin!" She wasn't smiling anymore. "What are you afraid of? For real."

For real? Spiders. People leaving me. Not being good enough. Rejection. Too much responsibility. Being buried alive by an escaped psychopath. Losing out on a chance to date the coolest girl I knew. Turning out like my dad. The list was endless. But mostly I was afraid of a future so terrifying in its unformed vastness that it pressed in on me with its bullying fists until I was afraid to take a real breath. I was afraid of being left behind while Dani and Dave spun toward that future. But admitting my fear only felt like giving it more power over me.

"I fear nothing," I said in a fake German accent. "For I am Van

Hotsprings, killer of vampire sperm at precisely one hundred and four degrees."

Dani's mouth settled into a sideways squiggle of disappointment. "Mm-m-m. Okay. Well, whatever. Let's go up," she said, flat, and hopped off the headstone.

Fuck. In my head, a new movie, *Night of the Living Dumbass*, played:

```
INT. Basement. Bad, bad, night.
    The zombie horde attacks Kevin but
stops when they realize that killing
him is redundant. Cut. Roll credits.
Fin.
```

When we got back upstairs, the lights were only operating at half power. The AC was still blasting, though. The sudden cold of it made me shiver. John-O had his DemonVision glasses on. He'd propped open the door with his foot and was watching the movie through the crack.

"John-O," I said. He didn't respond. "Yo, Earth to John. Did you set the popcorn maker for a fresh batch? John?"

I snapped my fingers near his ears. Finally, I yanked the glasses off his nose, and he blinked a few times. "Oh. Hey. When did you get here?"

"Son, haven't your mother and I warned you about the dangers of marijuana?" I said. John-O still seemed dazed. "Seriously. You okay, dude?"

"Yeah. I think so. It's so weird. I was watching the movie and, I don't know, for a minute there, it felt like I was actually inside of it."

"O-o-k-a-ay." Dani loaded fresh GMO-infected kernels into the popcorn hopper. With the bow slung over her shoulder and the arrow sticking up out of the back of her pants, she looked completely badass.

"The thing is, I *wanted* to be there. I didn't want to leave," John-O continued. "And then I thought I saw these creatures outside the window of the old mansion."

"Yeah, John-O. That's because it's a horror movie." I left him to join Dani behind the counter. I didn't have anything to do, really; I just wanted to be close to her. To look busy, I pushed the ice around in the big silver bin, breaking up the chunks with the scooper and wishing I could rewind this rapidly devolving night.

"No. That's not it." John-O sounded pissed. "The next thing I knew, those things were inside the mansion. And somebody was calling my name. He told me the creatures needed permission to come out. He asked me to grant them permission."

Dani looked concerned. "What did you say?"

"I said . . ." John-O twitched as if he were shaking off imaginary bugs. His voice deepened, like puberty on time lapse. "I said sure. Come on in."

John-O started to go really wrong then. His blue eyes went bright red, and the flesh of his face warped as if burned by acid. His whole body jerked as he lurched toward the concessions stand.

"Holy shit," Dani whispered, backing away.

John-O kept coming.

I leaped in front of Dani, lobbing boxes of Milk Duds like candy grenades. "Get back, freshman demon!"

The corner of one box caught John-O in the eye. Yowling, he yanked on the box, taking his eye with it.

"Dammit! I've got no service!" Beside me, Dani swished her cell above her head as if she could catch a connection in the air. "You piece of shit, Verizon!"

Two more demons pushed through the doors. One of them wore Bryan Jenks's John Deere baseball cap, and if I had been afraid of that asshole before, I was pants-soilingly frightened now. His mouth was huge and round, with sharp nubbins of teeth. Demon-faced Bryan Jenks pushed the screeching John-O to the floor and bit into his neck, nearly severing his waxwork-like head.

"Go, go, go!" I pushed Dani ahead of me toward the projection room. We were up the stairs and through the door in record time.

"Don't watch the movie!" I shouted, knocking Dave off his stool.

"What the hell?" Dave looked up, dazed. "Hey, it was just getting good. I felt like I was actually in the movie . . ."

"I think you were," I said, trying desperately to catch my breath and not pass out. "That thing about the movie being cursed? Not bullshit. I think it steals your soul and turns you into some kind of demon-zomboid thing."

Dani nodded, wide-eyed. "Truth. It got John-O. His face turned into fondue right in front of us! And then Bryan Jerks came out and started eating him!"

Through the window, the darkened theater still flashed black-and-white. Dave balled and flexed his fingers. It was the self-soother his therapist parents had taught him for whenever his OCD kicked in. "Kevin. Dani. You guys are seriously starting to freak me the fuck out."

Shrieks erupted from the theater like an all-the-souls-in-hell karaoke party.

"We have to get out of here. Now," I said.

"But what if it's turning into a total demon-zombie prom down there?" Dani asked.

"Plan A: we make a run for the back exit, then book it down the road to Taco Bell for help."

"What's plan B?" Kevin asked.

I'd seen hundreds of horror movies. The tropes and clichés, the zillions of ways people acted dumb or cocky and got killed? I knew them all. I felt smug and safe, thinking *I'd* never be that dumb. Now I knew: Some things you couldn't plan for; you just had to react in the moment and hope it was enough.

"We'll figure that out." I turned to Dani. "Walk behind me. If, you know, something happens, if one of those things gets me, just run." When she started to protest, I explained, "Your dad's already been through enough. And you've got a scholarship."

"What about you?"

I shrugged. "Who would miss me?"

Dani let out a gasp. Then she pursed her lips. "You're a fucking moron, okay?" She grabbed my hand, and if I hadn't been about to pass out from fear, I would've been the happiest dude alive.

Slowly, I opened the projection room door. It was clear. We crept down the stairs, listening to the hammering of rain on the roof. That's when I noticed the photo on the wall. Scratsche was gone. Was it a trick of the light? I wanted to ask Dani and Dave if they saw it, too, but Dani whispered urgently, "Kevin, *c'mon!*"

At the bottom of the steps, we stopped short. Four of the undead paced in front of the back doors, snapping at each other.

"What. The. Total. Fuck," Dave whispered, his panic evident. "Shit. What's plan B?"

"Front doors. Keep low." I crept along the wall. When we came around by the concessions stand I put up my hand and jerked my head to the spot in front of the *I Walk This Earth* poster, where two crouching demons were still munching down on John-O's destroyed body. "Just keep walking," I said, gently squeezing Dani's hand. "Don't attract attention."

I kept my eyes on the doors. Rain swept past sideways in metal-colored sheets. Fifteen feet. Ten. Five. Zero. Carefully, I pressed the handles, trying not to make any noise. They wouldn't budge.

"Stop fucking around, Kevin," Dave whispered.

"I'm *not!*"

A gargling shriek like a dying air-raid siren sounded behind us. The demons who'd been blocking the back exits had arrived. Their huge mouths opened, giving us a front-row view of the pulsing membranes of their anaconda-large throats. It was scarier than any special effect, and it was one hundred percent real. The John-O eaters stumbled away from his corpse and reached their clawlike fingers toward us.

"Dude. You're the manager. Tell them to get out. Show's over. Go home."

"Dave. You are seriously *losing* it," Dani growled.

"No. I lost it. It's totally lost. I'm trying not to shit myself here."

"Follow me." I ran for the concessions stand. The demons surrounded us, curious, but I couldn't count on that holding for long. "Grab anything you can use as a weapon."

"Like what?" Dave screamed.

"I don't know! I've never had to kick demon ass before, okay? Improvise!"

Dani threw scoopfuls of ice. Dave started flinging plates of nacho chips. I looked around. Popcorn salt shaker. Soda cups. Napkin holders. Soft pretzels. Butter vats. *Butter vats . . .*

"Hey! Help with this." I grabbed two dish towels to block the heat and removed the metal bedpan-looking thing that blessed the stale kernels with rancid oil.

Dave stared at me like I'd gone mental. "What are you going to do with that? Wait for their cholesterol to catch up with them?"

"Remember when we saw *Aliens from Planet 11 Ate My Brain*?" I said, loosening the top. "Remember how they finally killed the alien freaks?"

"The aliens couldn't take the heat. They melted 'em." Dani ran over to help me with the vat.

The thing formerly known as Bryan Jenks jumped onto the counter in a crouch, ready to strike.

"Hey, Bryan! You want butter with that?" I shouted, just like I was the hero in an action movie. Together, Dani and I threw the bubbling vat of yellow yuck. Bryan screamed and thrashed as the hot oil blistered his skin into ribbons, and even though Bryan was a total douche bag I'd often wanted to finish off with a series of cool-looking karate moves I didn't actually know, I felt sick watching him suffer, demon or not.

Dave let loose with a slightly crazy laugh. "'Hey, you want butter with that?' Dude, that was so fly." He tried to high-five me.

I let his hand hang out in space. "Not now."

"Nggzzzzraaahsss!" Creature Bryan screeched.

Dave's voice was choked with fear. "I think you pissed it off."

I grabbed both Dave's and Dani's hands. "Plan C: theater, on three. One. Two—"

With a warrior's cry, Dave took off running, dragging us behind him into the theater. We slammed our bodies against the doors. Dani grabbed the broom resting against the back wall, snapped it over her knee, and jammed the broken stick through the big gold door handles.

I shoved Dave. "I said on *three,* dumbass!"

"I couldn't take it anymore. Those things look like frozen beef jerky. And they *smell,*" Dave panted. He kicked at an empty soda cup. "This is a bad way to die, man. God damn it, I had tickets for Comic-Con."

This wasn't how tonight was supposed to go. I was supposed to ask Dani for a date. She was, hopefully, going to say yes. And now we were making a last stand in the Cinegore against a horde of soul-stealing, flesh-eating demons escaped from a cursed movie. The doors began to crack as the demon-zombies thumped against them. Soon, they'd break through the flimsy broom lock.

"This is for real, Kevin. Think," I said. All those horror movies in my head, and now, when it counted, I couldn't come up with a way out of this mess. And that's when the crazy idea hit me.

"Hey!" I shouted at the movie. "Hey, over here! Pay attention."

"What are you doing?" Dani touched my arm, and I wished it were a different night so I could just enjoy the lightness of her fingers.

"I'm not going down without a fight," I promised her. I yelled up at the screen again. "I know you can hear me. *Look. At. Me!*"

Natalia Marcova glanced in my direction. She'd been dead for five decades, but her image lived on, burning brightly, a beautiful, preserved fossil.

"I saw that! Yes! Over here," I said, waving my arms.

She gave me a little wave. "Hello."

"Help us. Please," I said. "You've seen this happen before—isn't that what you said, Jimmy?"

"Gee. I guess I did." He raked a hand through his wavy, 1960s, swoon-worthy hair. "I kinda got caught up in the emotion of the moment, y'know? I'm method."

"Why should we help you brats? You don't even know how to dress properly," Alastair Findlay-Cushing said from the sofa, nursing his tumbler of liquor.

"Because we're the future," I said. "In every movie, somebody has to live on to tell the story. Or else . . . or else there's no point."

"Not necessarily," Jimmy Reynolds said. "What about *Sunset*

Boulevard? It's narrated by a dead man."

"Thanks for the spoilers, ghost of John-O," Dave whispered irritably.

"Gee, honey. I want to tell you," Natalia purred, her native Brooklyn accent shining through. "But if I do, he'll send me to the bad place."

"Who?" I asked.

Natalia's eyes fixed on a point somewhere behind me. "Him."

Slow clapping echoed from the back of the theater. He emerged from the shadows, wearing the same sharkskin suit as in the photograph. "Bravo. Well done. I must say, this is quite a surprise."

"Mr. Scratsche?" I peered out through the haze-dust thrown off by the screen and into those dark, soulless eyes. He didn't look a day older than he had in 1963.

Mr. Scratsche gave a courtly bow. "At your service. In a manner of speaking."

His hand went up like a conductor's. The broken broomstick shot free of the door handles. The hungry, growling creatures staggered inside, shuffling into the rows, taking their seats, mesmerized by the flickering images.

Scratsche smiled. "Ah, you people. You never tire of staring up at that screen, imagining yourselves there—better, beautiful, immortal. Everywhere, it's always the same: people sitting in the dark, hungry for the light, for validation, for the idea that good defeats evil, for the smug safety of thinking that they will win in the end."

"You belong here with us, Scratsche, and you know it!" Jimmy Reynolds shouted, falling to his knees. "You escaped only by damning us *all*!"

"Whoa. Chill, Marlon Brando," Dani muttered.

"Jimmy, Jimmy." Mr. Scratsche shook his head like a mildly put out headmaster. "True, I offered all of you up in return for my escape. But you all signed the contract of your own free will." Like a magician's trick, Scratsche produced a scroll that unrolled to reveal hundreds of signatures. Another snap and the scroll rolled up and dropped back into his pocket. "I heard you earlier, Jimmy. You tried to warn people. Didn't I tell you last time that there would be consequences?"

"I'm sorry, Mr. Scratsche. I'm just awfully tired of being trapped in this movie." Jimmy sounded scared and tired. "I've been wearing this cravat for fifty-six years. It makes me look like an asshole."

"Understood." Mr. Scratsche flicked his fingers toward the screen and sudden flames consumed Jimmy Reynolds. Seconds later, all that remained was the singed cravat and a burned patch on the carpet. "*That's* for going off script."

Dave's eyes had a glazed look. He'd started humming the *Care Bears Movie* theme song. It was what he did when the world was too much.

"What do you want from us?" I shouted.

"I believe the question is what do *you* want, Kevin? What do you all want? Oh. That's rhetorical. I've read your questionnaires."

Mr. Scratsche strode down the center aisle with the grace of a leopard. He threaded his fingers together. His fingernails were long and curved. "I've been thinking that the time is right to bring the film out of retirement. You're correct that someone needs to keep the story alive. To be its caretaker, hmm? *I Walk This Earth*—a new version for a new audience, directed by Kevin Grant. How does that sound?"

No adult had ever said anything like that to me before, like they saw me. Like I was worth seeing. "Me? Why me?"

"I've been watching you for months. I know what lives inside you. The longing for what you cannot have." His eyes flicked to Dani, and she looked at me quizzically. My face went hot. "The world is hungry for new thrills. In the past, distribution was a problem. But, my goodness! The things you can find nowadays, right there on your devices. Imagine it, Kevin: Your take on *I Walk This Earth*, available on demand. Downloadable. Shareable. It only requires a bit of sacrifice."

The scroll was out again. In Scratsche's other clawed hand was a pen.

"That didn't seem to work out too well for these guys." I jerked my thumb at the screen.

Dave nodded. "You tell him, bro."

"They don't have your *vision*." Scratsche smiled. I knew it was a trick, but somewhere inside me it was like somebody had opened a bank vault and said, *Go ahead. Take what you want.* His smile hardened. "Or did you just want to stay home and look after your mother, like a good boy? Maybe end up at the bottom of a bottle like her?"

"Fuck you," I said, even though my voice trembled. "That's not my only choice." And I didn't know if that was true or if I just wanted it to be true.

Mr. Scratsche laughed. "Haven't you been paying attention, Kevin? The vampire rises again. The scientist revives the killer's brain. The zombie horde is reinfected. That's what accounts for all of those sequels and remakes. *You can't win against evil.* Oh, sure. If you were to destroy this last remaining print of the film now, before you'd committed your soul, you would. But the projector is all the way up there." Scratsche pointed to the thick glass of the narrow projection booth window. "Out of reach. Like your dreams." Scratsche's dark eyes blazed. "You've been out of options for some time, Mr. Grant. Deep down, you know that. Join me . . . or you'll all die. Have you ever been torn apart by demons? I'm told it hurts. Quite a lot."

On-screen, the fireplace hissed. I looked over my shoulder at the swirling circle of flame and the endless darkness inside, devoid of shape, like my futureless future. My eyes locked on Natalia's. "Please," I begged. "Just a hint."

For a moment, she stared at the floor. Then she whispered, "The movie feeds on your fear. That's what gives it power."

Mr. Scratsche put a hand to his chest. Tiny horns had sprouted at the top of his forehead, and his teeth had lengthened. "Ah, me. I really should have cast Yvonne De Carlo."

He flicked his fingers once more, and Natalia screamed in terror as she flew backward, pinned to the mansion wall, a dagger hovering inches from her neck.

"Be good, now, my dear," Scratsche said. "I know you'd hate to play out the rest of your contract with a slashed throat. Messy."

Dave shut his eyes tight and rocked. "Stop feeling fear. Stop feeling fear. Stop feeling fear."

I pulled the three of us into a tight huddle, draping my arms over both of their backs. I'd never been this physically close to Dani before. We were nearly nose to nose, and suddenly I was flooded with want for that future she'd asked me about under the tree. A future with her. "The movie lives on fear, right? So we have to stop feeding it. Quick! What's the opposite of fear?"

"Taylor Swift?" Dave said. Dani and I glared. "What? Taylor Swift makes me happy."

I turned to Dani. "What's a *normal* opposite of fear?"

Dani let out a shaky breath. "Um, courage? Joy. Love. Altruism. Hope."

"That's it," I said.

"What's it? That was, like, five things."

Shadows and light played across her face. I brushed a drop of popcorn oil from her cheek.

"Hope," I said.

The old movie's hazy glow turned me into a ghost of myself as I stepped to the front of the theater. "If these are going to be my last few minutes on earth, then I have something to say."

"Oh. He's one of those 'last profound words' kids. *Won-n-nderful*," Alastair mumbled into his glass.

"You know, you're kind of a dick," Dave said. "I revoke your hot-ness status. I might clap when you go back to hell."

Alastair shrugged. "I'm a B movie actor. Hell's redundant, kid." He drained his glass, which immediately refilled. "This isn't even real booze."

"Mr. Grant. This protracted endgame has begun to bore me. I'm not pleasant when bored," Scratsche threatened.

"Just a sec, okay?" I faced Dani. In those movies I'd made in-side my head, I was always cocky and cool, because there were no stakes. I'd been guilty of the very thing I'd railed against. But now, looking into her big brown eyes—seeing the fear and the anger and the worry—I felt all of my emotions at once. I hated that I'd wasted so much time, and I wished more than anything that I could be the hero I wanted to be, the hero worthy of her.

I cleared my throat. "Dani, I know this is really bad timing, considering we're about to be either eaten by demons or consigned to hell, neither of which is how I would've planned our first date. But the truth is, I'm crazy about you. Totally. Madly. Completely. And I know this is stupid, but I have to know: If this were a normal Saturday night, and I asked you out, would you say yes?"

Dani stared at me. I couldn't tell if she was mad or happy or sad or all of the above. "Wow. Your timing sucks."

"Yeah. Yeah, I know." My heart plummeted. "Sorry. Forget I said anything."

"Would you shut up for a second, Kevin?" She came closer. "For, like, *forever,* I've been waiting for you to ask me out, but you never did. You're the reason I took this stupid job. And now—*now*—when we're about to be sacrificed to hell, you finally work up the courage?"

"I—Wait. You like me?"

"Oh. My. God." Dani lifted up her arms in frustration and let them fall to her sides again. "Seriously? You mean you couldn't tell?"

"Not . . . really?"

"Damn, boys are dumb."

"Sexist."

"Sorry. I meant to say, 'Damn, Kevin is dumb.'"

"Better. So how come *you* didn't just ask *me* out?"

"Because . . ." Dani's brows furrowed. "Because it's scary putting yourself out there?"

"Yeah," I said, smiling in spite of everything. "It really, really is."

"Aw-w-w. You two are awfully cute," Natalia said. "I feel real bad that you'll either get eaten by demons or lose your souls."

"Thanks?" I said, and then I added, "ma'am," because I was inside a theater full of revenants led by the devil's henchman on my first and possibly last date with the girl of my dreams, and my mouth had given up trying to make sense of things.

"Kev!" Dave said, sounding panicked. "The hope thing's not working!"

Mr. Scratsche laughed. "You see, Kevin. There really is no way to stop it." He held out the scroll again. "Accept your fate."

"No! Wait!" I paced. Stopped. "Unless we destroy the movie."

"Yes, yes, but you can't," Scratsche said, impatient. "And even if you *could,* I doubt that someone like you would destroy the last remaining print of a rare film. After all, you know what it is to be thrown away."

I'd never wanted to be somebody like my dad, who could just cut ties and take off with only hope stuffed in his pockets. But now I saw it differently. Maybe sometimes the best thing you can do is to burn it all down and start over. If we survived this night, I'd apply to UT. Hell, I'd fill out twelve applications.

I ran back to Dani. "Hey," I whispered. "You pretty good with that bow?"

"For somebody who only took one semester of archery and ended up accidentally shooting Coach Pelson in the ass, yeah, I guess so."

"Who says there's only one way to stop a cursed film from playing?" I offered a lame half-smile. "Options."

Dani smiled back at me. "Options."

"Do you have an answer for me, Mr. Grant? Your audience is hungry." Scratsche gestured to the impatient demons.

"I do. I'd like to show you the trailer for my first short film, entitled *You're Not the Boss of Us*, in glorious 3-D." I removed Cthulhu Shortcake from my pocket. "Dave—lighter, please."

Dave handed over the blue Bic. "You sure you got this, bro?"

I took a deep breath. "Hope so."

Behind me, I could hear the muffled, curious voices of Natalia and Alastair. "What's he doing?" "Is this a thing kids do nowadays?" "It's strange." But they were the sounds of the past getting dimmer.

I stuck our plushie elder god to the tip of the arrow. "Sorry, Shortcake."

"Enough, Mr. Grant!" Mr. Scratsche's voice was a thundering roar.

"Please! No talking during the movie," I said, and with a shaking hand, I set Cthulhu Shortcake aflame. To Dani, I whispered, "Aim for the fireplace."

She nodded and let the imitation *Robin Hood: Prince of Darkness* arrow sail. It pierced the screen, smoked, and fizzled out.

"Shit," Dani said, and my heart sank.

"It's okay," I told her, and I wondered if that's what Dani's mom had said to her little brother in the seconds before the plane hit the ground.

"Well, I'll be damned." Alastair Findlay-Cushing was staring at the floor of the old movie mansion. A line of fire had traveled from our Cthulhu arrow through the screen and into the film. Natalia and Alastair coughed as their cinematic tomb filled with smoke.

Mr. Scratsche leaped to his feet. "No!"

"Betcha didn't see that twist coming," I said.

A huge bang sounded. The rickety walls of the mansion shook. Natalia screamed as the swirling hole of the fireplace opened up and sucked her inside. A visibly shaken Alastair went for his drink, remembering at the last second that it was fake.

"Oh, fuck," he grumbled, and then he, too, was gone.

Smoke billowed around the edges of the movie screen and spread into the theater. Mr. Scratsche pointed a gnarled finger at us. "Feed! Feed!" he roared to his demon minions. But they were confused by the order and began devouring each other in a bloody frenzy.

The scroll flew from Scratsche's pocket and hovered in the air. He made a desperate grab for it just before it disappeared. A hole opened in the center of the screen, a bottomless void that mirrored the black of Scratsche's widening eyes. Terrible sounds escaped from that darkness—howls of pain and sorrow, but also of loss and regret.

"No," Scratsche gasped. "No, wait, I—"

A giant, flaming hand shot out from the darkness and closed its fiery fingers around the screaming Scratsche. He beat against its grip, but it was no use. He really was out of options. As the flaming hand dragged him back to his eternal nonrest, we heard only one last whimper. The hole closed.

For a moment, it was silent. And then everything went apeshit.

The screen bowed out, vomiting fire. Flocked wallpaper bubbled and blackened. Scraps of ceiling rained down in chunks, as if the theater were built on a fault line whose time had finally come.

"We're trapped!" Dave yelled, dodging flaming ceiling scraps.

My chest tightened at the thought of this being Scratsche's last laugh, one of those last-second horror movie gotcha! moments.

"Dani!" I coughed, taking hold of her hands. "I love you. I'm sorry it's ending this way."

Dani's mouth settled into a tight line. "The fuck it's ending this way!" She ripped the edge of her shirt, wrapped it around the arrow, yanked it from the screen, and used it to pry open the fire exit door. "C'mon, y'all!" she yelled. "We out!"

This time, *she* reached for *my* hand, and we didn't waste any time running toward the open arms of the night.

Dani and I leaned against the trunk of her car in the light mist and watched the flames eat through the Cinegore. Fire truck sirens sounded in the distance. Just under their caterwauling, I could hear Dave on his phone. "Dude, you don't know what kind of night *I've* had. For starters, I've got brain goop on my jacket . . ."

The inferno intensified the oppressive stillness of the Texas night. We'd stripped down to our tanks and jeans. If I could've unzipped my skin and taken it off, I would have. Dani poured some Milk Duds into my palm. They were slightly melty, but that was the way I liked them best. She burst out laughing. I started laughing, too. It was the shock, for sure. Your emotions get super weird after you've been hunted by demons and forced to banish your boss to hell.

"Holy fuck," I said, trying to settle.

"You can say that again."

"Okay. Holy fuck."

Dani stepped in front of me. With the flames behind her, she made me think of an avenging angel in a movie I wanted to see over and over. "Just checking: That actually happened, right?"

"Yeah. Pretty much."

"Okay." Dani nodded, more to herself than to me. "Okay."

"This is insane!" Dave was selfie-ing the shit out of himself in front of the melting Cinegore. "I've already got one hundred and fifty-three retweets and over sixty favorites in just the last five minutes!"

"I need to sit down." Dani unlocked her car and dropped into the driver's seat, keeping the door open to let some of the hot air escape. I got in on the passenger side. The car smelled like her—like popcorn, vanilla perfume, and something I didn't yet know but knew I wanted more of.

Dani clutched her car keys in her fist. "So, technically, is this our first date?"

Now that the adrenaline-laced fear was gone, a different sort of fear seized me. I'd opened myself up pretty wide in there when I thought I was going to die. It was time to deal with the aftermath of my honesty. But I was feeling okay with that. More than okay, in fact. "Yeah." I let my head loll against the leather headrest. "Guess so. Sorry it's so weird—"

Dani leaned over and cut off my apology with a kiss. And when she did, all the movies went out of my head, because there was no invented story that could compete with the here-and-now feel of her lips on mine. Reluctantly, I broke away.

"Hold on," I said, and reclined my seat.

Grinning, Dani did the same. And then it was *on*. We were a tangle of mouths and tongues, hands and legs, and, once, an unfortunate parking brake intrusion. It was making-up-for-lost-time kissing. You've-been-granted-a-second-chance-don't-waste-it kissing. Kissing with plenty of options.

Panting heavily, Dani broke away and stared up at the car's top. "Wow. Um. Why the hell haven't we done that before?"

"Right?" I managed between gulps of air. I couldn't wait to kiss her again. The pessimistic past was slipping away like the last of the rain. I felt strangely good. Maybe when the new Starbucks was built, I'd get a Frappuccino there. Maybe over Christmas break, when Dani and I were both home from school.

The sirens sharpened as they arrived. We brought our seats up again. In the rearview mirror, Dave was still reading his phone. "Over three hundred and climbing! This is so fucking rad!"

I shook my head. "Can you get a double major in Oblivious and Narcissistic at Stanford?"

Dani smiled. "Think he'll be all right if we go?"

"In a few minutes this place will be crawling with hunky firemen. So, yeah."

Dani turned the key in the ignition. The car's first blast of AC was a blessing. "IHOP?"

"Mm-hmm."

I could practically taste the pancakes, sweet and sugary good. They tasted like the future. Dani gunned the motor and faced the road where the bulldozers slept. Through the Mustang's windshield, the horizon was a vague impression of clouds and stars, a long line of pleasant darkness just waiting to take shape. It was still a long, long way from dawn.

SICK PLEASURE

FRANCESCA LIA BLOCK

+ For A and U +

I was the first night of summer vacation when my friends M and L and I piled into J's VW Bug and drove to Phases, the teen dance club deep in the San Fernando Valley, to escape sorrow and find the thing that we were looking for.

The four of us had spent the day at the beach and were all sunburned, even M and L, who were naturally dark. Heat radiated off of us, and J's car was saturated with the rich coconut-and-chemical scent of Bain de Soleil suntan oil. I was the palest of all us, and by the end of the summer there would be actual blisters on my chest from lying in the sun so often. Later, the blisters would scar. On the radio, loud new wave music played and we bopped in our seats and screamed the lyrics—about broken glass and summer and driving and lust and the beat—out the windows. As hot winds blew us along the 101 freeway, stars that had died long ago burned holes in the night with their brightness.

My friends and I were intent on burning brightly that night, too. We had just graduated from high school and would all be leaving for college in a few months. No more SAT scores or college applications to worry about. But a lot of other things.

I felt safe with J driving. As a little kid, when people asked her what she wanted to be when she grew up, she'd say "a hero," but she'd settled on training to become a highway patrol officer after she graduated from college. She had learned to ski when she was three and to skateboard like a pro at ten, so I always felt I was in good hands when she was at the wheel. Once, coming back from a Knack concert, her Bug broke down in the fast lane of the freeway. J stayed calm while the rest of us screamed as we looked out the back window and saw headlights approaching, watched them swerve away just in time. A CHP officer rescued us. Maybe that's why J wanted to be one.

I'd known J and M since kindergarten. We'd met the first day. M and I were both drawing pictures when the teacher came over to look. I was used to getting a lot of praise for my artwork. But the teacher picked M's drawing of a horse and held it up.

"This is wonderful," the teacher announced.

In ballet, the same thing happened. I loved dancing in my living room to my mom's records more than anything, but I couldn't follow the steps in class. M could.

"What a beautiful turnout you have," the teacher told her.

She had always gotten better grades, too.

M, J, and I met L in our "gifted" classes in middle school. L was so quiet and mysterious with her smooth, brown skin and hair, her placid face. Even her frown was pretty. With her tiny nose, high forehead, and small, pointed ears, she sometimes looked like a slightly vexed cat. She was one of those girls that everyone has a crush on, but she didn't realize it and wouldn't have cared if she did. Or maybe she would have just found it annoying and stressful.

L and I did a science project together. Science was L's favorite subject, though she felt strongly about never experimenting on animals. She loved animals more than anything, probably more than people.

I went to L's house to work on the project. Her parents were kind, rather strict Mexican Americans, and she had two brothers who loved baseball. L and I baked batches of chocolate chip cookies, ate them all, and went on long runs together to burn off the calories. Then M and L started to go horseback riding or ice-skating after school and on weekends. I wasn't invited, so I hung out alone with J.

She took me skiing with her parents, who were old-fashioned Polish immigrants with a house full of tiny china figurines. While J skied the steepest slopes, I took a beginner lesson. It was fine while I was holding on to the waist of the cute instructor, but when I had to go by myself I lost control and fell, tumbling down the slope. I never tried it again. To soothe our sore muscles and my bruises, J and I took a Jacuzzi outside. Mist rose from the water and snow glowed around us as I felt myself start to relax.

Some skinny, long-haired boys in ski jackets were huddled by the pool, watching us. We smelled weed; they were smoking. J and I got out of the Jacuzzi and ran past them, through the freezing air, to the lodge, not even bothering to put on our clothes.

Later I wrote a poem about that night. The silvery pain of the cold, the way the boys' eyes made me feel warm, like gold.

I couldn't ski, horseback ride, or ice-skate well, but I had inherited a way with words from my screenwriter father and my poet mother. Maybe I wouldn't be a hero like J, a scientist like L, or an artist like M, but I wanted to do something with my life that would make people feel better, somehow. Words were the answer, but I didn't know it yet.

Because we would be leaving for college soon, that night at Phases was different from the other times we'd come. Even then, we were aware of the significance of this change. It made the lights shine bluer and gave the music an urgent, melancholy sound.

My friends and I were wearing our vintage Keds canvas sneakers with pointed toes that we had found at Cowboys and Poodles on Melrose. The shoes and clothing sold there were all from the fifties but, magically, still brand new. We wore the Keds with miniskirts and white cotton men's T-shirts, which we had altered by cutting off the sleeves and collar bands and writing on them with pink marker the words "Healthy Pleasure." This was in direct response to the punk boy gang who hung out at the same club and wore T-shirts that said "Sick Pleasure", written in black Sharpie.

We never spoke to these boys, but they fascinated us with their short, spiked hair and tattoos. We didn't know their actual names but M had nicknamed them Rat Catcher, Little Italy, Horse, Ken (for the doll), and Mohawk. They were hanging out in the corner, as usual, under the strobe lights, dumping little airplane-size bottles of vodka into their sodas and watching us with smirks on their faces.

We'd given them not only names but also histories. Rat Catcher lived with his single, alcoholic mom near Phases. He started going there when he was twelve. He started smoking and drinking then, too. At Phases, Rat Catcher met Ken and Horse, who were both older, taller, better looking. But Rat was smarter and became the leader. We imagined that Little Italy, who always looked somewhat disheveled, was homeless, and that the others took care of him. He was their mascot. We didn't try to make up a story about Mohawk. He seemed like he wasn't as close to the others, even sitting at a distance from them, arriving and leaving earlier. Mohawk was always well groomed, not a trace of stubble on his scalp, at least from what we could see in the dark, and he didn't wear the Sick Pleasure shirts either.

"Think Pink" by the Fabulous Poodles played, and my friends and I rushed the dance floor like wild things, skanking around, flailing our arms, tossing our hair. We knew the boys were watching, but we pretended to ignore them, as usual.

More songs: the B-52s, the Go-Go's, Blondie. Music is so powerful and mysterious because it can bring up emotions you've buried inside of you. Dancing is a way to experience those emotions and release them so they don't get stuck in your throat or stomach or chest. At that time it was the only thing that made me forget everything else. I became just a heartbeat, a part of the music. I was completely free.

When REO Speedwagon's ballad "Keep on Loving You" came on, we hurried off to sit on one of the shag-carpeted benches that surrounded the dance floor. Sometimes, if we were in the mood, we would dance by ourselves to the slow songs. Secretly, I found this particular song romantic, in spite of how cheesy it was and the guitar solo I hated, but I would never have admitted my affection for it to anyone.

I was leaning against M's bare, brown, bony shoulder, still warm from the sun. J was leaning her strong back against my knees, L sitting by herself on my other side. I was gazing up at the spinning disco ball when I felt a presence watching me and looked up. Mohawk was there, so close I could have reached out and touched his large hand. He smiled with crooked teeth under a big nose that had obviously been busted at least once. I was self-conscious about the bump on my own nose and was planning to have it shaved off as soon as possible.

"Hey," Mohawk said. "Want to dance?"

Another slow song was playing, and I hesitated. M elbowed me. We all did what M told us to do. She was going to Yale in the fall. She was the fastest girl on the track team. And she had won best dressed in school, even though her leopard print, stretch Fiorucci pants, patent leather motorcycle jacket, and vinyl purse with two cherubs wearing sunglasses on it were way too out there to become trendy in the Valley. I stood up without thinking and followed Mohawk onto the dance floor.

He put one arm on my waist and brought me close to him. His breath smelled clean, not like alcohol as I had expected, and his eyes were warm and twinkled.

"Why don't you and your friends ever talk to us?" he asked.

"You don't talk to us either."

He grinned, showing those rebellious teeth again. "Where are you from?"

"Studio City," I said. This was a small suburb of the Valley, on the other side of a canyon from Hollywood. "You?"

"Calabasas." That was a wealthy area farther north. This, like his breath and eyes, was also a surprise.

"Why do you come here?" I asked him.

"I love to dance," he said.

"But you guys never dance."

I felt his shoulder shrug under my hand. His voice sounded deeper. "Yeah. I watch you dance."

He pulled me a little closer, so our hips were almost touching. "Get on," he said.

"Get on where?" I wasn't sure I liked where this might be headed.

"My toes."

I looked down and saw that he was wearing heavy black engineer boots.

"The toes are steel." he said.

I stepped carefully on and balanced myself, clinging tighter to his back and shoulder. He moved with surprising ease, me on top of him like that.

M was waving at me from the edge of the dance floor. "We're going now," she was saying.

I stepped off of Mohawk's feet.

"Hey," he said. "What's your name?"

"I."

"I'm A," he said. And then I had to leave.

When we came back to Phases a few nights later, the Sick Pleasure boys weren't there. I felt a coldness sinking through my body, from the base of my throat to my pelvis. I'd wanted to see A. I'd spent the last few days imagining dancing with him again. The solid feel of his muscles under my hands. The light sweat that pressed his T-shirt to his back.

I danced with my friends, but I was forcing it. Without Sick Pleasure, especially A, watching, I didn't feel inspired by the music.

The chill sadness crept through my body again and I couldn't shake it off.

The music changed. Hardcore punk. The Adolescents, "Creatures." My friends and I left the dance floor. Then Sick Pleasure walked into the club. They stormed the floor, skanking and slamming into each other. The DJ cranked the music and my ears rang and the strobe lights were making me dizzy. Was A with them?

There he was.

I just stood watching, until he grabbed my arm and pulled me out with him. I imitated the movements of the boys but they ignored me, except for A, who backed up into me repeatedly until I finally grabbed his shoulders and he swung me up onto his back and danced with me like that. The room spun around and I shut my eyes and pressed my face into his sweaty neck. This is one way to leave your life for a while.

The song was over and another one played. "Wild in the Streets" by the Circle Jerks. And another. Dead Kennedys, "Holiday in Cambodia." I knew the songs from listening to Rodney on the Roq's show on KROQ. Rodney was odd, with his mullet and whiny voice, but he knew his music.

I kept dancing with A. Then the music switched back to my familiar upbeat new wave and, panting, A and I collapsed onto one of the carpeted seats. He showed me this little Xeroxed pamphlet he'd made.

"It's a zine," he said. I pretended to know what that was, but I didn't, yet. It had collages of ticket stubs and flyers from punk shows and ink drawings of a boy with a Mohawk, who looked just like A, skanking around the margins. There were reviews of record albums and lists of favorite songs and punk venues.

"You made this?" I asked.

It was the ninth edition called *Suburban Kaos*. I told him it was cool. I especially liked the drawings of the skanking boy.

He grinned with his funny teeth and warm eyes.

The DJ announced there was going to be a fifties dance contest the next night.

"Hey, we should enter," A said.

I was surprised that he'd ask me in front of his friends. I said yes.

I found an old dress of my mother's. She'd worn it to marry my father at the courthouse downtown. It was both of their second marriages, so white wasn't appropriate, she said. Since they'd gotten married, my parents hadn't been apart from each other a single night.

The dress was gold silk damask with a full skirt. The waist and chest were a little too big and the hem was longer than it should have been because my mother had always been taller and more voluptuous than I am. I belted the dress tightly and put on a pair of her cream-colored leather pumps with pointed toes and pearl buttons.

At Phases, I found A sitting by the DJ booth wearing a pair of black jeans, a white short-sleeved button-down shirt, and black and white creepers with heavy black rubber soles. He knew how to swing dance; it was crazy how good he was. The only other people in the contest were a couple of heavy metal kids, who seemed drunk, and some punk girl with bleached skunk stripes in her dyed-black hair and a silver nose ring, who danced by herself while watching A out of the corner of her eye. He and I won. The DJ gave us a mirror that said "Phases" on it. My charming partner, A, let me keep it. M said it was a coke mirror. Sick Pleasure sat in the corner and ignored the whole thing.

"Do you and your friends want to come to a party at my house this weekend?" A asked before M told me we had to leave.

Calabasas was dark at night, with fewer streetlamps and more trees than where my friends and I were from. A's house was surrounded by huge hedges. That Saturday night, M, J, L, and I walked up the lit path to a three-story mansion and went inside through tall doors. Loud punk music was playing, so we knew we were at the right place. Kids with punk hairstyles and clothes were hanging out drinking from plastic cups of beer. I wondered what A's parents did to have a house like this.

Where was he?

Rat Catcher and Ken were sitting on leather couches in the main room with a girl on either side of them. Rat Catcher eyed us narrowly. I felt self-conscious in my pink-and-lavender striped stretchy Betsey Johnson minidress that I had been so excited to wear. The girls all wore cutoff jeans or plaid skirts and torn T-shirts adorned with safety pins; their hair was bleached and teased.

We went looking for the beer in the kitchen and J filled our cups. I'd never drunk much before, and the beer tasted sour, but I chugged it anyway, hoping it would fortify me against my self-consciousness.

Warm hands around my waist. I turned and saw A grinning.

"You came," he said.

"Hey, nice house."

He took my hand firmly in his. "Come on, I'll show you."

M gave me the stink eye, L frowned, and J smiled as A led me outside through glass doors. The pool shimmered blue. Beyond it stretched dark gardens. The air smelled sweet, like jasmine, maybe, or roses, and crickets and frogs chirped and croaked.

"It's so cool here."

"Thanks. You look cute."

"Thanks. I thought maybe I wore the wrong thing."

"No. You look good."

We stopped and stared at each other. I was suddenly shy. I still hadn't even kissed a boy. Neither had J or L, but M had already had sex last year. She said it wasn't all that great but she did feel kind of different afterward. I asked her how and she shrugged and just said, "Mature," and the way she said it made me feel like a stupid little kid.

"You're the best dancer of your friends," A said. I wasn't used to being the best at much.

Once, the summer after junior year, M, J, and I had gone on a trip to our friend S's beach condo. L didn't go. Her parents wouldn't have let her, even if she'd wanted to, which she didn't. M, J, and I didn't tell our parents that S's parents would be out of town. My parents didn't even ask any questions about the trip; they trusted me.

M, J, S, and I went to the beach all day. Then we showered, put on tight jeans, and walked from the condo to a restaurant overlooking the water. Some older guys approached us and S flirted with them. The guys ordered us beers and oysters. They had a limo and offered to take us to their condo for more drinks. S said sure, and the rest of us nervously went along with it. The condo was decorated in silver and black with a mirrored ceiling. The guys lay back on the couch, watching us dance for them.

"Let's see. Yeah, you're the best looking," the blond one had said, pointing drunkenly at me.

Then he'd passed out, his friend went to take a piss, and we left, giggling, and ran home. We had no idea, at the time, how dangerous the whole thing could have been. And all I cared about was having been singled out for once.

I worried about S, but I didn't know what to do or even how to talk about it. There was something about her dad. I didn't like the way he looked at S. I wondered about her painfully bitten nails, her nervous laughter, and her flirtatious ways. The fact that she sometimes went out of the house without underpants on. Eventually her parents divorced and she moved away. I wish I'd said something.

Now A said, "Like, you dance like you mean it. Like you *have* to dance or something."

"I do," I said.

"Why?"

"Because I feel depressed otherwise."

"Why?"

I shrugged and tried to smile. I didn't want him to think of me as a depressed person.

"Let's swim," A said.

He pulled off his T-shirt and jeans and jumped into the pool in his boxer briefs. I stood there watching him bobbing up and down, spitting water out of his mouth.

"Come on."

So I finished my beer in a gulp, took off my pumps and my dress, and jumped into the water. It was cold, and when I started to shiver, A swam over and put his arms around me. His Mohawk had flattened out against his head. I wondered what he would have looked like with a full head of hair. In the dark I couldn't see his eyes, but I could feel the cool, smooth flesh of his arms and chest, and I could feel his heartbeat in the night. His dick pressed against my thigh and all my muscles loosened against him.

I'd never seen a penis in person, and I had mixed feelings about them. Fear. Aversion. Curiosity. A mild, tingling delight.

"Can I kiss you?" A asked.

I nodded. He put his hand behind my neck and brought my face to his. I closed my eyes and tilted my mouth up to him. His lips. His firm, gentle tongue. Then stronger. I ran my fingers over his busted nose, his bony cheekbones, his skull. I felt myself slipping away into the water and the night. Teenage boys are not so far away from being kids and are very far away from being men. Most of them. A seemed pretty close to both.

"We're going," M shouted. "Hurry up, I, or we're going to leave you."

I pulled away from A, suddenly aware that I was wearing only a bra and underpants, wet ones so that everything showed through. "I have to go," I said, getting out of the pool.

When A said he'd pick me up at my house, I told him I'd meet him outside, because I knew my mom would never let me go out on a motorcycle. It was really the only rule she had, and even though she was distracted with what was happening with my dad, I knew I couldn't get away with it.

I met A a little way down the street. He was wearing a leather jacket, leaning on his bike with his arms folded and his legs crossed like James Dean. He had two helmets and he put mine on for me. Then we got on his motorcycle. As I straddled the seat I felt A between my legs. Bikes are so dangerous and hot. Death and sex. I guess that's why people like them. Or hate them.

He revved the engine and we rode.

Laurel Canyon twisted like the river that had probably originally forged it, among the steep hillsides covered with wildflowers. Vines had grown across the telephone wires and hung down in green clumps above our heads. A girl in a black taffeta dress with black cowboy boots and a shock of magenta hair was hitchhiking. I wished I were dressed like her.

We drove down Sunset to the Whisky and parked. He helped me off the bike and we went inside the dark little club that smelled like smoke. I'd gotten a fake ID from this nerdy guy at my school who made them for you using a photo booth picture, but I'd always been too scared to use it. Unlike A, who didn't seem to be afraid of anything.

The club was packed. On the stage, five girls in shabby vintage dresses were playing their instruments badly and too fast. They were amazing. The lead singer had a round, cute face that reminded me of J's. "We've got the beat," the girl sang. I'd heard the song on the radio and at Phases, but it was different live. I thought, girls can do this punk thing? I had no idea. My life changed at that moment.

"Aren't they awesome?" A said, grinning at me in the dark. "The bass player reminds me of you."

She was petite and wore a kilt and moccasins. Her dark curly hair was cut short. I thought she was the most beautiful girl I'd ever seen. When she sang backup, her voice was a squeak. "That's Jane," he said. "My favorite."

Jane. I wanted to be Jane. He brought me a beer but said he wasn't going to drink, since he was driving. The beer was cold and I was starting to love the taste. I drank the whole thing and A took the empty bottle from me. He and I slammed together in the pit, his body shielding me from the writhing wall of boys. I knew I was safe. My hair stuck to my face as I sweated from my pores. I closed my eyes. I was falling, drifting far away. He put his arms around me and brought his face close to mine. We kissed. I could feel him so hard against me. His Mohawk dark and majestic in the darkness. I was with the best guy. The best one.

We went outside. The night was warm. I never wanted to go away to Berkeley and leave Los Angeles. I wanted to drink it down like a beer. I wanted to roll in it and put it inside of me. I got on the back of A's bike and we took off down the Strip. Billboard models watched us with their huge eyes. Frowned with their sexy mouths. I could feel the careful attention A was paying to everything around him. His body was quivering; he was alert, keeping me safe, just as he had on the dance floor.

We were stopped at a light, waiting to turn into a gas station at the corner of Crescent Heights and Sunset. I said, "I don't know why I was afraid of motorcycles. They're the greatest thing in the world."

We made the turn and a car going through a yellow light tapped against us. Just like that. Lightly but with surprising precision. We went down.

We weren't hurt at all. Not even a scrape.

"Hey," A said when we got to my house. "I want to tell you something."

The air smelled of eucalyptus and I could hear an owl in the distance.

"That's not my house. My mom works there. For that actor, John Davidson. He was out of town and my mom was at her boyfriend's when I had that party. We live in the guesthouse. Sometimes my friends crash with us when their parents won't let them come home."

"Oh," I said.

"Sorry."

"It's fine." I wanted to confess something, too. "My dad has cancer and I have to go away to college in the fall."

"Oh, that sucks." He squinted at me in that pained James Dean way.

"Yeah." I shrugged and tried to smile. Why had I told this to A? Why had I said it out loud?

"Where are you going to college?" he asked.

"Berkeley." I was going to ask him the same question, but then wondered if he was even going, if the question would make him uncomfortable.

When he kissed me good night my lips were hard; I didn't respond. Not because his parents didn't own that big house or he might not be going to college or he and I could have been badly hurt in the motorcycle accident. More because it had fully hit me that I was moving away and probably wouldn't see A again when I did. Because I wasn't as pretty as L, as cute as J, as powerful and cool as M, and maybe A would realize this. Because of the cancer that was spreading through my dad's body and would eventually take him away from me and my mom, leaving us grief stricken and alone. Or something.

I went into my little house and went to bed. I could hear my mother through the wall. She was sobbing. I thought, *When Dad dies it will kill her. And then I'll die, too.*

I didn't hear from A. My friends and I went back to Phases. The Sick Pleasure guys weren't there. Instead, there was a pack of surfers I'd never seen before. They were all tan, with blond hair, and wore plaid shorts and T-shirts with Vans sneakers, or Levi's with short-sleeved button-down plaid shirts and Topsiders, no socks.

M said, "Now those are some hot guys."

I didn't really think so. I mean, none of them were A.

J said, "Oh my God, that one's mine," and she pointed to the shortest one, who had angelic blond curls and a baby face.

"You got him," M said. "That's Angel. I get Swell." She nodded to the tallest, best looking of the guys. "L can have Hot. I, you get Tan-the-Man."

I didn't want Tan-the-Man. I wanted A. Why hadn't he called me? Did he think I didn't like him? Had he lost interest in me? I wished I'd kissed him back. I could never explain to him why I hadn't; I couldn't even explain it to myself. But maybe if there was another chance, I could kiss him properly. I could make it right.

M commanded that we all dance and we went onto the floor. The surfers watched us. I didn't feel the music the way I usually did. I kept thinking about A's body and the taste of beer and chlorine on my lips as he kissed me in the pool.

Swell danced over to M and loped in circles around her. He was so animated, he seemed like he was made out of electricity. He had dimples and a flashing white smile with perfect teeth, like a dentist's son. Or John Davidson. J and Angel had the same playful dancing style and shy grins. L danced with Hot but mostly she seemed to be ignoring him. I missed A as I made myself dance with Tan-the-Man. I remembered the way I'd balanced on A's big steel-toed boots, the way his big hands felt on my waist, the clean smell of his breath. Tan-the-Man smelled like alcohol and gaggingly strong Brut cologne. He leaped, rather than loped, around in circles like Swell, but Tan couldn't pull it off the same way. He was making me dizzy.

Just then, I saw Rat Catcher standing at the edge of the dance floor, watching me. M had given him his nickname because he had pointy features and a wiry body. I turned from Tan to look for A. He was there. He was standing next to a girl. He was standing next to the girl with skunk stripes from the fifties dance contest. They walked outside.

Part of my soul detached and tried to follow A, but it slammed into the closed door like an alcoholic or a dazed, wounded animal and collapsed onto the ground.

I turned back to Tan. And I started dancing as hard as I could.

Later I found out that Tan's name was B. He and his friends were from Camarillo. All I knew about that place was that there was a famous mental institution there.

Yes, the guys were surfers, as we had thought. Tan was going away to UC San Diego in the fall. He was going to study pre-law.

"Hey," Tan said. "We're having a party. You and your friends should come."

J drove the VW to Camarillo. The air smelled like the sea and strawberry fields. It was a nice community with midsize homes and green lawns. We parked and went up to a house. Loud new wave music was playing, so we knew it was the right place. Inside were girls with tan skin and tight striped dresses or white shorts and bikini tops, lying on couches with surfer boys. My friends and I must have looked exotic, the girls from LA. I was wearing a T-shirt, Levi's, and Converse sneakers, like I'd worn to the Whisky with A. I realized I'd worn the wrong thing to this party.

Swell ran up and grabbed M around her tiny waist and lifted her in the air and spun her. She squealed. M was not a squealer. Swell carried her out of the room, her legs dangling over his arms, her flip-flops falling off her feet. (M, of course, had dressed perfectly for the party). J and L looked at me. Angel came over with beers. He gave us each one. He and J were both wearing the same thing: short-sleeved Polo shirts, plaid shorts, and flip-flops. He took her hand and they walked away. Even from across the room I could see J's dimples and the light in her eyes.

L was wearing Topsiders and a white tank top that made her brown skin glow. She and I looked at each other; she frowned, as usual. Hot came over and she frowned at him. He shrugged and walked away. L and I sat on a couch. Tan-the-Man came over and joined us.

"Looking good, ladies," he said, putting his hand on my knee.

I realized that I wanted to lose my virginity. And A wasn't there. We'd won a fifties dance contest. He was a great kisser. He lived in John Davidson's guesthouse. He had a motorcycle. We'd had an accident. What if I'd gotten really hurt? My mom would have been so angry at me, I think. Or maybe she wouldn't have noticed because she was so worried about my dad. Maybe dying on a motorcycle with A would be better than watching my father die slowly of cancer and my mom die of grief soon after.

I swallowed some beer. "My dad has cancer," I said to Tan.

He leaned closer and cocked his head so his ear was near my mouth. "What?"

"Never mind," I said.

"Hey, you want to go see the upstairs?"

"Sure."

We left L sitting on the couch and rolling her eyes. That L, she was the smart one. She would attend Harvard in the fall.

She wanted to be a veterinarian.

Tan took me to a bedroom upstairs. He took out a vial of white powder and sprinkled it onto a mirror. I thought of the mirror I'd won at Phases. I'd put it on my dresser at home under a tangle of jewelry made of plastic and rhinestones.

Tan snorted and then offered me some. I snorted, too. It hurt my sinuses with a bright white pain. I didn't feel anything else except an accelerated heartbeat and a kind of shiny panic. Maybe it was bad coke. Then I left my body quietly while he pulled my jeans and underwear down over my hips and shoved himself inside of me. It actually didn't hurt that much, maybe because of all the dancing I'd done. I think I'd broken my hymen that way. Or maybe the coke worked to dull the pain. Or maybe it was my naturally high pain tolerance. Or the fact that I wasn't really there.

M was right; I felt different afterward. But not more mature. I got so sick the next day—I'd never been so sick. My whole body burned with poison fever. I wondered if I was just responding to the metaphor of feeling fucked.

I missed A with a longing as strong as those hot winds that ravaged us that summer, that hot sun that had burned blisters on my skin. But I had not chosen A. Somehow, with all the grief and confusion and fear and years of mild but persistent negative thoughts that had worn a path in my brain, I had chosen to get fucked by Tan-the-Man instead.

Love can be so strange and sad. It can be hard to understand why we run toward certain people and away from others at different times in our lives. Why we search so hard for that thing we are looking for, and then run so fast when we find it.

Years will go by.

M will be happily married and working as an art director on movies. She and I will have had a falling out after I finally let her know that I'm sick of her telling me what to do. She will say, "You don't know what love is. I've been the best friend you could have." Maybe she's right.

J will be a heroic CHP officer, married with two kids.

L will be a successful veterinarian, still single, still beautiful, and so smart.

None of us will be in touch.

Maybe A will be living in a bungalow in Hollywood, working as a graphic designer, still writing and drawing zines, still listening to punk music. If he is losing his hair, or even if he isn't, maybe he shaves his head. Maybe he still wears creepers. Maybe he has kids. A boy who is a musician in a garage band. A girl who is an artist. Maybe A will have just gone through a divorce and just be starting to think about dating again.

I will have lost my parents, one to cancer, one to cancer and grief. I will have two children I adore, and, a few years after my divorce, I will just be starting to think about dating again. I will like myself a lot more than I did when I met A, but I will still have to work at it every day.

Words will be the answer. They always were.

I will write a story about A for you. Maybe it will make you feel better. Or at least feel. Something. And the story will be for A, too. Maybe he'll read it.

NINETY MINUTES, TURN NORTH

STEPHANIE PERKINS

Marigold hated this time of year. July was hotter—and maybe even *wetter*—than the rest of summer, for one thing. The air swelled thick with humidity. Sweat trickled down the hollows of her body. And the rain showers, so frequent in the afternoons, caused more inconveniences than relief. Dark clouds became a weary sight.

She hated the sunscreen and the gluey white paths it left behind when smeared across her skin. She hated the bloodsuckers— the hidden ticks with their threat of Lyme disease and the inexhaustible mosquitoes, buzzing inside her eardrums and always preferring her above other people. She hated the texture of her hair, fattened and frizzed, unrecognizable as her own. And she especially hated the boiling hot parking lots.

Parking lots like this one.

Marigold Moon Ling's relationship with North Drummond had been bookended by parking lots. They'd met in an Ingles grocery store parking lot last winter, and he'd broken up with her in a Bed Bath & Beyond parking lot last spring. At the time, she'd been holding a small microwave purchased with one of those big, blue twenty-percent-off postcard coupons. It was her first appliance for her first apartment. She'd been leaving the laid-back mountain town of Asheville, North Carolina, for a job in the gridlocked urban sprawl of Atlanta, Georgia. Atlanta was a three-and-a-half-hour drive away. Three and a half hours seemed manageable to Marigold. They did not to her boyfriend.

Ex-boyfriend.

God. That prefix still stung, even in her head.

But it was this specific sting—this steadily intensifying sorrow, this oppressive sense of guilt—that was the reason Marigold was standing in the parking lot of Mount Mitchell, the highest peak east of the Mississippi, about to make what might be the most humiliating mistake of her newly adultish, nineteen-year-old life.

Marigold was here to save her ex-boyfriend.

Not save in the Southern, religious sense. Less dramatically and more specifically, Marigold was here to convince her ex-boyfriend to follow her back to her apartment in Atlanta, split her rent, and enroll in college.

It was still a tall order. She was aware. But the mission was platonic. It was about helping out a friend who had helped her, about repaying a massive cosmic debt. It felt both intolerable and unjust that Marigold got to leave while North believed that he had to stay.

What Marigold didn't understand was what North was doing *here*. She'd returned to North Carolina under the guise of visiting her mother, but, before even dropping off her weekend bag, she'd driven the extra thirty-two miles past Asheville to his family's Christmas tree farm near Spruce Pine. His mother had shocked her with the news that he no longer worked there. He'd been adamant about staying at home so he could manage the property for his ailing father, but now he was working another full hour's drive away—down endless winding roads, past countless overgrown campgrounds and churchyards—even deeper into the mountains at Mount Mitchell State Park.

As Marigold stared at her destination, her wariness about the task at hand sank to a new and distressing level. She was exhausted from the long drive, but, worse, she'd spent the last hour in increasing anger and bitterness. If Marigold could admit it to herself—Marigold wasn't quite ready to admit it to herself—she might recognize these feelings as betrayal. She'd told North everything there was to tell, but he'd either lied or withheld. She couldn't recall him once, not *once*, mentioning a plan that didn't involve working on his parents' farm (their ambition) or going to college (his).

So what in the hell was this?

When turned into a hard number, their four months together sounded more like a brief encounter than an actual relationship. But their connection had always been about more than romance or hormones or sex. Almost instantly, he'd become her best friend. They'd texted each other throughout the day, every day, even after she moved away. Until his texts grew sparse in May. Until he'd stopped texting her altogether in June.

Marigold had imagined many reasons for his textual disappearance: jealousy over her evolving life, shame for staying behind, a possessive new girlfriend, losing his phone in the river, losing his memory in a car accident, losing his thumbs to a tractor blade. But she'd never imagined that he'd gotten another job. That he *had* moved on with his life, and that it didn't involve her.

What am I doing here?

The heat, rising up from the parking lot.

What. Am I doing here?

The heat. It was suffocating. She couldn't breathe. Marigold backpedaled into her Kia and slammed the door shut. She turned the key in the ignition for a blast of cold air, and her phone blared on through the stereo. She'd been listening to *Mystery Show*, one of North's favorite podcasts. She'd never listened to podcasts before North. Now she listened to them more than music.

Fuck you, North. Fuck you for ignoring my messages. Fuck you for making me worry, for making me feel guilty, for making me drive into the middle of fucking nowhere, for fucking ruining fucking podcasts! Fuck!

She grabbed her phone, hit the music app, and her speakers exploded with a soul-belting roar from Beyoncé, but it wasn't enough—not even a teensy spark of enough—because her entire world had been tainted by North. He used to pretend that he hated Beyoncé, but once, after they'd gotten into an argument about something that didn't even matter, he'd stopped mid-debate and deadpan-recited every single word of "Halo." She'd laughed so hard that she'd cried, that it actually made her abdomen sore. North could say anything and make her laugh. He had one of those voices.

Marigold pounded her fists against the steering wheel, pounded and pounded and pounded and pounded, until one of her flailing hands hit the horn. Startled, she jumped back in her seat. The family of six getting out of the minivan beside her also jumped. Marigold waved in an embarrassed apology.

Fuck you for that, too, North.

But she didn't feel it so strongly.

Marigold lowered the volume on her playlist and kept her gaze downward, pretending to mess with her phone until the family left. She concentrated on her breath like her hippie mother had always instructed her to do. In. And out. In. And out. Their voices grew faint and then vanished completely. She raised her head.

Mount Mitchell loomed before her.

Marigold's heart sank. The peak didn't look particularly steep or foreboding—it actually looked pretty mild—but it did seem . . . somber. Amid the spruces and firs were a startling number of dead trees. It was like the mountainside had been scattered with broken toothpicks. Their skeletons were so white and empty beside the bushy evergreens that they were almost a negative space, despite their physical presence. They were a question. Something missing.

"What are you doing here?" Marigold asked aloud. But this time she wasn't talking to herself or to the dead trees.

She'd driven all this way. She might as well go ask him.

The funicular was at the end of the parking lot. It was an incline railway consisting of two slow-moving cable cars—one ascending, one descending—and it was for people who didn't want to hike their way to the summit. Judging by the sizable number of tourists waiting on the benches beside her, that meant it was for most people.

Marigold hadn't been here since an elementary school field trip. Her memories were of a rickety green car, shaking its way up the track, daring her not to become at least a *little* afraid of heights. Marigold wasn't afraid of heights. But as she listened for the descending car's approach, she crossed and uncrossed her arms. She glanced nervously at her reflection in the window of the park office—where she'd paid the exorbitant twelve-dollar ticket price—and then, alarmed, she ripped off her sunglasses for a closer inspection.

Her face was flushed, her T-zone glistened with grease, and her black hair was frizzing out from its braid. Every day, she wore her hair with a thick braid across the top of her head like a headband. The rest of her hair was pinned up in the back. Usually, this signature look made her feel spunky somewhat Heidi-ish and cute.

Right now, she did not feel so cute.

Vibrations. Behind her. The rolling hum of the pulleys grew louder, into whirs and clanks. The descending car was approaching. According to his mother, North was operating one of the cars. There was a fifty-fifty chance that he was almost here.

Marigold's stomach lurched. She was here to help out a friend, sure, but that didn't mean she wanted to look like a human garbagemonster. This was still a person who had seen her naked. In a burst of panic she yanked out the bobby pins, unbraided her hair, finger-smoothed it down, and then hurriedly redid the whole thing.

The clanking grew louder. As parents and children and couples all shuffled to their feet—she was the only person here without some type of partner—Marigold stayed planted, grabbing a compact from her purse. It took three oil-blotting sheets (*three*, for God's sake) and a layer of powder to hide the shine. It didn't cover her freckles, but nothing ever did. They were more prominent this time of year, and, to her, they seemed jarring with her Chinese American features. She used to hate them, but North had told her they were sweet. Once, he'd even connected the dots on her right cheek with a Sharpie to make a lopsided heart.

The car's shadow fell across her back. Some of the kids cheered, and she sensed the twenty or so assembled people surging toward it.

Fifty-fifty. Her real heart felt lopsided.

The gears locked into a complete stop, and there was a whoosh of accompanying wind. The flags beside the park office—US and NC—momentarily flapped harder as her nose was assaulted by the scent of fir. She closed her eyes and inhaled. *Christmas in July.* Rationally, she knew it was the mountain. Irrationally, she knew it was him.

Marigold shoved her sunglasses back on, grateful for any protection, however minimal, from the elements. In her short jean shorts and tight tank top, she suddenly felt vulnerable.

You're just here to talk. That's it. Whatever happens, it'll be fine.

Sometimes it was hard to believe the truth.

Marigold's knees quivered as she stood and turned around. A forest-green car was parked beside the platform. Above its large front window was a name: MARIA. It was written in gold lettering. She couldn't see the driver.

But then—*then*—

A single voice rose above the crowd, through a tinny, old-fashioned speaker. Her spine shivered in recognition. With North, you always noticed his voice first. It was deep and confident. Sardonic and dismissive. But the timbre also held an unexpected underpinning of amusement and warmth that let him get away with saying all sorts of outrageous things. People just liked hearing him talk. He was only a few months older than she was, but he sounded like a grown man. Except . . . even that wasn't quite true. No one sounded like North. It's what had attracted her in the first place.

"Please watch your step as you exit," he said through the intercom. "I'd feel terrible if you tripped and wrecked your face. Not you, sir," he added. "Your face is a disaster. No one would notice."

The crowd—on board and off—laughed jovially.

Marigold raised her eyebrows.

A door popped open and North Drummond stepped into view. Her heart hammered against her rib cage. He swiftly jumped down from a platform on the back of the car to the main platform and then held out a hand to help an elderly woman disembark. "Goodbye," he said. He wasn't using the intercom anymore, but Marigold could still hear every word. "Please tell your friends. We're trapped in the boonies, and we're desperately lonely. We could use the company."

The woman chuckled and patted his hand.

Marigold wasn't sure why she felt so startled. Maybe it was because she hadn't seen him since April, but it was as if North's expression had been frozen in time. Despite his droll smile, his eyes held the same heavy weariness. The same edge of exasperation. Or maybe it was his uniform, which made him look like a junior park ranger. He was dressed entirely in pale blue. *Powder* blue. A powder-blue, short-sleeved, button-up shirt, powder-blue shorts that hit just above his knees, and a powder-blue hat that looked sort of like a baseball cap, only taller. And more awkward. In tidy white letters, two words had been stitched onto the front of it: FUNICULAR OPERATOR.

When the last passenger exited, he hopped back onto the car's short platform, using its guardrail to help swing himself up as if he'd done it a hundred times before. Marigold realized, disconcertingly, that perhaps he had.

"Ladies and gentlemen, girls and boys," he announced, "I'll need you to board this car one at a time. Politely. Not like the jerks that you actually are."

The crowd laughed again as they queued into a single-file line. Marigold hesitated near the back, hiding between two bikers with thick arms and wizard beards. Trying to be invisible. Trying to *think*. She'd thought it would have been easy enough to get him alone, but she hadn't expected to find him . . . doing a routine? Was that what this was?

A ranger in khaki hurried past, signaling something to North. He nodded, the middle-aged woman took his place, and he jogged off toward the park office.

Marigold watched anxiously as he disappeared into the log-and-stone building. The line moved forward as passengers continued to board. Would he return? Should she wait out here? She couldn't see him through the office's windows.

"Come on, sweetheart. You're up."

Marigold looked back, agitated, to find the ranger signaling for her to board. "Um." It came out as a stammer. "Uh . . ."

The ranger's hand gestures grew more impatient.

"Is he—is that guy coming back?"

The woman nodded brusquely. "He's on his way right now."

Marigold glanced over her shoulder to find North striding toward them, halfway across the main platform. Like a startled rabbit, she shot up and into the car. It wasn't flat, like a cable car on the street. It was built to match the mountain's natural incline, and the wooden benches faced backward—toward the view. The front of the car, the best seats, were already taken, so she hustled down the sloping aisle and onto a middle bench. It was as far away from the back—where North would be standing—as she could get.

"Thank you, Kathy." His voice clicked on over the intercom, and Marigold heard him shut the door. "I'll take it again from here."

She could have at least *waved* to show him she was here. Why had her first instinct been to run? Marigold sank into her seat, flaming with regret. The car smelled like body odor and old machinery. Its windows were closed and revealed traces of rain earlier in the day. The atmosphere felt stuffy. Claustrophobic. It was too late, that was the worst part. At some point—some point very soon—North would discover her, and for the rest of his life, she'd be a silly anecdote he'd tell to friends and future girlfriends.

"Greetings, good afternoon, and welcome to Mount Mitchell State Park," he said. "Because you're all lazy, you've chosen to sit your way to the summit, when you could have easily walked it instead."

As the other passengers groaned with good nature, Marigold heard him pressing buttons and flipping a switch. The small car lumbered into motion.

"Out the front window, you'll find spectacular views of the Black Mountain range—part of the larger Blue Ridge range, part of the even larger Appalachian range—and out the *side* windows, you'll find that we're rising at a near-horizontal incline. I cannot stress this fact enough: It truly isn't a difficult hike. Denali, the tallest mountain *west* of the Mississippi, has an elevation of 20,310 feet. We're headed up to 6,684 feet. This funicular should not exist. Unfortunately, it does, so we're stuck here together for the next nine minutes."

More laughter and guffaws. The travel-fatigued parents seemed relieved to have someone else entertaining their children, if only for this fleeting respite. But Marigold felt surrounded by his voice. Cornered by it. Beside her, a couple in their late twenties with ironic hobo hairstyles was snapping carefree, square-shaped selfies. She hunkered down even lower and peered through the slats on the back of their bench.

North had one hiking boot–clad foot propped up on a metal box. His left hand held the intercom, while his right hand rested on his thigh. It was an oddly masculine pose for someone so casually flashing his bare knees and calves in such absurd blue shorts. "The first rails were laid over a century ago, and they've only undergone minimal repairs since. But have no fear; this antique rattletrap breadbox is safe and sound." He pounded on a wall for emphasis. It was not a sturdy noise.

The rickety car joggled and clattered, beneath and around her, but nothing else was matching up to her childhood memories. It was true that the mountain didn't seem very steep, and she also didn't remember the operator delivering such a gimmicky spiel.

He sounded like a skipper on the Jungle Cruise at Disney World.

"I'm delighted to say that it's been almost three weeks since my last derailment," North continued, "and I only lost half of my passengers."

Marigold marveled at his propped-up leg. They'd dated in colder weather, *pants* weather, so she'd never seen his legs outside in broad daylight. They were tan and muscular and hairy. She would've guessed that hairy legs might be kind of gross, but they weren't. They were manly.

Everything about North made him seem older than his age. It wasn't just his voice or his legs. He was tall and broad—*brawny* was the word that most frequently came to mind—from years of hard farm labor. He listened to NPR and had dreams of becoming a radio broadcaster. His vocabulary was considerable, and he'd consciously dropped his rural accent at a young age. He could also be a bit grumpy and curmudgeonly, though with a tenderness and thoughtfulness to his actual actions that she found rather charming. Marigold used to joke that he was born to be someone's grandfather.

The hipsters beside her had stopped Instagramming. Conscious of their wary side-eyes, Marigold whipped her head forward again, wincing with embarrassment. She slid back up, slowly, into an almost normal sitting position. As if there weren't anything suspicious about her behavior. As if she weren't being a total creep.

"Each car was christened upon the funicular's launch," North said, and Marigold heard a twinge of genuine distraction in his voice. Not the sort that meant he'd spotted her, but the sort that meant his mind was elsewhere. He was working on autopilot. "The first car was named *Elisha* after the Reverend Elisha Mitchell, the scientist who proved that this mountain was the tallest in Appalachia. At the time, Dr. Mitchell's claim was hotly contested, and tragically, he died on an expedition while trying to verify his original measurements. He fell from a nearby waterfall. Later, both the mountain and the waterfall were named after him, and his tomb was moved to the summit." A *thunk* indicated North's foot landing back on the floor. "Now. Did anyone catch the name of the second car—this car—as you were boarding?"

"Maria!" a man called out.

"Careful, sir. No one likes a show-off." After pausing for the inevitable laughter, North continued. "But you're correct. This car was named after Dr. Mitchell's wid—"

He stopped. Midword.

The hair rose on the nape of Marigold's neck. She felt him staring at her, staring *through* her, and the sensation was tense and electric and charged. She squeezed her eyes shut, willing him to continue. He didn't.

The other passengers shifted on their benches to see what was happening. North's silence was deafening. Her entire body burned as she removed her sunglasses. Suddenly, the mountainside car seemed precarious. She turned, dizzily, to face him.

North stared at her for several long seconds. His expression remained flat. Unyielding.

She grimaced and held up a hand, just barely, in acknowledgment.

He held her gaze for one last, pointed second. Blinked. And then turned away with a blithe smile for his audience. "His widow, Maria. The one left behind."

There was a collective exhale as everyone settled back into their seats. North didn't miss another beat, and Marigold knew he wouldn't deign to look at her again. She angled herself toward the closest window, ignoring the stares of the more curious passengers. North was her friend. She was here to *help* him. Why was this all so shameful and humiliating?

Since moving away, she must have accidentally said or done something awful to him, but she was flummoxed as to what this transgression might be. North was still talking. Her head buzzed, and her bra was lined with sweat. She wished she could crack open a window. The railway split into two sets of tracks, and they passed the other car—jokes were exchanged and hands were waved and bells were rung—and then the two tracks merged back into one. The ride was only half over. It was agonizing.

When they finally reached the top, she lingered behind while everyone else exited. Several people expressed their gratitude to North. "Save your thanks for the return trip," he replied with faux merriment. "There's still plenty of time to be mauled by a black bear."

The passengers had all disembarked.

For a surreal moment, Marigold thought he'd actually forgotten about her. But then she heard him jump back onto the car's platform. His movements sounded heavier, not like the easy swing she'd seen earlier. He reentered the car, held out a hand toward the new line preparing to board—a signal for them to wait—and then closed the door.

Marigold stood.

North stared at her with that same guarded expression. "I only have a second."

"I know."

"Are you here to see me?"

"Of course I'm here to see you." Marigold moved toward him, up the sloping aisle. "I wanted to talk."

"No."

She stopped. Her heart stuttered. "No?"

North glanced away. "I meant . . . my break isn't for another ninety minutes. And there's a line of tourists out there dying to hear my tremendous farewell speech."

"Oh. Yeah, sure. Of course."

They were staring at each other again. A lump rose in Marigold's throat. She remembered herself, forcibly, and hurried to the door. She waited for North to open it. He didn't. She glanced at him, hurt and unsure—*Am I supposed to do it?*—and that was the moment his hard expression crumbled and his warm eyes filled with remorse.

"You'll wait for me?" he asked. "You have the time to wait? I'm sorry. There's no one else here right now who could take my place."

The lump returned. "I can wait."

North reached for the door, but then, in an afterthought, kicked open the metal box near his feet, grabbed an object from inside it, and thrust it into her hands. "Here. To keep you occupied." But then he frowned as if he'd said something idiotic. "Meet you in front of the museum at four o'clock?"

Marigold clutched the object to her chest and nodded.

It was a sandwich. To keep her occupied, North had given her a vegetarian BLT with avocado and imitation B.

This was interesting for four reasons: One, he'd been flustered enough to misspeak. North rarely got flustered and even more rarely misspoke. Two, he'd given her a part of his own lunch. He must not *completely* hate her. Three, he'd forgotten about her lifelong aversion to the texture of raw tomatoes. This was disappointing to an extent that made Marigold feel uncomfortable. And four, he might be a vegetarian now. North had always wanted to be a vegetarian, but he'd needed the more complete proteins found in meat to do his farmwork without getting tired. Surely it took less energy to do this new job.

Marigold sighed as she rewrapped the sandwich. Her mother would be thrilled. She was the owner of a popular vegan restaurant in downtown Asheville, and she already believed that North hung the moon. This would cement it. Marigold wasn't a vegan or a vegetarian—she loved meat, probably because she'd always been denied it—but she was understanding toward those who were. Still, the tempeh bacon made her sad. It represented another change in North's life that she hadn't known about.

She watched the *Maria* clank its way down below her line of sight. At least the temperature was several degrees cooler up here. The accompanying breeze was a solace as she approached a cluster of old-looking buildings: restrooms, the museum, a concessions stand, and a gift shop. A wide pathway—asphalt imprinted to look like stone—ran behind them, winding its way up toward what could only be the summit. Marigold had a lot of time to kill, so she checked out each building, starting with the women's restroom. It had been a long drive.

After taking care of that, she wandered over to the concessions stand, which she found typically Southern in flavor. There were bottles of water and Gatorade, cans of soda, granola bars, candy bars, and those orange-colored peanut butter crackers. But they were also selling mason jars filled with apple butter, chow chow, pickled okra, and blackstrap molasses, and they had an entire shelf of fruit cider—strawberry, peach, muscadine, and scuppernong.

Marigold hadn't eaten since breakfast, over eight hours ago. North had guessed correctly; she was famished. She bought a package of trail mix and wolfed it down. She stared at North's sandwich. Then she removed the tomatoes and ate it, too. It tasted better than the trail mix.

Next up was the museum, which turned out to be one dimly lit room. Its displays explained the park's flora, fauna, geology, and topography. Marigold read each sign dutifully, but without the focus to comprehend any of their sentences, until she reached the corner dedicated to Dr. Elisha Mitchell. A single word jumped out, and her heart staggered.

North. His wife, Maria's maiden name had been North.

It was a coincidence. A first name versus a surname, and North had been named after—of all the hideous things—the North Pole. His seasonally passionate parents had also named his older brother Nicholas and his sister, Noelle. It was worse than her own mother naming her Marigold Moon. But Drummond Family Trees had been growing and selling Christmas trees for two generations, and they were aiming to extend it into a third. When North's father had been diagnosed with Parkinson's, the pressure had been put onto Nick, who'd run away in response. Noelle wanted the farm, but their parents had misguidedly offered it to North instead, because he was male. Then she'd run away, too. North didn't want it, but he was all they had left. His parents weren't cruel. However, they'd made an ugly mistake, and now North was the one paying for it. Except . . . maybe he wasn't anymore?

Maria S. North.

It meant nothing. But it felt like something. The word *north* always felt like something. Marigold wondered when that would stop, when the stilted female voice on Google Maps wouldn't crush her spirit every time it told her to turn north onto the interstate.

This is why you're here, she reminded herself. *To stop this sadness and guilt.*

Still, Marigold left the museum and hurried into the gift shop next door. A carved wooden bear with a WELCOME sign greeted her at its threshold. The smell of Christmas grew stronger, to the point of being overpowering.

Does this mean Christmas is ruined forever, too?

The shop was also one room, and a self-inflicted browse revealed the usual trinkets—souvenir postcards, magnets, pins, books, puzzles, T-shirts, and sweatshirts, all featuring the mountain or the Blue Ridge Parkway. A girl about her age stood behind the counter in a powder-blue polo and matching powder-blue pants. In an organized row in front of her register were a dozen tiny brown bottles with eyedroppers. Marigold picked one up. Pure balsam fir oil.

"It's what you're smelling right now," the girl explained.

"Mmm, it's nice." But as the lie tumbled from her lips, it evolved into the truth. Marigold wanted one of these tiny bottles. She *needed* one.

She bought one.

Outside the spell of the shop, her regret was instantaneous. She'd already spent too much on the funicular and the trail mix, not to mention the gas it took to drive here. But she was too embarrassed to return it. She'd just have to replace a few more meals next week with ramen. Marigold was already eating a lot of ramen. She had two jobs in Atlanta: an internship at an animation studio, which was what she hoped to be paid for doing some day, and a serving gig at an Outback Steakhouse. That was where the rest of her meals came from—the cheapest menu items, purchased with her employee discount. Sometimes her grandparents, who ran a popular Chinese restaurant in nearby Decatur, would leave food on her doorstep while she was at work. It always made her cry.

Marigold checked her phone and was dismayed to see only forty-five minutes had passed. The screen showed two bars on a 1x signal—it might as well be dead—so she couldn't even call her mom or go online. Her eyes rested on the funicular tracks as another green car crested the mountain. After some quick math, she realized it wasn't North. His car was at the bottom.

She shivered and rubbed her bare arms. Now that her body had cooled, the air seemed chilly and autumnal. Most of the park's visitors were wearing pants or jackets, as if they'd known—duh—they'd be going on top of a mountain today.

To be fair, I did not know I'd be going on top of a mountain today.

The only thing remaining was the summit itself, so Marigold trudged onto the pathway. It was even colder under the trees, but it was also more tranquil. The air tasted clean and newly born, and as she brought it deeper into her lungs, she discovered she'd been holding her breath. But here there was lichen-covered bark and moss-covered logs, pinky-purple wildflowers and spiky-soft bee balm, and even a chirping bird with fluffy blue feathers. It wouldn't have looked out of place on Snow White's finger.

A spotted dog in a bandana bounded past, followed by an older woman with a large backpack and walking sticks that looked like ski poles. It was the first actual hiker that Marigold had seen here. But the closer she got to the summit, the more crowded it was. The shelter of the trees disappeared, and the peaceful nature sounds grew into clamorous playground noises. Children laughed and cried and screamed with the freedom of summer vacation. A peculiar stone structure emerged. It resembled a stumpy castle tower, and it was packed with tourists.

Marigold wove through the throng, across a bridge, and around the packed observation deck. The 360-degree view was undeniably beautiful—if she were in a happy mental space, she might describe it as stunning, or even breathtaking—but she wasn't in a happy mental space. The wind whistled and nipped at her exposed skin, so she left after only a minute. She ducked beneath the bridge. Leaning against one of its concrete pillars, she slid down into the dirt. The gravel sparkled with flecks of mica, and the patches of grass were spotted with yellow dandelion flowers. Marigold hugged her knees against her chest.

It's not so bad, she told herself.

Ahead of her were rolling ridges and mountain ranges cloaked in mist. Below her, the twin cars of the funicular rose and fell. And behind her, inside the ground, was Dr. Elisha Mitchell. His tomb didn't look like much—a pile of flat rocks inside a rectangular wall made out of similar rocks—but she knew what it was, because people kept asking what it was and then reading the plaque out loud.

Marigold redid the calculations. North's car would make one more full trip before she saw him again. She rifled through her purse, searching for paper and a distraction, but could only find the receipt for the balsam oil. Slowly, perhaps unconsciously, she drew her favorite character onto the back of it, a cantankerous but lovable sloth named South.

South was North, of course. But . . . he actually *was*.

North had recorded the voice of the character. Marigold made comedic animated short films for YouTube, but she wanted to make them for television. It's why she had moved; Atlanta was home to several animation studios. She'd been fortunate—and talented enough—to score the internship, even though the grunt work often sucked. She trusted it would get better.

A boy with dirt on his nose appeared behind her. "I can see my echo."

Marigold wasn't in the mood, but she smiled anyway to be polite. "Oh, yeah?"

"Watch this." He cupped his hands around his mouth and shouted, "Mountain, mountain, mountain, mountain."

She nodded.

"Awesome, awesome, awesome, awesome."

She smiled again, for real this time.

He pointed at her drawing. "Can I have that?"

"I'm sorry." His mother, a harried-looking woman with stress between her brows and giant silver hoops in her ears, rushed up and grabbed his hand. "Emiliano Navarro Castellanos. What have I told you about bothering strangers?"

"It's okay. He's not bothering me." Marigold added a marigold into the sloth's hands and then held out the drawing for Emiliano. "His name is South. He only eats orange flowers and heirloom tomatoes."

Emiliano looked up at his mother. She nodded, and he eagerly accepted the drawing. "Thank you. Gracias!" His mother thanked her, too, but Emiliano was already skipping away and pulling her along with him.

Marigold felt inexplicably sad to see them go—a general, misdirected stirring of loneliness and fear. She didn't know how long she'd been staring at Dr. Mitchell's tomb when her heart compressed with a sudden and knowing panic. She checked her phone. And then she scrambled to her feet. Racing down the peak, she dodged strollers and a tour group in matching neon T-shirts. It was exactly four o'clock. Railways were punctual. *He* would be punctual. What if he left, thinking she'd changed her mind?

In the last ninety-three minutes, North's confidence had continued to spiral downward. His usual posture of self-assurance bordering upon arrogance had wilted into hunched shoulders and slack arms. As Marigold gasped and wheezed toward the museum, his back was to her, but she still registered the defeat in his body.

She slowed her pace. Her own confidence dared to grow.

His ears pricked up as if receiving some subtle signal, and he turned to face her. Shoulders pulling back. Chin rising.

Marigold stopped when she was still several feet shy. "Sorry I'm late. Thanks for waiting." Her voice was a little breathless.

"You, too," North said.

"And thanks for the sandwich."

He winced.

"I'm serious, it was good. I was really hungry."

"Sorry about the you-know-what. I didn't even think of it until you'd left."

A smile broke through her cautious reserve. North *had* remembered. "So, was my interpretation correct?" she asked. "Are you officially a vegetarian?"

"Your mom would be proud."

"She'd ask why you still eat dairy."

North laughed unexpectedly. Her heart panged in response. He had a great laugh—funny and deep. "How's she doing, anyway?"

"Good. Pretty good, at least."

"I'm glad to hear it," he said. The sentiment was sincere. North and her mother got along well, which was remarkable because Marigold's mother didn't care for most men. Marigold's father had always been sort of awful, but they hadn't known how awful until a year and a half ago when his *other* wife had surprised them on their doorstep.

It was taking a while to get over those scars.

Her father had never been around much—his work in orthopedic sales kept him away for weeks at a time, he'd claimed—but her mother had been fine with that. She clung to her free-spirit identity to an extent that verged upon irony. And she'd never been his legal wife, only a partner. It was why Marigold shared her mother's Chinese surname and not her white father's Irish surname. Unfortunately, this was also why, when his actual wife showed up, they'd lost their house and most of their savings. Those things had never belonged to them, either.

North had played a huge role in getting their lives back on track. When she met him, Marigold and her mother had been living in a dirty, crowded apartment and were saving up for a new house. Not only had North cleaned and organized their apartment to make it livable, but he'd also helped them find the house. And then, when *that* space had required a ton of work, he'd driven his truck over every night for the three weeks before their move-in date to paint the drab walls, fix the leaky plumbing, rip up the musty carpeting, refinish the damaged hardwood, and carry in the heavy furniture. And he'd done it the whole time knowing that as soon as her mother was settled, Marigold would leave. It wasn't what he'd wanted. North had helped because it was what her family had needed.

This was the debt that felt like it could never be repaid. *This* was why she was here.

It was why they understood each other, too. Marigold respected North's sense of duty to his family. She never would've left home if she felt that her mother wasn't stable enough to be alone. But Marigold also knew it was important to carve out your own life—something her mother had always encouraged, even when things were rough—and she was worried that North had given up trying.

The confident edge returned to his voice. "I have a tip."

Marigold arched an eyebrow.

"The next time you attempt to spy on someone who knows you, wear a hat." North pointed at her braid. "It's a dead giveaway."

"I wasn't spying."

"You were one hundred percent spying."

She shrugged it off. "Maybe . . . ten percent spying, ninety percent wondering what the hell you're doing here."

"I'm working. What the hell are *you* doing here?"

"Your mom told me you'd be here, so I came."

He was as stubborn as a boulder. "Why?"

"Because I wanted to talk to you."

"And how's that going for you so far?"

Marigold glared at him. *Glared.* And then she burst into laughter.

North looked away, trying to hide a grin. "All right. Okay."

"You're impossible."

"I know."

"And you look ridiculous in that uniform," she said.

"I look incredible."

"Incredibly ridiculous."

"Incredibly handsome."

She laughed again, and he smiled directly at her—for one brief, brilliant second—before turning around and striding away. "Come on," he said. "I know a place."

Marigold would follow North anywhere.

They trekked up the pathway, but instead of taking her back to the summit, North nodded toward an offshoot that led into the forest. A sign marked it as the Balsam Nature Trail. She hadn't noticed it earlier. "You came on a good day," he said. "It already rained.

Usually, it showers in the afternoon."

"How long until your break's over?"

North didn't even have to glance at his phone. "Twenty-two minutes."

"Then let's not waste any more time discussing the weather."

He didn't respond, so Marigold took his silence as assent. They entered the sanctuary of the woods. Pebbles crunched underfoot. "Except, okay," Marigold relented, a few seconds later, "I do have *one* question. What's up with all the dead trees? Is it acid rain or something?"

North ground to a halt. He stared at her.

"What?" She marched past him.

"You," he said, "are a terrible listener."

It dawned on her. "You told us on the funicular, didn't you?"

"I told you on the funicular."

"Well, I was a little distracted after that insane stare-down you gave me."

"Balsam woolly adelgid." North started moving behind her again. "It's an aphid-like pest that's been killing the Fraser firs. But . . . yes. Acid rain, too."

Marigold waited for him to catch up before giving it another try. "Please tell me what you're doing here. And don't you dare say 'working' again."

"I'm not."

Her blood pressure rose. "You're not working."

"No. I'm not."

She gritted her teeth, tired of the verbal games. But North seemed to regret his decision to be difficult, because he quickly acquiesced. He gestured to a patch on his shirtsleeve. Marigold's eyes widened as she read it. "Volunteer? You're a *volunteer*?"

"Rangers wear khaki. Volunteers and seasonal hires wear blue."

"You're not even a seasonal hire? You're not being paid? For operating *heavy machinery* filled with *live human beings*?"

"It's totally illegal."

"This park is run by the state government!"

"Crazy, right?"

"What? I just . . . *What?* How did this happen?"

He shrugged. "My dad knew a guy."

"North Drummond." Marigold stopped in her tracks. "You know perfectly well you'll have to give me more than that."

North stopped, too. He stared at her with that same unyieldingness . . . and then his eyes gradually softened. "Yeah, I know." He managed a faint smile. "Come on. It's just ahead."

The sounds of the other visitors disappeared as he led her past a trail marker with a blue diamond, white triangle, and white circle. Marigold looked up. They had walked underneath an immense overhang of rock.

North glanced at her, and she smiled back in relief. "Right?" he said.

Marigold nodded in agreement.

A bit farther, they arrived at a rock formation jutting out from the side of the mountain. It hung like a canopy over another slab of rock, creating an irresistible, human-sized place to rest. The sheltered stone was still damp, but there was a spot that looked mostly dry, so they sat down and crossed their legs. The butt of her shorts instantly grew wet. Marigold barely noticed. Her nerves were jangling again, but the anxiety was mixed with excitement.

She was glad to be here with him. Alone. In this secluded place.

North removed his hat and tossed it onto the rock beside him. He rubbed his chestnut-brown hair, trying to get rid of the hat shape. It only partially helped.

Marigold had always liked North's hair. It was the same warm brown shade as his eyes. She smiled again, and he smiled back. And then their smiles faded away together. It looked like he wanted to say something, but he was struggling to find the right words. For the first time, Marigold wondered if maybe it *wasn't* easy for him to explain what he was doing here. Maybe he didn't have a good answer, not even for himself.

At last, he spoke. "My sister came back. In May."

It shocked her. It would be difficult for her to feel *more* shocked.

"We'd been talking—me and Noelle—and . . . she came back.

And, this time, my parents listened to her."

Marigold hated to interrupt, but she couldn't help herself. "You mean they gave it to her? She's running the farm now?"

He nodded.

"Well, that's . . . that's great."

Another nod. He stared at his hiking boots.

What was she missing? Noelle had returned—something unexpected and wonderful had happened—but then North had cut off communications with Marigold. "Okay," she tried. "Your sister took over the farm . . . so you needed a new job? Except, as you pointed out, you're not actually working here."

"I'm here because I need something to do until I figure out what I *want* to do."

"You want to go to college. You want to work in radio."

North picked out a sharp rock from the tread on his right boot. "My dad's best friend is a ranger here, and he told us about the open volunteer position. I was stationed in the museum, but on my first week he overheard me giving an improvised lecture to a tour group and was taken aback. Impressed," he added, with a touch of embarrassment.

"Two of the operators had just quit, and the rangers were desperate. They don't like the funiculars—giving the same two speeches, twice per hour. My dad's friend knew I had a lot of experience with big machinery, so he sort of . . . threw me into it. That same day. It didn't take long for them to teach me how to operate it, and I already knew the trivia from the museum, and because I wasn't getting paid I didn't feel like I had to follow the park's usual monologue . . ."

"Let me guess," Marigold said. "The rangers received so many raves from the park's visitors that they switched you over permanently?"

"That's pretty much it."

"Wow." Now Marigold was the one staring at her shoes, a pair of red sneakers. "Wow," she said again. "You should be proud of that. Congratulations."

"The other volunteers aren't happy with me."

Marigold glanced up. "Because you were singled out for the better job?"

North shrugged. "Most of them will be gone after the summer season, anyway."

"So . . . you're staying, then."

When he didn't reply, her outrage exploded back to the surface. "But they should be paying you! You should have a salary and health insurance and a 401(k)."

North hesitated. As if he wasn't sure he wanted to say what he was about to say. "They are. If you'd come next week, I would've been wearing pants."

Marigold blinked.

"Only volunteers wear shorts," he explained. "If you're paid, they give you pants."

As quickly as it had arrived, Marigold's anger dissipated into disappointment. She pulled her knees up to her chest. "Oh."

North rubbed the back of his neck. "They told me today. Right before I saw you, actually."

"That's why you were called into the park office?"

He nodded. "They offered me a full-time job. I accepted."

"Oh," Marigold said again. The wind rustled the trees. A droplet of water fell from a dangling branch and landed beside her. She shivered.

"What is it?" His voice was quiet.

Marigold shook her head.

North didn't prod, but he did notice the goose bumps on her arms. "You're *freezing*. Why wouldn't you bring a jacket?"

She shot him another aggressive glare. "Nice. Shorts."

North laughed as he unbuttoned his shirt, revealing a plain white T-shirt underneath. He held out the work shirt.

Marigold continued to glare.

"Take it," he said.

She made him wait for another five seconds before accepting it. "Thank you."

He seemed pleased for the victory. "You're welcome."

Marigold draped it over her arms and legs like a blanket, and her eyes shuddered closed. The shirt smelled like North's sweat and North's detergent and North's Christmas tree farm and something else *North* that slipped even deeper, that reached inside her physical body to fan out her memories like a magician revealing a deck of unblemished cards.

She saw their first kiss in her old apartment, illuminated by the glow of the tree that he'd just helped her decorate. The snowy nighttime rides in his truck, his right hand clasped over her left on the center console. The hours at her computer, watching him record his voice, breathing life into her animations. The first time they made love. He was feeding his neighbors' alpacas while they were in Florida, and he led her inside their house. They both got rug burn from the dining room carpet. It was more romantic than it sounded. And then the last memory: clinging to that stupid microwave in that stupid parking lot while North told her that he had no interest in a long-distance relationship. *Better to stop this charade now.* That was the word he'd used. *Charade.*

"What are you thinking about?" North asked.

Marigold opened her eyes. She was still frowning, but it had grown into a frown of concern. "Where will you live when you move out of your parents' house?"

North winced.

"You're not going to," she said.

"I will."

"Bullshit."

He wouldn't meet her eyes, and her frustration rose. "Is it at least for a good reason?" she asked. "Do they still need your help or something?"

"My parents will always need my help."

"Bullshit," she said again.

North turned his full body toward her, furious. "Why are you even here? Why?"

"Because you wouldn't talk to me!"

"And that didn't tell you something? Like, that I didn't *want* to talk to you?"

It was a slap in the face. "You *ass.*"

His energy deflated the moment he realized how much he'd hurt her. "Yeah. Maybe. Probably."

Marigold felt like a fool. She wanted to cry, but she didn't want to cry in front of him. She pushed back the tears. "I'm here . . ."

North waited.

She tried again. "I came here . . . to rescue you."

Now he was the one who was surprised. His forehead wrinkled as she sprang to her feet, a Marigold-shaped ball of nerves. She clutched his shirt against her chest and paced before him. "So my plan was to help you look for someone who could run your parents' farm. I was going to convince you to move to Atlanta and enroll in community college. And then we'd save up, or you could get some grants or loans, or all of the above, and then you could finish at one of the other schools. By then, you'd qualify for in-state tuition. Atlanta *does* have the second-highest number of colleges after Boston, you know."

North's mouth was agape. "*We* would save up?"

"You. I meant you." Marigold felt flustered. "But yeah. So my apartment has a second bedroom, and I need someone to split my rent, because I'm broke. We'd be helping each other out, you see?"

His jaw grew wry with understanding. "Ah. You want me to help pay your rent."

But he didn't understand, not at all. "If I didn't care who my roommate was, I wouldn't be here. I'd be on Craigslist!" Marigold threw her arms above her head. "I want *you* to be my roommate."

North stared at her until she stopped pacing.

"What?" Her voice trembled.

"You want me . . . to be your roommate."

"Yes."

He swallowed and shook his head. "Marigold. I can't do that."

"Because of this job?"

"Because of *you*."

"Oh." His shirt dangled limply at her side. Marigold glanced down the trail, fighting the tears from welling up again. "Okay.

Yeah, I guess it would be weird for you to move in with your ex-girlfriend. Someone you'd dumped."

North looked strangely stung. He stumbled to his feet. "No."

"No? What do you mean, *no*?"

"I didn't dump you."

"North, I was there. You broke up with me."

"Because you were leaving and I couldn't go with you! I didn't want to."

Marigold shook her head in confusion. "You didn't want to leave?"

"I didn't want to break up with you."

"But . . . but you did."

His shoulders drooped miserably. "I know."

"Oh." It was a whisper.

North crossed his arms to protect his last shred of dignity. "I stopped texting you because it sucked, all right? It sucked hearing about your new life and your new job, and I knew any day you'd tell me about a new boyfriend, too."

"But we were *friends*. You could've told me this. You left me in the dark."

"You always wanted me to talk to Noelle, but I was so angry with her. It wasn't until after you left that I finally reached out to her, so when she returned . . . it felt worse than if she hadn't. Because it was already too late."

Everything was wrong inside Marigold's chest. Her heart was cracking, thumping, splitting, swelling. All at once.

North extracted his shirt from her death grip, put his arms through the holes, and buttoned it back up. "I'm telling you that I can't move to Atlanta because I don't want to be your roommate. Or your friend. I never liked you like that. I mean, I did, of course I did, but . . ." He snatched up his hat from the rock. "It was always more complicated for me than it was for you. My feelings were stronger."

Marigold was frozen. She'd never seen him look so vexed. Or so forlorn.

He tugged the hat onto his head. "Do you understand what I'm saying?"

She could only nod.

"I'm going back to work." North leaned over and kissed her cheek, lightly. "You should take the other car down."

Marigold held a hand to her cheek as she watched him disappear into the forest. He never looked back. His kiss had been the first time their skin had made contact in three months.

Her fingertips still smelled like him. It didn't make her feel good. The kiss hadn't felt good, either. Something was whipping circles inside of her, dizzying and nauseating, a realization as huge and terrifying and destructive as a tornado.

To have the strength to move away, Marigold had channeled all her energy into helping her mother, finding a job, finding an apartment, packing up everything she'd ever owned, and saying goodbye to the only hometown she'd ever had. Leaving required determination, so everything else had been placed on hold. From her first encounter with North, there'd been an expiration date on their relationship. It hadn't seemed smart to acknowledge the possibility of something else. Or to admit anything out loud.

Marigold thought she'd been here to rescue him, but the act had been selfish.

She wanted North to move in with her not because she wanted to see him succeed (although she did), and not because she needed help with her rent (although she also did), but because she couldn't bear to be away from him for another day.

It was obvious. It was so stupidly obvious.

Marigold was in pain because she was heart-crushingly, soul-achingly, bone marrow–deep in love with North Drummond. How was it possible that she hadn't known until this moment?

North loved her. He *loved* her.

Marigold cried aloud—a strange, strangled sound—as the information washed over her again. *That* is *what he was trying to say, right?* Marigold shook her head, dislodging this last seed of doubt. She grabbed her purse and bolted down the trail, over the stones and logs. The world grew louder. Talking, playing, laughing, shouting. She ran onto the main pathway, pulse in her throat. She came around the final bend—

Just as his green car slipped out of view down the mountain.

The funicular closed at six. It meant that North would arrive for his final load of passengers in another ninety minutes.

She'd waited all day. She could wait a bit longer.

Marigold headed toward the buildings for warmth. According to the thermometer beside the concessions stand, it was fifty-seven degrees. She rubbed her arms vigorously, unsure how much of her shivering was from the temperature and how much of it was from her fear of what was still to come. It didn't help when she realized the seat of her shorts was muddy and wet. She took her time in the restroom, trying to get the fabric as clean and dry as possible with paper towels while praying that North hadn't seen the damage when she was pacing in front of him.

North. *North.*

As the clock ticked, second after agonizing second, his name soared through her like a ballad. They felt the same way about each other. It wasn't too late. It couldn't be.

It was the longest ninety minutes of her life.

At six o'clock, Marigold was still freezing, but the sky was blue and bright. The summer sun was still a few hours away from setting. The rangers had done a good job of shepherding people down from the summit, because the waiting area was full when the *Maria* arrived. North flumped onto the platform. He looked exhausted. He ushered the passengers aboard wordlessly as Marigold hid at the end of the line, unable to resist one final surprise. Her stomach twisted with hope and butterflies.

When the tall man ahead of her stepped onto the car, North's eyes locked upon hers. His expression briefly lit up before sinking back into something that was even more dejected. It reshaped itself again into anger. North held up a hand to stop her. "Oh my God," he said. "You're a worse listener than I thought."

He still cared. He still felt strongly about her. His reaction made her feel brave.

Marigold smiled sweetly, knowing how to play this final game. "Please let me board."

"Do you or do you not see this official government hand stopping you?"

"*Volunteer* government hand. And it's your job to let me board."

"You're killing me today." But he dropped it, shaking his head and stepping aside. "And now you're doing it on purpose."

Marigold grinned as she swept past him. "I am."

There was an inhalation behind her, preparation for a retort, but then . . . nothing. As if he was suddenly bewildered. Marigold took a seat on the bench closest to his control panel. He shut the door. She glanced over her shoulder and gave him another coy smile.

North's brow furrowed, but his eyes were alight as he reached for the intercom. "Ladies and gentlemen, girls and boys. Appreciated guests and persistent interlopers."

The other passengers laughed.

Marigold placed an elbow over the back of her bench and stared up at him. She was only a foot away. She batted her eyes.

His steady gaze never left hers as he engaged with the outdated controls, and the car lurched into its downward trajectory. "We, of the North Carolina State Parks System, *do* hope you've enjoyed your visit to Mount Mitchell today—"

Marigold smiled and nodded her head.

"—but not so much that you feel the urge to visit us again. We're very busy, and there are other tourists to meet. The world is *brimming* with tourists. We won't be thinking about you, so you should stop thinking about us. Just stop it. Right now."

The other passengers continued to laugh.

Marigold gave North an exaggerated pout.

"I know. It's hard." His mischievous gleam intensified. "This is a magnificent mountain. It's tall and stately and—some might say—incredibly handsome."

Marigold covered a snort with her hand.

"The other mountains you'll meet on future road trips will have far less appeal, but . . . you had your chance." North gave a rueful shake of his head. "You chose to come down. There's no going back up."

The rest of the car still didn't realize anything out of the ordinary was happening, until Marigold's voice rang out, loud and clear: "But what if we like *this* mountain? What if we can't even see the other mountains because we're so infatuated with the one standing right before us?"

She felt a growing number of eyes on the back of her head, but she kept her own eyes on North. The lines of his face were solemn. Mock, at first. And then something more genuine. "It sounds like you like this mountain a lot," he said.

"I do."

"I see."

"Today wasn't my first visit. When I left the last time, it destroyed me, but I didn't understand why. I just . . . couldn't stop thinking about it. The mountain," she clarified. "So I returned to uncover the reason."

North paused. "And what did you discover?"

"That my feelings were stronger than I'd realized."

"Exactly . . . how strong?"

"Very strong."

"I see," North said again.

Their audience oohed behind them. No one was looking at the view outside as Marigold placed a hand on the center of her chest. "And now my heart is breaking to be back in this same position. Leaving." Her tone turned pleading. "I wish the mountain would come with me, but even I know that's impossible. It takes millions and millions of years to move a mountain. It takes shifting plates. Violent earthquakes."

"Dynamite helps." He'd forgotten to use the intercom.

She smiled sadly. "I'm all out."

"You might've used more than you realized."

Marigold's veins throbbed as North reached out and gently touched her elbow, which was still hanging over the back of the bench. His fingers were warm.

"Besides," he said, "this isn't *that* big of a mountain. It's not like it's Denali or anything."

Marigold moved her arm and took North's hand. She squeezed. He squeezed back. They were both smiling.

North picked up the intercom with his other hand and returned his attention to the crowd. "Ladies and gentlemen, girls and boys, in case you were wondering: Yes. This does happen on every descent."

"Give her a kiss!" someone shouted.

"As you can see from the patch on my shirtsleeve," North said, "I'm a volunteer. Providing that level of entertainment would be above my pay grade."

Everyone laughed again.

As North launched into his regularly scheduled monologue, he was in a dazzling mood, engaging them all in jokes and debates. They passed the other car, empty except for its driver, and North gave the *Maria*'s bell a hearty ring. The driver of the *Elisha* followed suit. Marigold basked in North's glow. A soft wind drifted in through the open windows, and the car wasn't nearly as uncomfortable as it had been on her ascent. It wasn't uncomfortable at all.

North didn't let go of her hand until they reached the bottom and he had to help the others disembark. Several of them teased her as they passed by. At last, North reentered the car. He removed his hat and knelt beside her, eye-level. "Hi," he said.

Heat rose to Marigold's cheeks. "Hi."

"I'm glad you waited for my car."

"I'm glad you're glad. Are you done for the day?"

"I saw you," he said, ignoring the question, "right after I left you on top of the mountain."

Marigold cocked her head. She didn't know what he meant.

"I saw the drawing you gave to that boy. He was sitting in the second row, and he was holding it in his lap. Holding *me* in his lap. It felt like a sign."

"A good sign or a bad sign?"

"I wasn't sure."

She smiled. "You've always been my favorite character."

North held her gaze, a smile forming on his own lips. "I'm almost ready to go." It was the reply to her earlier question. "There's only one last thing I need to do."

Marigold leaned forward. Her heart pounded like a timpani, and her eyes closed—as he jumped to his feet with a thunderous *clang*. Her eyes shot back open.

He grinned and reoffered his hand.

"You're a tease," she said, blushing harder. But she took it.

They strolled out of the funicular. Unlike summer afternoons, summer evenings were magical. The rays of the sun stretched onward and outward in a mellow caress, the cicadas clicked and hummed in an insect orchestration, and the asphalt shimmered in a lazy and delicious heat.

North nodded toward the far end of the lot where her car was parked. "I'll meet you there in a few minutes. I need to stop by the park office first." His warm hand squeezed hers once more—tightly, reluctantly—before he vanished into the building.

Marigold ambled to her car and unlocked the door. When she opened it, a wave of hot air blasted her with the force of a nuclear explosion. She rolled down the windows and slammed the door shut again.

A split-rail fence ran along the edge of the lot, so Marigold hopped up and sat there instead, feet perched on the bottom rail. The sunshine felt like a tonic. The scent of honeysuckle drifted through the breeze. Marigold still didn't know what was about to happen, but at least now she understood why she was here.

Ten minutes later, North appeared. He wore the plain white T-shirt, and he'd changed into jeans. The shorts were gone. Did that mean he was still accepting the pants? The new job? Fresh panic struck Marigold with as much force as the air inside her car.

North headed for her in a straight line. The lot had emptied, and they were alone. Her heartbeat flew into an erratic state. *His reluctance to kiss me. His reluctant release of my hand.*

Was this the beginning or the end?

He stopped several feet away, sensing her fear. Or maybe he

was afraid, too. "I had to turn in my uniform. I'll really miss those shorts."

Marigold tried to steady her voice. "Because . . . the pants. The promotion."

He shook his head. A small smile appeared.

"Because . . . you quit? Did–did you just quit?"

His smile grew bigger. He nodded.

Marigold burst into tears. North sprang forward, enfolding her in his arms. She was still sitting on top of the fence, and her knee-caps jammed into his ribs, but he only crushed her against his chest tighter. She was still crying. She was also laughing. "You are such an asshole," she said against his neck.

"I'm sorry." He was laughing, too. "I thought it would be obvious."

"Well, it wasn't!"

"I'm sorry," he said again.

"I am, too."

North pulled away to look her in the eyes. "You have nothing to be sorry for. I needed you to come here. I *did* need you to rescue me."

Marigold smiled as she wiped away her tears. She widened her stance and he slipped forward into the empty space, pressing against the rails. Pressing against her. "It feels good to be able to pay you back," she said. "You rescued me first, you know."

North's hands slid onto her bare legs, and his smile changed into a grin. "You know . . . this is the first time I've seen *you* in shorts, too."

She laughed.

"Summer looks good on you."

Marigold sighed, relishing his touch after such a long drought. Her slender arms wrapped around his strong shoulders. "It looks good on you, too."

But as they stared at each other—up close, in wonder and amazement—North's expression slowly collapsed into vulnerability. She tilted her head in silent question.

"Marigold," he said. All traces of joking had disappeared. "Before this goes any further—before I move in with you—there's something I need to say. Out loud."

She nodded. Her heartbeat rushed into her ears.

"Just in case it wasn't absolutely, unequivocally clear when I said good-bye to you on top of the mountain . . ."

She nodded. Once more.

"I'm in love with you."

Her eyes widened.

"I've been in love with you for a long time. So if that's too much for you, if that's too far—"

Marigold pulled him into a kiss, and they sank into the embrace with a sense of openness and exposure and passion that they'd never experienced before. Her legs wrapped around his waist, locking him into place. His hands slid underneath the back of her shirt, hers underneath the back of his. They were hungry. They devoured each other. Their bodies were hot with sweat, but there was something both honest and revealing about sweating together.

She pushed away from him, panting. "North?"

"Yes?" He could barely get the word out.

"Before this goes any further, there's something I need to say. Out loud."

He nodded. Smiling.

"Just in case that wasn't absolutely, unequivocally clear . . ."

He nodded. Once more.

"I'm in love with you, too."

And then North was kissing her again. And when, at last, they pulled apart—minutes, hours, days, years, a lifetime later—it was clear. They were finally traveling in the same direction.

"Home," Marigold said. She was filled with happiness and sunlight.

Between the evergreens, the first fireflies of the night materialized. They blinked in the dusk of the setting sun, a reminder that light was a recurring state.

North helped her off the fence. "Let's go home."

SOUVENIRS

Tim Federle

Maybe I've just been reading too much Charles Dickens recently, but today doesn't seem dreary enough for a breakup, you know?

Yeah, about the Dickens thing: Not my choice. It's on our AP summer reading list, and I want to get into a good college, and summer's almost over. That said, the breakup thing wasn't exactly my choice either. But today's the day—breakup day—that Kieth and I agreed to, that we've been circling all summer like two gay buzzards. Unless, wait, maybe I mean vultures? Are those the same thing? Which one is the bird that waits until something's dead before it swoops down?

If that sounds dramatic, blame Kieth. He's kind of rubbed off on me this summer. He's an actor. For God's sake, he spells his name *Kieth*, even though he was born regular old Keith.

Not that my Kieth is any kind of regular.

It was his idea, for example, to pick out our breakup day in the first place, the way some couples might look forward to an anniversary or a camping trip. I don't really know. It's all new to me. He's my first boyfriend. (I'm his third, which he likes to remind me.)

Customers!

A mom in a Pittsburgh Pirates baseball hat approaches my booth, followed by two girls in identical teal tank tops. They're local—but then, they're all locals here. Nobody drives more than forty miles to come to Wish-a-World. We are as regional and rickety as it comes, one degree removed from a traveling carnival.

"Good afternoon," I say, doing my best to act casual. "Can I help you?" I've been back here thumbing my copy of *A Tale of Two Cities*, pondering how a book so heavy could be considered so classic.

"We were just wondering," this lady says to me (she's about to ask where the bathroom is), "if you knew where the bathr—"

"Head past the log flume," I say, "and duck under the sign for snow cones, and then make a hard right past the gazebo where everyone smokes, even though they're not allowed to. Can't miss it!"

Already, *poof*, they're gone. At the beginning of the summer, I would've tried to upsell them on a key chain, a hat, an anything. That's my job, and I like to do a good job. But one thing you learn when you man a souvenir stand at a regional amusement park is that mostly what people want is bathroom directions. What they rarely want is a twenty-dollar T-shirt, let alone a thirty-dollar *sweat*-shirt, and who can blame them? The average temperature around here is hell with a chance of thunder.

I scan the sky for that cloudy, Dickensian day that doesn't seem to be showing up. "The good news," I mumble at a seagull, "is that I've gotten over love before."

Yep, I love Kieth. Or I think I do. But, hey, I loved pizza once, too, before I became lactose intolerant—and now I barely even miss it. I barely even think about pizza, I mean.

A cluster of tweens screams past my booth without stopping, one of them holding a Mylar Wish-a-World balloon that flits behind her like a metallic kite. I crack open *A Tale of Two Cities* and attempt to read the same paragraph I've been attempting to read for about three days now. Maybe four.

But then: "Excuse me—*sir*?"

And against all odds, I'm smiling.

It's Kieth, sneaking up on my booth. Who else would call me sir? Sirs don't have zits. Sirs can grow respectable sideburns.

"Could you," he continues, "direct me to the Tunnel of Love?"

I shut the book. My eyes are already watering. Basically, my eyes are Pavlov's dogs, and Kieth's voice is the bell.

"We don't have a Tunnel of Love," I say, just like I did on the day we met. He's recreating the whole scene—the way he tiptoed up to my booth "looking for the Tunnel of Love" after a full week of us stealing quiet glances at each other in the moldy employee locker room. Even under those harsh fluorescents, he was adorable. And unlike guys in my PE class at school, Kieth actually looked *back*. I was smitten.

"What kind of an amusement park *is* this if you don't have a Tunnel of Love?" he says, putting on a show here. Always putting on a show *any*where. "I'd like to speak to management." Kieth places his hand on my book, but I jerk it away from him, for secret reasons.

"Ha-ha," I say, "you can stop now." He's in his show costume. Against park regulations. This is my in. "You're not allowed out here wearing that!" I only say it to change the subject, to get mad at him about something. When I'm mad at Kieth, I love him less.

I glance at the time on my phone. His next show starts in ten minutes. "You don't even have your makeup on!"

Three times a day, Kieth performs in a spirited theme park revue. It's a really cheesy show. Wish-a-World couldn't get the rights to any good songs, so it's this oddly generic mash-up of different knockoff styles. The fifties medley contains no hits from the fifties. The seventies medley sounds just like the eighties medley. Only the wigs offer a vague clue to the era.

"Eh." Kieth rubs his chin like he's checking for bruises on a peach. "It's the last day. I'm gonna skip the makeup and give my skin a break."

He already has perfect skin.

I cross my arms. A small line has formed behind Kieth.

"People need to know where the bathroom is," I say, gesturing at the antsy park patrons fanning themselves with our famously outdated park maps. "And *you* have a show!" I look at my phone again. "In seven minutes!"

But he doesn't budge. He touches my hands and makes them stop playing this made-up song that I've been thumping into my glass stand. Every time Kieth touches me, I feel the same jolt I felt in the second grade when I plugged in my mom's hair dryer and got my finger caught between the prongs and the outlet.

"Actually, Matty," he says, "I wanted to invite you to this little wrap party the cast is having. Backstage."

Ugh. I've avoided going backstage all summer. All those theater people in one room, all those loud voices, all that *hugging*—it's a lot. Kieth is enough. Kieth is, I remind myself, almost too much.

"Why didn't you just text me?" I ask. Because, really, it's a big deal to be in costume outside of his amphitheater. Kieth could get written up. I'm no goody two-shoes, but I hate breaking rules for no reason.

"I had a feeling you'd put up a fight, is why," Kieth says. "You know, all those theater people . . . So I thought I'd ask you to the party face-to-face. Plus, I like your face."

I hate that he knows me so well. No—I *love* that he knows me so well, and I hate that today it's over.

To catch you up: Tomorrow, Kieth's off to freshman year in college and I'm off to senior year in high school, both of us traveling in opposite directions on a map. You couldn't mastermind a more geographically literal breakup.

Ba-da-boom, ba-da-boom, ba-da-boom.

This canned music starts pumping from inside the half-tented amphitheater, twenty feet away across our faux-cobblestone Maine Street. It used to be called *Main* Street, but Disney apparently sued us in the nineties, so the owners painted an *e* onto the word *Main*—even though nothing about Maine Street is evocative of Maine. There are no lobster shacks. There are no fishermen. We are in Pennsylvania. There's just my souvenir stand and the amphitheater and a dozen "shoppes" with faded striped awnings, all of them selling the same Wish-a-World candy.

"Can we move it along, guys?" this dad type calls out from my line.

"I gotta work the booth," I say to Kieth.

He releases my hand. "So? The wrap party, at lunch? Be my plus-one?"

Please note that he can't even say "Be my *date*," after five weeks and two days of, you know, dating.

"I thought we were having lunch *together*," I say. "Just us. For the *last* time." This all comes out more emphatic than I mean it to, LIKE WHEN YOUR BEST FRIEND TEXTS YOU IN ALL CAPS.

Buh-du-beeeep, buh-du-beeeep, bu-duh-beeeep.

The music has switched to this annoying bleep, which signals the three-minute countdown to the top of Kieth's show. Several potential patrons leave my line altogether, openly scowling at me as they hightail it to find bathrooms unknown. There goes my commission.

Kieth glances at the amphitheater entrance—an unwelcoming wall of concrete speckled with wadded-up gum, a Wish-a-World rite of passage—and then back at me. "See you after the show . . . *please*?"

Man, you should see the way he twinkles. Kieth can turn on the charm like it's, I don't know, a faucet. A faucet that's powered by a geyser.

"*Pretty* please?"

I take *A Tale of Two Cities* and use it to gently bop his forehead. "Okay."

He leans forward and kisses me, something we don't do in public. It's against park policy for employees to date each other—but I let him. I have to stand on my tippytoes because he's taller than me. What if I never meet another guy who is the perfect kissing height, a four-and-a-half-inch difference if I'm in my favorite pair of white Converse (which don't technically fit me anymore but are the ideal level of smudged)?

Our first kiss happened beneath a murky moon, with mosquitoes buzzing around me like a halo. Every one of my senses went *boing*. I could smell Kieth's sweat-concealing cologne, I could taste his gum, I could see his eyelids flutter. I didn't close my own eyes, because what if *this*—the hottest, happiest moment of my life—was a dream? When he came up for air and said, "Holy crap, Matty, you're a really good kisser," I still wasn't sure if I was awake.

But today, "No crying!" is all Kieth says, after he pulls away from our public kiss and sees my face. He's always teasing me (in a sweet way, I think?) for being emotional. By now, he's learned that once I start crying you'd better back away or find a snorkel. "At least save it for the parking lot!"

That's where we always say good night. Every night. A tradition.

"Fine," I say. "Look—presto—I'm not crying." But he's not really listening. He's getting in his performance zone, which I have to respect. I love a job well done.

"I'm outtie, cutie," he shouts back at me, scurrying away with only one minute left till he's due on stage.

And as I look at his ridiculously cute butt in those polyester black pants, the thing that dawns on me, weirdly, is that maybe I do miss pizza. Very badly. That maybe, if I'm being honest with myself, I haven't stopped thinking about pizza since the day I had to stop eating it, when the allergist said I have an oversensitive disposition.

Something is off about Wish-a-World today. No theme park is exactly an epicenter of civic responsibility, but even by our lax standards there is a lawless vibe in the air.

Adults are hiding behind our overgrown topiary bushes (is that a hippo? a . . . *dragon*?) before springing out to soak their friends with water guns. Skateboarders are blazing down the Maine Street sidewalk in coordinated, flock-like V's. Twice already today I've watched the manager of the Candy Shoppe chase after kids who were dashing out of his store with shoplifted sweets, their pockets bulging like chipmunk cheeks.

Last month, Kieth bought me these humongous candy lips from

the Candy Shoppe and wrote "But your kisses are sweeter" on the price tag in purple Magic Marker.

Across the courtyard in the amphitheater, they're midway into their thirty-five-minute show, at the top of the all-girl doo-wop section. Kieth's not on again for another forty-five seconds, so I leisurely open my book again, and—

Really, who am I kidding? I'm not going to digest a word of this. Not today anyway.

So I take off my sunglasses and pull out my bookmark, which isn't a bookmark at all but a handwritten, top secret list that I've slowly been compiling. A list of everything about Kieth that drives me crazy. I figure it'll be easier to put him in the past if I can remember how annoying he makes my present.

Thing number one: *He always looks like he's waiting for me to stop talking.* Like, his eyes kind of fade out when I'm sharing something. Kieth's like a kid in Kiddie Land, waiting his turn to hop on a ride. But the thing about the kids at Kiddie Land—and I know this because I was a ride operator last summer, and made three dollars less per hour—is that they are terrible about waiting their turn. And so is Kieth.

I squint against the sun, toward Kieth's stage. The girls are taking all sorts of bizarre vocal liberties in the medley today, making it sound totally contemporary. They're acting up, since it's the last day at the park. "Prank day," Kieth called it, preparing me for it last night, "because what are they going to do, fire us? None of us want to work at this deadbeat park again, anyway."

He said all this, by the way, forgetting that yours truly is back for his second summer in a row. Because Kieth forgets everything.

I accidentally bite my tongue and take the hot frustration as a cue to continue reviewing my list.

Thing number two: *Kieth isn't always sensitive about my feelings.* He's got that actor thing where his eyebrows are permanently lifted, judging every last everything that passes by. It can be intoxicatingly fun to hang with Kieth—nobody is funnier, nobody is faster. But as my mom always says, "There's a fine line between charming and manipulative."

Oh, my mom: a nurse, a real bleeding heart. Like, she had a COEXIST bumper sticker on her car before it was trendy, et cetera. The only nicer person is my dad, who my friends have anointed "the strangely buff vegetarian." My parents are so nice that when I brought Kieth home for dinner a couple weeks ago my dad tried three different neutral topics—the weather, the wonky mass transportation system in Pittsburgh, and "What about your folks, Kieth? What do they do?"—before giving up, since Kieth likes to be in total control of conversation topics. (Kieth wanted to talk about religion, since he's proud to have recently left the Catholic church. My mom got up three times during dinner—to get the salt, to get the pepper, and then to get a different kind of salt.)

Thing number three: *Kieth won't say the word "love."*

But I will. My grandparents were all hippies. Love is my family's currency. We spend love like it's money, like we're the richest people in the world.

Thing number four: *He never asks about my job!* Maybe he thinks my job isn't interesting, but I think it is. Now look, I am *paid* to sell T-shirts and squeeze bottles—and I've personally outsold every other booth in the park, thank you, for five weeks running—but I've decided my bosses are really funding my future as a social scientist. A people researcher. A Pittsburgh primatologist.

See, for an amateur studier of strangers, Wish-a-World offers four distinct categories of patrons: (1) older couples who are over each other; (2) high school couples who are *all* over each other; (3) large groups wearing matching neon-colored shirts, making their way through the park with an air of accomplishment that Columbus probably reserved for discovering America; and (4) punks.

A classic number four is approaching my booth now, which gets me tense. Kieth is almost back on, and I love the way he, like, bops around in his spacesuit costume for the "Future and Beyond" medley. I don't want to miss it. I never miss it, even though I have to kind of crane my neck to even halfway see the platform stage.

"Hey there, *Matthew*," this kid says. Total punk. He's reading my name tag, saying "Matthew" to make his friends laugh. (Please make a note that any employee you come across who's got a name tag on—at a grocery store, at an amusement park—hates it when you actually formally address them by their name. Free tip.) "How much are the firecrackers?"

I pretend to scratch my shoulder. "We don't sell firecrackers. Want a T-shirt?" As if this guy could afford a twenty-dollar T-shirt.

One quick check of the amphitheater stage—at Kieth, doing this incredible jump-split move I could no more describe than actually pull off myself—and every one of my bookmark bulletin points is rendered obsolete.

I mean, the way his little face lights up when he does that move ... My boyfriend is *cute*, and that means something about me, right? That I can attract such a certifiably cute boyfriend— even with my unpredictable skin and strangely large feet, even if I put off summer reading until the last week of summer—must mean *something* good about me.

"Really, Matthew?" the number four at my counter says. "'cause I could've sworn I saw some firecrackers back there."

I am in what you might call a Kieth haze, so when this punk kid's punk friend lurches forward and shouts "Boom!" in my face, I shriek. (Shrieking is one of my specialties, right after: developing rashes for no medical reason.)

The firecracker gang saunters away, high-fiving each other as they disappear into a thicket of ropes left over from the entrance of an ancient, dangerous pirate ride.

"Punks," I say, like I'm ninety. I wish I had a cane to wave at them.

At least there's still time to catch my favorite/least favorite part of the show. At the end of Kieth's spacesuit solo, he jumps down into the crowd, pulls a stranger with him up on stage, and asks them their name. And he makes this big-ass deal out of it. Nine times out of ten, the stranger is semi-mortified and yet also semi-tickled, standing exposed on a stage in the sun, being forced to boogie around with Kieth.

Sometimes, I don't know, I think he picks out the *most* awkward-looking person, just to make himself look better.

Even so, you gotta admit. Today he looks especially amazing.

You want one good reason? One thing about Kieth that keeps me coming back for more, in spite of the fact that he never asks about my job and seems physically incapable of saying the word *love*?

Because he laughs at my categorically terrible jokes is why.

Oh, another thing: because there was a night back in June when it was weirdly chilly out, and he gave me his jean jacket to wear in the parking lot, and the collar smelled like his Aveda hair pomade stuff, so I took it home and haven't given it back yet. (Up until that night, I had always hated jean jackets on guys.)

And also: because the third time we kissed in my car, I forgot I had my retainer in and he didn't pull away and say, "Eww." He pulled away and said, "That's hilarious." And when I said, "No, that's so friggin *me*," he cut me off and said, "I still think you're a really good kisser."

Kieth himself had just gotten out of a relationship, at the beginning of the summer, and planned on staying "purposefully single" for his entire time at the park. But on day one he reportedly walked by me in my booth, on his way into rehearsal, and said to this girl in his cast, "However, if *that* boy is gay, I'm in trouble."

Nobody had ever considered me "trouble" before. Who am I kidding? Nobody had ever considered me "*that*" boy," either.

But the number one reason why I dated Kieth this summer is: He doesn't let me talk down about myself. Ever.

Even with my supposed friends at school, I am their easiest target—the donkey in a game where nobody has blindfolds and everyone has tails, except for me. But when I'm with Kieth, and I slip into my old "Ugh, I look so weird in this photo" act, or my "*Yeah, my sense of direction is the worst*" shenanigans, he always stops me and asks, "Why don't you give yourself credit for all the things you're amazing at, Matty?"

He's never quite told me what all those things are, but it's nice to know he's keeping his own list. You know?

"Let's give a bi-i-ig round of applause to our 'Music: Through the Ages!' singers and dancers!"

Oh, man. The show is over and the crowds are exiting. That means lunch. That means this cast party nonsense.

I slide *A Tale of Two Cities* into my cubby behind the booth, and I stare at Kieth's stage door across the squiggly-with-humidity courtyard, and I say a little prayer. But the thing is, I suck at praying.

My parents raised me to be Buddhist.

So, it's the best of parties, it's the worst of parties.

It has my favorite flavor of diet pop and a respectable assortment of cookies, true. But it also has all-new people who I'm expected to chat with.

Aha, you might say. *You're a T-shirt salesman. You make small talk all day.* Not so, I'd counter. I attempt to make *sales,* a purpose that I can hide behind. Here, I feel as if I have to sell myself. (I still don't know the product well enough to really sell it.)

Also, the air smells like fast food and feet. Cinderblock bricks give the space an overall vibe of a low-security, highly theatrical prison. Also, why is everything painted black, when this is a "green room"? I don't know any of the rules.

"You want another soda?" Kieth asks. I'm slurping mine down double time, in lieu of that small talk thing I hate.

"I don't know what a *soda* is," I say, "but another *pop*, sure." I'm obsessed with regional dialect differences. Kieth is from Delaware. He calls gum bands "rubber bands." He calls pop "soda."

And he calls *me* Matt—not Matty, like he always does—when he tells me I'm "doing great, Matt," as if I've never been to a party. But the longer I stand here—the only introvert, bopping terribly to this music (I cannot dance; people always think I'm kidding when they see me try)—the more I realize he's not going to introduce me to anyone. And it bugs me.

All summer long, we've kept our relationship secret—a Romeo and Romeo situation, so we wouldn't get in trouble with our bosses. At first it seems clandestine, sexy even, the way we'd meet in the last bathroom stall, beneath the Monster Maze, to fumble around. To laugh when we couldn't undo our button fly jean shorts fast enough. But now—the way I'm hanging out here like a ghost who nobody's noticing . . . the way it's hitting me that Kieth and I barely got together, *ever,* outside of work—I am struck by the fact that *Romeo and Juliet* ends pretty tragically.

(It was on my summer reading list last year.)

"Yo, everyone!" shouts a girl in hoop earrings and fake eyelashes. She motions to cut the playlist, and then she holds her fist against her lips and attempts a weak *doot-do-do-doooo* trumpet call.

Kieth shushes his cast.

"It's time for the summer-end awards!" the girl announces, producing a thick stack of colorful papers from behind her back.

There are cheers.

Oh, gosh. I hunt for more ice to add to my drink, to give myself something to do.

"So, we all voted," she continues from on top of this ratty brown sofa. "And the very first award, and some would argue *most* important—for Most Likely to Get to Broadway First, obvi—goes to . . ."

"Wait!" hollers the one straight guy (according to Kieth). "Let's do a drumroll!" And so they do, this entire team of performers smacking their thighs in unison, a thundering sound that makes a lightbulb flicker.

I stand, dumbstruck, trying to think of this as free social research. As if I've discovered an Inca tribe whose chief form of communication is being louder than necessary.

"In a unanimous vote, Most Likely to Get to Broadway First goes to . . . Erica!"

Erica, I guess, launches into what can only be described as a dance routine, twirling across the scuffed-up floor, nearly knocking over a strange, out-of-place vacuum cleaner, and grasping her printed out MOST LIKELY sign as if it's a scholarship to Juilliard.

I and I alone clap, not realizing that a speech from Erica is implied, and thus I should shut up and trust my introvert instincts to never get involved, ever.

"When I first arrived at the park this summer . . ." Erica begins—and, within moments, she is crying. In fact, everyone sort of is, except for me and Kieth. Instead, he puts his hand on my non-existent butt and leans over. "You're being a good sport," he says, and I reply, "I am." And when he squeezes my nonexistent butt cheek, presto: If I had to choose a superpower right now it would be to stop time forever.

Screw invisibility.

Erica yammers on for approximately a thousand years (at one point, without irony, she thanks both "God and freedom"), and then we're on to goofier awards, the lunch hour disappearing in front of me, my stomach rumbling at the smell and sight of a stack of forbidden pizzas that nobody seems to be touching.

And I bet none of them are even lactose intolerant.

Somehow a walkie-talkie-wielding girl in a ripped black T-shirt appears among us. She's the only person wearing less makeup than either me or Kieth. "Ten minutes till the next show, gang," she announces, "so let's wrap this sobfest up."

On cue, Kieth presents her with the Best Snarky Stage Manager award, pulled from his book bag. I guess he's part of the . . . awards committee? It's like, how much about Kieth do I still not know?

When this walkie-talkie chick is asked to give remarks, she says, "They don't pay me enough to babysit you all, but I love yinz, and you better keep in touch with me or I'll kill you." She gets a little weepy herself, and then the metal stage door slams shut behind her, and we're already down to the last two awards as the spotty air conditioner putters itself back on with a *clank*.

And really, should I be surprised? Kieth is voted Flirtiest Guy. When it's his turn to give a speech, he says, "Okay, okay, sue me. I like to make eyes," and he unzips his book bag and fishes for something inside. "But only *one* guy this summer stole my heart . . ."

He looks right at me. I debate if this is the moment to step forward and make myself known or to step backward and give Kieth the spotlight. And so I do nothing at all.

Have I mentioned I dropped out of the debate club at school because I'm such a slow debater?

"But, uh, *names*," Kieth says, stammering and dropping his bookbag to the floor, "will be withheld to protect the guilty."

Everyone kind of *aww*s, but then we're right on to The Flirtiest Girl award—another category that Erica sweeps.

I'd look outside to scan for those storm clouds, but the green room doesn't have windows.

The thing is, Kieth knows I hate being the center of attention—but he could have said my *name*, you know? I am aware that my feelings are contradictory, but sue me. Historically, I am always the final person named for stuff. I mean, my last name starts with a friggin' *V.* I am neither short nor tall. I am remarkably unremarkable at sports, at the arts, at academics. I am a Matt-of-all-trades, a walking 3.2 GPA. But today, during this stupid backstage celebration, I had one last chance at being *declared*. This summer, anyway.

"Nice award," I manage to say, when Kieth bounds over and helps himself to my last sip of pop.

"Stupid award," he says, and he goes to kiss my cheek just as I sneeze.

After I've recovered (because it became a series of *four* sneezes; aren't I irresistible?), Kieth cups my hip and pulls me in and goes, "Did you forget to take your allergy meds again, young man?" Like he's my mom or something.

Except, I *did* forget them. And I *love* that he's worried about me. It is so nice to be worried about. It is maybe the best thing about being in a relationship: that you can share the heavy load of being alive.

"My allergy meds make me jittery," I say, looking away and concentrating all my energy into not sneezing on him. "I'll survive."

A bell rings and the overhead lights flash on-off, on-off, on. The air buzzes for a second—that fluorescent lamp sound—and it's time for the cast to get back into their wigs and prep for their next show. Party's over.

Pizza's untouched.

I grab a handful of Pringles and refill my pop, but they're out of ice. I'm hunting for the metaphor when Kieth says, "You know I flirt with *everyone,* right?" He's leading me to the stage door now, and I guess he can tell it isn't just my allergies that are acting up. "Boys, girls. It's not personal."

"Maybe it's not personal to *you*."

"Mat—"

"It's fine. Of course I know you flirt with everyone." I step out onto the baking concrete. "You're a theater person." Man, if I thought it was hot inside, I was incorrect, because the sun is going all-in on the bet that it can send me into senior year with a sunburn.

"Hey." Kieth jiggles my shoulder with his hand. "At least we never have to become *that*." He points at the concrete path, just past the fake trees whose vinyl leaves shimmer with moisture. "Ya know?"

I do know, because we spot them at the same time: a pair of classic number ones. This middle-aged couple walking side by side but out of tempo, looking overheated and just plain . . . used to each other.

"Yeah, I guess," I say quietly.

I should admit that Kieth was totally up front about not wanting to call us a couple. Or an anything. It was all me. "Can we just *not* do labels this summer?" he asked, in a way that wasn't really asking, roughly one week into dating. "Can we just have *fun*?" Days later, when he mentioned that it might be hyper-mature to name our breakup day ahead of time—to save us "the awkwardness" of some big final goodbye—my heart actually lifted. At least a breakup signaled an end to something real.

I almost sneeze again. "Gotta go," I say, shaking Kieth's hand off my shoulder. "A bunch of number threes are loitering outside my booth."

A multitude of people and yet solitude.

I read it again: "A multitude of people and yet solitude." It's a quote from my book, underlined and circled in light-blue pen. I didn't underline or circle it. It came premarked, purchased from a used bookstore bin for fifty whole cents. Probably some other kid had to read *A Tale of Two Cities* for AP summer English, and probably his teacher made him circle important quotes. I wonder if I have good teachers. My teachers don't make us do that.

I keep putting the book aside to appear attentive whenever a group passes my souvenir stand. But they never stop today. They coast right on by me, most of them pausing only to whap the swinging Ye Olde Funnel Cakes sign.

A multitude of people and yet solitude.

And so, this time when I go head-down, I dare myself to dive into the prose and push through. For longer than two sentences. Without checking my phone. Strangely, it works—I get, like, *enchanted* by a series of Dickens paragraphs that are actually short and, believe it or not, readable. Some of them are even kinda funny. And so I am taken by utter surprise—I am every synonym for *startled*—when I feel a hot exhale on my cheeks followed by the signature scent of Kieth's off-brand spearmint gum.

"What are you doing?" I ask, but he's already flipping up the wooden bar and grabbing my hand. They're almost at the end of their show, and he's wearing his space suit costume. I *know* what he's doing.

"Come on!" he says, giddy, almost violent with intent.

I go floppy, but Kieth is strong—a quality I'd always found supremely hot until this very moment—as he drags me across the bumpy Maine Street courtyard, past the wall of gum wads, and down through the amphitheater audience.

I am the only guy he has chosen to dance his solo with all summer.

This hits me as we motor past aisle after aisle of girls, sitting stadium style under gauzy strips of circus tent ceiling. The music rumbles so much louder inside the amphitheater.

I am the only guy all summer, and I am in a fog of panic.

"Just go with it!" Kieth says, right as we reach the lip of the stage. Right as his entire cast motions for me to join them up there, and the audience (twenty people, tops) lets out a tired version of a cheer.

I never "just go" with anything. I study on weekends for tests that aren't happening until Wednesday. I plan out dinners for the week with Mom (on a spreadsheet). I take a half million selfies before posting the most chill-looking one. And even then I usually delete it.

Somehow, though, I am now standing center stage on a rickety riser that feels so much less solid than it looks from my booth. And, like, the way Kieth's lip is glistening under the lights, and the way his eyes are midperformance jittery, and the way the synthe-sized guitar sound is blaring us into another dimension . . . I don't know. I close my eyes, and kind of bounce up and down, and in-deed try to just go with it.

Pretend it's your wedding, I chant like a mantra. *Pretend he's your husband.* Like I'm marrying an astronaut and this is our first dance.

Except that when I open my eyes again, shaken by rowdy laughter from the audience, my astronaut isn't even dancing with me. Kieth is way off to the side. He's grinning a new kind of grin, either smug or self-satisfied. He never lets people dance alone—if anything, he dances *hardest* when he's got competition next to him—and when I look out at the crowd, it's those number four punks from earlier who are laughing. Hard. And pointing. And I am so sweaty and disoriented that I genuinely don't know if I'm in on the joke or if I *am* the joke.

I flip around and instinctively reach for my fly, but before I can even check it, Kieth turns me back to face the audience. And as he holds up this microphone to my mouth, the embarrassment and confusion of, well, *everything,* smacks me like a bird against a window. The way he wouldn't even introduce me to his cast today, let alone invite me to go see a movie with them this summer—and now he's making me stumble around in front of them, by myself, like some kind of Hollywood chimpanzee. Whether my fly is down or not, I feel completely unzipped.

"And *what*," Kieth says, his voice booming from surround sound speakers, "is *your* name, sir?"

"You know my fucking name," I say, pushing his microphone away, hard, and definitely not taking the mandatory bow. I leap off the stage and race two steps at a time up the amphitheater aisle, toward the exit. But I pause at the top to crouch into the faces of those firecracker punks. And this time *I* yell "Boom!" And they aren't laughing anymore.

"that was seriously uncool," I text Kieth, as I'm limp-jogging away to my booth, not five seconds later, to throw down my CLOSED sign and hide. And get mad.

When I'm mad at Kieth, I love him less.

It takes three tries, but I get Mom on the phone.

"Hi, hon. Is everything okay?"

"Kind of sort of." But my voice is already betraying me. It does this thing where it cries before my eyes do. Annoying.

"Aw, honey, what happened? Are you all right?"

The exit music from the amphitheater blasts so forcefully that the cobblestones shudder beneath my sneakers. I pivot and beeline toward the all-pastel Kiddie Land, where at least I won't be the only person crying. (No toddler escapes Kiddie Land without at least one breakdown. It is so much less stressful to work souvenirs.)

"I don't want to get into it. I mean, I'm not technically *hurt* or anything. Other than, you know."

"Breakup day," Mom says. Have I mentioned she's the best?

"Wait, am I catching you in the middle of a shift?" I ask, suddenly aware she could be prepping for a procedure.

"Yes, but it's nice to have a breather. Today has been a nonstop car accident."

I come upon this concessions stand that's been out of commission all summer on account of a broken cotton candy dispenser. When a machine breaks at Wish-a-World, it doesn't get repaired. It just sort of sits there in the sun, rusting in the weather, becoming a kind of monument to itself. "Mom . . . do you think I'll, like, meet somebody legitimately amazing someday?"

I know she can't read the future, but it sometimes helps to just feed your mom what you want to hear said back to you.

"Of course you will! You're so handsome and smart. You're so *young.*"

"You're just saying that because you're my mom."

"Well, yeah, but it's true. I know I can't prove it to you, but it's true."

In the relative quiet behind the abandoned cotton candy booth, I can make out the steady beeps and squeaky wheels of Mom's hospital. There is some comfort in knowing that her opinion of me comes from a somewhat objective medical background. I think she had to sign some kind of oath as a nurse, stating she'd never lie to a patient.

"Hon?" she says, after I sink to my butt to sit on the curb. I suppose you'd say I'm fully crying now.

"Yes?" I manage.

"How can I make you feel better?"

"Maybe you can just listen to me cry for ten more seconds and then tell me to man up."

So she does. She listens to me cry for ten seconds, maybe even twenty, maybe even a minute, and then she goes, "Hon?"

"Yeah? Time to man up?"

"No. I think there's nothing more manly than showing your emotions. That's going to really serve you well, in the long ru—"

"You know, the thing is," I say, basically choking at this point. I turn it into a cackle so I don't freak her out. "I don't even think Kieth is the right fit for me. I'm just sort of, like, in *general* upset."

"He's not the all-time most considerate boy," Mom says. "That's for sure." It's so rare to hear her judge somebody, anybody, that I relish and hang on to it as another guy might relish and hang on to the last quarter of a football game.

And yet I am still a blubbering idiot.

I look up to see a boy holding his dad's hand. The boy is eight, maybe even nine—older than I would have ever been to be holding my dad's hand in public. (Dad and I are close, but affection isn't our specialty; respect is.) In the kid's other hand, he is managing both a Wish-a-World balloon and an extravagantly overloaded ice cream cone. We're talking three scoops. It's all too much. He's just a kid, not a ninja or a magician. The ice cream rolls off the top, and the dad lunges—like a superhero in pleated shorts—and he *almost* catches it, but he doesn't. The ice cream falls to the asphalt, practically in slo-mo in this heat, and splatters an ugly green splatter.

My dad would have caught it.

"Matty-love?" Mom asks. "Did you hear what I said? Should I not have said that about Kieth being inconsiderate?" Beeps, squeaks, so much happening on her end. "Do you want to just cry some more?"

I wait for it, for the kid with the empty cone to burst into tears. But he doesn't. He tilts his head curiously at the mess, as if watching a caterpillar morph into a butterfly. And then he looks up at his dad and goes, "Can I get another one?"

And when his dad says, "Of course you can," I realize it's time to stop crying.

By now the sky is fully purple, because this part of Pittsburgh never gets totally black, even at 11:15 p.m. Cricket wings and cicada chirps make the air pulse in a sonic way. I had wanted to be home by this hour. To take off early and to block Kieth from being able to text me. To pull into my driveway and find that Mom's shift ended at nine, and hope she'd thought to make me corn fritters, my favorite thing when I feel like crap. They are literally the greasiest. The grease soaks up your feelings.

But I just couldn't do it.

"You're alive," Kieth says, when he finds me in the parking lot on the front hood of Dad's rusted-out Honda, trying to knock out another chapter of Dickens. It seemed like a good pose to be in, something cool but detached. But I don't know.

"I'm alive." I'm folding and refolding Kieth's jean jacket in my lap. I had it marked on my calendar to bring it back to him, and to have Mom wash it first. I managed the first part, but I didn't have her wash it. I guess I wanted to smell him on the ride to work, one more time.

"You totally disappeared," he says. "And now the day's over."

Kieth's older than me, but he looks like a kid right now.

"Why did you pull me up on stage?" I steady my voice. "You *know* that I have, like, off-the-charts stage fright."

Accidentally, I begin to slide down the hood, but Kieth catches me by a shin and holds me there, teetering off the car like the world's most low-stakes trapeze act.

"My jacket," he says, like he's psyched to see an old friend. "I forgot I gave it to you."

Because he forgets *everything* is why. I am so not going to miss him.

"Why did you pull me up on stage?" I ask again.

"I saw the look on your face when I didn't say your name at the wrap party. It threw me off. So I thought, I don't know—I thought it would be, like, sweet and memorable or something. Or bold. To pull you on stage. To push you outside of your comfort zone."

"On breakup day, you want to dance with me in public." I stare at the Milky Way. During one of my obsessive nerd phases, when I never left the house, I memorized every major constellation I could see from my window. "Of *course* I'd be stupid enough to be surprised. Of *course* I'd be lame enough to—"

"Matt, you know it kills me when you talk down about yourself. So, please, just, st—"

"Okay, okay, got it. I'll stop."

I set the jacket and the book on my car, and when I look back at Kieth, he's digging around in this big cardboard box under his arm, which is full of all his junk from the dressing room. He removes a neon-blue sheet of paper and hands it to me.

"What is this?"

"Read it."

I flip it over.

"The Best Boyfriend award," it says—exactly like the flimsy awards they gave out five hours ago—with "Matty Vukovich" written below, in Kieth's autograph. (The guy practices his signature on everything. His cursive is probably prettier than your grandma's.)

"What does this mean?" I say, too excitedly. I slide off the hood and land on my feet. The gravel coughs. My ankle still aches from jumping off the stage, but it's like my blood is carbonated. "What *is* this?"

"It just means you were the best catch I ever caught," Kieth says.

I drop the award to my side. "That sounds pretty past tense."

"Matt. It's breakup day. It's a tribute to how sensitive you are. I was actually gonna give it to you at the summer-end awards thing—I made it for you last night, and everything—but I chickened out. All those people."

"All that hugging."

He holds up his free hand, as if to show me he's not carrying a pistol. "I guess I was afraid the award would make you, like, *cry*."

A few cars take off around us, kicking up pebbles and fumes. Music blares from Devil Isle, the sixteen-plus section of the park. The whole place was supposed to close at eleven tonight, but it seems they're struggling to get everybody out.

"Well, *thanks*," I say, looking back at the award. Maybe I'll adopt a parakeet, just so I can line the bottom of a cage with it. "I'm not sure how I'm your best boyfriend *ever* if you're breaking up with me . . ."

Kieth takes my hand. He does the quiet-voice thing, rare for an actor, where I have to lean in to hear him. "We're breaking up with each *other*, Matt. We agreed to this. It's the right thing. I'm going away, and—"

I press the printout against his face. It crinkles around his big (beautiful, perfect) nose. He laughs. "Quiet," I say. "I know. I get it."

He doesn't want to cheat on me. That's why, by the way. He's going to arrive at his conservatory and be surrounded by (beautiful, perfect) theater boys, and he doesn't want to cheat on me. And he's known this since the beginning of the summer. Since the beginning of our no-labels showmance.

I slide the Best Boyfriend award through the crack at the top of my window and it falls like a giant feather onto the front seat. I plant my hands on my hips and wait for Kieth to talk. It works.

"I mean, listen. I could make a list of all the reasons *why* you're the best."

"Could you?"

"You aren't afraid to make eye contact," he says, right away. "That was a first for me. Every other guy I dated was afraid to make eye contact."

"That's funny. I didn't know that about myself." I'm about to change topics so that I won't have to watch him immediately run out of all the supposed reasons why I am the best whatever ever.

But, remarkably, he isn't done.

"You have amazing parents, is another thing. And I love your big feet. And the last guy I dated pressured me to drink all the time, and you and I never even drank together, once. And I didn't miss it at all."

I hate beer. I hate beer, and I love that Kieth's list about me is kind of endless.

"And you take your work seriously, Matty, which is a big turn-on." Now his nose is running. Like, a lot. But it isn't gross. "Do you want me to keep going?"

"Yes."

"Okay." He takes a deep breath. "You aren't afraid to have real conversations about life—it's like you're thirty years old sometimes—and that freaked me out. But I was getting used to it. I mean, basically you've raised the bar for anyone else I'm ever going to meet."

I shift around on the big feet that he apparently loves, but I don't say anything.

"So, in a unanimous vote of one," he says, "you get the Best Boyfriend award. Which beats the Flirtiest Guy in any race, every time."

I look back at the car, because otherwise I'll try to get him to kiss me. And, as a joke, I guess—thinking it might lighten the mood—I grab *A Tale of Two Cities* off the hood. "Well, I have something for you, too," I say, stalling and half turning away from Kieth. I covertly tear out a random page and then hand it to him as if it is a deep and poignant present. "Here."

But Kieth studies the page like it's a treasure map, and when he looks back up, his eyes are rain clouds. The weather has finally arrived.

"There is prodigious strength in sorrow and despair," he says.

I'm not sure why, but he says it again. And then again, like he's memorizing something. Forever an actor. Then I realize, duh, he's reading from the book. He holds up the page for me to see, and those words—"There is prodigious strength in sorrow and despair"—are circled three times in light-blue pen.

"That is beautiful, Matty," Kieth says, now all-out crying. I'm talking *me*-level tears. It is both impressive and disconcerting. All summer long I've wanted him to lose it, just once, and now I'm like *Wait, you're stealing my routine.* "Thanks, seriously."

Holy Buddha. He thinks *I* underlined it. And had the page all picked out to give to him, like it's a real gift.

"I've been too hard on you for being emotional." He waves the page around, laughing at himself, wiping his nose across his arms. They are lean and long, punctuated only by this turquoise-bead bracelet that I won for him at the arcade, that he wasn't supposed to wear during the show—but that he never took off, ever.

I remain quiet.

"There's nothing weak about crying, you're right. I'm sorry I gave you crap for that. I'm gonna frame this quote for my dorm, maybe."

Come on, roller coasters. Come on, distant screaming crowds. Now isn't the moment for silence, but even Pennsylvania's infamous cicadas have shut up.

"Can you just *not* be the sweetest guy of all time today?" I finally say. "I've been waiting for this since June."

It's not fair. With him coming down and me tearing up, we have evened out. We are together, at last, a matching level of emotion. Just in time to say good-bye.

The box under Kieth's arm shifts—*ca-chunk*—the sound of lip-stick and mouthwash and a weird, lone Adidas soccer sandal. The whole thing nearly topples from his grip, so I reach to help him. We lower the box to the ground and I notice a glimmering wedge of foil shining from on top of his otherwise dull belongings.

"You want that?" he asks, just when I'm back in love.

"What is it?"

"Pizza, from the awards party. Left over. I lost my appetite. You should take it."

Well, *dammit*.

I pick the pizza wedge up and am about to launch into an "I am lactose intolerant, and you know that! I told you that on our first *and* second dates!" speech, when Kieth pulls me into a hug.

He smells like the jean jacket smell I've come to associate with the concept of "boyfriend." Boyfriends smell like Tide detergent and Degree deodorant and a little bit of sweat and a little bit of Aveda and a little bit just Kieth. But maybe I'm all wrong. Maybe that isn't the boyfriend smell.

"Having you out there every day made it so easy to perform this summer," he says. We're still hugging. *Theater* people. "Like, it gave me an incentive to give it my all. Nobody else in my cast had that."

Kieth pulls away. I don't know what to say back. My heart throbs. My ankle throbs. I hope none of this will hurt so much once he's in a different time zone.

"Good luck," I say, "at school."

"You're supposed to say 'break a leg.' It's bad luck to say good luck." His lip trembles. His face is red. I really am the best boyfriend he ever had. I get to own that.

Both of us go to kiss each other, and so neither one of us does.

"Jinx," I say. A schoolyard joke for myself.

"I should probably take off." Kieth picks the box back up. "I've got this early flight, and I'm already annoyed because—"

"You're sitting on the aisle, but you're pissed the seat won't recline because it's in front of an exit row."

He smiles and nods. "You remember everything. It's freaky."

You remember nothing, I'm thinking, *it's annoying.*

But I just say, "Get outta here."

And he does.

He glances at my dad's Honda, pauses for a sec, and then disappears between two vintage VW Bugs. I am somehow reminded of when Stacy Hoffner, my best friend in third grade, moved away to Youngstown, Ohio. We were going to be best friends forever, and then we weren't. I was going to have a hole in my heart for all time, and then I didn't. I moved on—even if some part of me stayed scarred by Stacy leaving me. But the thing about scars is that, as much as they knot you up, they can make you stronger, too. Collect enough scars and you get a whole extra layer of skin, for free.

I wave at the back of Kieth's head, though I might just be seeing things at this point.

Yeah. He's gone.

But when I turn to get inside the car, Kieth's jean jacket is still on the hood, next to my book, set a foot apart like an old couple. I take out my phone to text him *"you forgot something!!"* And right as I'm about to hit Send, his own message dings in.

"Keep the jacket," it says. *"it was cuter on u anyway ☺"*

And against all odds, I'm smiling.

I fold the book and the pizza wedge inside the jacket and slide into the front seat, where my butt crunches into something foreign. It's the damn *Best Boyfriend* award. I uncrumple it and place it on the passenger side, and then it's all too quiet in here. Quiet in that loud way. So, when I turn on the car and this old-school song comes on the radio, I let it play. Let it *blast,* even, like Dad's car is the amphitheater inside the park. Except that in here I'm safe.

It's a decent song, as sixties songs go. At least it isn't a knock-off. And not to be the grandchild of hippies but, like a trance, the optimistic thrum of the acoustic guitar sort of hypnotizes me into reaching over, to rip open the foil, and—I guess for old times' sake—take a giant, careless bite out of the forbidden pizza.

It's more delicious than a memory can possibly live up to.

See, a memory doesn't remember the way the congealed tomato sauce comes back to life when you bite into it. The way the greasy crust tastes like sleepovers and inside jokes and curfews. The way the cheese holds it all together.

It's going to make my stomach hurt, but it's worth it. It's pizza. What is life without the occasional risk of pizza?

After I demolish the slice, I switch on my lights, shift into drive, and—without even thinking twice—reach across the seat, pick up the Best Boyfriend award, and use the back of it to wipe off my mouth. Then I'm outtie, past the state's second-tallest roller coaster and onto the familiar country road. Two songs later, I merge extra-smooth onto the parkway. Usually I suck at yielding, but tonight I nail it, winding the bend toward the underpass, licking my lips into a guilty pizza grin, and holding my breath when I go through the mountain tunnel that always takes me back home.

Inertia

Veronica Roth

T here must have been some kind of mistake," I said.

My clock—one of the old digitals with the red block numbers—read 2:07 a.m. It was so dark outside I couldn't see the front walk.

"What do you mean?" Mom said absently, as she pulled clothes from my closet. A pair of jeans, T-shirt, sweatshirt, socks, shoes. It was summer, and I had woken to sweat pooling on my stomach, so there was no reason for the sweatshirt, but I didn't mention it to her. I felt like a fish in a tank, blinking slowly at the outsiders peering in.

"A mistake," I said, again in that measured way. Normally I would have felt weird being around Mom in my underwear, but that was what I had been wearing when I fell asleep on top of my summer school homework earlier that night, and Mom seeing the belly button piercing I had given myself the year before was the least of my worries. "Matt hasn't talked to me in months. There's no way he asked for me. He must have been delirious."

The paramedic had recorded the aftermath of the car accident from a camera in her vest. In it, Matthew Hernandez—my former best friend—had, apparently, requested my presence at the Last Visitation, a rite that had become common practice in cases like these, when hospital analytics suggested a life would end regardless of surgical intervention. They calculated the odds, stabilized the patient as best they could, and summoned the last visitors, one at a time, to connect to the consciousness of the just barely living.

"He didn't just make the request at the accident, Claire, you know that." Mom was trying to sound gentle, I could tell, but everything was coming out clipped. She handed me the T-shirt, skimming the ring through my belly button with her eyes but saying nothing. I pulled the T-shirt over my head, then grabbed the jeans. "Matt is eighteen now."

At eighteen, everyone who wanted to participate in the Last Visitation program—which was everyone, these days—had to make a will listing their last visitors. I wouldn't do it myself until next spring. Matt was one of the oldest in our class.

"I don't . . ." I put my head in a hand. "I can't . . ."

"You can say no, if you want." Mom's hand rested gently on my shoulder.

"No." I ground my head into the heel of my hand. "If it was one of his last wishes . . ."

I stopped talking before I choked.

I didn't want to share a consciousness with Matt. I didn't even want to be in the same room as him. We'd been friends once—the closest kind—but things had changed. And now he wasn't giving me any choice. What was I supposed to do, refuse to honor his will?

"The doctor said to hurry. They do the visitation while they prepare him for surgery, so they only have an hour to give to you and his mother." Mom was crouched in front of me, tying my shoes, the way she had when I was a little kid. She was wearing her silk bathrobe with the flowers stitched into it. It was worn near the elbows and fraying at the cuffs. I had seen that bathrobe every day since Dad gave it to her for Christmas when I was seven.

"Yeah." I understood. Every second was precious, like every drop of water in a drought.

"Are you sure you don't want me to take you?" she said. I was staring at the pink flower near her shoulder; lost, for a second, in the familiar pattern.

"Yeah," I said again. "I'm sure."

I sat on the crinkly paper, tearing it as I shifted back to get more comfortable. This table was not like the others I had sat on, for blood tests and pelvic exams and reflex tests; it was softer, more comfortable. Designed for what I was about to do.

On the way here I had passed nurses in teal scrubs, carrying clipboards. I passed worried families, their hands clutched in front of them, sweaters balled up over their fists to cover themselves. We became protective at the first sign of grief, hunching in, shielding our most vulnerable parts.

I was not one of them. I was not worried or afraid; I was empty. I had glided here like a ghost in a movie, floating.

Dr. Linda Albertson came in with a thermometer and blood pressure monitor in hand, to check my vitals. She gave me a reassuring smile. I wondered if she practiced it in a mirror, her softest eyes and her gentlest grins, so she wouldn't make her patients' grief any worse. Such a careful operation it must have been.

"One hundred fifteen over fifty," she said, after reading my blood pressure. They always said that like you were supposed to know what the numbers meant. And then, like she was reading my mind, she added, "It's a little low. But fine. Have you eaten today?"

I rubbed my eyes with my free hand. "I don't know. I don't—it's the middle of the night."

"Right." Her nails were painted sky blue. She was so proper in her starched white coat, her hair pulled back into a bun, but I couldn't figure out those nails. Every time she moved her hands, they caught my attention. "Well, I'm sure you'll be fine. This is not a particularly taxing procedure." I must have given her a look, because she added, "Physically, I mean."

"So where is he?" I said.

"He's in the next room," Dr. Albertson said. "He's ready for the procedure."

I stared at the wall like I would develop X-ray vision through sheer determination alone. I tried to imagine what Matt looked like, stretched out on a hospital bed with a pale green blanket over his legs. Was he bruised beyond recognition? Or were his injuries the worse kind, the ones that hid under the surface of the skin, giving false hope?

She hooked me up to the monitors like it was a dance, sky-blue fingernails swooping, tapping, pressing. Electrodes touched to my head like a crown, an IV needle gliding into my arm. She was my lady-in-waiting, adorning me for a ball.

"How much do you know about the technology?" Dr. Albertson said. "Some of our older patients need the full orientation, but most of the time our younger ones don't."

"I know we'll be able to revisit memories we both shared, places we both went to, but nowhere else." My toes brushed the cold tile. "And that it'll happen faster than real life."

"That's correct. Your brain will generate half the image, and his will generate the other. The gaps will be filled by the program, which determines—by the electrical feedback in your brain—what best completes the space," she said. "You may have to explain to Matthew what's happening, because you're going before his mother, and the first few minutes can be disorienting. Do you think you can do that?"

"Yeah," I said. "I mean, I won't really have a choice, will I?"

"I guess not, no." Pressed lips. "Lean back, please."

I lay down, shivering in my hospital gown, and the crinkly paper shivered along with me. I closed my eyes. It was only a half hour. A half hour to give to someone who had once been my best friend.

"Count backward from ten," she said.

Like counting steps in a waltz. I did it in German. I didn't know why.

It wasn't like sleeping—that sinking, heavy feeling. It was like the world disappearing in pieces around me—first sight, then sound, then the touch of the paper and the plush hospital table. I tasted something bitter, like alcohol, and then the world came back again, but not in the right way.

Instead of the exam room, I was standing in a crowd, warm bodies all around me, the pulsing of breaths, eyes guided up to a stage, everyone waiting as the roadies set up for the band. I turned to Matt and grinned, bouncing on my toes to show him how excited I was.

But that was just the memory. I felt that it was wrong before I understood why, sinking back to my heels. My stomach squeezed as I remembered that this was the last visitation, that I had chosen this memory because it was the first time I felt like we were really friends. That the real, present-day Matthew was *actually* standing in those beat-up sneakers, black hair hanging over his forehead.

His eyes met mine, bewildered and wide. All around us, the crowd was unchanged, and the roadies still screwed the drum set into place and twisted the knobs on the amplifiers.

"Matt," I said, creaky like an old door. "Are you there?"

"Claire," he said.

"Matt, this is a visitation," I said. I couldn't bear to say the word *last* to him. He would know what I meant without it. "We're in our shared memories. Do you . . . understand?"

He looked around, at the girl to his left with the cigarette dangling from her lips, lipstick marking it in places, and the skinny boy in front of him with the too-tight plaid shirt and the patchy facial hair.

"The accident," he said, all dreamy voice and unfocused eyes. "The paramedic kind of reminded me of you."

He reached past the boy to skim the front of the stage with his fingertips, drawing away dust. And he smiled. I didn't usually think this way, but Matt had looked so good that day, his brown skin even darker from a summer in the sun and his smile, by contrast, so bright.

"Are you . . . okay?" I said. For someone who had just found out that he was about to die, he seemed pretty calm.

"I guess," he said. "I'm sure it has more to do with the drug cocktail they have me on than some kind of 'inner peace, surrendering to fate' thing."

He had a point. Dr. Albertson had to have perfected the unique combination of substances that made a dying person calm, capable of appreciating their Last Visitation, instead of panicking the whole time. But then again, Matt had never reacted to things quite the way I expected him to, so it wouldn't have surprised me to learn that, in the face of death, he was as calm as still water.

He glanced at me. "This is our first Chase Wolcott concert. Right?"

"Yeah," I said. "I know that because the girl next to you is going to give you a cigarette burn at some point."

"Ah, yes, she was a gem. Lapis lazuli. Maybe ruby."

"You don't have to *pick* the gem."

"That's what you always say."

My smile fell away. Some habits of friendship were like muscle memory, rising up even when everything else had changed. I knew our jokes, our rhythms, the choreography of our friendship. But that didn't take away what we were now. Any normal person would have been stumbling through their second apology by now, desperate to make things right before our time was over. Any normal person would have been crying, too, at the last sight of him.

Be normal, I told myself, willing the tears to come. *Just now, just for him.*

"Why am I here, Matt?" I said.

Dry eyed.

"You didn't want to see me?" he said.

"It's not that." It wasn't a lie. I both did and didn't want to see him—wanted to, because this was one of the last times I would get to, and didn't want to, because . . . well, because of what I had done to him. Because it hurt too much and I'd never been any good at feeling pain.

"I'm not so sure." He tilted his head. "I want to tell you a story, that's all. And you'll bear with me, because you know this is all the time I get."

"Matt . . ." But there was no point in arguing with him. He was right—this was probably all the time he would get.

"Come on. This isn't where the story starts." He reached for my hand, and the scene changed.

I knew Matt's car by the smell: old crackers and a stale "new car scent" air freshener, which was dangling from the rearview mirror. My feet crunched receipts and spilled potato chips in the foot well. Unlike new cars, powered by electricity, this one was an old hybrid, so it made a sound somewhere between a whistle and a hum.

The dashboard lit his face blue from beneath, making the whites of his eyes glow. He had driven the others home—all the people from the party who lived in this general area—and saved me for last, because I was closest. He and I had never really spoken before that night, when we had stumbled across each other in a game of strip poker. I had lost a sweater and two socks. He had been on the verge of losing his boxers when he declared that he was about to miss his curfew. How convenient.

Even inside the memory, I blushed, thinking of his bare skin at the poker table. He'd had the kind of body someone got right after a growth spurt, long and lanky and a little hunched, like he was uncomfortable with how tall he'd gotten.

I picked up one of the receipts from the foot well and pressed it flat against my knee.

"You know Chase Wolcott?" I said. The receipt was for their new album.

"Do I *know* them," he said, glancing at me. "I bought it the day it came out."

"Yeah, well, I preordered it three months in advance."

"But did you buy it on *CD*?"

"No," I admitted. "That's retro hip of you. Should I bow before the One True Fan?"

He laughed. He had a nice laugh, half an octave higher than his deep, speaking voice. There was an ease to it that made me comfortable, though I wasn't usually comfortable sitting in cars alone with people I barely knew.

"I will take homage in curtsies only," he said.

He pressed a few buttons on the dashboard and the album came on. The first track, "Traditional Panic," was faster than the rest, a strange blend of handbells and electric guitar. The singer was a woman, a true contralto who sometimes sounded like a man. I had dressed up as her for the last two Halloweens, and no one had ever guessed my costume right.

"What do you think of it? The album, I mean."

"Not my favorite. It's so much more upbeat than their other stuff, it's a little . . . I don't know, like they went too mainstream with it, or something."

"I read this article about the lead guitarist, the one who writes the songs—apparently he's been struggling with depression all his life, and when he wrote this album he was coming out of a low period. Now he's like . . . really into his wife, and expecting a kid. So now when I listen to it, all I can hear is that he feels better, you know?"

"I've always had trouble connecting to the happy stuff." I drummed my fingers on the dashboard. I was wearing all my rings—one made of rubber bands, one an old mood ring, one made of resin with an ant preserved inside it, and one with spikes across the top. "It just doesn't make me feel as much."

He quirked his eyebrows. "Sadness and anger aren't the only feelings that count as feelings."

"That's not what you said," I said, pulling us out of the memory and back into the visitation. "You just went quiet for a while until you got to my driveway, and then you asked me if I wanted to go to a show with you."

"I just thought you might want to know what I was thinking at that particular moment." He shrugged, his hands still on the wheel.

"I still don't agree with you about that album."

"Well, how long has it been since you even listened to it?"

I didn't answer at first. I had stopped listening to music altogether a couple months ago, when it started to pierce me right in the chest like a needle. Talk radio, though, I kept going all day, letting the soothing voices yammer in my ears even when I wasn't listening to what they were saying.

"A while," I said.

"Listen to it now, then."

I did, staring out the window at our neighborhood. I lived on the good side and he lived on the bad side, going by the usual definitions. But Matthew's house—small as it was—was always warm, packed full of kitschy objects from his parents' pasts. They had all the clay pots he had made in a childhood pottery class lined up on one of the windowsills, even though they were glazed in garish colors and deeply—*deeply*—lopsided. On the wall above them were his Mom's needlepoints, stitched with rhymes about home and blessings and family.

My house—coming up on our right—was stately, spotlights illuminating its white sides, pillars out front like someone was trying to create a miniature Monticello. I remembered, somewhere buried inside the memory, that feeling of dread I had felt as we pulled in the driveway. I hadn't wanted to go in. I didn't want to go in now.

For a while I sat and listened to the second track—"Inertia"—which was one of the only love songs on the album, about inertia carrying the guitarist toward his wife. The first time I'd heard it, I'd thought about how unromantic a sentiment that was—like he had only found her and married her because some outside force hurled him at her and he couldn't stop it. But now I heard in it this sense of propulsion toward a particular goal, like everything in life had buoyed him there. Like even his mistakes, even his darkness, had been taking him toward her.

I blinked tears from my eyes, despite myself.

"What are you trying to do, Matt?" I said.

He lifted a shoulder. "I just want to relive the good times with my best friend."

"Fine," I said. "Then take us to your favorite time."

"You first."

"Fine," I said again. "This is your party, after all."

"And I'll cry if I want to," he crooned, as the car and its cracker smell disappeared.

I had known his name, the way you sometimes knew people's names when they went to school with you, even if you hadn't spoken to them. We had had a class or two together, but never sat next to each other, never had a conversation.

In the space between our memories, I thought of my first sight of him, in the hallway at school, bag slung over one shoulder, hair tickling the corner of his eye. He had black hair, floppy then and curling around the ears. His eyes were hazel, stark against his brown skin—they came from his mother, who was German, not his father, who was Mexican—and he had pimples in the middle of each cheek. Now they were acne scars, only visible in bright light, little reminders of when we were greasy and fourteen.

Now, watching him materialize, I wondered how it was that I hadn't been able to see from the very first moment the potential for friendship living inside him, like a little candle flame. He had just been another person to me, for so long. And then he had been the *only* person—the only one who understood me, and then, later, the last one who could stand me. Now no one could. Not even me.

I felt the grains of sand between my toes first—still hot from the day's sun, though it had set hours before—and then I smelled the rich smoke of the bonfire, heard its crackle. Beneath me was rough bark, a log on its side, and next to me, Matt, bongos in his lap.

They weren't his bongos—as far as I knew, Matt didn't own any kind of drum—but he had stolen them from our friend Jack, and now he drumrolled every so often like he was setting someone up for a joke. He had gotten yelled at three times already. Matt had a way of annoying people and amusing them at the same time.

Waves crashed against the rocks to my right, big stones that people sometimes spray painted with love messages when the tide was low. Some were so worn that only fragments of letters remained. My freshman year of high school I had done an art project on them, documenting each stone and displaying them from newest-looking to oldest. Showing how love faded with time. Or something. I cringed to think of it now, how new I had been, and how impressed with myself.

Across the fire, Jack was strumming a guitar, and Lacey—my oldest friend—was singing a dirge version of "Twinkle, Twinkle, Little Star," laughing through most of the words. I was holding a stick I had found in the brush at the edge of the sand. I had stripped it of bark and stuck a marshmallow on it; now that marshmallow was a fireball.

"So your plan is to waste a perfectly good marshmallow," Matt said to me.

"Well, do *you* know what a marshmallow becomes when you cook it too long?" I said. "No. Because you can never resist them, so you've never let it get that far."

"Some questions about the world don't *need* to be answered, you know. I'm perfectly content with just eating the toasted marshmallows for the rest of my days."

"This is why you had to drop art."

"Because I'm not curious about charred marshmallows?"

"No." I laughed. "Because you can be perfectly content instead of . . . perpetually unsettled."

He raised his eyebrows. "Are you calling me simpleminded? Like a golden retriever or something?"

"No!" I shook my head. "I mean, for one thing, if you were a dog, you would obviously be a labradoodle—"

"A *labradoodle*?"

"—and for another, if we were all the same, it would be a boring world."

"I still think you were being a little condescending." He paused, and smiled at me. "I can give it a pass, though, because you're obviously still in your idealistic adolescent art student phase—"

"Hypocrisy!" I cried, pointing at him. "The *definition* of 'condescending' may as well be telling someone they're going through a phase."

Matt's response was to seize the stick from my hand, blow out the flames of the disintegrating marshmallow, and pull it free, tossing it from hand to hand until it cooled. Then he shoved it—charred, but still gooey on the inside—into his mouth.

"Experiment over," he said, with a full mouth. "Come on, let's go."

"Go where?"

He didn't answer, just grabbed me by the elbow and steered me away from the bonfire. When we had found the path just before the rocks, he took off running, and I had no choice but to follow him. I chased him up the path, laughing, the warm summer air blowing over my cheeks and through my hair.

Then I remembered.

He was leading us to the dune cliff—a low sand cliff jutting out over the water. It was against beach rules to jump off it, but people did it anyway, mostly people our age who hadn't yet developed that part of the brain that thought about consequences. A gift as well as a curse.

I watched as Matt sprinted off the cliff, flailing in the air for a breathless moment before he hit the water.

I stopped a few feet from the edge. Then I heard him laughing.

"Come on!" he shouted.

I was more comfortable just watching antics like these, turning them into a myth in my mind, a legend. I watched life so that I could find the story inside it—it helped me make sense of things. But sometimes I got tired of my own brain, perpetually unsettled as it was.

This time I didn't just watch. I backed up a few steps, shook out my trembling hands, and burst into a run. I ran straight off the edge of the cliff, shoes and jeans and all.

A heart-stopping moment, weightless and free.

Wind on my ankles, stomach sinking, and then I sliced into the water like a knife. The current wrapped around me. I kicked like a bullfrog, pushing myself to the surface.

"Now that's what I'm talking about," Matt said, as I surfaced.

As our eyes met across the water, I remembered where I really was. Lying in a hospital room. Unaware of how much time had actually passed.

"I like this memory, too," he said to me, smiling, this time in the visitation instead of the memory. "Except for the part when I realized my dad's old wallet was in my pocket when I jumped. It was completely ruined."

"Oh, shit," I breathed. "You never said."

He shrugged. "It was just a wallet."

That was a lie, of course. No object that had belonged to Matt's father was "just" something, now that he was gone.

He said, "So this is your favorite memory?"

"It's . . . I . . ." I paused, kicking to keep myself afloat. The water was cool but not cold. "I never would have done something like this without you."

"You know what?" He tilted back, so he was floating. "I wouldn't have done it without you, either."

"It's your turn," I said. "Favorite memory. Go."

"Okay. But don't forget, you asked for this."

I had always thought he was cute—there was no way around it, really, short of covering my eyes every time he was around. Especially after he cut the floppy mess of hair short and you could see his face, strong jaw and all. He had a dimple in his left cheek but not his right one. His smile was crooked. He had long eyelashes.

I might have developed a crush on him, if he hadn't been dating someone when we first became friends. And it seemed like Matt was always dating someone. In fact, I counseled him through exactly three girlfriends in our friendship: the first was Lauren Gallagher, a tiny but demanding gymnast who drove him up the wall; the second, Lacey Underhill, my friend from first grade, who didn't have anything in common with him except an infectious laugh; and the third, our mutual acquaintance Tori Slaughter (an unfortunate last name), who got drunk and made out with another guy at a Halloween party shortly after their fifth date. Literally—just two hours after their fifth date, she had another guy's tongue in her mouth. That was the hardest one, because she seemed really sad afterward, so he hadn't been able to stay mad at her, even while he was ending things. Matt never could hang on to anger, even when he had a right to; it slipped away like water in a fist. Unless it had to do with me. He had been angry at me for longer than he was ever angry with a girlfriend.

For my part, I had had a brief interlude with Paul (nickname: Paul the Appalling, courtesy of Matt) involving a few hot make-out sessions on the beach one summer, before I discovered a dried-up-booger collection in the glove box of his car, which effectively killed the mood. Otherwise, I preferred to stay solitary.

Judging by what Lacey had told me while they were dating, girls had trouble getting Matt to stop joking around for more than five seconds at a time, which got annoying when they were trying to get to know him. I had never had that problem.

I heard rain splattering and the jingle of a wind chime—the one hanging next to Matt's front door. My hair was plastered to the side of my face. Before I rang the bell, I raked it back with my fingers and tied it in a knot. It had been long then, but now its weight was unfamiliar. I was used to it tickling my jaw.

He answered the door, so the screen was between us. He was wearing his gym shorts—his name was written on the front of them, right above his knee—and a ragged T-shirt that was a little too small. He had dark circles under his eyes—darker than usual, that is, because Matt always had a sleepy look to his face, like he had just woken up from a nap.

He glanced over his shoulder to the living room, where his mother was sitting on the couch, watching television. He drew the door shut behind him, stepping out onto the porch.

"What is it?" he said, and at the sound of his voice—so hollowed out by grief—I felt a catch in my own throat. In the memory as well as in the visitation. It never got easier to see him this way.

"Can you get away for an hour?" I said.

"I'm sorry, Claire, I'm just . . . not up for hanging out right now."

"Oh, we're not going to hang out. Just humor me, okay?"

"Fine. I'll tell Mom."

A minute later he was in his old flip-flops (taped back together at the bottom), walking through the rain with me to my car. His gravel driveway was long. In the heat of summer the brush had grown high, crowding the edge, so I had parked on the road.

Matt's house was old and small and musty. He had had a bedroom once, before his grandmother had to move in, but now he slept on the couch in the living room. Despite how packed in his family always was, though, his house was always open to guests, expanding to accommodate whoever wanted to occupy it. His father had referred to me as "daughter" so many times, I had lost track.

His father had died three days before. Yesterday had been the funeral. Matt had helped carry the coffin, wearing an overlarge suit with moth-eaten cuffs that had belonged to his grandfather. I had gone with Lacey and Jack and all our other friends, in black pants instead of a dress—I hated dresses—and we had eaten the finger food and told him we were sorry. I had been sweaty the whole time because my pants were made of wool and Matt's house didn't have air-conditioning, and I was pretty sure he could feel it through my shirt when he hugged me.

He had thanked us all for coming, distractedly. His mother had wandered around the whole time with tears in her eyes, like she had forgotten where she was and what she was supposed to do there.

Matt and I got in the car, soaking my seats with rainwater. In the cup holder were two cups: one with a cherry slushie (mine) and the other with a strawberry milk shake (for him). I didn't mention them, and he didn't ask before he started drinking.

I felt struck, looking back on the memory, by how easy it was to sit in the silence, listening to the pounding rain and the *whoosh-whoosh* of the windshield wipers, without talking about where we were heading or what was going on with either of us. That kind of silence between two people was even rarer than easy conversation. I didn't have it with anyone else.

I navigated the soaked roads slowly, guiding us to the parking lot next to the beach, then I parked. The sky was getting darker, not from the waning of the day but from the worsening storm. I undid my seat belt.

"Claire, I—"

"We don't need to talk," I said, interrupting. "If all you want to do is sit here and finish your milk shake and then go home, that's fine."

He looked down at his lap.

"Okay," he said.

He unbuckled his seat belt, too, and picked up his milk shake. We stared at the water, the waves raging with the storm. Lightning lit up the sky, and I felt the thunder in my chest and vibrating in my seat. I drained the sugar syrup from the slushie, my mouth stained cherry bright.

Lightning struck the water ahead of us, a long bright line from cloud to horizon, and I smiled a little.

Matt's hand crept across the center console, reaching for me, and I grabbed it. I felt a jolt as his skin met mine, and I wasn't sure if I had felt it then, in the memory, or if I was just feeling it now. Wouldn't I have noticed something like that at the time?

His hand trembled as he cried, and I blinked tears from my eyes, too, but I didn't let go. I held him, firm, even as our hands got sweaty, even as the milk shake melted in his lap.

After a while, it occurred to me that this was where the moment had ended—Matt had let go of me, and I had driven him back home. But in the visitation, Matt was holding us here, hands clutched together, warm and strong. I didn't pull away.

He set the milk shake down at his feet and wiped his cheeks with his palm.

"*This* is your favorite memory?" I said, quietly.

"You knew exactly what to do," he said, just as quietly. "Everyone else wanted something from me—some kind of reassurance that I was okay, even though I *wasn't* okay. Or they wanted to make it easier for me, like losing your father is supposed to be easy." He shook his head. "But you just wanted me to know you were there."

"Well," I said, "I didn't know what to say."

It was more than that, of course. I hated it when I was upset and people tried to reassure me, like they were stuffing my pain into a little box and handing it back to me like, *See? It's actually not that big a deal.* I hadn't wanted to do that to Matt.

"No one knows what to say," he said. "But they sure are determined to try, aren't they? Goddamn."

Everyone saw Matt a particular way: the guy who gave a drumroll for jokes that weren't jokes, the guy who teased and poked and prodded until you wanted to throttle him. Always smiling. But I knew a different person. The one who made breakfast for his mother every Saturday, who bickered with me about art and music and meaning. The only person I trusted to tell me when I was being pretentious or naive. I wondered if I was the only one who got to access this part of him. Who got to access the whole of him.

"Now, looking back, this is also one of my least favorite memories." He pulled his hand away, his eyes averted. "Not because it's painful, but because it just reminds me that when I was in pain, you knew how to be there for me . . . but when you were in pain, I abandoned you."

I winced at the brutality of the phrase, like he had smacked me.

"You didn't . . ." I started. "I didn't make it easy. I know that."

We fell back into silence. The rain continued to pound, relentless, against the roof of my car. I watched it bounce off the windshield, which had smeared the ocean into an abstract painting, a blur of color.

"I was worried about you," he said. "Instead of getting angry, I should have just told you that."

I tried to say the words I wanted to say: *Don't worry about me.*

I'm fine. I wanted to smile through them and touch his arm and make a joke. After all, this was his Last Visitation. It was about him, not about me; about the last moments that we would likely share with each other, given that he was about to die.

"I'm still worried about you," he said, when I didn't answer.

I didn't carry him to this memory; *the* memory. It was weird how much intention mattered with the Visitation tech, in this strange space between our two consciousnesses. I had to summon a memory, like pulling up a fishing line, in order to bring us both to it. Otherwise I was alone in my mind, for instants that felt much longer, little half-lifetimes.

After Matt's dad died, there was a wake and a funeral. There were people from Matt's church and from his mother's work who brought over meals; there were group attempts to get him out of his house, involving me and Lacey and Jack and a water gun aimed at his living room window. The long, slow process of sorting through his father's possessions and deciding which ones to keep and which ones to give away—I had been at his house for that, as his mother wept into the piles of clothing and Matt and I pretended not to notice. Over time, the pain seemed to dull, and his mother smiled more, and Matt returned to the world, not quite the same as he had been before but steady nonetheless.

And then my mother came back.

I had two mothers: the one who had raised me from childhood, and the one who had left my father without warning when I was five, packing a bag of her things and disappearing with the old Toyota. She had returned when I was fourteen, pudgier and older than she had been when my father last saw her, but otherwise the same.

Dad had insisted that I spend time with her, and she had brought me to her darkroom, an hour from where we lived, to show me photographs she had taken. Mostly they had been of people caught in the middle of expressions or in moments when they didn't think anyone was watching. Sometimes out of focus, but always interesting. She touched their corners in the red-lit room as she told me about each one, her favorites and her least favorites.

I hated myself for liking those photographs. I hated seeing myself in that darkroom, picking the same favorites as her, speaking to her in that secret language of art. But I could not help but love her, like shared genes also meant shared hearts, no point in fighting it.

I saw her a few times, and then one day she was gone again. Again with no warning, again with no good-byes, no forwarding address, no explanations. The darkroom empty, the house rented out to new people. No proof she had ever been there at all.

I had never really had her, so it wasn't fair to think that I had lost her. And my stepmother, who was my *real* mother in all the ways that mattered, was still there, a little aloof, but still she loved me. I had no right to feel anything, I told myself, and moreover, I didn't want to.

But still, I retreated deep inside myself, like an animal burrowing underground and curling up for warmth. I started falling asleep in class, falling asleep on top of my homework. Waking in the middle of the night to a gnawing stomach and an irrepressible sob. I stopped going out on Friday nights, and then Saturdays, and then weekdays. The desk I kept reserved strictly for art projects went unused. My mother—stepmother, whatever she was—took me to specialists in chronic fatigue; she had me tested for anemia; she spent hours researching conditions on the Internet, until one doctor finally suggested depression. I left the office with a prescription that was supposed to fix everything. But I never filled it.

It was at school, of all places, that Matt and I found our ending. Three months ago. It was just him and me in fifth period lunch, in April, when the air-conditioning was on full blast inside so we sat under an apple tree on the front lawn. I had been going to the library to sleep during our lunch hour for the past few weeks, claiming that I had homework to do, but today he had insisted that I eat with him.

He tried to speak to me, but I had trouble focusing on what he was saying, so mostly I just chewed. At one point I dropped my orange and it tumbled away from me, settling in the tree roots a few feet away. I reached for it, and my sleeve pulled back, revealing a healing wound, sealed but unmistakable. I had dug into myself with a blade to make myself feel *full* of something instead of empty—the rush of adrenaline, of pain, was better than the hollowness. I had looked it up beforehand to figure out how to sterilize the edge, to know how far to go so I wouldn't puncture something essential. I wanted to know, to have my body *tell* me, that I was still alive.

I didn't bother to explain it away. Matt wasn't an idiot. He wouldn't buy that I had slipped while shaving or something. As if I shaved my arm hair.

"Did you go off the meds?" he said, his tone grave.

"What are you, my dad?" I pulled my sleeve down and cradled the orange in my lap. "Lay off, Matt."

"Well, did you?"

"No. I didn't go off them. Because I never started taking them."

"What?" He scowled at me. "You have a doctor who tells you that you have a problem, and you don't even try the solution?"

"The doctor wants me to be like everybody else. *I* am not a problem."

"No, you're a kid refusing to take her vitamins," he said, incredulous.

"I don't need to be drugged just because I don't act the way other people want me to!"

"People like me?"

I shrugged.

"Oh, so you're saying you feeling like shit all the time is a *choice*." His face was red. "Forgive me, I didn't realize."

"You think I want to pump my body full of chemicals just so I can feel flat all the time?" I snapped. "How am I supposed to be myself when something is altering the chemistry of my brain? How can I make anything, say anything, do anything worthwhile when I'm practically lobotomized?"

"That isn't what—"

"Stop arguing with me like you know something about this. Just because you have this emotional trump card in your back pocket doesn't mean you get to decide everyone else's mental state."

"Emotional *trump card*?" he repeated, eyebrows raised.

"Yeah!" I exclaimed. "How can I possibly have a legitimate problem when I'm talking to Matt 'my dad died' Hernandez?"

It had just . . . *come out*. I hadn't thought about it.

I knew that Matt's father's death wasn't a tool he used to control other people. I had just wanted to hurt him. It had been a year, but he was still raw with grief, right under the surface, and embarrassed by it. I knew that, too. Between us was the memory of him sobbing in the car while he held tight to my hand.

After weeks of ignoring his texts, and lying to him about why I couldn't come hang out, and snapping at every little thing, I guess me using his dad's death against him was the last straw. Even then, I hadn't blamed him. It was practically a reflex to blame myself anyway.

"Matt," I started to say.

"You know what?" he said, getting to his feet. "Do whatever you want. I'm done here."

"I made a mistake," Matt said, and his mouth was the first thing to materialize in the new memory—the lower lip bigger than the top one, even his speech a little lopsided, favoring the dimpled side. "I should have started the story here."

We were in the art room. It was bright white and always smelled like paint and crayons. There were racks along the back wall, where people put their projects to dry at the end of each class period. Before I had started failing art because I didn't turn in two of my projects, I had come here after school every other day to work. I liked the hum of the lights, the peace of the place. Peace wasn't something that came easily to me.

My classmates were in a half circle in front of me. I was sitting in a chair, a desk to my right, and there were wires stretching from electrodes on my head to a machine beside me. The screen faced my classmates. Even without the electrodes, I knew how old I was by the color of my fingernails—my freshman year of high school, I had been obsessed with painting my nails in increasingly garish and ugly colors, lime green and sparkly purple, glow-in-the-dark blue and burnt orange. I liked to take something that was supposed to be pretty and make it ugly instead. Or interesting. Sometimes I couldn't tell the difference between the two.

This was the second major art project of my freshman year, after the photographs of the love rocks. I had become fascinated by the inside of the brain, like it would give me explanations for everything that had happened to me and everything happening inside me. A strange stroke of inspiration, and I had applied for a young artists' grant to purchase this portable equipment, at the forefront of medical advances in neuroscience. A doctor had taught me how to use it, spending several hours with me after school one day, and I had wheeled it into my art class soon afterward.

I didn't say anything to explain it, just hooked myself up to the machine and showed the class my brain waves and how I could alter them. I did a relaxation exercise first, showing my brain on meditation; then I did math problems. I listened to one of my favorite comedians. I recounted my most embarrassing memory: sneezing and getting snot all over my face during a school presentation in sixth grade. My brain waves shifted and changed depending on what I was doing.

I kept my brain waves clean of emotional turmoil—the muck of my mother not coming downstairs for breakfast that one morning when I was five, the empty space in the driveway where her car had been. I kept secret the chaos of my heart and guts. I was only interested in showing the mechanics of my mind, like the gears in a clock.

When I finished, the class greeted me with scattered applause. Unenthused, but that wasn't surprising. They never liked anything I did. One of the girls raised her hand and asked our teacher, "Um . . . Mr. Gregory? Does that even count as art? I mean, she just showed us her brain."

"It counts as performance art, Jessa," Mr. Gregory said, taking off his glasses. "Think about what you just said—she *showed us* her *brain*. An act of vulnerability. That is incredibly rare, in life and in art. Art is, above all things, both vulnerable and brave."

He gave me a wink. Mr. Gregory was part of the peace of this room. He always seemed to understand what I was getting at, even if I couldn't quite get myself there.

"Why are we here?" I said to Visitation Matthew, frowning. "We didn't even *know* each other yet."

Matt was sitting near the back of the class, on the side, his head bent over a notebook. He smiled at me within the visitation. Dimpled cheek, crinkled eyes, a flash of white teeth.

"This is where our story started," he said. "You were so . . . I mean, their opinions were completely irrelevant to you. It's like while everyone else was listening to one song, you were listening to another. And God, I loved that. I wanted it for myself."

It made me feel strange—weightless in places, like I was turning into tissue paper and butterfly wings.

"You think I didn't care what they thought of me?" I shook my head. I couldn't let him believe a lie about me, not now. "Of course I cared. I still can't think about it without blushing."

"Fair enough," he said. "But I went to that party sophomore year because I found out you were going and . . . I wanted to get to know you. I loved this project. I loved everything you did in art class. I felt like you had showed yourself to me, and I wanted to return the favor."

My cheeks felt a little warm. "You never said."

"Well, you've said before that talking about old projects embarrasses you," he said, shrugging. "So I never wanted to bring it up."

"*This* is what I was worried about, you know," I said, softly. "About the medication. That it would mean I couldn't do this—art—anymore. I mean, feeling things—feeling intense things, sometimes—is part of what drives me to make things."

"You think you can't feel better and do great work at the same time?"

"I don't know." I chewed on my lip. "I'm used to being this way. Volatile. Like a walking ball of nerves. I'm worried that if I get rid of the highs, and even the lows—*especially* the lows—there won't be anything about me that's interesting anymore."

"Claire." He stood, weaving through the chairs, and crouched in front of me, putting his hands on my knees. "That nerve ball isn't you. It's just this thing that lives in your head, telling you lies. If you get rid of it . . . think of what you could do. Think of what you could be."

"But what if . . . what if I go on medication and it makes me into this flat, dull person?" I said, choking a little.

"It's not supposed to do that. But if it does, you'll try something else." His hands squeezed my knees. "And can you really tell me 'flat' is that much different from how you feel now?"

I didn't say anything. Most of the time I was so close to falling into the darkest, emptiest place inside me that I tried to feel nothing at all. So the only difference between this and some kind of flat, medicated state was that I knew I *could* still go there if I needed to, even if I wouldn't. And that place, I had told myself, was where the real me was. Where the art was, too.

But maybe—maybe it *wasn't* where it was. I was so convinced that changing my brain would take away my art, but maybe it would give me new art. Maybe without the monster in my mind, I could actually do more, not less. It was probably equally likely. But I believed more in my possible doom than in my possible healing.

"It's okay to want to feel better." He touched my hand.

I didn't know why—they were such simple words, but they pierced me the way music did, these days. Like a needle in my sternum, penetrating to my heart. I didn't bother to blink away my tears. Instead of pulling myself away from them, away from sensation entirely, I let myself sink into it. I let the pain in.

"But how can I feel better now?" I covered my eyes. "How can I *ever* . . . ever feel better if you die?"

I was sobbing the way he had sobbed in the car with me, holding onto his hands, which were still on top of my legs. He slipped his fingers between mine and squeezed.

"Because," he said. "You just have to."

"Who says?" I demanded, scowling at him. "Who says I have to feel anything?"

"I do. I chose you for one of my Last Visitors because . . . I wanted one last chance to tell you that you're worth so much more than your pain." He ran his fingers over my bent knuckles. "You can carry all these memories around. They'll last longer than your grief, I promise, and someday you'll be able to think of them and feel like I'm right there with you again."

"You might not be correctly estimating my capacity for grief," I said, laughing through a sob. "Pro-level moper right here."

"Some people might leave you," he said, for once ignoring a joke in favor of something real. "But it doesn't mean you're worth leaving. It doesn't mean that at all."

I didn't quite believe him. But I almost did.

"Don't go," I whispered.

After that, I carried him back to the ocean, the ripples reflecting the moon, where we had treaded water after jumping off the cliff. The water had filled my shoes, which were now heavy on my feet, making it harder to stay afloat.

"You have makeup all over your face," he said, laughing a little. "You look like you got punched in both eyes."

"Yeah, well, your nipples are totally showing through that shirt."

"Claire Lowell, are you checking out my nipples?"

"Always."

We laughed together, the laughs echoing over the water. Then I dove at him, not to dunk him—though he flinched like that's what he expected—but to wrap my arms around his neck. He clutched at me, holding me, arms looped around my back, fingers tight in the bend of my waist.

"I'll miss you," I said, looking down at him. Pressed against him like this, I was paper again, eggshell and sugar glass and autumn leaf. How had I not noticed this feeling the first time through?

It was the most powerful thing I had felt in days, weeks, months.

"It was a good story, right?" he said. "Our story, I mean."

"The best."

He pressed a kiss to my jaw, and with his cheek still against mine he whispered, "You know I love you, right?"

And then he stopped treading water, pulling us down into the waves together.

When I woke in the hospital room, an unfamiliar nurse took the IV needle from my arm and pressed a strip of tape to a cotton ball in the crook of my elbow. Dr. Albertson came in to make sure I had come out of the procedure with my faculties intact. I stared at her blue fingernails to steady myself as she talked, as I talked, another dance.

The second she said I could go, I did, leaving my useless sweatshirt behind, like Cinderella with her glass slipper. And maybe, I thought, she hadn't left it so the prince would find her . . . but because she was in such a hurry to escape the pain of never getting what she wanted that she didn't care what she lost in the process.

It was almost sunrise when I escaped the hospital, out of a side exit so I wouldn't run into any of Matt's family. I couldn't stand the thought of going home, so instead I drove to the beach and parked in the parking lot where I had once brought Matt to see the storm. This time, though, I was alone, and I had that strange, breathless feeling in my chest, like I was about to pass out.

My mind had a refrain for moments like these. *Feel nothing,* it said. *Feel nothing and it will be easier that way.*

Burrow down, it said, *and cover yourself in earth. Curl into yourself to stay warm,* it said, *and pretend the rest of the world is not moving. Pretend you are alone, underground, where pain can't reach you.*

Sightless eyes staring into the dark. Heartbeat slowing. A living corpse is better than a dying heart.

The problem with that refrain was that once I had burrowed, I often couldn't find my way out, except on the edge of a razor, which reached into my numbness and brought back sensation.

But it struck me, as I listened to the waves, that I didn't want to feel nothing for Matt. Not even for a little while. He had earned my grief, at least, if that was the only thing I had left to give him.

I stretched out a shaky hand for my car's volume buttons, jabbing at the plus sign until music poured out of the speakers. The right album was cued up, of course, the handbells and electric guitar jarring compared to the soft roar of the ocean.

I rested my head on the steering wheel and listened to "Traditional Panic" as the sun rose.

My cell phone woke me, the ring startling me from sleep. I had fallen asleep sitting up in my car with my head on the steering wheel. The sun was high now, and I was soaked with sweat from the building heat of the day. I glanced at my reflection in the rearview mirror as I answered, and the stitching from the wheel was pressed deep into my forehead. I rubbed it to get rid of the mark.

"What is it, Mom?" I said.

"Are you still at the hospital?"

"No, I fell asleep in the parking lot by the beach."

"Is that sarcasm? I can't tell over the phone."

"No, I'm serious. What's going on?"

"I'm calling to tell you they finished the surgery," she said. "Matt made it through. They're still not sure that he'll wake up, but it's a good first step."

"He . . . what?" I said, squinting into the bright flash of the sun on the ocean. "But the analytics . . ."

"Statistics aren't everything, sweetie. In 'ten to one,' there's always a 'one,' and this time, we got him."

It's a strange thing to be smiling so hard it hurts your face, and sobbing at the same time.

"Are you okay?" Mom said. "You went quiet."

"No," I said. "Not really, no."

No one ever told me how small antidepressants were, so it was kind of a shock when I tipped them into my palm for the first time. How was I afraid of such a tiny thing, such a pretty, pale green color? How was I more afraid of that little pill than I was of the sobbing fit that took me to my knees in the shower?

But in his way, he had asked me to try. *Just try.*

And he loved me. Maybe he just meant he loved me like a friend, or a brother, or maybe he meant something else. There was no way for me to know. What I did know was that love was a tiny firefly in the distance, blinking on right when I needed it to. Even in his forced sleep, his body broken by the accident and mended by surgery after surgery, he spoke to me.

Just try.

So I did, as we all waited to see if he would ever wake up. I tried just enough to get the chemicals into my mouth. I tried just enough to drive myself to the doctor every week, to force myself not to lie when she asked me how I felt. To eat meals and take showers and endure summer school. To wake myself up after eight hours of sleep instead of letting sleep swallow me for the entire summer.

When I spoke to the doctor about the Last Visitation, all I could talk about was regret. The Visitation had showed me things I had never noticed before, even though they seemed obvious, looking back. There were things I should have told him in case he didn't wake up. All I could do now was hope that he already knew them.

But he did wake up.

He woke up during the last week of summer, when it was so humid that I changed shirts twice a day just to stay dry. The sun had given me a freckled nose and a perpetual squint. Senior year started next week, but for me, it didn't mean anything without him.

When Matt's mom said it was okay for me to visit, I packed my art box into my car and drove back to the hospital. I parked by the letter *F*, like I always did, so I could remember later. *F* was for my favorite swear.

I carried the box into the building and registered at the front desk, like I was supposed to. The bored woman there printed out an ID sticker for me without even looking up. I stuck it to my shirt, which I had made myself, dripping bleach all over it so it turned reddish orange in places. It was my second attempt. In the first one, I had accidentally bleached the areas right over my breasts, which wasn't a good look.

I walked slowly to Matt's room, trying to steady myself with deep breaths. His mother had given me the number at least four times, as well as two sets of directions that didn't make sense together. I asked at the nurses' station, and she pointed me to the last room on the left.

Dr. Albertson was standing outside one of the other rooms, flipping through a chart. She glanced at me without recognition. She probably met so many people during Last Visitations that they ran together in her mind. When she turned away, I caught sight of her nails, no longer sky blue but an electric, poison green. Almost the same color that was chipping off my thumbnail.

I entered Matt's room. He was there, lying flat on the bed with his eyes closed. But he was only sleeping, not in a coma, I had been told. He had woken up last week, too disoriented at first for them to be sure he could still function. And then, slowly, he had returned to himself.

Apparently. I would believe it only when I saw it, and maybe not even then.

I set the box down and opened the lid. This particular project had a lot of pieces to it. I took the table where they put his food tray, and the bedside table, and I lined them up side by side. I found a plug for the speakers and the old CD player that I had bought online. It was bright purple and covered with stickers.

Sometime in the middle of this, Matt's eyes opened and shifted to mine. He was slow to turn his head—his spine was still healing from the accident—but he could do it. His fingers twitched. I swallowed a smile and a sob in favor of a neutral expression.

"Claire," he said, and my body thrilled to the sound of my name. He knew me. "I think I had a dream about you. Or maybe a series of dreams, in a very definite order, selected by yours truly . . ."

"Sh-h-h. I'm in the middle of some art."

"Oh," he said. "Forgive me. I'm in the middle of recovering from some death."

"Too soon," I replied.

"Sorry. Coping mechanism."

I sat down next to him and started to unbutton my shirt.

His eyebrows raised. "What are you doing?"

"Multitasking. I have to stick these electrodes on my chest. Remember them?" I held up the electrodes with the wires attached to them. They were the same ones I had used to show the art class my brain waves. "And I also want to stack the odds in my favor."

"Stack the . . . Am I on drugs again?"

"No. If you *were* on drugs, would you be hallucinating me shirtless, though?" I grinned and touched one electrode to the right side of my chest and another one under it. Together they would read my heartbeat.

"No comment," he said. "That's a surprisingly girly bra you're wearing."

It was navy blue, patterned with little white and pink flowers. I had saved it all week for today, even though it was my favorite and I always wanted to wear it first after laundry day.

"Just because I don't like dresses doesn't mean I hate flowers," I replied. "Okay, be quiet."

I turned up the speakers, which were connected directly to the electrodes on my chest. My heartbeat played over them, its pulse even and steady. I breathed deep, through my nose and out my mouth. Then I turned on the CD player and set the track to the second one: "Inertia," by Chase Wolcott.

Inertia
I'm carried in a straight line toward you
A force I can't resist; don't want to resist
Carried straight toward you

The drums pounded out a steady rhythm, the guitars throbbed, driving a tune propulsive and circular. My heartbeat responded accordingly, picking up the longer I listened.

"Your heart," he said. "You like the song now?"

"I told you the meds would mess with my mind," I said softly. "I'm just getting used to them, though, so don't get too excited. I may hate the album again someday."

"The meds," he repeated. "You're on them?"

"Still adjusting the dose, but yes, I'm on them, thanks in part to the encouragement of this guy I know," I said. "So far, side effects include headaches and nausea and a feeling that life might turn out okay after all. That last one is the peskiest."

The dimple appeared in his cheek.

"If you think *this* heartbeat change is cool, I'll show you something even more fascinating." I turned the music off.

"Okay," he said, eyes narrowed.

I stood and touched a hand to the bed next to his shoulder. My heartbeat played faster over the speakers. I leaned in close and pressed my lips lightly to his.

His mouth moved against mine, finally responding. His hand lifted to my cheek, brushed my hair back from my face. Found the curve of my neck.

My heart was like a speeding train. That thing inside me—that pulsing organ that said I was alive, I was all right, I was carving a better shape out of my own life—was the sound track of our first kiss, and it was much better than any music, no matter how good the band might be.

"Art," I said, as we parted, "is both vulnerable and brave."

I sat on the edge of the bed, right next to his hip, careful. His hazel eyes followed my every movement. There wasn't a hint of a smile on his face, in his furrowed brow.

"The Last Visitation is supposed to give you the chance to say everything you need to, before you lose someone," I said. "But when I drove away from here, thinking you were about to leave me for good, I realized there was one thing I still hadn't said."

I pinched his blanket between my first two fingers, suddenly shy again.

Heartbeat picking up again, faster and faster.

"So," he said quietly. "Say it, then."

"Okay." I cleared my throat. "Okay, I will. I will say it."

He smiled, broad, lopsided. "Claire . . . do you love me?"

"Yeah," I said. "I love you."

He closed his eyes, just for a second, a soft smile forming on his lips.

"The bra is a nice touch," he said, "but you didn't need to stack the odds in your favor." He smiled, if possible, even wider. "Everything has always been carrying me toward you."

I smiled. Reached out with one hand to press Play on the CD player. Eased myself next to him on the hospital bed, careful not to hurt him.

He ran his fingers through my hair, drew my lips to his again.

Quiet, no need for words, we listened to "Inertia" on repeat.

LOVE IS THE LAST RESORT

JON SKOVRON

Dear reader, I want to assure you that this is not a story about love or romance, regardless of what you may have read on the cover. There are quite enough of those stories already, thank you very much. No, this is a story about two people who insisted that love was only for fools.

The first of our two heroes was Lena Cole. She had piercing blue eyes, beautifully precise features, and long black hair pulled back in a practical yet not unattractive way. She moved through the grounds of the Hotel del Arte Spa and Resort with the confidence that came from experience and routine. Although just shy of eighteen, in the few summers she had worked at the resort, she had made herself an indispensable member of the staff.

She passed the dining room, laid for breakfast. "Good morning, Ms. Nalone."

An older woman with bleach-blond hair and a deep tan sipped her mimosa. "Good morning, Lena."

Lena Cole knew the name and habits of every guest of the past three years and could recognize them on sight. Ms. Nalone, a divorcée several times over, was a regular. Her son, Vito Nalone, age nineteen, would not be out of bed for at least another hour.

Lena continued down the hallway. As she passed the game room, she said, "Nearly time to start work, Zeke."

A spritely boy of sixteen with spiky black hair sat on a beanbag, destroying zombies on a massive flat-screen TV. He wore the white polo shirt and tan khaki shorts that were required of all the resort staff. He shut off the game and gave Lena a sharp salute.

Lena smiled and moved on, greeting guests and nodding cordially to other staff members. When she reached the lobby, she saw the manager. Like Lena and Zeke, Brice Ghello wore the staff uniform. His hair was very short, with only a little fringe of bangs that jutted out perfectly parallel to the ground.

"Lena, good, I was just about to text you." Brice examined his clipboard as if it contained all the truths of the universe, which, to his mind, it did. "I need you to pick up Arlo Kean at the train station."

"Oh yes," said Lena. "The new boy. Have you decided where to put him yet?"

Brice shook his head. "Bring him to orientation at noon. I'll decide then. Oh, but make sure you check on the Ficollos before you go."

"I was just on my way."

Lena rode the elevator up to the penthouse suite. Magnus Ficollo was the owner. But he was not the sort of owner who saved the penthouse for special VIPs. To his mind, the whole point of owning a resort was so he could take the penthouse whenever he and his daughter liked. And at the beginning of summer—when the spring rains had stopped but the intense heat of midsummer had not yet begun—they liked it very much.

It was Lena's primary responsibility to ensure that Mr. Ficollo and his beloved daughter, Isabella, had everything they needed. When she knocked on their door, Isabella opened it.

Isabella's eyes went wide, and she threw her arms around Lena. "It's so great to see you! How was your school year?"

Lena smiled warmly and took a moment to return the embrace before gently disentangling herself. In the years that she had worked for the Ficollos, she had learned that Isabella, like many international jet-setting heiresses to billions of dollars, already had everything she needed, except a good friend. "Productive as always, Miss Ficollo."

"But did you have any *fun*?" Isabella's eyes were bright, and her smile was as relentlessly perky as it had been the previous summer.

"I'm sure I did, Miss Ficollo."

Isabella squeezed her hands. "Did you see? My hedge maze is finished!"

"It turned out beautifully."

Isabella towed Lena over to the balcony, where they could see the layout of the entire resort. There was the pool and wet bar, the tennis and basketball courts, the gardens, the golf course, and the latest edition to the grounds—the hedge maze, installed especially for Isabella. She sighed happily. "It's everything I wanted. This is going to be an *amazing* summer."

"Just as wonderful as last year," said Lena.

"Are you up for a tennis match this morning?"

"I'm afraid I have to pick up the new staff member from the train station," said Lena. "Can we postpone until the afternoon?"

"Of course we can," said Isabella. "A new staff member? How exciting! I love new people."

Lena wrinkled her pert nose. "New people bring change."

If you haven't already guessed, the second of our heroes is the aforementioned new employee, Arlo Kean. Unlike Lena, Arlo was quite accustomed to change. Three schools in as many years, each more strict than the last. His mother might have been mad at him for being expelled with such frequency, except she had a habit of changing jobs and boyfriends every year as well. But what Arlo and his mother lacked in reliability, they made up for in adaptability. That was how his mother had started dating one of the wealthiest men in New York City. This latest boyfriend had found a summer job for Arlo at a fancy country resort. Compared to his warehouse job last summer, this one sounded like three months of heaven.

As Arlo disembarked from the train, he raked his fingers through his light-brown, curly hair. It needed a trim, and it fell in his eyes often enough that it was probably on purpose. He scanned the crowd, looking for the person who was supposed to pick him up. He grinned when he saw a girl around his age holding a sign that said "Kean." This girl had the sort of beauty that changed depending on the angle you viewed her. Looking at her one way, her features were as elegant and sharp as a blade. Looking at her another, her eyes blazed with an inner fire. As it happened, Arlo liked to play with both knives and matches.

Still smiling, he stepped up to her and pointed at the sign. "That's me."

She looked at him appraisingly. "Well, I suppose you'll add to the aesthetics, if nothing else. Come on. You're the last staff member to arrive. We have to be back at the resort by noon."

As he followed her to the small parking lot beside the train station, he decided that adding to the aesthetics was a compliment. "You're staff at the resort?"

"Yep." She pushed the key chain button to unlock the black hybrid SUV.

"Then I can't imagine how the aesthetics could possibly be improved," he said, as he climbed into the passenger seat.

She smiled faintly as she started the car. "I believe there is always room for improvement."

"So, do you have a boyfriend?"

"Nope," she said calmly, her eyes not leaving the road.

"Want one?"

"Nope."

"Oh," said Arlo. "Yeah. I like to keep things casual, too."

She turned her sharp gaze upon him. "I bet you do."

"Hey, I didn't mean it like that."

She returned her attention to the road. "What way did you mean it?"

"Uh . . ." Arlo flipped through several possible responses and rejected each in turn. "Maybe I should just shut up and look pretty."

"I was about to suggest that," she said.

Thus ended the first meeting of our two heroes, dear reader, without a meet cute or love-at-first-sight moment. After all, such things only happen in silly romances. Even if this *were* a love story—which it most certainly isn't—I know that discerning readers like you would never tolerate such banal contrivances.

Ms. Patricia Nalone lounged poolside. Her doctor had told her, more than once, that at her age she should not be sunbathing. That it was practically an invitation to skin cancer. But without a deep copper tan, Ms. Nalone would no more feel herself than if she allowed her blond hair to devolve into its natural gray. So she lay on a chaise longue, her leathery skin gleaming with lotion, a glass of iced wine in her hand, though it was not quite noon.

"Really, Vito," she said to her son, in a voice that had once been sultry but was now ravaged from a half century of smoke and drink. "I don't know what's wrong with you."

"Nothing is wrong with me, Mother," said Vito Nalone absently. The majority of his focus was on his form as he curled a dumbbell. Weight training wasn't just about how much you could lift. Flinging a heavy dumbbell around wouldn't do you any good if your form wasn't perfected to maximize both definition and size.

In some ways, Vito was a lot like his mother. Suntan lotion gleamed on his bronze skin, too, though the skin was smooth and taut over his young, well-cared-for physique. He didn't dye his dark hair completely, but he had indulged in a few blond highlights.

"Then why won't you ask out Isabella Ficollo?" His mother

would have frowned, but the recent Botox treatment prevented it.

Vito shrugged his muscular shoulders. "I'm just not interested in her."

"How can you not be interested in the sole heir to billions of dollars?"

Vito put his dumbbell down on the pool deck and leaned back into his chair. He watched the staff manager, Brice Ghello, walk quickly past, brow furrowed as he examined his clipboard. There was something sincere to the point of fussy about Brice that Vito found extremely charming. He sighed. "I don't know, Mother. I'm just not into her."

The Hotel del Arte staff convened on the basketball court at precisely noon. It was a large gathering of mostly high school and college students. Arlo looked up at the hoops longingly. He wondered if staff were ever allowed to use them. Not that a rule against it would prevent him, but it would certainly factor into his plans.

A younger boy of perhaps fifteen or sixteen came and stood beside him. He was also staring up at the hoop.

"What do you think?" asked Arlo. "Maybe they'll let us play at night?"

The boy put his hands together as if praying or begging.

"This is Zeke Zanni," Lena said, nearby.

"Hey, Zeke." Arlo held out his hand.

Zeke shook his hand and smiled, but said nothing.

"Zeke doesn't talk," said Lena.

"Why not?" asked Arlo.

Lena shrugged. "He never said." She pointed to the front of the crowd. "Brice is about to start."

Brice Ghello looked to be a little older than Arlo, perhaps twenty. "Hello, everyone, I'd like to get started, please." He examined his clipboard as he waited for conversation to stop. "As the manager here at Hotel del Arte, I want to welcome you to the first day of summer and the beginning of our peak season. Some of our guests have already arrived. Many will be arriving soon. For the few of you who are new this year, come see me after orientation to receive your uniform and assignment. You are expected to wear your uniform at all times while on duty so that guests know who they can approach for assistance."

Arlo eyed the white polo and the tight—and what seemed to him excessively short—shorts. He whispered to Lena, "Do all the shorts fit like that?"

She gave him a wolfish grin. "It's one of my favorite things about working here."

"I thought you didn't want a boyfriend."

"There's a wide spectrum between appreciating the sight of cute boys in tight shorts and having a boyfriend."

"And where do I fall on your spectrum?"

Lena leaned back and examined his backside. "If you don't prove to be a complete imbecile, there might be some room for advancement."

Zeke nudged Arlo with his elbow and gave him an encouraging look.

"Is that her version of a compliment?" asked Arlo.

Zeke nodded.

"I want it completely understood," Brice was saying, "that even though you have your individual responsibilities, the happiness of our guests comes first. Whatever you are doing, if a guest asks for *anything*, you do it. Got it? Okay, newbies up here to see me, everyone else to your stations."

The crowd dispersed, and Lena nudged Arlo. "Let's see what he gives you. Brice has an uncanny talent for giving a person just the right job."

They walked against the flow of people to Brice. Arlo noticed Zeke following behind.

"What's your job, Zeke?" asked Arlo. He wasn't sure how Zeke would answer, but he felt rude asking Lena a question meant for him.

Zeke held his hands together like he was holding an invisible golf club, then took a swing, shading his eyes as he watched the pretend ball fly through the air.

"Caddy? Not a bad gig. Maybe I'll get something like that."

"Hey, Brice." Lena jerked her thumb at Arlo. "New guy. Hasn't proved to be a complete idiot yet."

"Okay." Brice tugged at his chin and narrowed his eyes as he contemplated Arlo.

"What, no Sorting Hat?" asked Arlo.

"Pool boy," said Brice.

"Are you serious?" Arlo ignored Lena and Zeke, who were both silently chuckling.

"Absolutely," said Brice earnestly. "The pool is one of the most popular stations in the resort. I need someone good looking but also smart enough to handle himself and others on the deck. You can swim, can't you?"

"Well, yeah—"

"Excellent," said Brice. "It's an important position. In fact, it's probably best I train you myself."

Arlo assessed the sincere expression on his new boss's face and forced a smile. "Perfect."

"Oh, Lena!" called a perky voice from the other side of basketball court. A girl around Arlo's age, wearing a pink polo shirt and white skirt, waved a tennis racket. The sunlight framed her, so Arlo had to squint when he looked at her. It gave her an almost eerily angelic quality. "Are you free to play yet?"

Lena smiled warmly. "Of course, Miss Ficollo. I'll be right over." She turned back to them. "Well, boys. Duty calls." Arlo watched her jog away, realizing that the tight uniform shorts worked both ways. He let out a quiet sigh.

Brice followed Arlo's gaze to Lena. "That's never going to happen."

"I consider myself an optimist," said Arlo.

"Good luck with that." He took Arlo by the shoulders and turned him in the direction of the pool. "I think you'll find the role of pool boy to be incredibly rewarding in other ways. Why, *I* was pool boy my first year here. You'll be amazed at how interesting it can be."

"Can't wait," said Arlo. As Brice steered him toward the water,

Arlo looked over his shoulder at Zeke and mouthed, "B-ball after work?"

Zeke gave him two thumbs up.

"Now," said Brice, his eyes sparkling with delight. "The two most important responsibilities of being a pool boy are making sure the chemicals are always in balance, and skimming the surface of the water so it always looks pristine!"

"Was that the new staff member I saw you and Brice talking to?" asked Isabella, as she served the tennis ball with an artful perkiness that had taken years to perfect.

"Yeah. The new pool boy," said Lena, as she returned the ball.

"Are you trying to pretend that you don't know his name?" Isabella hit the ball back. "You, Lena Cole, who knows everyone?"

Lena missed the return. She calmly retrieved the ball by the fence. "His name is Arlo Kean."

"He's cute," said Isabella.

"He's trouble." If compelled, Lena would have admitted that she found him attractive. And the way he so easily communicated with Zeke was another trait she found appealing. But there was something about Arlo Kean that made her ever so slightly unsure of herself. And *that* was a feeling she didn't like at all.

"Do you know what your problem is, Lena?"

"Please tell me, Miss Ficollo," said Lena, as she bounced the ball on her racket.

"You judge too quickly. Maybe he only seems like a trouble-maker when you first meet him. Some boys, you have to look a little deeper to find the true beauty."

"Such as young Mr. Elore?" Lena pointed her racket past the tennis courts to the entrance, where Franklyn Elore and his mother were just arriving.

"Oh, Franklyn . . ." As Isabella caught sight of him, her perky demeanor melted like taffy in the sun. "He looks even dreamier than last summer, don't you think?"

"If by *dreamy*, you mean with his head in the clouds."

Franklyn reminded Lena of one of those Romantic-era poets like Byron or Shelley. He had soulful eyes, eternally rumpled clothes, and an air of wistful innocence combined with a complete lack of awareness regarding what was actually happening around him. She watched now as he struggled to steer a handcart stacked with books along the sidewalk without allowing it to veer into the gardens. His hair and glasses were both askew, and his shoelaces were untied.

Lena supposed he couldn't be blamed too much, however, since his mother was little better. Dr. Elore followed behind him, e-book reader in hand, somehow managing to just barely not run into things as she read. Her hair also was askew, her clothes equally rumpled. But where Franklyn was reminiscent of a Romantic poet, his mother looked more like a stuffy Ivy League professor who rarely saw the light of day, which was exactly what she was. Every year, Mr. Elore sent his wife and son to Hotel del Arte for the summer, and Lena didn't blame him for staying behind.

"Franklyn, dear," said Dr. Elore, her eyes not leaving her e-reader. "Given the superior pedigree of *Caesar's Gallic Commentaries,* I see no reason for you to focus your Summer Latin curriculum on sentimental drivel like Virgil."

"Because, Mother," said Franklyn, still trying to negotiate his handcart past their tennis court, "I'm more interested in the *soul* of the language than its politics."

"Ready for my serve, Miss Ficollo?" Lena asked pointedly.

Isabella shook herself and, with supreme effort, gathered her melty taffy bits back into the shape of an attractive heiress. "Yes, of course. Ready when you are."

But at the precise moment Lena served the ball, Franklyn's handcart tipped forward, spilling books across the sidewalk like a stack of thick Latin playing cards. "Oh, dear!" Franklyn's soft voice turned Isabella's gaze just as the tennis ball arrived. Instead of connecting with her racket, the ball connected with her head, and she dropped to the court with a very unperky flop.

"Isabella!" Lena leaped over the net and ran to her side.

Franklyn turned at the name. "Miss Ficollo!" He stumbled over his books, nearly losing his footing on a copy of the *Aeneid* before catching himself and making his way hastily to Isabella's side.

Lena helped her into a sitting position and examined the red mark on her forehead. It was entirely possible that Lena, somewhat irritated by Isabella's endless infatuation with Franklyn, had served the ball just a little too hard. A tiny bruise was already forming.

Franklyn stood over her awkwardly, wringing his hands. "Miss Ficollo! Are you all right?"

Isabella's eyes fluttered open. A gentle smile formed on her pink lips as she said, "Please, Franklyn. Call me Isabella."

"Is-a-bell-a." He took apart each syllable as if he were examining an orchestral piece, one section at a time, to see how it all fit together to make such a beautiful sound. "Isabella . . ."

"Yes, Franklyn?" she asked breathlessly.

"I'm glad you're okay." Then he fled.

Isabella sighed. "Perhaps he doesn't like me after all."

She was so used to everyone being demonstratively affectionate to her that she'd never needed to develop the skill of detecting its subtler clues.

"I don't think that's it," said Lena.

Isabella frowned, and even slightly concussed and frowning, she remained perky, which goes to show what years of training and commitment can do. "You're just trying to make me feel better."

Lena looked down at Isabella's bruised forehead and felt a prickle of guilt. "I tell you what. To make up for braining you with a tennis ball, would you like me to find out?"

"It's all in the wrist," said Brice, as he demonstrated the proper way to skim dead and dying bugs from the surface of the pool. He held the long metal pole loosely in his hands and dipped the square-framed net into the bright blue, chlorinated water. "You submerge sideways so as not to create wake, and then come up *under* it."

"Got it." Arlo attempted to shift his tight staff shorts into a position that gave a bit more relief.

"I don't want to overwhelm you. Maybe we should cover using the pool vacuum for the bottom tomorrow."

"Ooh, really? I'd hate to let it go that long," Arlo said blithely.

Brice nodded. "Yes, maybe you're right. Let's do it now."

Arlo winced. One of these days, he'd learn to keep his big mouth shut. Now he needed a diversion. "Hey, that tanned muscly dude is totally checking you out."

Brice flushed from his forehead to his neck. "Don't be ridiculous. That is the son of Ms. Nalone, one of our most valued guests."

"So?"

"So, even if he *was* checking me out, which he probably isn't—"

"Go ahead and look. He's still doing it. Pretty blatantly, I'd say."

"I will *not* look, and anyway, it doesn't matter, because we are strictly forbidden from . . . getting involved with guests."

"Huh." Arlo watched his boss fiddle with the long metal skimmer pole. "That a *firm* rule, is it?"

Brice's face went so red it was nearly purple.

"Just wondering how *hard* you plan to enforce it," continued Arlo.

"I, uh, look at the time." Brice made a show of looking at his watch. "Dr. Elore and her son should have arrived by now. I'd better make sure they have everything they need." He shoved the metal pole at Arlo. "You, uh, continue with the skimming." Then he hurried toward the hotel.

Arlo smiled. Vacuuming successfully deferred until another day. His big mouth just as often got him out of trouble, which was likely why he had never learned his lesson.

"I nearly forgot." Brice reappeared and said in a hushed tone, "If you see Dr. Elore, whatever you do, keep her and Ms. Nalone apart. I promised Mr. Ficollo there would be no need to call the police or an ambulance this year."

"Understood," said Arlo, although he didn't really. He figured it would become obvious when it needed to be.

Once Brice was gone, Arlo surveyed the pool area. There wasn't much to it. The pool itself was L-shaped, its long part dedicated to lap swimming. There was also a hot tub, a wet bar, and a shed where the pool supplies were kept. The entire deck was ringed with lounge chairs. There were a few lap swimmers moving slowly back and forth, and several people lying on deck chairs, among them valued guest Ms. Nalone and son.

So this was his summer. It was definitely better than a warehouse, but Arlo considered how it might be improved. The most obvious way would be to have his boss relax. And the most expedient way he knew to do that was getting him laid.

Arlo skimmed the pool, working his way slowly towards the Nalones. He didn't have a plan yet, but thought eavesdropping might offer some clues.

"You're being impossible, Vito." Ms. Nalone's face was half covered by enormous sunglasses. She looked like a Barbie who had been dropped into a deep fryer. "It's not like I expect you to ask out an *ugly* heiress."

"Isabella is very pretty," agreed Vito without enthusiasm.

"She's entirely boinkable," said Ms. Nalone.

"*Boinkable,* Mother?"

"The kids don't say that anymore?" Ms. Nalone shrugged. "Anyway, she looks fantastic. I wish I had such naturally perky tits."

"Mother!"

"What? It would have saved me a fortune." She took a large swallow of chardonnay, then turned to Arlo. "You! Pool boy!"

"Yes, ma'am?" asked Arlo.

Ms. Nalone frowned behind her massive sunglasses. "Are you new?"

"Yes, ma'am. My first day."

"*Really,*" she said in a way that made Arlo a tad nervous. "What's your name?"

"Arlo, ma'am."

"After the folk singer?"

"Yes, ma'am."

Ms. Nalone made a quiet noise of disgust. "I hate folk music. I'll just call you Pool Boy."

"Whatever you like, ma'am," said Arlo, remembering Brice's emphasis on keeping the guests happy. He could play along with this. It was better than skimming the pool.

"Oh, I *do* like you." Ms. Nalone licked her red, lipstick-caked lips.

"Mother," chided Vito.

Ms. Nalone waved her hand at him as she continued to address Arlo. "Have you met Miss Ficollo, the owner's daughter?"

"I saw her briefly from a distance, ma'am."

"Good enough. Would you say she is boinkable?"

Arlo looked over at Vito, unsure how to respond.

Vito sighed. "You might as well humor her."

Arlo turned back to Ms. Nalone. "Yes, ma'am."

"*How* boinkable?" pressed Ms. Nalone.

"Exceedingly."

"And do you have anything in particular," asked Ms. Nalone, "against inheriting billions of dollars?"

"Not at all, ma'am."

Ms. Nalone leaned back in her chair, a look of satisfaction on the lower half of her face. "See? Pool Boy has far more sense than you do, Vito." She tilted her sunglasses down to give him the full impact of her glare. Vito squirmed, his eyes looking around for some means of escape.

Arlo felt bad for him. It was also very informative, regarding his plan to get Brice laid, though not particularly encouraging. The fact that Vito might not be out, at least to his mother, complicated the situation.

Vito broke into a smile. "Look, Mom. The Elores are here."

Ms. Nalone sat up in her chair. "Really?"

She jumped to her feet and moved swiftly to the wet bar. There stood a woman dressed more for a safari than a pool, in tan shorts and matching short-sleeved button-down. She had thick glasses and an exceptionally large forehead.

"Is that Dr. Elore?" Arlo asked Vito.

"Sure is."

"Huh." Arlo watched the two women smile and hug each other.

"My boss told me to keep them separated."

"Yes, that comes later." Vito stood and walked off toward the golf course. "It's the first day, so . . . maybe as late as dinner?"

"Her lips are like . . . organically grown roses. Her hair, like . . . gluten-free pasta."

Having a poetic mind did not necessarily guarantee that one could compose poetry. However, this was not the first bad poem Franklyn had composed about Isabella, and Zeke had developed a tolerance. He lay on a gentle hill and ran his fingers through the carefully manicured grass while Franklyn Elore slumped on a nearby bench, pen and notebook in hand. Both sets of golf clubs lay on the grass and would see no action today.

Franklyn frowned as he examined his writing. "Not pasta. That gets a bit clumpy. Isabella's hair is never clumpy." He groaned and rolled off the bench to lie beside Zeke, his arms and legs spread wide. "Don't you think Isabella is the most beautiful girl who ever lived?"

Zeke smiled and nodded encouragingly.

Franklyn held up his notebook. "It's no use, Zeke. There's simply no way I could hope to capture such transcendent charm in mere words."

Again, Zeke smiled and nodded.

Franklyn narrowed his eyes. "Are you humoring me?"

Zeke shrugged.

Franklyn sighed, letting his notebook drop. "You placate me like I was a sick invalid. Is that what love is? An affliction?"

Zeke patted his head sympathetically.

"I *am* sick with it. And sick *of* it." Franklyn closed his eyes, the afternoon sun on his face. "I wish there was some way I could tell her . . ." He sighed again. "No, it's impossible. I'm sure she's not even interested in me. How could she be?"

The two boys lay on the golf course, their eyes closed. Gradually, they became aware of the sound of approaching footsteps.

"Well, well. With all that sighing and groaning in the air, I knew

Franklyn Elore had to be here."

Franklyn opened his eyes to see Vito grinning down at him. He lifted his hand. "Will you help me up?"

"Actually, I thought I might join you down there." Vito flopped down on the other side of Zeke. "I take it you've already seen Isabella."

"She's even more lovely than last summer."

"She's certainly filled out. My mother is insanely jealous."

"Does she still want you to ask her out?"

"Of course. She could swallow any amount of jealousy with a billion-dollar chaser."

"What if you just . . . you know, told her the truth?"

"You're kidding, right?"

"It would solve the problem," said Franklyn defensively.

"I know. I've come close. *Really* close, but then . . ." He shook his head. "I just can't."

Zeke patted Vito sympathetically on the head.

Then Vito said, "You know, Franklyn, if *you* just asked Isabella out, that would help both of us."

"Now *you're* the one who's joking."

"It's not so crazy," said Vito defensively.

"She's out of my league."

"True," admitted Vito.

"And, even if by some miracle she said yes, you know my mother would never approve."

"Your mother's GPA requirement is a little strict," said Vito. "Not everyone can nail a three point seven five every quarter."

"I actually talked her down from a four point oh, arguing that the occasional imperfect grade builds character."

"Still, I hear Isabella gets a three point five, which is better than I ever got. She's not exactly stupid."

"Of course she isn't. But trying to explain that to my mother . . ."

Now it was Franklyn's turn to get a sympathetic pat from Zeke.

They lay there listening to the birdsong, the wind rustling the grass, and far in the distance, the sound of an actual golf club striking a golf ball.

"I saw Brice today, training the new pool boy," said Vito. "He takes it all so seriously. It's adorable."

"You should ask him out," said Franklyn.

"Right after I tell my mom I'm gay?"

"You could do it in secret. In the old days, people did that all the time."

"She would know," said Vito. "Even if she didn't, I'd hate lying about it. Besides, I don't even think he's interested in me."

"With all your muscles and things?" Franklyn reached across Zeke and poked Vito's large bicep.

"I know, right?" said Vito. "But he never even looks at me. So maybe he just . . . doesn't like muscles."

"Which would be so unfair."

"Love is unfair," said Vito.

"And hopeless," said Franklyn.

Zeke patted them both on their heads at the same time.

"Sometimes I feel guilty that Vito and I always dump everything on you, Zeke," said Franklyn.

"Oh, Zeke doesn't mind, do you?" asked Vito.

Zeke smiled in a self-satisfied way. Dear reader, if you have ever had to tromp around on a hot golf course for hours, lugging someone else's ungainly golf bag filled with long metal objects, then you too would most likely prefer lying in the shade, half-listening to rich boys complain, instead.

Lena and Isabella sat in their bathing suits in the sauna. Lena didn't much care for any room designed specifically to make one uncomfortably hot. She was even less fond of jumping into the bracingly cold pool immediately after. But Dr. Elore had suggested it to Isabella the previous summer as being good for her complexion, and even though Lena pointed out that Dr. Elore's PhD was in ancient history, not dermatology, it had become a daily late afternoon ritual.

"Why won't you tell me anything about this new pool boy?" asked Isabella. The heat challenged even her perkiness. In the sauna, the best she could manage was vivaciousness.

"There isn't much to tell," said Lena dismissively. "I only just met him this morning."

The thing about being vivacious was that it sometimes led one to poke at topics another person clearly wished to avoid talking about.

"Where's he from? Where does he go to school? Is he single?"

"He's from the city but moves around a lot. He goes to a different school every year, too. Honestly, looking at his résumé, I wouldn't have hired him. But he's somehow acquainted with one of your father's friends."

"So he has connections," said Isabella. "How mysterious!"

Lena wiped the excessive sweat from her forehead. "Why do you keep pushing this?"

Isabella pouted. "Because it would be a lot more fun to pine over Franklyn if you had someone to pine over as well."

"Let us say, for the sake of argument, that I found young Mr. Kean attractive. Even so, I am not the kind of girl who *pines*."

Isabella rubbed her sweaty hands together. "Still, it wouldn't hurt to show him a *little* encouragement. He might be handy to have around this summer."

"Use him, you mean?" asked Lena.

"Of course! What other purpose do boys serve? You can use them for all sorts of things—carrying, building, fixing, remembering. And some of them are quite nice to look at."

"There are practical and aesthetic advantages to the idea of keeping one on hand," admitted Lena.

"Just think about it. Are you ready to jump in the pool?"

The women's sauna opened out to the locker rooms. Lena and Isabella walked past a cluster of elderly naked women and toward the pool. As they neared the entrance, they heard the distinct scratchy tones of Ms. Nalone.

"The reason your son is still single is because he's a clumsy nerd who never takes his nose out of a book!"

"Well," came the flat tone of Dr. Elore, "the reason *your* son is still single is because he's a brutish lout who can hardly form a coherent sentence!"

"Is it that time already?" asked Lena.

"I hope they haven't started throwing things yet," said Isabella.

The two girls hurried out to the pool deck. Ms. Nalone and Dr. Elore stood glaring at each other. It appeared they hadn't thrown anything yet, but that phase wasn't far off. This was particularly unfortunate for Arlo, who stood between them, directly in the line of fire.

He held up his hands. "Now, ladies, please. Let's just take a moment to calm down."

"Eggheaded sow!" yelled Ms. Nalone.

"Withered bimbo!" yelled Dr. Elore.

"What is that boy doing?" muttered Lena.

"Being brave and heroic," said Isabella, and gave her a nudge.

"Heroism is overrated, and bravery often accompanies stupidity," said Lena. "Besides, he won't be much use if he's knocked unconscious with that bottle of wine."

"I've always thought of a ninety-eight sauvignon blanc as rather light," said Isabella.

"I'm afraid the bottle will hurt the same, regardless of the grape and vintage."

With two hands, Ms. Nalone held the bottle of wine by the neck, ready to bring it down on Arlo's head if he didn't get out of the way. But he stood steadfastly between them. No, Lena corrected herself. "Steadfast" sounded far too appealing and complimentary. He stood *obstinately*. Yes, that sounded more disagreeable.

"Bimbo, am I?" Ms. Nalone snarled. "I'll crack that egg head of yours wide open!"

"I doubt your withered arms even have the muscle mass to swing that bottle!" said Dr. Elore.

"*Do* something, Lena," said Isabella. "We don't want poor Arlo to get hurt."

Lena sighed. "I suppose I must."

"That's it, you pompous, bloated tick," shouted Ms. Nalone. "Let's settle this once and for all!"

"Agreed!" Dr. Elore shouted back.

"Now, ladies." Lena stepped coolly into the fray, beside Arlo. "This simply won't do."

"Don't try to stop me!" said Ms. Nalone, hefting her wine bottle.

"Naturally not," said Lena. "But if you're going to settle this once and for all, as you suggest, then you should do it properly."

Ms. Nalone's bottle lowered slightly. "Properly?"

"A duel, of course," said Lena. "I assume you'll name your sons as your seconds. Shall I ask Arlo to fetch the pistols?" She looked first at Ms. Nalone, then at Dr. Elore, both of whom seemed nonplussed by the suggestion.

"Why . . . I . . ." spluttered Ms. Nalone. "I've never fired a pistol in my life!"

"That would be somewhat of a disadvantage," agreed Lena. "Should I have him fetch the rapiers instead? It's a bit old-fashioned, but far less likely to be fatal. Generally, duels with swords result in minor dismemberment at worst."

"Dismemberment?" Dr. Elore's large eyes widened further behind her glasses.

"I shouldn't worry too much, doctor," said Lena. "They have made astonishing strides in prosthetics these days."

"But . . . I've never fought anyone with a sword, either," said Ms. Nalone.

"I don't see how that should make much difference," said Lena. "After all, I doubt you've ever fought someone with a hundred-dollar bottle of wine. And I'm sure I don't need to tell you that, regardless of the outcome of the duel, should the bottle break, it would be charged to your room."

"A hundred dollars?" Ms. Nalone looked down at the bottle.

"Yes," said Lena. "So it would be preferable if you selected a more appropriately durable weapon. What will it be, then? Spears? Bow and arrow? Knives?"

Ms. Nalone stared at her.

Lena turned to Dr. Elore. "It appears Ms. Nalone is deferring to your choice, doctor. Gallant, under the circumstances. What is *your* weapon preference? If you want to keep the bleeding to a minimum, may I suggest something blunt, such as billy clubs? Or perhaps baseball bats. It is baseball season."

Dr. Elore looked pale.

"Well, if neither of you are willing to select a weapon, we will need to postpone the duel."

"Yes . . ." said Ms. Nalone. "I suppose we must . . ."

"Agreed," said Dr. Elore.

There was a long pause while everyone stared at one another. Nothing like this had ever happened before at the Hotel del Arte.

Brice appeared in the doorway. He looked around, noting the oddly subdued tone. "Is everything all right?"

"Perfectly," said Lena.

"Great. Well, everyone, it's time to dress for dinner."

The entire pool deck took a collective breath.

"Thanks for the assist," Arlo said to Lena, as the guests headed into the hotel to change into their evening wear.

"Assist?" asked Lena.

"Yeah. I mean, I had it under control, but I appreciate the help."

Lena was about to inform Arlo that he'd had absolutely nothing under control. But as she looked into his smiling face, a lock of curly hair dangling over one eye, she recalled Isabella's suggestion. Perhaps it wouldn't hurt to expend *some* effort. So instead, she smiled. "It was courageous of you to step in like that on your first day. Dumb. But courageous."

This scrap of encouragement worked on Arlo like a plant starved for water. He positively bloomed—his back straightened, his smile broadened, and his eyes brightened. Lena, who was generally not in the habit of lavishing praise, found it an interesting and potentially useful reaction.

"It was really smart how you talked them out of it, though," said Arlo.

"I suppose," said Lena, "we make a good team."

Arlo's chest puffed up with pride. "I agree."

"Well, I must change and see to the Ficollos," said Lena.

"I have to admit, I didn't peg you for a girl who would wear a bikini," said Arlo.

"Why not?" Lena turned and headed toward the door. "I happen to know I look fantastic in a bikini."

"Another thing we agree on," Arlo said quietly. Then louder, "Oh, hey, Zeke and I will be at the basketball courts after work. If you don't have other plans, you could stop by."

Lena stopped and considered the invitation. It was nicely done, she had to admit. Including Zeke gave it a cordial, no-pressure tone that eliminated the risk of those awkward professions of love she had so disliked having thrust upon her in the past. Also, there was something she needed to ask Zeke. "Perhaps I will."

"Great!" The resulting smile looked at risk of splitting Arlo's face in half.

As Lena headed for the dining room, she wondered what she had just set in motion. Arlo reacted to her kindness like an eager puppy. A decidedly adorable puppy, she had to admit. If she wasn't more careful with how she dispensed future praise, she could very well find herself making a habit of it.

"You should have seen it, Zeke," said Arlo as he shot the basketball. "She *handled* those two old biddies." The ball banked off the backboard and dropped through the hoop. Zeke caught the rebound and passed it back to Arlo. "And get this. She told me that we make a *good team*." He chuckled and shot the ball again. "How about that."

The ball rolled around the hoop and fell out. Zeke got the rebound again, but this time dribbled back to the three-point line.

"Oh, I hope you don't mind, I told her she could meet us here after work," said Arlo.

Zeke shrugged, then sank the three-pointer.

"Nice one." Arlo rebounded. He dribbled a few times as he stared up into the evening sky. There were so many more stars out here in the country. "It's just, I've never met a girl like Lena before. And I've met a *lot* of girls. She's . . . interesting . . . and beautiful . . . and she calls me on shit. I kinda like that." He passed the ball back to Zeke. "Not that I'm in love or anything ridiculous like that. Love is the worst thing that can happen to a guy. It makes them idiots."

Zeke rolled his eyes and bounced the ball hard at Arlo, who caught it and spun it on his finger. Zeke clapped, looking impressed.

"You think that's cool? Watch this." Arlo kept the ball spinning as he passed it back and forth between his hands, then under one leg, then behind his back.

Zeke clapped again.

"More Harlem Globetrotter than NBA all-star." Lena had just arrived and now stood courtside, her arms crossed. "Why am I not surprised?"

Arlo tossed the ball high, gave her a quick bow, then caught the ball again.

"How was your first day?" she asked.

"More exciting than I expected," he said.

"And how was *your* first day back, Zeke?" she asked.

Zeke gave her a thumbs-up, then caught the ball from Arlo and took another shot.

"Zeke, I hate to put you on the spot, but I promised Isabella I'd ask," said Lena. "You caddied for Franklyn this afternoon, didn't you?"

Zeke smirked and nodded, perhaps wondering if it should be referred to as caddying or as therapy.

"Did he talk about Isabella at all?"

Zeke pressed one hand to his heart and the other to his forehead, making an expression somewhere between rapture and swoon.

"I thought so," said Lena. "Still too frightened to ask her out. Ah well. Same as last summer, I suppose. The two of them stealing longing looks at each other across the table."

Zeke stuck out his tongue.

"True," she said. "But there's nothing to be done."

"What's this?" asked Arlo.

"Franklyn and Isabella have been secretly pining for each other for years, but neither has the courage to act on it."

Arlo dribbled the ball between his legs. "Sounds like they just need a push."

"From whom?" Lena looked genuinely perplexed.

"Us, of course."

Lena and Zeke exchanged an uncomfortable glance. Then she said, "That seems rather meddlesome, not to mention presumptuous."

"I prefer 'solicitous' and 'proactive,'" said Arlo.

"Spin it as much as you spin that ball," said Lena. "It amounts to the same thing."

"Sounds like you're afraid of shaking things up." Arlo took a shot, and the ball went through the hoop with a swish.

"Sounds like you enjoy it," said Lena.

"Only when it suits me," said Arlo. "Think about it. There's Isabella and that Franklyn, then there's Brice and Vito. All four of them pining for each other and nobody doing a thing about it."

"How did you know about Brice and Vito?" asked Lena.

"Because I have eyeballs. Don't tell me—that's been going on for years, too."

Lena and Zeke exchanged a guilty look.

"Think how much happier both couples might be together," Arlo continued. "And think about how much easier it would be for us if they stopped whining all the time."

Zeke put his hand on Lena's shoulder and gave her a pleading look.

"You want to do this, too?" she asked.

He gave a serious, emphatic nod.

"If you feel that strongly about it . . ." She crossed her arms and looked warily at Arlo. "What did you have in mind?"

Arlo grinned. "Something that's going to take all three of us to pull off."

The next day, at Lena's suggestion, Isabella invited Dr. Elore, Franklyn, Ms. Nalone, and Vito to join her in exploring the new hedge maze that her father had installed for her. Additionally, and also at Lena's suggestion, Isabella insisted that Arlo and Brice be on hand in case anyone became lost or needed assistance.

Dr. Elore and Franklyn were mildly intrigued by the idea of a labyrinth, both being enamored with intellectual puzzles. And of course Franklyn relished any event that might put him in close proximity to Miss Ficollo.

Ms. Nalone and Vito were less enthusiastic about the invitation. Ms. Nalone chafed at the hours missed from direct sunlight, and the event cut into Vito's usual weight training time. But Ms. Nalone saw it as an opportunity to get Vito and Miss Ficollo together, and Vito became much more interested when he learned Brice would be there.

Brice was beside himself with worry about what might happen to the resort while it wasn't under his watchful eye, but he could hardly decline Miss Ficollo's request.

"Thank you all for coming," said Isabella as everyone gathered at the maze's southern entrance. She gave them a smile that, had it been properly witnessed and documented, might have stood in the *Guinness Book of World Records* as the perkiest ever achieved. "I'd like to get started on our adventure!"

"Is there a program?" asked the doctor, who approved of plans, programs, and schedules.

"I'm so glad you asked, doctor," said Isabella. "Yes. We can't wander the maze in one big clump, so we'll break into groups. There are several entrances to the maze. Ms. Nalone, Vito, and I, accompanied by Lena, will take the southern entrance here. Dr. Elore and Franklyn, accompanied by Arlo and Brice, will take the east entrance. We'll converge at the center of the maze, which has a beautiful fountain and a delicious picnic lunch laid out for us. Doesn't that sound lovely?"

"It certainly does!" said Ms. Nalone, who was pleased that Vito and Miss Ficollo would have so much time together. Perhaps a spark or two might ignite.

The other responses of approval were more forced. Franklyn had hoped to be in Isabella's group, and Vito had hoped to be with Brice.

"Marvelous!" said Isabella. "Then let's begin. And try not to get lost. It would be a shame if the picnic spoiled."

So the groups divided and entered at the same time, from separate entrances. What Lena and Arlo had neglected to tell anyone else was that Zeke was already inside the maze, waiting for the signal.

There are hedge mazes that are like charming paths, and then there are actual mazes made of ten-foot-tall, impenetrably dense hedges. This was the latter. Those who did not know Isabella well might have been surprised that she had a true passion for them. She not only had requested the maze but also had designed it herself. That had been a year ago, though. She knew she might not recall every twist and turn, so she had intended to bring her blueprints, in case one of her guests became lost and needed to be rescued. But she was unable to locate them. Lena had assured her they would turn up eventually, and for the purposes of the day, she had complete confidence in Isabella to lead them through by memory.

Lena continued to exhibit that confidence, even after it became abundantly clear to Ms. Nalone and Vito that Isabella had a dreadful memory.

"I could have sworn it was *this* turn that brought us into the next section," Isabella said, mostly to herself.

"Vito, why don't you see if you can help," said Ms. Nalone, giving her son a meaningful look. In her mind, there were few things more attractive than some masculine, take-charge action. She assumed, incorrectly, that Isabella felt the same.

"But I'm awful at mazes," said Vito, who didn't mind taking masculine action, but only when it was something he was actually knowledgeable about or skilled at.

Ms. Nalone sighed in exasperation. She pulled Vito aside, letting Isabella and Lena turn a corner.

"Don't you get it?" she hissed. "This is your chance to make a move!"

"Don't *you* get that I'm not going to?" he asked.

Ms. Nalone released his arm and hurried to catch up with the girls. It was clear that Vito would be no help. Perhaps he was worried that Isabella would reject his advances, crazy as that seemed. Maybe if she spoke to Isabella on his behalf, she could get her to show some glimmer of interest in him, and it would give him the confidence to ask her out. Yes, that's how it would work.

"Isabella, dear."

But when Ms. Nalone turned the corner, Isabella and Lena were gone.

"How did you know about this bypass?" Isabella asked Lena, as they walked alone down a long, straight path.

"Oh, I just remember it from the first time we tested out the maze." Lena felt a stab of guilt. She didn't like lying to Isabella. But she had promised Arlo she wouldn't confess that they'd stolen (*secretly borrowed*, he'd insisted on calling it) the blueprints until after their plan came to fruition.

"I wish I had your memory," Isabella said wistfully. "Still, it seems a bit like cheating, don't you think?"

"It was more to get us away from Ms. Nalone," said Lena. "I hope you don't mind."

"Not at all. You were the one who insisted they be in our group. I would have much preferred the Elores."

"I didn't expect Ms. Nalone to start pushing her son on you so intensely," said Lena.

"Pushing Vito on *me*?" asked Isabella, looking bewildered.

"Hadn't you noticed? She's been trying for years."

"But Vito's gay, isn't he?"

"I don't think she realizes."

"Good gracious, then she's the only one," said Isabella. "Do you think she'll keep trying all summer? How tedious."

"She might give up if you were to make your interest in someone else more plain."

"Franklyn, you mean?" Isabella sighed. "Every time I try to get less formal with him, he runs away. He's made it plain he's not interested in pursuing that course."

"On the contrary," said Lena.

"How do you mean?"

"Would you say young Mr. Elore has a gentle nature?"

"Why, yes of course."

"And a poetic soul?"

"The most poetic I've ever encountered."

"Wouldn't it be feasible, then, that your overtures so overwhelm his sensitive nature with feelings of affection that he simply doesn't know how to handle his own ardor?"

Isabella's eyes grew wide. "Could I have that much of an effect on him?"

Lena smiled. "I have it on good authority you do."

"Oh, Lena!" Isabella took her friend's hands. "What must I do then to sway his delicate heart?"

"Perhaps a poem to win the poet? Something that allows you to express your feelings for him without overwhelming him with your beauty at the same time."

"But I'm *terrible* at poetry. I adore it, but I couldn't rhyme a couplet if my life depended on it."

"Then I will help you," said Lena.

Isabella squeezed her hands. "Would you? When should we do it?"

"Why not now?" Lena produced a small notebook and pen from her pocket.

Isabella's eyes narrowed. "There's some scheme at work here."

"Scheme, Miss Ficollo?" asked Lena. "I'm not sure what you mean. I always have pen and paper on hand."

"In the three years we have been together, I have never known that to be the case."

"Very well," Lena said gravely. "Then may I ask you to simply trust me this once?"

"Silly Lena," said Isabella, taking the pen and notebook. "I trust you always. Now, how should it begin?"

"What do you mean, there's a plan?" Brice whispered to Arlo. The Elores were far ahead of them, but Brice was never one to take chances. And at the moment, that was the problem.

"I mean exactly that," said Arlo. "Lena, Zeke, and I have devised a scheme to get Franklyn and Isabella together that requires your help." Arlo decided it would be premature to let him know that far more than his help would be requested. "And don't chew your nails."

"What?" Brice guiltily pulled his hand away from his mouth.

"Lena said when I sprang this on you, you might be tempted to fall back on nail-biting as a means of coping."

"Nonsense." Brice turned up his nose in disdain. "And so is this whole wretched idea. What business is it of ours if Franklyn and Isabella get together or not?"

"Don't be like that, Brice," said Arlo. "Think of the looks of joy on their faces when they're finally united."

"Think of the cooing and giggling and hand-holding," said Brice. "The public displays of affection."

"I promise you'll hardly notice," said Arlo, who was of the firm belief that the only people who disliked seeing other people kiss were those not being kissed themselves—something he hoped to remedy for Brice. "Look, all I need you to do is take the good doctor ahead while I work on Franklyn."

Brice gave him a disgruntled look. "This won't end well."

"That depends on your personal feelings regarding the fulfillment of true love," said Arlo.

"Fine," said Brice. "But you *owe* me. All three of you."

Arlo winked. "Agreed. Now, let's catch up with our guests." They hurried toward the Elores as they made a turn.

"The history of garden mazes is a curious one," the doctor was saying to Franklyn.

"Mmm," said Franklyn, who did not seem at all interested.

"Really, doctor?" asked Brice, with perhaps more enthusiasm than might realistically be expressed. "I'd be so grateful to know about it!"

"You would?" asked the doctor.

"I always love to impart tidbits of knowledge on guests." Brice smiled. "It gives them a more well-rounded experience here at the Hotel del Arte."

The doctor looked pleased. "That is certainly an insightful and admirable goal. Very well, then. I believe the first true hedge mazes were constructed in the mid-sixteenth century, although there are some gardens with mazelike qualities dating back to as early as the fifteenth . . ."

As the doctor began her discourse, she and Brice moved slowly ahead, while Arlo and Franklyn lagged behind.

"You're the new pool boy, right?" Franklyn asked.

"Arlo Kean, at your service, Mr. Elore."

"Second day on the job, Arlo, and already being invited on special events. You must have made quite an impression."

"I'm happy to say, Miss Cole finds me indispensable."

"Is that so?" Franklyn looked impressed. "Lena Cole is a devastatingly intelligent and capable woman. You could not come more highly recommended."

They had reached a four-way intersection in the maze. The doctor and Brice turned to the west. Franklyn was about to follow them when Arlo said, "Mr. Elore, do you see that?" He pointed to a rolled-up piece of paper sticking out of the hedges in the north corridor, where Zeke had notified him by text that he'd planted it, after retrieving it from Lena.

Franklyn stopped and stared at it. "A note of some kind?"

"Should I retrieve it, sir?" asked Arlo.

"Do you think we should?" Franklyn asked nervously.

"Fortune favors the bold," said Arlo. Without waiting for further waffling, he pulled the paper from the hedge. He unrolled it and made some small show of surprise. Nothing too dramatic. "It appears to be addressed to you, sir."

"Me?" asked Franklyn, with the sort of surprise normally reserved for statements like "You have been accepted at Hogwarts School of Witchcraft and Wizardry."

Arlo held out the note. "See for yourself."

Franklyn timidly took the offered sheet of paper. Arlo was glad to see that Brice had taken the doctor down another passageway, out of both hearing and sight.

"Oh, my . . ." said Franklyn. "Listen to this!"

"Do you think that's okay?" asked Arlo. "I'd hate to pry."

"I *need* you to hear it. To tell me if I'm awake rather than dreaming! To make sure I understand the contents of this missive and am not deluded with wishful thinking."

"I'll do my best, sir," said Arlo.

Franklyn cleared his throat.

To my own, dearest Franklyn:
These gentle words are for your gentle heart.
Forgive me if I do not play the part—
I know I should be shy and blushing sweet,
But Love insists I cannot be discreet.
I offer you these lines from which we start,
Though they be more of sentiment than art,
For without you I'll never feel complete.
If you feel the same, tell me next we meet.
With fondest love and affection, your own dearest Isabella.

Franklyn gripped the paper, which ruffled as tremors of passion washed through him. He looked pleadingly at Arlo. "Could this be real? I have never thought life could be so cruel as to show me dreams come true, then yank them away. But neither have I ever found it to be so benevolent as to fulfill them so completely."

Arlo nodded shrewdly. "You're wise to be cautious, sir. For all we know, it could have been written by someone else."

Franklyn examined the paper. "It does appear to be her handwriting, which I have noted in the past to possess a distinctive perkiness."

Arlo peered over his shoulder. "It *looks* like hers. But could it be a forgery?"

"I suppose," admitted Franklyn. "But to what end? Furthermore, the tone of the letter is very much in keeping with her speech."

Arlo thought he heard a bit too much Lena coming through, but was grateful Franklyn was not particularly objective in his analysis. "True. So the evidence confirms that this letter is from Isabella."

Franklyn shook his head in wonder. "How can a man be so lucky?"

"Lucky?" asked Arlo. "More like doomed."

"Doomed? What do you mean?"

"It seems clear she means to have you for her own," said Arlo sadly.

"Yes," said Franklyn, a dreamy smile spreading across his face.

"With passion that deep," continued Arlo, his voice mournful as he adopted the more poetical speech of his companion, "she will be satisfied with nothing less than the union of your two souls."

"Do you really think so?" Franklyn stared at the note, glassy-eyed and beatific.

"I'm afraid you can kiss freedom good-bye. From now on, your lips belong to Miss Ficollo."

"Oh, God." Tears sprang from Franklyn's eyes.

"There, there." Arlo patted his back. Then his eyes narrowed thoughtfully. "Wait. Maybe if we leave this garden maze right now, you can still escape love in the arms of Miss Ficollo."

Franklyn looked at him in horror. "You must be joking!"

"You would prefer love and Miss Ficollo to freedom?" demanded Arlo.

"I would prefer love and Miss Ficollo to all the riches in the world! To all the knowledge one could gain! You say I should avoid her embrace, but I have longed for it since the moment I first saw her. Her eyes transport me. Her voice soothes me. Her words move me. There is no one in this world I find more beautiful, more noble, or more true."

"That's how you really feel about Miss Ficollo?" asked Arlo.

"That times a thousand and more!" declared Franklyn.

"Why have you never told her?" asked Arlo.

"It is my own damned shyness that betrays me," admitted Franklyn. "When I look into her radiant face, words abandon me."

"Well," said Arlo, "you do a fine job telling her how you feel when you're *not* looking into her radiant face."

"I beg your pardon?" Franklyn looked confused.

Arlo took Franklyn by the shoulders and spun him around. Standing a short way down the south corridor were Isabella and Lena.

"Dearest Franklyn." Isabella's eyes were wet with tears. "Is that truly how you feel?"

Franklyn seemed frozen, unable to move. But then he broke free from the ice of his own dread. "Fortune *does* favor the bold. And so I say yes, Isabella! I have loved you for so long, I cannot remember a time when I didn't! You are my one true love, now and forever!"

"This is the part where you kiss her," murmured Arlo, and gave him a push.

Franklyn first stumbled, then ran into Isabella's waiting arms. They kissed, long and deep.

Lena strolled over to stand beside Arlo. "So far, the plan is going well."

"I'd say so," agreed Arlo. "Lovely verse, by the way."

"It was easier than I expected," said Lena.

"Careful," said Arlo. "Some people say love is contagious. You might start writing verses of your own next."

"I believe my constitution can handle it," said Lena. "But what about yours?"

"Fortunately, I have been vaccinated against love by a mixture of intelligence and good common sense," said Arlo.

"That is a relief," said Lena.

They watched the lovers kiss in silence.

It is this author's considered opinion that people talk entirely too much. Words, which should be used to communicate, are often used for the exact opposite purpose. As our two heroes stood next to each other, unprotected by their word shields, witnessing the union they orchestrated together, each could not help but be intensely aware of the other's presence. Of the other's warmth, of their distinctive scent, of the rise and fall of their chest. Of any perceptible movement toward them. Perhaps Arlo leaned ever so slightly in Lena's direction. We might even suppose it was unintentional. But, as all the world knows, there are naturally attractive forces between particles, and the closer the particles, the stronger the attraction. So that slight movement exerted itself upon Lena, who in turn leaned slightly toward Arlo. This continued for several minutes, the space between them gradually shrinking as the longing for each other grew. But before contact could be made, an opposing force appeared.

"What on earth is going on here?" Dr. Elore appeared with crossed arms, her formidable brow folded over the top of her thick glasses. Brice stood beside her, looking apologetic. "Franklyn, what do you and Miss Ficollo think you're doing?"

Franklyn and Isabella broke apart, embarrassed.

Brice hurried over to Arlo and Lena, who had regained some of the space between them. "Sorry! Zeke brought us back. I guess too soon."

"Not at all," said Lena. "I texted him a few minutes ago to bring you." She turned to Franklyn's mother. "Dr. Elore, you know perfectly well what they're doing, and it should come as no surprise to you since your son has been in love with Miss Ficollo for years."

"It *is* a surprise," said Dr. Elore. "Because I expressly forbid him from seeing her."

"And why is that?" asked Lena.

"It's none of your business, but if you must know, she is simply not smart enough for him."

"Mother!" Franklyn placed an arm protectively around Isabella. "Must you be so insensitive?"

"How do you *know* she's not smart enough?" pressed Lena.

"Her grade point average, of course," said the doctor, "which she freely admits to being a mere three point five last quarter."

"But do you know *why* it was a three point five?" asked Lena.

"Oh, Lena." Isabella blushed even harder than before. "I don't know if we need to go into all that . . ."

Lena inclined her head to Isabella. "I hope you will forgive my boldness, Miss Ficollo." She turned back to Dr. Elore. "The reason she received a three point five is because she walked out on her Women's History elective. The teacher was a man, and his view of women's history was so narrow that he did not even acknowledge Rosalind Franklin as being instrumental in the discovery of DNA. Miss Ficollo found his perspective troubling and met with him privately to ask that he broaden his views. The teacher refused. Of course, Miss Ficollo could have accepted the class for what it was, or she could have changed her elective. But she couldn't bear the thought of such narrow-mindedness in the vaunted halls of education. So she staged a walkout, and three-fourths of the class, both girls and boys, followed her. The teacher failed them all in retaliation, but because of Miss Ficollo's bold actions, he and his course are now being reevaluated by the school administration."

Dr. Elore turned to Isabella. "Is this true, Miss Ficollo? Is the integrity of education so important to you that you would sacrifice your own grade?"

"It is, Dr. Elore."

The doctor looked at her son. "Franklyn, it appears I owe you an apology. Your taste in women is impeccable."

"Does this mean . . . ?" he asked.

"You and Miss Ficollo have my blessing."

"Oh, Franklyn!" said Isabella.

"Oh, Isabella!" said Franklyn.

And the kissing began again. Dr. Elore decided this would be an excellent time to forge ahead and locate the picnic on her own.

"You promised I wouldn't have to watch this," Brice said to Arlo.

"Don't worry," said Arlo. "Soon you'll be far too busy to notice."

"What does *that* mean?" asked Brice.

But before Arlo could answer, a raspy female voice said, "What the hell is this?"

Everyone turned to the north corridor, where Ms. Nalone and Vito stared at Franklyn and Isabella. Ms. Nalone looked horrified, while Vito looked overjoyed. Behind them, Zeke stood with a quiet smirk on his face.

"I just . . . don't understand!" continued Ms. Nalone. "Miss Ficollo, you prefer nerdy Franklyn over my Vito?"

"Well . . ." Isabella glanced awkwardly at Vito for a moment, then to his mother. "I love Franklyn. And it isn't as if Vito has shown any interest."

"See?" Ms. Nalone turned on Vito. "You missed your window!"

"Oh well," he said dryly.

"Why have you been so impossible? It's like you've purposefully set out to deny my wishes! Do you hate me that much, that you're willing to throw away this gem of a girl just to spite me?"

"Forgodsake, Mother, it's not about you at all!" Vito said. "It's because I'm in love with Brice!"

Ms. Nalone's mouth opened, then closed, then opened again. It seemed likely that a riot of emotions would have contorted her face, if not for the aforementioned Botox injections. "Vito, that's absurd!"

"Why, Mother? Are you homophobic?"

"Of course not, dear. Homophobia is terribly out of fashion," said Ms. Nalone. "What I object to is you falling in love with a *resort manager*. What kind of living is that?"

Brice, by this time, had turned a shade of red typically reserved for tomatoes. "Ms. Nalone. If I may speak for a moment not as the staff manager of Hotel del Arte but as a man, plain and simple, I can assure you that if Mr. Nalone and I were to enter into a relationship, I could provide him with the lifestyle he is accustomed to."

"But what about *me*?" said Ms. Nalone.

"Mother . . ." Vito looked stricken.

"Excuse me?" asked Brice.

"Who will support *me*?" demanded Ms. Nalone.

There was a moment of total silence.

"If you need money, Ms. Nalone," said Isabella tentatively, "I'm sure my father would be happy to find some employment for you."

Ms. Nalone could only stare at her in horror.

"If I may," said Lena. "There is a more pressing question than Ms. Nalone's employment viability."

"What question is that?" asked Franklyn.

"We have established that Vito is in love with Brice. We have established that Brice is able to support Vito in a lifestyle to which he is accustomed. What we have not established is whether Brice wishes to do so."

"*Thank* you," said Brice. "It's—"

"So presumptuous!" said Arlo. "Do you all think the staff of the Hotel del Arte are here to cater to your every whim?"

Franklyn, Isabella, and Vito looked at each other in confusion.

"Of course not," said Isabella. "I cherish my friendship with Lena immensely."

"I don't know how I would have gotten through all these summers without Zeke's silent but unflagging support," said Franklyn.

"And I would never *assume* Brice cares for me as I do for him," said Vito.

"Good!" said Arlo. "Because he doesn't!"

"Wait a minute—" said Brice.

"First of all," continued Arlo, "Hotel del Arte staff are expressly forbidden from getting romantically involved with guests."

"Are they?" asked Isabella.

"I don't recall seeing that in the employee handbook," said Lena.

"Not expressly, no . . ." admitted Brice. "It's more of a . . . uh, guideline?"

"So it's not a rule!" said Arlo. "So what? Because our own sweet Mr. Ghello isn't even *interested* in dating you, Mr. Nalone."

"I didn't say that . . ." said Brice.

"Because he's straight!" said Arlo.

"Are you?" Vito asked Brice.

"No, I'm pretty gay," said Brice.

"But who cares!" said Arlo. "You can't assume he likes all those big, tanned muscles just because he's gay. In fact, he *hates* big, tanned muscles!"

"Actually, I like the muscles," said Brice.

"Fine!" said Arlo. "So he likes muscles. But you can't expect him to be attracted to a man so submissive to his mother!"

"It's really quite sweet," Brice told Vito. "Honestly, it's one of the reasons I didn't want to push anything. I didn't want to put a strain on your relationship with your mother."

"So he finds Vito's relationship with his mother sweet!" said Arlo. "But you can't expect a wild, vibrant, hedonist to settle down in the prime of his life. Mr. Ghello has seeds to sow! Conquests to make! Hearts to break!"

"I'm really more of a domestic," said Brice.

"Yes! But all of that aside, he still doesn't want to involve himself romantically with Mr. Nalone because . . ." Arlo looked expectantly at Brice. "Come on, I can't come up with *all* the reasons. What else?"

"I can't think of anything," said Brice.

"Oh." Arlo looked deflated. "You're sure?"

"What I'm sure of," said Brice as he took Vito's hand, "is that I would love to take you to dinner off the resort and get to know you better. If that interests you?"

Vito smiled. "Very much."

Lena nudged Arlo. He tried to ignore the warmth her touch kindled within his chest.

"You almost overplayed that," she whispered in his ear. It was more or less impossible to ignore the shiver that ran through him as her breath touched his ear, so he thought the fair thing to do was retaliate in kind.

"Nah, it was perfect," Arlo whispered back, noting with satisfaction that Lena shivered slightly.

"I suppose everything worked out, regardless," said Lena.

Arlo grinned. "You have to admit, it was a lot of fun."

A smile slowly worked its way onto Lena's face. "Yes. As a matter of fact, it was."

"All right, Miss Cole." Isabella gave her a steely, decidedly unperky look. "And you, too, Mr. Kean. I suppose you're both quite pleased with your little matchmaking schemes."

Arlo shrugged. "I suppose we are."

"It was with your best interests at heart," said Lena.

"I don't doubt it," said Isabella. "But there's an aspect of this you both missed. Wouldn't you say, Franklyn?" Isabella gave him a wink.

Franklyn frowned. "Is there?"

Isabella sighed and whispered something in his ear. His eyes widened, and he gave Lena and Arlo a wicked smile. "There is indeed, my dearest Isabella."

"You don't think . . ." said Brice.

"I think she does," said Vito.

"What are we missing?" demanded Arlo.

"It's perfectly obvious that they mean us," said Lena.

"You and me? In love?" Arlo asked incredulously.

"It would seem that is their intent."

"Love? Me?" he asked. "Ridiculous!"

"People who fall in love lose all ability to think logically," said Lena.

"Common sense leaps right out the window," said Arlo, nodding his agreement as he leaned in toward her again.

"Any wit they might have had leaves them," said Lena, leaning in as well.

"I don't think I could ever fall in love," said Arlo, leaning in just a little more. "Not even with a woman as brilliant and attractive as you."

"I couldn't agree more," said Lena, matching him in closeness. "It doesn't matter that you might be nearly my intellectual equal and look fantastic in tight khaki shorts. I would never allow myself to succumb to something as banal as love."

By this time, the two had leaned in to each other so closely that they were staring directly into each other's eyes. Still they had not touched, and the tiny space between them crackled. If longing could be converted into electricity, they would have powered the resort for a year.

"I would go so far as to say," said Arlo, his breath coming fast, obviously from talking so much and not from the effort of maintaining that tiny space between them, "that the only person I could ever truly spend my life with is someone who loathes love as much as I do."

"Agreed," said Lena, her breath as fast as his, no doubt because she wished to show that she could respire just as strongly as him. "And now that we have firmly established this fact, that neither of us would ever consider love as an option, I suppose"—she took his hands in hers, feeling the spark run through her body—"there would be no risk in forming some sort of intimate relationship."

Arlo entwined their hands further until he could feel her strident pulse pound. "Since we're the only two sane people on earth, common sense dictates we are perfectly suited for each other."

"There's only one final test before we know that for certain." Lena leaned in so close their noses almost touched.

"What is that?" asked Arlo, his eyes a little glassy.

"I loathe bad kissers. So I'm afraid I'll need to verify your skill in that area."

"Verify away," said Arlo.

So she did. And it was a very long verification process. It could never be said that Lena Cole was not thorough. By the time Arlo had demonstrated his alacrity with kissing to her satisfaction, nearly everyone had retired to the picnic.

"That was sufficient, Mr. Kean," she said breathlessly against his cheek.

"I am beyond relieved that you approve, Miss Cole," he sighed against her cheek.

A slow, polite clap began nearby. They both turned to see Zeke laughing silently at them.

"It appears Mr. Zanni anticipated this outcome," said Arlo. "Perhaps from the beginning."

"It would explain why he wanted us to cooperate so badly in the first place," said Lena. "I suppose you think you're very clever, Mr. Zanni."

Zeke nodded.

"Don't worry, Miss Cole," said Arlo. "The summer has just begun. I'm sure you and I can find a suitable match for young Mr. Zanni."

Zeke vehemently shook his head.

"I will bend all my thoughts toward it, Mr. Kean," said Lena.

I regret to inform you, dear reader, that they made good on their promise. For there are none so insistent on the virtues of love as those already in its thrall. Which is why I chose to set this story down for you.

You see, I am Zeke Zanni, and I am sorry to admit that I have deceived you. As you have no doubt figured out, this is, indeed, a story about love. And as I am in love, I have penned this tale in the hope that you should join me in this folly by falling in love with someone yourself. Because if we are *all* fools, then perhaps there is some wisdom in falling in love.

GOOD LUCK *and* FAREWELL

BRANDY COLBERT

A udrey and I are lounging on the sandy banks of Foster Avenue Beach when she tells me she's going to San Francisco.

Some people would beg to differ, but Foster Beach is the best beach in Chicago. A breeze floats up from the lake and skims across our bare legs and arms before moving over to the plain of well-tended grass shaded by tall, leafy trees, where people grill out and throw balls around. Down the sand from us, kids splash each other in the shallow water, their parents parked a few feet away with noses stuck in grocery store paperbacks. It's not the type of beach people think of when you say "beach"—there's no salt water, and the city is far from tropical. But it's nice to sit here on a blanket in the middle of July, eating pastries with my cousin while we sun our legs.

"San Francisco? For a protest?" I ask, reaching into the paper bag between us for a cherry boat. It's my favorite treat from the Swedish Bakery, the flaky pastry filled with dark, sticky-sweet preserves. I met Audrey on Clark Street around ten this morning and we walked straight from the bakery to the beach, leisurely strolling as we ate pecan rolls and scones.

"No," Audrey replies. She was leaning back on her elbows, with her legs stretched in front of her, but she sits up when she says this.

I hold out the bag; she still has a mini loaf of banana bread sitting in the bottom. She shakes her head, and it's only then that I notice her hands are clenched in her lap. That her lips, usually painted a berry red that stands out against her brown skin, are colorless and drawn in a tight line. I pause, too. I don't dare lick the dollop of preserves from the tip of my pinkie, because I can feel it, the bad news in the warm summer air.

"I'm moving there . . . with Gillian."

The pastry drops from my fingers and lands on the sand, cherry side down. Of course.

"She found a job," Audrey says slowly, watching to see what I'll do next. "A *good* job."

What I do next is grab the sand-covered pastry. I don't bother holding it around the edges. She's leaving. The only person, besides my mother, who has ever understood me—*really* got me—is moving over two thousand miles away. California seems like another planet compared to Chicago. We won't even be in the same time zone.

I squeeze my hand, let the preserves ooze onto my skin, staining my palm.

"Rashida—" Audrey begins, but I cut her off.

My throat aches from the lump that just took up residence, but I manage to get out, "I'm happy for you." Because it is the thing to say to the cousin who has always been there for me. It is the *mature* thing to say, which is something I think about too often at the age of seventeen. I guess that's what happens when you're forced to grow up too early.

"You are?" Audrey relaxes, relieved by my lie, even as she looks down at the mangled pastry. "I was afraid you'd be mad at me."

Mad isn't the word. Disappointed? Possibly. But anything I express besides happiness right now won't do anyone any good. She's leaving because Gillian wants to leave, and she wants to be with Gillian. And Audrey's not my actual mom, even if she took on the unofficial role of surrogate four years ago.

"It's really only one year here without you, right?" I reply. "I mean, I'll be going off to school at the end of next summer, anyway. Maybe I'll end up out West."

I've never considered living in California; the thought has never even crossed my mind, let alone my lips. But it's what I needed to say to convince Audrey that I won't break down when she leaves, and that's more important than a few small lies.

"I need to toss this," I say, standing up with the sad little cherry boat. The trash can is at the edge of the beach, where the sand meets the grass. I brush off the butt of my cutoffs, slip away from Audrey on bare feet, and throw the pastry into the can.

I hold my arm out in front of me as I walk. The jam has somehow worked its way up my skin, leaving a sticky spot near my elbow. Shrieking children and snoozing sunbathers line my path to the water, along with a few people dressed in jeans and long-sleeved shirts, as if they accidentally wandered onto the beach and decided to stay and sweat it out.

The lake water is cool at my feet, lapping over my toes and then frothing at my ankles as it rises. I walk in a bit farther before plunging my hands in. As I wash away the stickiness, I look across the water, at the small waves rolling so slowly it's like they're barely moving at all. Maybe I should keep walking—tread out into Lake Michigan and float away. Not like my mother floated away on an entire bottle of antidepressants, but just . . . to a life where I don't have to keep watching people leave.

When I get back to our spot, Gillian is standing there, helping Audrey shake the sand out of our blanket. What is she doing here? And how did she get here so quickly? I wasn't gone even five minutes. She's good at sweeping in—she and Audrey have been together for barely a year, after all. I take a deep breath, pretend like

I don't notice the fake smiles plastered on both their faces.

"Hey, Rashida," Gillian says, the smile increasing in breadth. "How are you?"

"Fine. Good," I say.

Audrey tucks the thick square of blanket underneath her arm. She's watching me again, and I know I should say something to make her and Gillian more comfortable, but I can't.

"I was in the neighborhood so I thought I'd give you guys a ride back," Gillian says.

"Cool," I say. Then, "Thanks."

She doesn't try to talk to me anymore. I trudge behind them to the car, watching her as I chew on my thumbnail. She has an athletic build—Audrey told me she ran track through college—and thick, dark box braids that touch the small of her back. Her skin is a light, light brown, the sort of ambiguous shade that makes people she's never met wonder aloud if she's biracial. She pronounces her name with a hard *G* that always makes me think of fish gills.

Gillian gets into the driver's side of her old Toyota and unlocks the passenger door, which apparently doesn't open from the outside. I wonder if they're driving this car to San Francisco, if it will break down in every state they pass through, and if Audrey will regret saying yes to the move—to what would surely be a foreshadowing of their new life together.

"Hey," Audrey says in a quiet voice before she opens the door. She touches my shoulder so I'll look at her instead of staring down at the pavement. "I love her. I need you to know that I wouldn't leave if I weren't sure. But I am. I love her too much to not go."

Love.

It's such a bullshit word. She loves me, but that's a different kind of love, and it's not enough to make her stay.

Three weeks later, when Audrey's apartment is stacked with boxes and her refrigerator holds a lone egg and jar of sweet pickles, I find myself at her parents' house, nibbling on cubed cheese beside the dining room table.

Audrey didn't want us to fuss over her leaving. It's not her style. She hates drawing attention to herself, probably because of her work as an activist. She's used to doing so much for others—organizing rallies, contacting politicians, raising funds for nonprofits that fight injustice. But her mother insisted on sending her off with a proper good-bye, so soon all of Audrey's and Gillian's friends and family and now-former coworkers will be gathered in my aunt Farrah and uncle Howard's Rogers Park home.

It's still early, and I'm still eating cheese, when I spot Audrey across the room, huddled in front of the record player with Gillian, sifting through a pile of vinyl. Gillian squeals and holds up an album, and I watch Audrey lean in toward her girlfriend's head to check it out. I pop a bite of sharp cheddar into my mouth and wish it weren't so hard to be nice to the person my cousin loves. And it *wouldn't* be so hard, if Audrey loving Gillian didn't mean Audrey leaving us.

Music suddenly emerges from the speakers, and my uncle Howard walks over to the food table, bopping his head in time to the beat. "And they say you kids don't have good taste in music. Not my daughter. *My* girl"—he snaps his fingers for emphasis—"knows the greats."

"I've never heard this," I say, shrugging and not smiling, because I don't have to pretend I'm in a good mood for Uncle Howard.

He is unyieldingly cheerful, but not the sort of person who constantly reminds you to be grateful for what you have. He genuinely looks on the bright side of things, even after all the shitty stuff he's seen, living in Chicago for nearly sixty years.

"Well, then *you* are getting a free lesson in classic Motown." He pulls on the brim of the tweed Kangol hat perched on his shaved brown head. "The Marvelettes—one of the greatest girl groups of all time."

"Better than the Supremes?"

He gasps and pretends to look over his shoulder, then leans in close. "Don't ever let your aunt hear you say that. It's a hot debate around here." I smile, but only a little, so he puts a hand on my shoulder and says, "San Francisco will be nice to visit, yeah? We can get out of here when it's all nasty and cold."

I glance over at Audrey, who's standing alone at the record player now, staring down at her phone. She always looks pretty, but she's dressed up tonight in a black lace minidress with long sleeves. Her dark hair is sleek, pulled back into a tight bun. And the lipstick is back.

"Isn't San Francisco kind of cold anyway?" I say, remembering the time my mother came back from an art show held there in August and said she'd had to buy a sweater during the trip.

Uncle Howard shoots me a smile that assures me he knows my grumpiness has nothing to do with him before he starts in on the bowl of olives.

I walk to the kitchen for a glass of water but stop abruptly in the doorway. Gillian is standing at the counter with a guy, their backs facing me, and I consider turning and walking out before they see me. This is a party to say farewell to her, too, but I don't have anything nice to say to Gillian, so maybe it would be better if I just avoided her.

But then my foot presses on a squeaky part beneath the linoleum and they both swivel around. And I'm stuck.

"Oh, hi Rashida." Gillian's eyes are as bright as her voice. A blue plastic cup sits on the counter by her elbow, next to an open bottle of vodka and a jug of orange juice. "This is my brother, Pierre."

First, I notice the dimple in his chin. It's so perfectly sculpted that I want to touch it to see if my finger would get lost. But every part of him is worth a second glance, from his rich, dark skin to the black-framed glasses on his face to the soft brown eyes behind them.

"Hi." He crosses the room and sticks out his hand. "Rashida? Nice to meet you."

I knew Gillian had a brother, but I didn't know he was my age. Or that he looked like *this*. I glance at his short, neatly trimmed Afro and think about how soft it must be. He smiles, showing teeth that I'd be sure had been subjected to braces except that one on the bottom is just a little bit crooked.

Gillian coughs and giggles at the sink, and that's when I realize Pierre is still standing there, holding out his hand, and I've not moved or even said a word. I'm simply staring. I brush my fingers over the front of the full, flowered skirt that stops a few inches above my knees, then shake his hand. I smile at him briefly, my gaze shifting back to Gillian, who is taking a long drink from the blue cup, before I say, "Nice to meet you, too."

Gillian gestures toward the vodka. "Want a drink?"

I give her a funny look. "You can't be serious right now."

"Well, I don't mean to brag, but I make a mean screwdriver," she says, laughing.

"Well, I think it's a pretty terrible idea, Gillian. My *family* is here."

Excluding my father, of course. He was supposed to be here by now, but he must be having too much fun at dinner with Bev. Which makes me want to take Gillian up on the offer of the drink, after all. But I don't actually like booze that much. I've choked down a beer and had a couple of cocktails, stealthily made with the spoils of unattended liquor cabinets, but alcohol mostly makes me sleepy.

Pierre glances at me with a furrowed brow, as if he can't believe how rude I was to his sister.

She doesn't seem to take offense, though, or if she does, it's hidden behind the vodka. She smiles the same type of smile that she wore at the beach, caps the bottle, and says, "You know where to find me if you change your mind," before exiting the room.

I slide past Pierre to grab a bottled water and think I should say something—anything to get rid of that look on his face—but I don't know what to say, so I walk away, too.

Aunt Farrah is sitting at the bottom of the staircase on my way to the bathroom. She's not preoccupied with anything, just sitting and staring down at her hands, but there's a sadness to the way her body leans into the railing, so I take a seat beside her. A huge family portrait hangs in a wooden frame on the opposite wall—

Farrah and Howard and little Audrey, when she still wore pink barrettes in her hair.

I rest my head against her shoulder. "I kind of want tonight to be over, but then I don't, because that means we'll only have another couple of days before she leaves."

Being around Farrah is easier now, but at first, after my mother was gone, I was uncomfortable looking at my aunt. They were sisters, and they were so much alike. Not in looks—my aunt is curvy, like me, with boobs and an ass, where my mother was tall and slim. I have my mom's russet-colored skin, brown with red undertones, and Farrah has the same medium-brown complexion as Audrey. But they share so many mannerisms that I'd never noticed before, like the way my aunt tugs on her ear when she's thinking hard about something, or how she chews on the stem of her eyeglasses when she's anxious.

Farrah probably should have been the one to take over my mothering, but Audrey stepped up before anyone else could claim the spot. She's seven years older than me, which used to seem like such a big difference, but the gap feels smaller now that I'll be a senior in high school. And maybe that's why she's leaving. Maybe she thinks I'm old enough to no longer need her.

"I know, baby." Aunt Farrah sighs. "I keep thinking she'll change her mind or tell us it was all a joke. Howard says I have to let her go; she's twenty-four years old. But it's not that easy for mothers. It never is."

She realizes what she's said at the exact moment my body stiffens. And I want to run away, to stop being the one who makes people second-guess what they say, but she puts her arm around me and pulls me close.

"You know I'm here for you, girl." Aunt Farrah smells like strawberries. "Anytime you start missing her, you come over or call or do both, okay?"

The *her* could be my mother or Audrey, and I worry that the combination of missing them both will be too much for me.

A few minutes later, I run my fingers under the cold tap in the bathroom and press them to the sides of my cheeks, the hill of my forehead. I fluff my hands through my hair, which is short and black and big and curly. Then I rummage through my aunt's medicine cabinet, same as every time I'm at her house.

I hold my breath as I look to see if anything has changed. There's a sepia-toned bottle of melatonin. Multivitamins for women. Blood pressure medication. But still no antidepressants.

I breathe out in relief and am just replacing the orange pill bottle when the bathroom door bursts open. I startle and drop it onto the tiled floor, where the top pops off and Aunt Farrah's blood pressure meds go scattering in every direction.

"*Shit*." I don't even look up before crouching down to collect them. It's bad enough to go through my aunt's medicine cabinet on a regular basis, but to have been caught doing so by—

"Let me help."

His feet give him away. Black Chuck Taylors with dirty white laces and ballpoint ink winding around the sides of the rubber soles. I noticed them in the kitchen, but I was too far away to read what they said. Now I'm too embarrassed to take a longer look.

"Thanks." I move aside the bottom of the shower curtain to rescue a few pills.

I expect Pierre to apologize for not bothering to knock, but he's become as cranky as me in the last half hour. "You know, whatever you're feeling . . . you shouldn't take it out on my sister," he says, bending down to sweep his hand around the base of the pedestal sink.

"Excuse me?" That's enough to make me look at him. "She was offering alcohol to a teenager at a family party. Do *you* think that's a good idea?"

"First of all, it's not a family party—it's a party. This is for Gillian's people, too." He stands and sets a few pills on the wide lip of the sink. "And you aren't seriously concerned about the drinking. You were being a jerk to her."

My mouth opens to tell him he's wrong, but everyone in that room knows I was a jerk, most of all me. Still. I'm not quite ready to admit that out loud, and especially not to him.

"I'm allowed to feel how I feel," I say, just barely holding the orange bottle steady enough to drop in the collected pills.

Pierre frowns and pushes his glasses up the bridge of his nose. "I never said you weren't, but you don't have to be rude to my sister. You're not the only one who's upset about the move. You're being dramatic. It's not like they're dying."

At that, my entire body starts shaking. I'm still able to secure the lid and shove the bottle back into the cabinet. But he notices. And he starts to say something, reaches for my arm, but I slip past him wordlessly for the second time this evening.

And somehow I manage to get out of the room without telling Pierre to go fuck himself.

The house has filled with a good-size crowd that's eating, dancing, laughing, and talking at volumes that confirm it is a full-fledged party. I recognize Audrey and Gillian's friends from protests and some people from Aunt Farrah and Uncle Howard's Baptist church, where I've been to a few services over the years. But there are plenty of people I don't know. I remember Pierre's comment, that this isn't just a party for my family, and it makes me cringe.

My father has arrived which should put me at ease but doesn't. He's accompanied by his new girlfriend, Bev, a secretary at the School of the Art Institute of Chicago, where he works as an art history professor. Bev is whatever. Nice enough, I guess, but I have to wonder what my father likes about her. That she's stable? Predictable? Reserved? My mother was none of those things, and it never occurred to me that she should be.

Dad waves me over, so I join them by the record player, weaving through guests holding glasses of wine and beer bottles still dripping with icy water, freshly plucked from the cooler. I pass Gillian, who's standing by the big window behind the sofa, talking to someone I don't know. Gillian is always energetic, but I've never seen her like this—gesticulating grandly to punctuate each word of her sentence, twisting her face into expressions that I don't think are supposed to be as comical as they appear. I glance at her hands, and sure enough, the blue cup is sitting firmly in one of them.

"How was dinner?" I'm asking only to be polite.

They invited me but I declined, saying I'd agreed to come over early and help my aunt and uncle with the setup. Which was true, but by the time I got here they'd already finished cleaning and had hung the banner (GOOD LUCK AND FAREWELL!) and set out the food, so I mostly gnawed on pretzels and weighed in on my aunt's prospective party outfits. But my father doesn't need to know that, because standing around idly before a party celebrating the departure of my favorite person on the planet was still preferable to sitting in a restaurant with him and his girlfriend.

"Oh, we went to this fantastic new seafood place in River North," Bev says a little breathlessly, the most excited I've heard her sound about anything. "The mussels were outstanding!"

"You missed out, Rashida." Dad leans down to kiss the top of my head. "Some of the best oysters I've ever had."

"I'm allergic to shellfish," I remind him. "So it's probably good that I missed out."

"Well, I knew that," he says quickly, stroking his beard. His professor's beard, my mother used to call it. Silver hairs started growing in among the black ones after she died. "We only decided to go there when you said you couldn't come."

I don't believe that. At his best my father is absentminded, but lately it seems like he's even more forgetful when it comes to me. I'll be heading off to college in a year, and sometimes I wonder if he'll be happier once I'm gone.

"So, how have you been, Rashida?" Bev tucks a piece of her light-brown bob behind her ear. "Have you started thinking about college yet?"

She looks more nervous than usual. I've watched her glance around the room at least three times, and I realize—only after she visibly relaxes when she catches sight of a blond guy—that she's anxious about being one of the few white people at the party. I wonder if she notices when she's out with my father and he's one of the only black people in the room. Does his potential discomfort ever cross her mind?

"I've thought about it," I say, and stop just short of shrugging. I can't *not* think about it, with a college professor as a father. He's not pushing me to study a particular subject, but he brings up the topic often, asking if I've narrowed down my first-choice and safety schools yet. He'll be okay with whatever I study, so long as the program isn't based in Chicago. I think having me around reminds him too much of my mother.

"Any idea what you want to major in?" Bev presses on. Clearly not reading me, not seeing that I don't want to talk about this with her right now. Or ever, really.

"I'm not sure," I respond. "Maybe linguistics. Or sociology."

Or horticulture, if I'm being honest. There wasn't a week that went by in the spring and summer that my mother and I weren't in the backyard before the sun got too hot, working our fingers through the soil of our vegetable garden. Tending the garden was relaxing, and it made me feel accomplished. I let everything die after she did.

I tilt my head to the side. "What did *you* study in school, Bev?"

My father's head swivels toward me, but I don't look at him because I don't want to see his face. He knows I'm being mean, that I'm aware there's a good chance Bev isn't using whatever degree she has to work in reception.

Audrey saves me. She swoops in from out of nowhere to greet my father with a hearty "So good to see you, Uncle!" and a kiss on the cheek. She tells Bev it's nice to see her, too, then turns to me. "We're going to play bocce out back and we need another person. You in?"

I can't say yes fast enough. And as I take her hand and head out to the backyard, I wonder how I'll survive when she's no longer around to rescue me.

My heart only sinks further as we step outside. Audrey didn't tell me Pierre would be here.

He's standing at the edge of the lawn, a tall shadow beyond the light that spills off the porch and onto the bocce balls lined up on the freshly mown grass. His gaze shifts to me, and neither of us smiles before he looks away. Gillian is swaying to imaginary music by the deck railing, cup in hand. Her eyes are unfocused—a little wild, even, as they flit about the yard.

The air is humid and warm, scented with the sweet perfume of Aunt Farrah's rosebushes, the fat pastel blooms dotting the trellis at the end of the deck. Earlier, Uncle Howard strung white Christmas lights along the porch, and they glow softly around us, working months ahead of their usual gig. Tonight is beautiful. It could even be romantic, if I were with someone besides my cousin, her tipsy girlfriend, and a guy who hates me.

Even Audrey and Gillian can't enjoy it. Audrey is holding her girlfriend by the elbow, and I can't tell if it's to show affection or to keep her steady. Gillian slams her cup on the railing and takes Audrey's face in her hands, smashing their mouths together. It doesn't look pleasant, and my cousin pulls away quickly, shaking her head. She says something so quietly I can't hear it. Pierre stares at the detached garage at the back of the yard, mortified.

A few moments later, we're spread out across the lawn, standing in teams. Audrey started to pair off with Gillian, but the look I shot her made it clear that wasn't an option. Pierre must have been relieved, too, though he doesn't look so happy next to Gillian, either. She's wrapped her braids around her chin in a makeshift beard, prattling on about the Gettysburg Address.

I turn to my cousin. "Is she—"

I don't get out another word before Audrey snaps, "She's fine. It's fine. Let's play."

Oh. Audrey doesn't snap at me. She's even-keeled in general, always with a soft spot where I'm concerned. But a deep groove rests between her eyebrows, and her lips are pursed tight enough to crack, and she doesn't even give me an apologetic smile.

Audrey and I win the quarter toss; I motion for her to go first. Gillian screams, *"Go, babe, go!,"* loudly enough to be heard down the block, and I think maybe her unbridled enthusiasm will make

Audrey smile, but Audrey ignores her as she rolls the small white ball across the grass.

We get through the first round without incident, if you don't count Pierre shushing his sister every two seconds. Gillian talks loudly, incessantly. I glance at Audrey. She's not even trying to hide her annoyance, crossing her arms and pointedly looking straight ahead. I toss a red ball too hard and it rolls to the back of the yard, bouncing off the fence.

"Dead ball," Pierre says in a smug voice.

I glare at him. He's probably just glad the attention is off his sister, for once.

It's her turn, but she's wandered away. Gillian stumbles through the cluster of green and red bocce balls, displacing a few in the process and cackling as she effectively ruins our game. She's a firecracker let loose too many days after the Fourth of July, a jack-in-the-box that's broken free from its prison, a toddler who has discovered her legs. Gillian is officially wasted.

Audrey sighs. "Well, I guess we're done here."

"She's done for the night," Pierre concludes.

Gillian leaps toward the back of the lawn and spins underneath the empty clothesline, singing a song that's so off-key and slurred it's unintelligible. Her braids fly wild around her face, swinging across her sweaty forehead as she moves to the chorus of crickets in the air. Is this what Audrey will have to put up with when they get to San Francisco? Is this new? Or maybe Gillian has never been able to hold her liquor and I'm only finding out now.

"We need to get her out of here," Audrey says. "I could take her back to my apartment, but everyone will notice if I leave."

"I'd drive us home, but I don't have a license." Pierre sticks his hands into the pockets of his dark blue jeans. "I guess we could take a cab, but—"

Audrey shakes her head. "You're not taking a cab back to the suburbs. It'll be, like, a million dollars, and I'm pretty sure none of us have that kind of cash right now." She pauses for a moment, then nods toward me. "Rashida, what if you drive the three of you back to my place?"

My mouth drops open. "Why do all of us need to go?"

"Because she's hammered," Audrey says in a matter-of-fact way that makes me wish I'd kept my mouth shut. "It'll take more than one person to get her back there and into bed."

"What are you going to tell our family . . . and her friends?" Pierre asks, clearly as worried as I am about taking on this challenge together. He gestures to the house, where the sounds of the party have started to float onto the porch. "Should I go in and say something?"

Audrey bites her lip as she glances toward the back door, the outlines of guests in the kitchen visible through the screen. "I'll tell them she got food poisoning from lunch."

"But what if she doesn't *want* to crash at your place?" I ask. Pierre and I are doing our best to think of every excuse possible to make this not happen, but Gillian doesn't look ready to leave, anyway. She looks as if she'd be content to frolic around for quite a while.

"Oh, she's about ten minutes from passing out." My cousin puts her hands on her slender hips. "You won't get much of an argument."

Just like Audrey knew she wouldn't get much of an argument from us, because Audrey is the sort of person people listen to. I've seen her take charge in a crowd of protestors hundreds deep.

The three of us manage to hustle Gillian from the backyard to the side of the house just as the first guests venture out onto the deck. Pierre and Audrey hold Gillian's arms on either side. She's distracted by everything in her line of sight—a glittery red, white, and blue party hat smashed against the curb, cream-colored petals floating from the tree that hangs over the sidewalk, a stray cat wandering down the path ahead of us.

"*Kitty!*" she cries out, lunging after the scrawny tabby.

The cat escapes, wide-eyed and lithe, and we herd Gillian to the car. Audrey was right. Her eyes are closing, her words slurring more as her lips find it harder to move.

Pierre opens the door, and Gillian immediately falls inside, sprawling across both seats. Her legs are completely slack, loose as cooked spaghetti. Pierre lets them dangle over the edge of the car for a moment, then says, "I should probably ride in back with her."

I shrug, trying to make it clear that I don't have an opinion about any of this. I'm here only because I have to be.

Audrey watches them get settled in the back, leaning down to peer in the window at Gillian before turning to me. Her shoulders slump with fatigue but her eyes are appreciative. "Good luck. See you soon." She drops Gillian's car keys into my palm and briefly closes her hand around mine. "And thanks."

Once I'm inside the car, I put on my seat belt. Gillian is no longer awake. Pierre has shifted his sister so that her head is resting on the edge of his thigh. I'm reluctant to speak to him, but I have to ask: "Seat belt?"

"Yup," he replies, just as brusquely. He pauses for a moment. "How far are we going?"

"Andersonville."

"Is that far?"

Oh, right. Gillian's family is from the west suburbs, out in Oak Park. I wonder how often he comes into the city—if he's familiar with other parts and if it's just this area that he doesn't know. And then I'm mad at myself for wondering. I know everything about Gillian and her family that I need to know.

"We can probably make it there in ten minutes," I say, checking my seat belt again.

I see him nod in the rearview mirror as I adjust it. Then I turn on the headlights. And still I don't touch the ignition.

"What's up?" Pierre asks.

"I . . . It's been a while since I've driven. Especially at night." Dad has a car that I can drive whenever he's not using it, but we live in Bucktown, right near the Blue Line and buses, and there's never a shortage of cabs if I'm really desperate. Lately he's been complaining that the area is too busy, that we'd be happier someplace more quiet. But it's the house we lived in with my mother, dead garden and all, and I think he recognizes that our fragile relationship will hold up longer if we stay there until I leave for school.

"There's no rush," Pierre says. "And you said it's not far."

"Right," I say. It's not far.

I turn the key and classical music fills the car as the engine rumbles to life. I'm surprised, because I don't know anyone who listens to classical besides people my dad's age. Gillian seems as if she'd be more into pop or hip-hop or electronic—something with a good beat that fits her boundless energy. But I'm grateful for the strains of string instruments floating through the car. It's soothing.

I keep my hands at ten and two and drive a few miles under the speed limit; some people pass me, but no one looks mad. Just as I'm getting comfortable, Gillian whimpers in her sleep, a noise that becomes increasingly louder by the second. I glance at them in the rearview mirror when I stop at a red light, thinking maybe I should pull over, but Pierre seems to have it under control. In the dim streetlights filtering through the car, I see him rub her shoulder, whispering a barely audible, "It's okay, Gilly. We're almost there."

He continues comforting her until the whimpers stop, soon replaced by soft snoring. The uneven breaths mingle with the classical music coming from her speakers and, once, her snores are timed so perfectly with a particularly dramatic part in the music that Pierre and I can't help but laugh. We catch each other's eyes in the mirror as the laughter fades.

"You're a good driver," he says quietly, and then looks out his window for the remainder of the ride.

Which is just as well, because it takes much too long for me to stop furiously blushing at a compliment so decidedly innocuous. And I want to know what's changed since we've been in the car. Because five minutes ago I could barely stand to look at him, and now my cheeks are on fire. Audrey always says I should give people the benefit of the doubt, and I don't always agree with her, but maybe Pierre isn't as bad as I thought. Maybe.

By some miracle, I find a parking spot a few doors down from Audrey's apartment building, and it's even wide enough that I don't have to parallel park. I sigh in relief—witnessing me try to squeeze a strange car into a tight space would most definitely make Pierre retract his previous statement—but it doesn't last long. Because Gillian won't wake up long enough for us to get her out of the car. She swats at Pierre with her eyes closed when he softly pats her face and tells her it's time to sit up. She doesn't respond at all when I say her name loudly and tug on the bottom of her pants.

"Audrey lives on the third floor," I announce, once it's obvious we'll have to carry her upstairs. "And it's a walk-up."

"Shit." But then he sighs and adjusts his glasses. "Help me get her over my shoulder?"

The whole undertaking is a struggle from start to finish. Gillian may still be in great shape from her days as an athlete, but her limbs are deadweight as we try to maneuver her over Pierre's shoulder. She becomes alert every so often and tries to push us away. She shoves at me so hard that I stamp my foot and step back.

"This is really shitty," I say, wiping my damp forehead.

"I'm the one who has to carry her up three flights of stairs," Pierre counters, his arms wrapped tightly around Gillian's middle.

"We wouldn't have to do this at all if—" I stop myself, but not fast enough.

Pierre looks up sharply. "If what?"

"Never mind."

"You're not the only one who feels this way." His voice is strained, and I can tell that whatever silent truce we called back in the car has expired. "Can we just stop complaining and get her up there so we can be done with this?"

I've never noticed how many entryways you have to pass through to get to Audrey's front door—the gate, the main entrance, the interior door that leads to the staircase—but by the time I'm inserting my copy of her house key into the lock, fifteen minutes later, I think maybe security measures are overrated.

"How . . . can such a small person . . . be . . . so . . . *heavy* . . . when she's . . . passed . . . out?" Pierre grunts as he carries Gillian to the bedroom at the back of the apartment.

The bed is gone, along with the rest of the furniture. All that remains is the air mattress Audrey will sleep on until they leave for San Francisco. Pierre deposits Gillian on the slightly saggy mattress and I pull the covers up to her chin. She kicks them off and turns on her side, which saves us a step, because movies have taught me that you're not supposed to let drunk people sleep on their backs.

"Fuck," Pierre says as we exit the bedroom. "That *was* shitty." His breathing is steady but heavy as he bends at the waist, his palms planted firmly against the tops of his thighs.

"Want something to drink before we go back?" It seems like the polite thing to suggest.

He nods, and we head to Audrey's tiny kitchen, where I hope she still has something to drink from. A short stack of paper cups sits on the counter beside a freestanding roll of paper towels. "I guess tap water is the best I can do."

"Tap water is still water," he says, and I fill up a cup, which he quickly drains, his Adam's apple bobbing along as he chugs.

I step aside so he can refill the cup himself, and open Audrey's refrigerator. The jar of sweet pickles has disappeared, leaving the single brown egg sitting on the top rack. Audrey loves to cook. I feel unsettled, seeing her kitchen so bare.

A groan emerges from down the hall, guttural and urgent. "Aud," Gillian croaks, just loud enough for us to hear her. "Audie, I need . . . *Aud* . . ."

We rush back to the bedroom where Gillian is trying unsuccessfully to get out of bed. She gives up, her head draping over the side of the air mattress. "I'm . . . gonna . . ."

I dash across the hall to grab the bathroom trash can and slip it under her head just in time. She heaves and vomits, and it smells terrible. I stand back while Pierre holds her braids away from her face. Her light-brown skin has gone almost pale, but he tells her everything will be fine, the same voice he used in the car.

He sits with her while she spits and moans and then dry heaves and falls back onto the mattress. I bring her a cup of water, and Pierre convinces her to take a few sips before she rolls back over.

"Listen, I don't want you to think Gilly's a drunk asshole," Pierre says as he stands. "Sometimes she drinks too much when she gets nervous, and she was nervous about tonight."

I frown, confused. "About a party?"

"About watching everyone say good-bye to Audrey. She thinks . . ." He lowers his voice, even with the impossibly loud snores now coming from the air mattress. "She thinks you guys hate her for taking your cousin away."

I should reassure him that of course we don't hate her, because Audrey is an adult and she wouldn't leave if she didn't want to. But I don't say any of that. Unfair or not, a part of me does hate Gillian. She *is* taking away my cousin. Audrey would stay in Chicago if she'd never met Gillian, because Audrey *loves* Chicago. Even when it's covered in sheets of ice and piles of black, slushy snow and the windchill registers at negative double digits, Audrey says this is her favorite city.

"Ah." Pierre raises his eyebrows. "She's not wrong."

"Nobody hates Gillian." *Not really.* I hesitate, because I'm afraid my voice will become too thick, like it does every time I think about Audrey leaving. "We just really love Audrey is all."

He nods. Not dismissively, but a nod where he makes eye contact with me, one that says he hears me. He understands.

"Well, we can't leave her like this." Pierre sighs as we move to the front of the apartment. "She'll be really confused if she wakes up and she's alone. And if something happened to her because of me . . . I should stick around. I mean, if your cousin's cool with me being here."

"She'll be cool with it, but what will you do?" I look around the empty apartment. There's no television, not even an idle magazine or book. Everything has already been taken away or boxed up and moved to the edge of the room. My voice echoes against the nothingness, and I think about how depressing it would be to sit in here all alone.

"Quiet isn't so bad." He shrugs. "And I'm sure you want to get back to the party . . ."

Part of me wants to do that—Audrey *is* leaving in a couple of days. But it wasn't the sort of party where you have fun. The bocce, drinks, and Motown-themed merriment felt forced, like we were all pretending it was an ordinary Saturday night gathering. And I can't even hide out with my father, not with Bev around, being awkward and asking the wrong questions.

Considering the way things started out between us, I can't believe hanging out with Pierre is the better alternative. But I think about the car ride over, how sweet he's been with his sister. And I can't ignore the fact that the only moments tonight that I haven't felt wrapped up in a cloud of anxiety are the ones I've spent with him. Maybe arguing isn't much better, but I'll take any emotion over crippling sadness. And, well . . . we're not arguing *now*.

"Or I could stay," I say, shocked at how confident the words sound in my mouth.

Like they belong there.

Like *we* belong here. Together.

A slow grin spreads across Pierre's smooth, dark skin. "Or you could stay."

I've made a mistake.

A few minutes later, and we're still standing here in the living room, staring at the hardwood floor, the ceiling. Anywhere but each other. What if our silent truce is just that—effective only when it's silent?

"I'm starving," Pierre says bluntly, blessedly breaking the tension. "I saw a pizza place up the street. Know if it's any good?"

"It's good enough."

That makes him smile. "You want to split a pie? I can do anything but deep-dish."

My eyes widen. "Wait—seriously?"

Pizza can be a controversial topic in Chicago. When your city is known for a specific type of food, it feels downright traitorous to choose anything else. But the truth is I don't like deep-dish pizza and I don't think I ever will.

"I know it makes me a freak around here, but I really hate it." He makes a face. "There's too much damn bread."

"Make that two freaks, then," I say with a small smile.

He leaves and I check on Gillian. She's sleeping soundly on her side, but the room still smells awful, so I tiptoe around the air mattress to push the window all the way up. The summer moon is fat, and it shines through the pane brightly enough that I can see the rectangular patches on the wall where Audrey's pictures used to hang. I've spent so much time here that I can envision her bedroom exactly as it looked before she packed everything away, from the Fannie Lou Hamer quote that sat framed on her nightstand ("I am sick and tired of being sick and tired") to the bookshelves full of Baldwin and hooks and Lorde and Morrison to the nubby stuffed elephant named Freddie who sat on her bed.

A memory lies in every corner of this apartment: the bistro table where I calculated equations and ate leftovers from Aunt Farrah's, the love seat where I took countless afternoon naps, the space between the coffee table and the armchair, where I sat cross-legged while Audrey put twists in my hair.

All of it is gone now. But maybe that's the best part—that I won't be able to come back here after Audrey moves away. Because some days I think I'm doing okay, and then it hits me, in my own house—a nick in the bathroom tile where my mother dropped her flatiron, a birthday card, buried under a pile of old papers, that says "Love you forever, Rah." I gasp and it is the worst kind of surprise, the permanent reminder that life is only temporary.

Pierre comes back, in possession of a large pizza box and two bags from the convenience store filled with drinks. "I didn't know what you like, so I just got as much as I could carry."

There is a blue sports drink and a purple sports drink and three types of soda and a canned energy drink and apple juice and sparkling water. I thank him but quickly turn away to load them in the refrigerator, because I am embarrassed by his thoughtfulness. My father has known me his whole life and he wouldn't go to this trouble. If he wasn't sure which drink I wanted—and he wouldn't be, not without asking—he'd likely bypass the cooler altogether.

Pierre takes the blue drink and I choose the apple juice and we sit in the middle of the empty living room with the pizza box and roll of paper towels. He opens the box to reveal a glorious thin-crust pizza with mushrooms and red peppers on my half, sausage and pepperoni on his.

"Are you a vegetarian?" he asks, removing a slice.

"I used to be." I pull out my own piece and hold it in the air. "My mom never ate meat, but my dad is, like, the biggest carnivore on the planet. Sometimes it's easier to eat what he makes, since it's just the two of us."

"Is your mom . . . ?"

"Dead."

Pierre swallows a bite and washes it down with a swig of blue water. "Sorry."

"It's okay," I say.

And this is the part of the conversation where people wait for me to tell them how she died, also known as the part where I start resenting them. But I don't get that vibe from Pierre. He's just here, in the now, not demanding an explanation. It fills me with an unnerving but pleasant sort of comfort.

We're silent as we plow through our first slices of pizza, and maybe I should be worried about the possibility of grease on my chin, but I'm too hungry for that.

Halfway through the second piece, Pierre says, "I had an older brother."

I wipe my mouth with a paper towel and look at him, confused, but before I can respond, he goes on. "He got shot on our street and died when I was fifteen."

"Oh my God." I don't mean to say it, but of course I'm surprised— by the way his brother died and that I didn't already know this, but also because Pierre is in the same club as me. Lots of people lose grandparents by the time they reach high school, but things are different when a parent dies. It's probably the same with a sibling. Nobody *talks* about the secret club, but you know when you meet someone else who belongs.

"I'm sorry," I say. Because I know how it feels, when people are so horrified by the way someone who was close to you died that you end up trying to make them feel better about their reaction. "I didn't know . . . Gillian never said anything."

He finishes his slice, scrunches a paper towel between his fingers, and sits with his legs bent in front of him, arms hanging lazily over his knees. "It didn't happen in Oak Park. I was born on the South Side. Parents never married, and my dad was around some but not a lot. Mom's a nurse in the maternity ward at a hospital."

The South Side? I know less about Gillian than I thought, because Audrey never mentioned she had lived there. Maybe they moved after Pierre was born. Though I could have sworn she said Gillian's parents are still together.

Pierre clears his throat. "After what happened to my brother, my mom wanted me out of our neighborhood. Someone on our street knows who shot Braden and nobody talked. *Nobody*. My brother was, like, a fucking golden boy. Straight-A student, good at every sport, nice to people who didn't deserve it. She didn't want the same thing to happen to me, so I went to live with Gillian and her family. She's not my real sister—we're, like, foster siblings. My mom knows her dad from the hospital."

I'm surprised I didn't catch on before now; they don't look anything alike. But lots of brothers and sisters don't resemble each other. And Audrey and Gillian have always referred to him as her brother—no clarifiers.

"Is it weird?" I ask. "Living with them?"

"It was at first." He glances back toward the bedroom, as if Gillian can hear him, but she's still passed out. "I miss my house and living with my mom. And I wish she didn't blame herself for what happened to Braden. She still talks about how maybe if she hadn't been working so much and—God, I hate that she does that. She couldn't have helped it. Braden couldn't help it. He was doing everything right. Sometimes really bad shit just happens."

"Yeah," I say, my voice quiet. "It does."

"Gillian's family is great. They make me feel like I'm part of them. And . . . just so you know, Gilly is the reason I'm living with them at all."

"I thought you said your parents knew each other?"

"They do, but we didn't know that. Not at first. She was part of the rally some people organized when Braden died, and she came up and introduced herself. Everyone knew my mom and me from the news." He pauses. "She started hanging around. Showing up after school, offering to take me to the library or White Sox games on the weekends. People talked about how sad it was, what happened to our family, but Gilly was the only one who stepped up and really made sure I was okay."

Maybe Gillian is more like Audrey than I realized. Everyone was concerned about the kid left behind after my mother swallowed a bottle of pills, but their concern tapered off in the weeks after the funeral. Besides my father, Audrey was the only one who checked in every day, who made sure I ate and did my schoolwork, who took me to the lake and museums to keep me busy and get me out of the house.

"I'm sorry about Braden." I touch Pierre's arm without thinking, then quickly pull my hand away, even though it felt good, my fingers against his skin.

He looks at me now, his eyes serious but kind behind his glasses. Then he nods, his head dipping down in one quick movement, as if he's putting a period onto the end of a sentence. "Thanks. It'll be three years next month."

"Sometimes I get mad when people don't remember the day my mom died," I offer. "My dad and I used to spend the whole day together, but then last year I woke up and he was gone and I just . . . I felt so . . ."

"Abandoned?"

"Yeah." I squeeze a hand around my curls. "Exactly that."

We used to get up early and eat her favorite breakfast, mushroom and spinach frittatas, then we'd visit the most expensive florist in the neighborhood and leave tulips on her grave.

She loved flowers, especially the tulips that overtake downtown Chicago in the spring. But her love for them became a family joke, because she had the greenest thumb of anyone we knew but always forgot to plant tulip bulbs in the fall. So we harvested delicate asparagus stalks, and plots of Swiss chard and arugula, and bulbous, blood-red beets that stained our fingers when we chopped them. And after we'd spent whole days in the backyard digging and pulling and planting and watering, we'd ride the train down to the Magnificent Mile just so she could see the tulips, the brightly colored blooms and pointed leaves lining the tourist-filled sidewalks with simple beauty. She'd lean into me as we walked among the crowds and say, "Just wait until we have our own next year—we'll make this look like amateur hour." And every year she'd forget about them until the soil was too hard to dig into, refusing new life.

Pierre and I sit there not saying anything, and I wonder if I've ruined our evening. Even friends and family members get uncomfortable when I bring up my mother. They try not to be, and yet their body language gives them away every time. But Pierre doesn't look like that, so I keep talking.

"My mom was a painter," I say. "I don't have any brothers or sisters, and honestly, she and my dad spoiled me a lot. Everything was pretty perfect until . . . I didn't know she was dealing with depression. My dad knew, of course, and I can remember some days when she wouldn't get out of bed, but I didn't understand. No one talked to me about it. And then she was gone, and I was only thirteen. Now I'm obsessed with looking in my aunt's medicine cabinet . . ." I glance at him to see if my confession registers, but his expression doesn't change. "I want to know exactly when she starts feeling anxious or depressed, because what if it runs in the family?"

"Do you think it does?" Pierre sits up taller as he looks at me.

I focus on the dimple in his chin and wonder if I'll ever get the chance to touch it. "No. I mean, I don't think so. But I was too stupid to see it in my mom, and what if I'm too dumb to see it in my aunt . . . or me?"

Pierre lets out a breath and I know instantly that what I said was too heavy for this room, for this night. Even for someone else in the secret club, even when we are sharing our life stories.

"You know, I feel like black people think we're not supposed to take medication for mental illness. Like we're supposed to be stronger than that. And that's fucking bullshit," he says, without an ounce of hesitation. "We're not superhuman. I was on antidepressants for a while after my brother died. And I never thought I would be on them . . . but it helped."

"I think that's the worst part." My eyes are dry but my voice is faint. "She was *trying* to get better. She knew she needed help, but it wasn't enough."

"But you'll always know she tried, right? I knew I had to stick around for my mom. The meds helped with that . . . And you were close with your mom, right?"

I nod, staring at my feet.

"She was trying for you. I'm sure of it."

I've always known that, deep down, but to hear it said out loud, directly to me . . . It means more than any sympathy card or phone call or "I'm sorry about your mother" that I've received in the past four years. It means the world to me.

"It sucks to lose people," Pierre says, and I feel him watching me, so I meet his gaze with a newfound respect. Because he's looking straight at me. Not away, where it would be comfortable for everyone else. "But I have to keep telling myself I'm not losing Gillian. She's leaving, but she'll still be around."

"Yeah." But then I break eye contact, because it's too much. He's too . . . *him*. Knowing what to say and when to say it. I don't know how he's so good at that when he's just met me.

"And I bet . . . well, I know it's the same with Audrey. I heard about you so much before I even met you. She's not going to forget you, Rashida."

"What did you hear about me?" I blurt.

It lightens the moment. It makes him smile.

"Well," he says, "all good things. That you're smart. And sweet, even if you try to hide it. And that Audrey loves you more than anyone."

I don't say anything to that. I concentrate on breathing and I blink hard and I try to ignore the tightness in my chest, the strange pressure that makes me feel as if my sternum might break like a faulty dam. I stare at his sneakers to distract myself, at the blue ink running along the cracked, off-white sides. At first I think it's doodles, words and sentences strung together nonsensically. But I make out a *thou* and a *hast*. "Are those Bible verses?"

278 • BRANDY COLBERT

"No." His smile is sheepish. "They're lines from *Hamlet*. I'm . . . kind of a Shakespeare nerd. I'm going to DePaul in the fall, and sometimes I think I need to go the practical route and study biology, but I really want to get into the playwriting program."

"What does the quote say?"

"It's . . ." He pauses, deciding how to respond. "It's that quote that says, 'This above all: to thine own self be true.' It saved me after Braden died. I wanted to find out who shot him, do whatever I had to do to get revenge. But I'm not . . . I couldn't have lived with myself if anything happened. And it could have. I knew people who would've . . ." He shrugs. Trying to shake off the memory. "But that's not who I am. So I looked at that quote every day to remind myself that revenge wouldn't get me anywhere except in jail, or maybe even dead, too."

I know nothing about Shakespeare besides *Romeo and Juliet*, but I could listen to Pierre talk about *Hamlet* and what Shakespeare means to him all night.

We stare at each other. Our eyes drop away—his back down to his Converse, mine to the grease-stained pizza box—but when I glance at him again he's already looking at me. I think . . . no, I'm *sure* I want to kiss him. And the way he considers every part of my face with his gentle brown eyes, from my cheekbones to my eyelashes to my lips—especially my lips—I think he might feel the same way.

I swallow hard, but not hard enough to drown out the rapid beating of my heart. It must be loud enough that he can hear it, too; animated enough that he can see my actual heart protruding, back and forth, back and forth, through my heather-gray shirt.

We should have heard the footsteps pounding up the stairs outside the apartment, or the commotion on the landing, or the jiggling of the key in the door. But Pierre moved closer to me. Close enough that I could make out the individual coils of his hair, pick up the clean scent of soap on his skin.

So when Audrey explodes into the apartment with a wall-shaking "Oh my *God*, you're still here?" We're startled, to say the least. When I see my father standing behind her, my surprise turns into supreme mortification. We weren't doing anything, but it's obvious we were about to start doing *something*.

"Well, at least now I know why you weren't answering my texts," Audrey says, a smile breaking out on her face once she realizes everyone is accounted for.

"We, um . . ." But I don't know how to finish. I almost kissed Pierre, and everyone in this room can tell. My face is flaming.

Pierre stands, holding out a hand to help me up from the floor. "Gillian got sick," he explains, and I don't know how his voice is so controlled. "We didn't want to leave her, and I guess we forgot to call."

Audrey goes back to check on Gillian. I could kill her for leaving us alone with my father. I smile weakly in his direction. "Sorry for making you worry, Dad."

"You can't just disappear like that and not let anyone know your plans, Rashida." He shakes his head. "What if you weren't here? What then?"

His voice rises as he keeps talking, but I don't want him to calm down. I've upset my father, but he's thinking about me. He was *worried* about me, and I didn't know I'd ever see such concern from him again. Even if this isn't how I wanted it to manifest.

"I'll be more thoughtful next time," I promise. "I forgot to check my phone and . . . well, I didn't think anyone would miss me."

"How could you possibly think that?" He walks closer to me. Near enough that I can see the genuine worry in his eyes and how quickly it would have turned into despair if I hadn't been here. "Rashida, you . . . I always miss you when you're gone, honey. Always."

And the earnest tone in his voice makes me think about the way he still peeks into my room each night before he goes to bed, even if we've already said good night. Or how he seemed more upset than me when I let knee-high weeds take over the garden, how each year he asks if I want to get seed packets from the nursery and start over. And I remember how, the day I met Bev, she told me that one of her first sets of instructions after she started at the school was to always put my calls through to him, no matter what.

My father's love isn't effusive; that was Mom's area. She loved big and full and in color, and that translated to her art and our garden and, most of all, to my father and me. But he's always been here. In his own way, but he's been here.

Dad smiles behind his beard before he turns toward Pierre and says, "Who's this?"

"I'm Pierre, sir." He steps forward to give my father a strong handshake. "Gillian's brother. I'm sorry we didn't check in, but I want you to know Rashida is safe with me."

Dad doesn't look so reassured, but he lifts his hand to meet Pierre's. Audrey comes back from the bedroom and announces Gillian is still "out like a light."

"Do you all want a ride back to the party?" My father rubs a hand over the back of his head as he inches toward the door. He is clearly over this whole situation.

And that's when I finally notice Bev isn't standing nervously by his side. I can't believe he'd leave her at the party where she knew no one and seemed so anxious about it. Maybe my father told her this was a family thing, that it was better if she stayed behind. Or maybe she suggested that herself. But either way, it isn't lost on me that my well-being was considered more important than her comfort.

Audrey yawns and scratches the side of her nose. "I should go back to say good-bye to some people, but I can't leave Gillian here . . ."

"We could stay," I say, not looking at my father or Pierre. But really, *really* wanting Dad to agree, because despite everything that's happened in the last five minutes, I haven't forgotten what *almost* happened between Pierre and me. And I want to get back to that moment. I want it to not have been ruined forever.

Audrey shrugs. "Why not? I'll be home soon, Uncle, and I'll make sure Rashida gets home okay."

My father doesn't like this. I can tell by the way he strokes his beard. But he agrees to it.

Maybe it's because I'm seventeen now. Or maybe it's because he realizes that, in the last year or so, he no longer has the ability to make decisions for me. Or maybe he sees that Pierre might be someone who can make me happy.

I hug Dad and Audrey before they leave, with much less fanfare than when they arrived. Audrey looks over her shoulder before she exits and mouths, "You'd better tell me *everything*" in such an exaggerated fashion that she might as well have shouted it.

I blush, the door closes, and Pierre looks at me.

I smile, though I feel just as timid now that we're alone again. "Well, that was . . ."

"Awkward?" he finishes.

"For starters."

The cacophony of snores starts up again from the bedroom, which makes us both laugh. Pierre points to the sliding glass door off the kitchen. "Does that open?"

"Yeah, there's a balcony," I say, and when I walk over, I'm surprised to see the small plastic table and two chairs are still sitting on the wooden planks.

"And we've been cooped up in here the whole night? Come on." He slips his hand around mine to lead me out outside, and that feeling from earlier, when I briefly touched his arm—this is one thousand times better. His hand is warm and soft and dry, and he doesn't let go, even after we're standing on the balcony.

The string of twinkle lights that was intertwined around the railing is gone, sacrificed to my aunt and uncle's deck, but the moonlight shines softly through the slats, creating a similar effect. The balcony looks out over the alley, so the view of overstuffed Dumpsters and pitted asphalt isn't impressive, but it is private. And it's peaceful out here, made even more so by the piano music playing in a building across the way. It's not nearly as polished as what we listened to in Gillian's car, but the tune is classical and pretty and perfect for this evening.

Pierre takes the seat farthest from the door, brushing it off before sinking down. I start to take the other chair, but he tugs lightly on my arm and pulls me down so I'm sitting in his lap.

"Is this okay?" he says, as I turn to face him.

"Yes." Then I gently press my pinkie into his chin dimple. "Is this okay?"

"Not really." But he says it with a smile, and he is still smiling as he outlines my bottom lip with the pad of his thumb.

I shiver, torn between wanting that particular tingle to last forever and wanting so much more. Our heads move toward each other at the same time. Slowly, but with purpose. And when we finally kiss, it is everything. Pierre's hands slipping around my waist and then dipping a little lower, his fingers grazing the small of my back. His mouth, tender and sweet on mine, but full of an energy that convinces me he wants this as much as I do. We pull back for a moment, but only so he can remove his glasses.

"Wait," I say, because I want to see what he looks like without them.

He blinks at me, and I'm relieved to see he's still the same Pierre. The same Pierre who loves Shakespeare and hates deep-dish pizza and who understands what it means to lose the person you always expected to be there—and how to love the ones who do their best to make that absence less painful.

As my lips meet his for a second kiss, I think maybe saying good-bye isn't all bad.

Maybe it means I'm making room for someone new.

BRAND NEW ATTRACTION

Cassandra Clare

t was a dark carnival. You know the drill. Evil clowns lurching out of the shadows, blood on their puffy white gloves. Tattered Big Top, blowing in a hot summer breeze. Insane giggling children running in and out of the shadows. The hall of mirrors that throws back terrifying, distorted reflections. The tattooed man whose tattoos move and crawl on his skin, the merry-go-round that turns back time, the bearded lady who comes at you with a carving knife, and the fortune-teller who gives you only bad news.

You know, your basic dark carnival. You've seen a thousand of them in movies or on television, read about them in books, heard about them in song lyrics. But you probably don't know as much about them as I do, given that I grew up in one.

Yep, that's me. Lulu Darke, only daughter of Ted Darke, the

owner of Ted Darke's Dark Carnival of Mystery, Magic, and That Which Is Better Left Unseen. My mom died when I was little, and my father raised me, traveling the country with the carnival. Mostly small towns where the inhabitants like a good scare. Summer's our best time, when the nights are hot and restless and couples want an excuse to cling to each other in either of the tunnels—the Tunnel of Love or the Tunnel of Terror, depending on their mood. The rest of the year is when we hole up somewhere, do our hiring, and I take my high school courses online.

Some people might think it's weird I don't have friends my age. My closest pals growing up were the bearded lady and Otto, the strongman. Most people stereotype strongmen as being dumb, but Otto's a borderline genius who reads Proust in the original French and taught me geometry when I was ten. All I've ever needed is the carnival and my dad.

That was before this May, when my dad packed up and disappeared.

Not that I wanted to think about that right now. We'd just arrived in a new town. It was Saturday night, our first night open, and the place was packed. We'd spread out in an open field, close enough to town that you could walk to us but not so close that anyone would call in a noise complaint.

Horrible screams were coming from the Big Top, which meant the show was going swimmingly. Melvin the Moaner was taking tickets. He didn't really have any talents besides moaning in a ghostly way, but we kept him on anyway, out of kindness.

Despite the satisfied crowd, ticket sales were slow. They had been for a while now, since before Dad vanished. He'd left behind a note on a Hallmark card covered with balloons. The note said he owed money all over the country and he had to run. Don't blame yourself, he'd said. Don't expect to hear from me. And I hadn't.

The only thing keeping the carnival afloat was an infusion of cash from my uncle Walter, my dad's older brother. He'd been the one running the fair until he'd married a rich woman with a teenage kid and settled down into a life of stable mediocrity. The one time I'd met Walter's stepson, he'd eaten too much cotton candy and thrown up on me. That was ten years ago.

Now we were running on borrowed cash and Walter's promise that he'd show up soon and help bail us out. His wife had died, and apparently he was eager to get back into the carnival business. Maybe he would, maybe he wouldn't. All I knew was that my family business, *my* dark carnival, was on the verge of going under. No wonder my nails were bitten to the raggedy quick.

"Lulu." It was Ariadne, the sexy mermaid. She was out of her tank for the night, wheeling around the fair in her motorized chair. "Reggie's got the flu. He needs you to take over in the Tunnel."

"Terror?" I asked.

"As if Reggie has ever stepped foot inside the Tunnel of Love."

I groaned. I was engaged in my preferred job, manning the Snack Shack. You might think evil clowns would put people off their food, but it's the opposite. Being scared makes people hungry, just like it makes them want to make out with each other's faces. We sold a ton of snacks, including funnel cakes, sugar-skull lollipops, neon-colored cotton candy, and bright red slushies MADE WITH REAL HUMAN BLOOD!

The blood was just corn syrup, but whatever. People ate it up, metaphorically and literally.

"Can't you do it?" I asked.

Ariadne flapped her tail and gave me a meaningful look.

Reggie's job was to lurk in the shadows and jump out at people with an earsplitting shriek. It was exhausting. I sighed. "Fine. But I'm taking a slushie with me."

Even though I knew I was on my way to a sucky job, my spirits lifted as I crossed the midway. Summer was in the air. Summer, my favorite time of year. I loved the hot nights, the smell of popcorn and bug spray, the occasional breeze that would lift my hair and cool my neck. I loved jumping in Ariadne's tank during the daytime, when the carnival was closed, and sunbathing out on the grass with a book.

I saw people giving me odd looks as I ducked into the Tunnel entrance. They probably thought I was breaking in to vandalize it. We didn't have uniforms at the carnival, but even so, my black eyelet sundress, spider-pattern tights, and Doc Martens didn't exactly scream "I work here!" Also, I'd recently dyed my hair in rainbow stripes, mostly because my dad had always forbidden me to dye my hair, so it was a way of flipping him the bird now that he was gone.

I navigated through the Tunnel, keeping to the employee area, where the machinery whirred and the floor was greasy with oil. Through the wall I could hear marks—sorry, *customers*—screaming as they enjoyed their jolting ride through darkness, where luminous piles of bones glowed on either side and vampires, ghouls, and demons leaped out to grab at their moving carriages.

The carnival had always been Dad's life. I remembered him talking about it to me when I was little, his eyes shining. "People come to shows like ours to be scared, yeah. But they also come to *live*. To feel magic. No regular hick circus will give you that. They come to feel brave, like they've faced the dark forces." He tugged on my hair. "There are some shows out there that don't know when to stop," he'd said in a more subdued voice. "They say if people want darkness, even if they think it's make-believe, give it to them. But the price you pay for that kind of evil, Lulubee . . . that's a high one. I say, if people want darkness, give them shadows cut with sunlight."

"Scary *and* funny," I said. "Like clowns."

He'd laughed and ruffled my hair, and I'd thought that we were the most important things to him, the carnival and me. But he'd taken off on us without a second thought, and we were both showing the effects. I hadn't been sleeping or eating, really. I kept waking up with nightmares of the carnival being repossessed, the pieces carted away, and me left in an empty field with a couple of unemployed evil clowns.

Unemployment is no joke for carnival people. It's not easy to get another job—there just aren't enough fairs like ours anymore. Everyone who worked here was like family to me, even Mephit, the scaly demon who lived under the Big Top. And my whole carnival family was depressed: Ariadne wouldn't stay in her tank, the acrobats were always drunk and couldn't walk the tightrope, Otto was too bummed to lift weights, and Etta, the bearded lady, had alopecia, which was making her hair fall out. Only the clowns were happy, and that was because they had fallen in love with each other and were cheerful all the time, which is the last thing you want from clowns who are supposed to represent everyone's worst nightmares.

My mood had plunged back down into the basement.

I'd just reached the place where Reggie hung out—a dark alcove between a stack of cursed pirate gold and a pile of open caskets—and flipped in my plastic vampire fangs, when I heard voices.

"This place is a wreck." It was a male voice, snotty and superior. "Did you see that bearded lady? She looked like she had mange."

"You couldn't be more right." Another male voice, deeper and even more superior. It instantly put me on edge. "The carousel is broken, the hall of mirrors needs a good Windexing, and where's the gentleman who bites the heads off chickens?"

Hmph. No one did that anymore, the chicken-biting thing. Too many upset vegetarian customers. This guy was a jerk.

"The whole place is coming apart," said the first voice, growing louder. Great. Their carriage was coming toward me, which meant I was supposed to jump out and scare them. Maybe I could skip it. They probably wouldn't be impressed with me, either. "They must have a seriously pathetic demon familiar."

You've probably been wondering how much of the dark carnival was real and how much was fake. Marks always do. The answer is some, and some. The answer is that it's as real as you want, and as fake as you hope. And the answer is that everything at the carnival that couldn't be explained, everything that sparked of *real* magic, was because of Mephit. Mephit was like a battery, and he made us light up.

Pathetic. At that I felt an explosion of rage. Mephit was *not* pathetic. He was an avatar of ancient evil! How dare they!

Without pausing to think, I leaped out of the alcove as their carriage swung into view. With an eldritch scream, I hurled my slushie at the oncoming carriage.

There was a bellow of rage. The carriage jerked to a halt, and I found myself staring into the angry, scarlet-soaked faces of my uncle Walter and his stepson, Lucas, the boy who'd thrown up on me ten years ago.

Fifteen minutes later, I was still in shock. Uncle Walter had ushered me into the well-appointed trailer he'd driven onto the fairground. I had to admit, it was fancy. The walls were real wood paneling, and there was gleaming chrome and brass everywhere.

Uncle Walter helped me onto a velvet sofa while Lucas disappeared, glowering, down the hallway to wash off the slushie. A door banged closed and then a shower turned on.

"I'm really sorry," I said.

"Nonsense." Uncle Walter looked like a picture of my dad taken with an unfocused lens. Everything about him was sort of blurry, including his blurry brownish eyes and indistinct jawline. His hands were pink and soft. "A girlish prank. Nothing to apologize for."

More thumping came from the back of the trailer. Lucas had stalked behind us all the way from the Tunnel of Terror, refusing to look at or speak to me. He'd taken the full force of the cherry-flavored ice. Uncle Walter had been spattered, but Lucas looked like he'd been slaughtering Muppets.

Uncle Walter leaned forward. "I hope you can think of me as a second father."

"My father's not dead."

"Well, no. I didn't mean as a replacement. More just . . . as an addition."

"Can't I think of you as an uncle?" I asked hopefully.

At that moment, Lucas stomped out into the living room. He was scowling and pulling on a T-shirt. I'm an honest kind of girl, so I'll admit I stared. He was wearing low-slung jeans and a gray, much-washed concert tee that clung to him in all the right places. I hadn't noticed his muscles, on the walk back from the Tunnel, or the fact that he had jet-black hair and green eyes, my favorite combination.

A silver chain with all sorts of lockets and pendants on it was slung around his neck, but the jewelry didn't make him look girly. Quite the opposite.

I shut my mouth, not wanting Uncle Walter to catch me leering at his stepson. I didn't remember Lucas having blazing sex appeal from the last time we'd met, but nobody looks their best when they're throwing up on you.

"You ruined my shirt," he said. "My *favorite* shirt."

"Lucas," Uncle Walter said. "Lulu has been through a time of personal tragedy. Don't you think we should be generous?"

Lucas thought about it. "No."

Someone knocked on the door. Scowling, Lucas opened it. It was Strombo, the animal trainer. Mostly he was in charge of the cats—the lions and tigers—but he also trained the rats to perform the Dance of Death. People get really freaked out by rats; I don't know why. I like them, myself.

"Boss," he said, and I saw with a pang that he was looking at Uncle Walter. My dad had always been *boss*. "We've locked up for the night. Everyone's gathered in the tent for the meeting."

"Thank you, my good man," Walter said. "I'll be there momentarily. I'm sure they'll find what I have to say about the future direction of the carnival . . . inspiring."

"If you say so, boss." Strombo was about to leave when Walter placed a hand on his shoulder.

"I'll be inspecting the animals tomorrow." Walter's voice dropped. "I'll be deciding which stay and which go. Prepare yourself for a new regime."

Strombo looked worried. He never let go of any animals, not even Throckmorton, the toothless panther. And he probably didn't know what *regime* meant.

There was an awkward silence when the door shut behind Strombo. Walter heaved himself to his feet. He was a skinny guy, but he gave the impression of someone with a weight on his shoulders. "I need the trailer to myself for a moment. Lulu, Lucas, perhaps you can show yourselves to the tent for the meeting." He chuckled. "Lulu and Lucas. Sounds like you were made for each other!"

My cheeks grew warm. Lucas glared. His hair was still dripping. He reminded me of a cup of coffee: wet, hot, and bitter. I tried to decide if it was immoral to lust after your step-cousin. I figured it wasn't. We weren't actually related. No shared blood.

I bounced up off the couch. "Not a problem."

It was a perfect summer night, with fireflies blinking in the fields surrounding the carnival. I led Lucas toward the center of the fair, taking my own zigzag path between the stands.

"When did you get here?" I asked, after a few beats of silence. Mostly because I was desperate for something to say. He was looking around, expressionless, taking in the sights. Carnivals are creepy after hours, and dark carnivals are doubly creepy. Shadows drifted eerily between the tents.

"A couple hours ago," he said. The last customers, girls in tank tops and boys in shorts, were filing out of the gates. The grass was littered with empty popcorn boxes, napkins, and ice cream cones, though it would all be cleaned up by morning. "So do the people coming here think it's make-believe? Or real?"

"They think what they think." I shrugged. "Do they think they're really drinking blood and seeing vampires and watching Strombo get eaten by a lion? They have to not believe it, or it'd be too scary."

"So is it dangerous? Do people get killed?"

"Of course not!" I was mortally offended. "My dad always said it takes a lot of magic to make something real look fake in the right way."

Lucas shook his head, his dark hair falling in his face. "I don't get it."

"Well, if you don't like ghost brides or the sinister sounds of giggling children, there's always the Tunnel of Love." I pointed toward its sparkling entrance, a dot of bright pink in a sea of dark.

He smiled. It changed his whole face. My heart bumped. "What's the story there?"

"They drizzle love potion through the air," I said, as we paused at the Snack Shack. I unlocked the little gate that blocked off the space behind the counter and went in. "Not too much. Just enough to make you feel affectionate."

I fished around in the big steel refrigerator until I found what I was looking for—a red slushie, premade—and fitted a lid onto it.

Lucas watched me with his eyebrows drawn together. "Are you thirsty?"

"Not exactly."

"Didn't get to finish your previous slushie because it ended up all over my face?"

"You were talking crap about the carnival." I headed back out into the night. "No one talks crap about the carnival. Also, the last time we met, you threw up on me, so we're even."

"I threw up out of nerves," Lucas said. "I was a nervous child."

We passed by the Mysterious and Macabre Museum of Mirrors. When I was a kid, it had been my favorite attraction, with its many corridors lined with shining reflective surfaces leading to a massive central square of huge mirrors that showed you tall and short, doubled and cut in half, old and young. Now I tried not to focus on any of them if I had to go in there. Their silvery faces could surprise you, and not in a good way.

"What were you nervous about?" I asked. The merry-go-round loomed up under the moon. The horses were snarling, rearing, terrified. The rounding boards and central cylinder were painted with a pattern of screaming faces.

It was a good place to come and be alone and think.

Lucas looked incredulous. "The terrifying demon your dad was shoving me in front of?"

I laughed. "That was Mephit. I thought you said he was pathetic."

Lucas's incredulity only grew. "Mephit's your carnival demon?"

So Lucas knew more than I thought. The real truth is, every dark carnival has a familiar. A demon. A real one is the heart of a carnival, powering its darkness, infusing attractions with a sense of menace and the customers with jumpy nerves.

"That's right." I hopped onto the carousel and wove between the horses to get to the central cylinder. It glittered with light when the carnival was open, but it was dark now. I knocked on a central panel and it popped open, revealing a descending staircase. I was halfway inside when I turned around to look at Lucas. "You coming?"

He shrugged a resigned shrug and followed me in.

The staircase led to a hastily dug area, lit with a couple generator-powered lamps. It was hot down here, even on the ledge. The pit underneath the ledge was hotter still.

"Mephit!" I called. "Mephit, dinnertime!"

Lucas looked horrified, though to his credit, he stood his ground. "You're going to *feed* me to the demon?"

"Don't be ridiculous," I said, as Mephit uncurled from the depths.

It's hard to describe a demon—they all look different, and they all look like nothing else on earth. Mephit most closely resembled a giant hairless cat with huge blue eyes and triangular ears. If, you know, a hairless cat had a snout full of fangs and black bat's wings and a long, scaly tail that slapped the ground impatiently. I held out the red slushie. Unlike the others sold in the Snack Shack, this one really was made with blood. Cow blood, but Mephit didn't mind. As long as it was cold, he liked it fine. His tongue shot out like a frog's and nabbed the cup from my hand. He swallowed it in one gulp, crunching the bloody ice between his teeth, and grinned.

"Whoa," Lucas said, as I scratched Mephit between the ears. He felt like warm rubber. Mephit had been around long enough that he'd developed a fondness for humanity. Lucas edged closer. "Can I . . . pet him?"

"Sure," I said, surprised. I backed away, and Lucas approached Mephit, rubbing him gently on the nose and between the ears. A purr rose up like the sound of a rusty motor. Blazing sex appeal *and* Mephit liked him? I was in trouble.

We were late to Uncle Walter's big speech in the main tent, and I could feel his glare as Lucas and I arrived. The carnival staff sat in the bleachers, looking grim. Otto winked at me, but I could tell he was in a bad mood. The clowns were holding each other and crying. Strombo was crouched on the floor with Throckmorton. Ariadne glanced over at us and gave Lucas an appraising look.

Walter stood before an enormous square that was covered in a velvet drape. "And so," he was saying, "this is the beginning of a brand-new day for Walter's Darke Carnival of the Unnatural, Unreal, Frightful, and Grotesque."

Reggie raised his hand.

"Yes, my good man?" Walter asked. I was beginning to suspect that he called everyone that to avoid remembering their names.

"That's great and all," Reggie said hesitantly, "but how will we get that much power? I mean, you're talking big stuff, really evil stuff. It's out of our league, you know? You'd need the demon equivalent of a ten-ton generator."

Walter smirked. "Fortunately, we have just that." He whipped the cover off the cage. It was a real carny gesture, I'll give him that. "Meet Azatoth!"

Lucas put his hands on my shoulders as if he was worried I would scream. I didn't, though his hands felt nice and warm.

The thing in the cage wasn't that huge, but it was sleek and slippery and sharklike in a subtle, unpleasant way. Unlike most demons, it didn't have claws or stingers or anything like that, just featureless steely-gray skin and a body that ended in a head that was all mouth. The teeth looked like they'd been found in a dozen different places. Jagged teeth, pointed teeth, teeth like ice picks, teeth made out of broken glass. Its eyes were black and dead as pits on the moon. They made me feel dizzy. Dizzy and a little sick.

Otto stood up. "No."

Walter gave him a dark look. "What do you mean, *no*?"

"That's a Keres demon." Otto picked up his jacket, slung it on. "No good ever comes from running a carnival on that kind of energy. There's dark, and then there's evil, and they ain't the same."

I thought of my dad. *But the price you pay for that kind of evil, Lulubee . . . that's a high one.*

Walter's face soured. "Does anyone else feel that way? Because you're quite welcome to follow Mr.—"

"Otto," Otto said.

"Mr. Otto right out that door," he said. "Just don't expect to ever come back." There was something slippery and cold in his voice. As if he'd learned to talk just like his demon looked.

A few people scrambled to their feet. Ariadne rolled her chair out, her head held high. Strombo followed Otto, carrying Throckmorton. Overall, though, it was fewer people than I would have thought. Most everyone stayed put. Curious, maybe—or maybe, like me, they didn't have anywhere else to go.

Lucas walked me back to my trailer. The rest of the staff shambled off to their own trailers and tents, looking like zombies.

As we crossed the midway, I saw Walter in the distance, leading Azatoth on a long, black metal leash that shimmered in the moonlight. He ushered him toward the structure I'd noticed earlier, the weird brushed-metal dome near his trailer that gleamed like a spaceship.

"Where did your dad get Azatoth?" I asked.

"Not my dad," Lucas said. "My stepdad." There wasn't any hostility in it, though; he just sounded sad. "I don't know. After my mom died, he was restless. He drove around a lot, disappearing at night. I thought maybe he was depressed. Then he came home with Azatoth. Said he wanted to get back into the carnival business. It was the first time he looked happy since she died."

"Was that before my dad left?" I asked.

He nodded. "Walter was looking forward to setting up his own show, but when he heard about your dad, he said we should come back here, make sure you were okay. He said he'd always loved this place."

I knew I ought to feel grateful. But I couldn't. Everything was changing, and not in ways I wanted it to change. "I'm sorry about your mom. My dad, he's still alive but—I know what it feels like to lose someone." I swallowed, and the next words spilled out of me. "Having somebody leave you like that on purpose, you end up asking yourself what you did. To make them go."

His eyes softened. "Nothing. You didn't do anything." He paused. "Is this your place?"

We'd reached my trailer. It wasn't hard to spot. Otto had spelled out *Lulu* in gold glitter paint along the sides. I had a brief urge to invite Lucas in, maybe sit and talk, but he was already turning away.

"Night, Lulu." He touched my arm lightly and disappeared into the shadows.

The carnival changed a lot over the next few weeks.

Carnivorous mermaids were installed in a massive tank, with a sign that read "Brand-New Attraction." Our happy evil clowns were replaced by clowns who carried carving knives and had a murderous gleam in their eyes. Walter hired a hag with bleeding cheeks and a howling screech to roam the carnival warning people about death. Couples emerged from the Tunnel of Terror looking groggy, bite marks on their necks. Ticket prices were jacked up one hundred percent. We were making money—lots of money—but it didn't feel good.

I stuck to my job at the Snack Shack, but I started to see something different about the customers buying hot dogs and Cokes. Their hands shook. There was a genuinely haunted look in their eyes. Some of them were crying, especially the ones who'd staggered out of the Museum of Mirrors.

As they exited the carnival, trembling and shocked, they'd pass Walter, who would grin and hold out a hand to shake. "You had a good time," he'd say. "Tell your friends." And they'd nod, looking convinced, their eyes as blank and dark as Azatoth's.

These days I was keeping a stack of college brochures under the counter. I'd always planned to enroll in business classes online and then take over the carnival from my dad. I wanted to update it, brighten the place up, maybe bring in some fireworks and dancing and technology—nothing too weird, just a little modernization. But now I was wondering if I'd have anything to come back to. The smiling young people on the brochure covers seemed to mock me—would they get where I'd come from? Would they think I was weird? How would I fit in with them? And, even more importantly, who would pay for me to go?

There was only one bright spot in the summer. Every night, Lucas came with me to feed Mephit. Walter hadn't tried to move Mephit, but now that Azatoth was powering the carnival, there wasn't much for our old demon to do. Lucas and I would scramble into the merry-go-round and climb down to Mephit's pit with his cup of icy blood. He would open his glowing blue eyes and stare at us sadly, like he missed being the heart of the fair. Like he missed Dad and how things used to be.

I would pet him on the nose. "You're not the only one."

After that, Lucas and I would go and talk. It wasn't a planned thing, but something about having him around made me realize how much I didn't know what normal teenage girls were like. Sometimes, when they watched their boyfriends lose games on the midway and stamp and swear, they'd look over at me, and our eyes would catch for a rueful second. Then I liked them, and I'd think about what it would mean to go to high school in a real building and not online.

But I didn't long for it. I'd grown up in the dust and smell and music of the carnival, and that was home to me. It was why those college brochures scared me so damn much, but it was also why I looked forward to the nights, when I could talk to Lucas.

We'd sit on the dry grass under the big summer moon, eating shaved ice from the Snack Shack, or sticky-sweet cotton candy. We had an unspoken pact not to talk about anything related to our parents or the carnival. We talked about music—I knew some, because it blared from the speakers of the rides—and about the places we'd been. I'd been all over America, seen every state, from the Golden Gate Bridge to the Tappan Zee.

Lucas had been all over the world. He told me about the Eiffel Tower and I told him about the Paris casino in Las Vegas. He told me about Stonehenge and I told him about Carhenge. He told me about eating lemon gelato on the Amalfi Coast and I told him about the oil spill I'd seen on the Gulf Coast. I found out that he laughed a lot, actually, and he was good at making me laugh, too. Enough that I didn't mind that sometimes we were up so late I'd see the sunrise.

I was fighting off a yawn while dishing up snow cones on a Wednesday night when I heard a yell. It sounded like a yell of pain. A *familiar* yell.

I dropped the paper cone full of ice and dashed past my puzzled customer toward the midway, where the yell had come from.

It was Lucas.

Walter had been giving him all the crappiest jobs—cleaning up after shows in the Big Top, washing down the merry-go-round, Windexing the Museum of Mirrors.

Tonight he'd been the "victim" in the dunk tank, and a lot of town girls had lined up to drop the hot guy into the water. I didn't blame them. I did, however, blame the carnivorous mermaid who'd been hiding in the tank. She'd bided her time and then taken a bite out of Lucas's ankle.

By the time I arrived, people were shouting and Lucas was climbing over the side of the tank. He'd yanked off the collapsible seat and used it to fend off the mermaid. She was drifting around, holding her elbow and glaring.

"Everything's okay, folks! Nothing to see here!" I called as I helped Lucas to his feet. His ankle was bleeding, though it was hard to tell how much, since the blood had mixed with the water. He looked dazed. "Come with me," I hissed, and steered him away as fast as I could toward my trailer.

Lucas sat on a pile of towels on the end of my bed as I put the finishing touches on his bandage. He'd used up the rest of my towels drying himself off, and his black hair stuck up like duck fluff around his head.

"Walter's going to be pissed," he said, as I stood up, dusting off my hands. It was an unwieldy contraption of Band-Aids and gauze, but I figured it would hold.

"He'll be glad you're okay," I said, surprised. Lucas glanced around my trailer. It was strange for me to realize that he'd never been inside it before. It was my sanctum, my private space, where no one could bother me. A velvet bedspread covered the bed, and everywhere else there was cloth and tape and sewing supplies. When you're always on the move, it's hard to buy clothes, so I had learned to make my own. That night, I was wearing a fifties circle skirt with pink poodles and a short red sweater.

I wondered if Lucas thought it was weird, not like a normal teenage girl's room. After all, it was a caravan, meant to be hitched to a truck and dragged along the highway. Then again, if Lucas didn't realize by now that I wasn't a normal teenage girl, he never would.

He shook his dark head. "My stepdad doesn't care. Not really."

I sat down on the bed, not too close to him. "I'm sorry he's been giving you the crap jobs. But that doesn't mean he doesn't care about you."

He turned toward me. His eyes reminded me of lime snow cone syrup. "Can I tell you something no one else knows?"

I nodded.

"My mom didn't die. She ran off and left. Abandoned me and Walter." He studied the bandage on his ankle. "It was years ago, but she's never tried to call or see how I'm doing or anything."

I was shocked silent.

"I've been a burden to Walter since then. All he wanted was to get back into the carnival business. But he had to wait for me to be done with high school. I graduated in May."

"So . . . you're going to college in the fall?"

"I don't know. I haven't decided." His eyes had darkened. Now they were more the color of pine needles.

I reached out and took his hand. "You couldn't be a burden to anyone. I've seen how hard you've been trying to help out—taking those jobs and all. No one who was a burden would do that."

Our eyes locked. He leaned forward, and I leaned forward. Our lips were a millimeter apart. I could feel him breathing. I couldn't move. It felt like my whole body had locked up in anticipation.

He made an impatient noise. "Come here." He pulled me into

him, and then we were kissing.

I closed my eyes and saw carnival lights. Lucas tasted like sugar and water. His mouth moved over mine, sweet and hot. I reached up a hand to cup his cheek. It was soft, with just a hint of scruff under my palm. I stroked my fingers down to his shoulder, and we drew away from each other, shaky and smiling.

"I feel like I maybe wandered into the Tunnel of Love and inhaled some of that stuff," Lucas said, his voice warm and soft.

I laughed, shivery all over. "Trust me, you didn't. I wandered in there once when I was younger, and it was like . . ." I wrinkled my nose. "My head felt like it was full of bad poetry and chocolate boxes. I told Otto I loved him. And Throckmorton."

"So"—he kissed along my ear—"it's like . . . Hallmark love in there. Not real love."

"Exactly." I wanted to kiss him again, but the image of a Hallmark card, the one with a bunch of balloons on the front, was suddenly vivid in my mind.

I pulled away from Lucas. "Wait a second."

He looked dazed, and my lipstick had left pink marks on his skin. "What? What's wrong?"

"Nothing. Or potentially everything." I put my hands flat on his chest. "How do you know your mom ran away?"

"My *mom*?" He stared at me. "You want to talk about my mom? Okay. She left a note."

"Do you remember what it said?"

Still looking at me like I was out of my mind, he reached into his pocket and produced his wallet. It was the kind with lots of small plastic compartments. Inside one of them, untouched by the water, was a folded-up piece of paper.

He handed it to me. It was creased and crushed and torn, but I could still read the words: *Can't stay . . . Don't blame yourself . . . Don't expect to hear from me.*

I pressed the note to my chest and stared at him. "Lucas. We have a problem."

In the morning, a loud bang woke me up. It was followed by a hair-raising growl. I went to the door, wrapped in a fuzzy pink bathrobe, with a candelabra in one hand, ready to bash any threatening beasties over the head with it.

I threw the door open. Uncle Walter stood on my front steps. Azatoth slurked behind him on his black metal chain, an unwholesome dent of darkness in the middle of the trampled grass.

"I've got something for you, Lulu." Uncle Walter held out a manila envelope. "Your daddy running off like he did, well, it made for something of a legal tangle. You and me, we're going to have to make some decisions about the carnival. I was thinking of keeping it open through September, for instance, maybe heading south where it's warmer."

"Okay." Was it me, or did Walter sound folksier than usual? I took the envelope, which was stuffed with a thick sheaf of papers. I didn't see any harm in staying open into the fall. "I'll sign it and give it back to you later."

He grinned—not a very nice grin. "Why? You got company?"

I was suddenly glad Lucas had left. We'd stopped kissing the night before so we could discuss the notes from our parents and argue about what to do next. When I kicked him out at three a.m., we were still arguing.

"None of your business," I said, starting to close the door.

He grabbed the door and held it. I tried to push it closed, but I couldn't. Walter was a lot stronger than he looked.

"See you at the Shack, Lulu," he said, and let go. The door banged shut. Even through it, I could hear Azatoth hiss.

"Fast Eddie?" Lucas said. "You know a guy named *Fast Eddie*?"

"Yep," I said. It was the next night, and I was manning the Snack Shack. I'd put up a hand-lettered sign saying "Out Of Everything No Food" so people would leave me alone. "He's a lawyer. He's fast at producing contracts."

"Lulu . . ." He leaned on the counter. Lucas was wearing a black shirt tonight, and, for some reason, it made his skin look tan and his eyes really green. I wanted to jump across the counter and kiss him, but business first.

"Something *is* going on. My dad ran off *and* your mom ran off. They left notes that were practically identical. They both said to expect not to hear from them." I crossed my arms across my chest. "You know what else is weird? Otto left me his number and a forwarding address when he left, but no matter how often I call, no one ever picks up."

"People are unreliable," Lucas said. "You can't depend on them. You want to talk about weird? Walter's been squirreling away potions. He's definitely up to something, I just don't know what."

"Lulu! Over here, Lulu!" It was Fast Eddie, waving.

Fast Eddie had come up through the carnival world. When I was little, he used to run the carousel. Then he'd gone to law school. He said the dark carnival had been perfect training. He came from a carnival family; people said they had some vampire in them. Maybe they did. I only ever saw Eddie at night, and he was awfully pale. But I try not to judge.

"Hey, Eddie. Snow cone? It's on the house."

He shook his head. "What's happening? Why the urgent summons?"

"It's about my dad. And—"

"Speedy Edward!" It was my uncle Walter. I reached to yank down the OUT OF EVERYTHING sign, but Lucas had already done it. He dropped the sign behind the counter and turned to his stepfather. Walter was beaming, but it was that slippery-shark smile. "Edward, it's been a long time."

Fast Eddie touched the brim of his hat. "It's Eddie, thanks. Fast Eddie."

"You're in law now, I hear," Walter said. "Why I remember when you used to run the carousel." He glanced over at me. "Decided to have a lawyer look over those papers I gave you, huh?"

Lucas shot me a weird look. I hadn't mentioned the papers to him yet. I'd told Eddie about them on the phone.

"I look over everything for Lulu," Fast Eddie said, although this was a lie. "Family friend and all that."

"Good to see you've got business sense. Not like your dad." He gave me a nod, but he didn't look pleased. "Drop the papers off at my trailer when you're done with them, you hear?"

I made a face. No one liked going to Walter's trailer because Azatoth slept nearby, chained to a giant tree stump. In the middle of the night, he howled like a lonely train. I didn't know how Lucas could stand it.

Walter walked off, shoulders hunched. I took the manila envelope out from underneath the counter and handed it to Eddie. He pulled out the thick stack of papers and whistled.

"Lulu, what's this? Why is your uncle giving you a bunch of papers that say you're signing the carnival over to him? You don't own the carnival—your dad does. Where *is* he, anyway?"

"He ran off. Didn't you hear? Apparently he owed money all over."

But Fast Eddie was already shaking his head. "No chance. Your dad was great with money. He had a college fund for you, a 401(k), a SEP IRA—"

"This is alphabet soup, Eddie," I said. "What are you talking about?"

"Your dad didn't owe anyone," he said firmly. "And, anyway, if anything did happen to him, the carnival belongs to you as long as Mephit's alive."

"As long as Mephit's alive?" I echoed. "Really?"

Fast Eddie nodded. "A demon is what makes a carnival what it is. A different demon means a different carnival. But Mephit's one of the old ones—he ought to live a thousand years. So why would you want to sign over the fair?"

"I wouldn't." I glanced over to see Lucas's reaction, but he had slipped away into the night, following his stepfather. I turned back to Eddie. "I'd never give up this place, or Mephit, or any of it."

"I didn't think so." He handed the envelope back to me. "You be careful, Lulu, you hear me? I don't think much of any of this."

I clutched it to my chest. My mind was already racing, and I didn't like what I was figuring out. "Me neither."

His eyes darted behind me. "Also, there's holy water in

that slushie machine. Did you know?"

He turned and faded away, back into the shadows.

Holy water.

I stared at the slushie machine, horror spreading over me. Real horror, not the kind you get from clowns in scary makeup or ghouls jumping out at you in the Tunnel of Terror. The kind that comes from betrayal.

I thought about grabbing that ice every day, dumping the blood over it, carrying it to Mephit . . .

I ran toward the carousel. The summer night was hot, and the air was thick. I heard the merry-go-round, even at this distance, spraying tinny melodies up into the sky. When I was halfway there, a figure stepped out of the shadows, blocking my way. I screamed.

"Lulu," a rough voice said. It was Lucas. We were on the midway, between the Crossbow Shoot and the High Striker, the strongman tower that Otto used to operate. He'd been replaced by a shady guy with a huge mallet. Every once in a while he'd slam the mallet down, the bell would ring, and the crowd would cheer weakly. I wanted to tell him the point was to let customers have a chance, but there was no time.

"Your stepfather has been feeding Mephit holy water." I grabbed Lucas by the hand and towed him toward the carousel. "I don't know how long he's been doing it. Mephit's a *demon*—he's been poisoning him."

"Lulu," Lucas said, spinning me to face him. "Forget about that."

"I'm not going to *forget* about it! Mephit's like—he's like family! And your stepfather is trying to get me to sign the carnival over to him—"

"Lulu." His gaze was intent. "I love you."

That did stop me. "*What?*"

"I love you. I've loved you since we first met."

He pulled me close to him. The sounds of the carnival surrounded us, the shouts from the midway and the big tent, the clashing music. The night was hot, and our bodies melded into each other. His hands slid up my back.

"Lulu," he whispered. "Tell me you love me."

I blinked. I'd never liked a boy as much, and I loved talking to him and the way he made me laugh, but . . .

But he looked dazed. Unfocused. Like he'd walked into a tree. I narrowed my eyes.

"What's wrong with you, Lucas?" I demanded. "Are you drunk?"

He shook his head. "Walter tried to convince me to help him. He could tell I wasn't buying it, and he gave me . . . something."

"What was it?"

"Not what he thought it was. There were two bottles on the table, and I switched them when he turned away for a moment. I think he meant to knock me out . . ."

I recognized his moony look then. "Love potion. It was love potion from the Tunnel."

He rubbed his eyes. "It tasted like strawberry bubble gum. I pretended to be unconscious until he left the trailer. He must have already known that if he got rid of Mephit he wouldn't need your signature . . ."

"Oh my God." I pushed free of Lucas and stalked toward the carousel. He followed, calling my name.

A bunch of other people were shouting as well, mostly angry people who thought I was jumping ahead of them in line. Some kids were crying, too. Maybe they thought I'd take their painted horses. Maybe Lucas's wild eyes were freaking them out.

I dived for the central cylinder of the ride and threw open the door. Lucas was still calling my name. I jumped inside, and he jumped after me, yanking the door shut behind us.

"Lulu," he gasped, as I hurried down the stairs. "Look, I don't want to be part of my stepfather's plans. I'd never hurt you like that."

"Go somewhere and lie down. Sober up." I'd never had a weirder evening. We reached the ledge and I looked down. Mephit was lying in a curled ball at the bottom of the pit. Terror seized my heart.

"Mephit!" I shouted. *"Mephit!"*

He raised his head slowly. His blue eyes were washed out, almost to pale white. Poor Mephit. He'd been poisoned, and I'd inadvertently been helping the poisoner. If anything happened to him, I'd never forgive myself.

I dropped to my knees. "Mephit. You have to get the holy water out of your system. You have to throw up."

Mephit made a glum noise and put his head back down.

"You can't just tell a demon to throw up," Lucas said, sounding almost normal. "I don't think that's something they can do on command."

I glared at him.

"Lulu," he said, gently. "My love. I'd spare you this if I could."

Mephit groaned as if in pain. I eyed Lucas speculatively, then stuck out my hand. "Help me up."

He did. I fell against his chest, not accidentally. His eyes softened.

"Do you love me?" I asked.

"I adore you."

Mephit definitely groaned this time, a sound of complete disgust.

I shut my eyes and hoped I would be forgiven for what I was about to do. "Kiss me. Kiss me, Lucas."

Lucas pulled me toward him and kissed me. "I love you," he said, between dotting kisses along my cheekbone. "You're the most beautiful girl I've ever seen. I love your crazy clothes, and your rainbow hair, and the way you make me laugh, and the way you smell like roses . . ."

Mephit made a horrible urping, yowling sound. I broke away from Lucas just as Mephit threw up what looked like glowing golden syrup all over the floor of the pit.

"That's *disgusting*," Lucas said.

"Do I really smell like roses?" I asked him, intrigued, as Mephit eyed the gold stuff with suspicion. The blue color was already returning to his eyes, and the bare patches where his fur had seemed to rub away were growing back in.

"Lulu . . ." Lucas's eyes widened. "I think it's starting to wear off."

I giggled. It might have been a touch of hysteria, given that I was trapped between a boy who was high on love potion and a vomiting demon.

"Oh, hell. What did I say to you?" Lucas demanded, grabbing fistfuls of his own hair. "Lulu, what?"

"Just that you loved me, and—*Mephit!*"

I screamed the last bit, because Mephit had burst out of his pit. In all the years I'd known him, he'd never used his bat wings. He used them now, sailing over the ledge and hurtling up the stairwell, a determined look on his face.

"Oh, *no!*" I took after the demon at a run, but he was really moving. He burst out of the carousel, knocking the door off its hinges, and sailed between the painted horses.

Lucas and I careered after him as the ticket takers screamed. The carnival was oddly empty. Walter must have shut things down while we were underneath the carousel. The midway was deserted as we tore after Mephit, who was flying straight for the hall of mirrors.

"Stop!" Lucas yelled. Maybe he thought Mephit was going to eat someone. Maybe Mephit *was* going to eat someone.

People were gathering . . . other carnival workers, drawn by our shouting and the sight of a demon sailing through the air. Mephit dived inside the museum.

I hesitated at the entrance. I heard Mephit inside, growling, and another noise, too—a hissing that chilled my bones. Seconds later, Lucas appeared at my side; he'd paused to grab up the strongman's mallet and was carrying it in his right hand.

"I'll go in." He looked grimly determined. "You stay out here."

"I thought the potion was wearing off?"

Before Lucas could reply, there was the sound of shattering glass. He bolted into the hall, and I went after him.

Funhouse versions of ourselves loomed on both sides as we dashed for the heart of the mirrors. When we burst in, we found Mephit and Azatoth facing off in the dead center of the central square. Neither of them cast reflections in the huge mirrors that lined all four walls, but Lucas and I did. For a moment I thought I caught a glimpse of my dad in one of the mirrors, but then again, I thought I saw my dad all the time. Mirrors don't always tell the truth. That was why I hated it in here.

"I see," said a voice from the doorway. A third reflection stepped between ours as Walter appeared in the doorway. Everyone turned to look, even the demons. Surprise and displeasure flashed across Walter's face when he saw his stepson, but he wiped the expression away quickly. "You disobeyed me, Lucas. You've betrayed our family. And you helped this girl save that nasty, scabby demon of hers."

Mephit snarled.

Walter's eyes were mean and ugly. "This carnival is mine. It always was mine. I was the older son, but our parents were too stupid to understand what that meant. They left the whole thing to Ted. I had to marry a rich woman just to make ends meet. And put up with her brat."

He glared at Lucas. Lucas gripped his mallet. I felt for him, in that moment, suffering the contempt of the only father he'd ever really known. If I were him, I would have pounded Walter with the mallet. But Lucas is a good person.

"It's over, Walter," he said. "We know you poisoned Mephit. We know you faked the notes from our parents."

If I'd still had a shred of doubt, the look of hate and surprise on Walter's bony face confirmed everything.

"Did you kill them?" Lucas demanded. "Is that what happened? Are they dead?"

It was the question I hadn't wanted to ask.

Walter's face contorted into a grin. "Brace yourself. Because you're about to go where they went, boy—"

Lucas threw the mallet.

Walter ducked; it sailed past his head and smashed the mirror behind him.

Out of the gaping hole stepped . . . my dad.

He looked just how my dad always looked. Slouchy cargo pants, sweater with leather patches on the elbows. Peacoat. It had been cold the night he'd run off. He stared daggers at Walter. "You weasel," he said. "Thinking you could get the carnival from me—locking me up like this, trapping me with black magic—"

"Thaddeus." Walter paled, backing up. "I can explain—" His head whipped around. "Azatoth! Get him! Get my brother!"

Azatoth hissed and shot forward—only to be seized in Mephit's jaws. Mephit's eyes glowed like gaslights as he tossed back his head and swallowed the other demon in two gulps.

Mephit began to swell. It was like consuming the other demon had plugged him into some kind of demonic power source. He grew and grew, and his eyes turned the color of the night sky, and his teeth shot out in jagged rows like a shark's. He lunged toward Walter, a low rumble emanating from his throat.

Walter yowled in terror and leaped backward—into the gaping hole of the broken mirror. There was a distant, echoing scream, and then the mirror sealed itself back up. Only a plain, silvery surface was visible now.

"Dad!" I threw myself at my father, who wrapped me in his wool-covered arms and hugged me tight. Mephit sat down on the ground and licked his spatulate foot thoughtfully.

"Lulu." My dad rubbed the top of my head. "Lulu, baby."

I turned around in his embrace to look at Lucas. His expression was tight and sad. "So, your dad's back, huh? I'm happy for you, Lulu."

He meant it, too.

My dad smiled. "Come on, kid. There are other mirrors."

Lucas stared at him uncomprehendingly—then his eyes lit up. A moment later, the mallet was back in his hand and he was smashing all the glass. Every single mirror but Walter's. Otto spilled out, and Strombo, and the clowns who loved each other, and finally, a brown-haired woman with Lucas's green eyes.

"Mom," he said, and threw the mallet aside so they could hug like two people who thought they'd never see each other again. And I guess they were.

The next night was the Fourth of July, and we had a party out on the midway. Otto found some fireworks and set them off, and I watched the sky turn red, white, and blue while my carnival family raced around, reuniting. Those who had worked for Walter mostly slunk away. A few stayed, promising my dad they'd be good—or, at least, they would only be bad according to his rules.

The carousel—with the help of Mephit—played "The Star-Spangled Banner" and "The Yellow Rose of Texas."

My dad told me that he'd been in his trailer one day, when Walter showed up out of the blue. Walter claimed he'd spent his wife's money to buy Azatoth, a demon so nasty he could power anything. He told my dad he could give up the carnival and walk away, or Walter would make him sorry. My dad said he'd never give up the carnival and that he found the disappearance of Walter's wife suspicious, to boot. That was it. Using Azatoth, Walter tossed my dad into the mirror. It was where he sent everyone who displeased him, including his wife.

My dad had become good friends with Lucas's mom while they were in there. "She's a nice woman," he said. Walter had manipulated her, too. He wasn't much of a carny, but he was a good con man.

"There were two things Walter didn't count on," my dad said, resting a hand affectionately on my head. We were sitting on a rise of grass, eating caramel popcorn. "He underestimated Mephit. Just because our carnival doesn't go around hurting people, doesn't mean Mephit's not powerful. He's one of the oldest, most powerful demons in the world. No surprise he ate Azatoth up as soon as his power returned."

"And the second thing?" I asked.

"You." My dad dropped his hand. "Clever Lulu, figuring Walter out, and his schemes besides. I'm so proud of you."

I hugged him. "Thanks, Dad."

He let go. "I saw those college brochures in the Snack Shack. I wasn't sure what to do with the money the carnival made while Walter was running it—I might give it to charity—but I'm sure there's enough for me to set aside some for you to go to school."

I nodded. "I want to study business. Learn how to run this place so I can take over from you someday."

He smiled proudly, but before he could reply, a nervous voice interrupted us. "Could I . . . could I talk to Lulu for a second?"

It was Lucas. He'd changed out of his usual T-shirt and jeans into khakis and a button-down white shirt. He was tan, and he looked like summertime.

My dad glanced at me. I nodded. He stood up, giving Lucas an exaggerated look of warning before wandering off to talk to the others. Otto was explaining the Saxons and the Normans to Strombo, Lucas's mom, and Ariadne. Strombo was petting Throckmorton.

Lucas sat down beside me. The fireworks were still exploding overhead, and in their light I could see his face—green eyes and solemn mouth and brushed-back hair. He looked nice, but I remembered kissing him and I knew he wasn't *too* nice.

"Those things I said before," he said, "when I took the love potion. I—"

"You didn't mean them," I said, quickly. "I know. I get it."

"No, I wasn't going to say that." He looked hard into the distance, biting his lip. "I remember what you said about taking the love potion and how it made your head feel like it was full of bad poetry. And I understood what you meant, because the thing is, real love wouldn't have made Mephit throw up."

I laughed shakily.

"Okay, that didn't come out right," he said. "But I've watched everything you've been doing to fight so hard for this carnival. To fight to keep it going, for your friends here, for your dad, even for Mephit. I love . . . how much you love this place. And it made me think that real love, not the Hallmark kind or the love potion kind, is scary and fierce and amazing. And I think . . . I think I'm falling in love with you."

My heart rang like the bell on the High Striker. "For real?"

He looked at me. Smiled softly. "For real."

I put my hand against his cheek. "Me, too." And I kissed him. I think I messed up his nice-guy look a little, running my hands through his hair until it stuck up, and rumpling his shirt. And I think he probably did the same to me.

When we finally broke apart, we were both smiling.

"But you're going to leave," I said, suddenly panicked. "You're going to go home with your mom. I won't see you again."

Lucas shook his head. "My mom wants to invest in the carnival. I told her I was really happy while I was here. That this was the only place I was ever happy while I was with Walter." He smiled, and it lit up the night. "She said I could stay, and your dad would teach me how to run a fair. If you don't mind."

I pulled him toward me for a kiss. "As long as I don't have to save you from the dunk tank again."

Lucas laughed.

I snuggled into his arms as the last of the fireworks faded, and high above, Mephit flapped across the sky, his wings silhouetted against the moon.

A Thousand Ways This Could All Go Wrong

JENNIFER E. SMITH

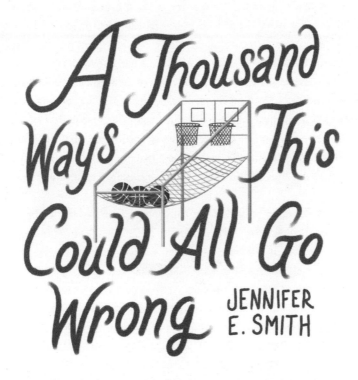

When I spot him at the other end of the grocery aisle, I freeze.

It's not that I don't want to see him. In fact, all summer I've been hoping to run into him. Looking at him now—in his same old khakis and a pale-blue button-down, his flips-flops worn thin at the heels, and his hair a bit longer than it was when I'd last spent an entire period of Spanish class staring at it—it's hard to believe it's been only six weeks.

It feels like it's been forever.

Lately, I've been daydreaming about running into him, imagining elaborate scenarios where he walks by while I'm at the beach with friends, and we decide to go for a stroll by the lake to catch up, or where he'll wander into the sandwich shop in town just as I'm telling a particularly great joke, and everyone at the table will be laughing at my dazzling wit as he casually drops by the table to say hello.

But now I've just finished work, which means I'm a total mess. There's a big purple splotch near the bottom of my white camp T-shirt, from someone's Popsicle, and a grass stain on my shoulder from where Andrew Mitchell knocked me over during an unusually aggressive game of red rover this afternoon. I have dirt on my knees, and duct tape on my sandals where the strap broke while I was chasing Henry Ascher during duck, duck, goose. I'm sweaty and sunburned and exhausted, not to mention that I'm still wearing the name tag I made in arts and crafts, which says "Annie" in such uneven, blocky lettering that it looks like it belongs to one of the kids.

But still, when I see Griffin Reilly at the end of the aisle, I can't quite bring myself to walk away.

He's examining a bag of candy, and while I watch, he turns it over in his hands, gripping it like a basketball, then pivots and sends it arcing toward his cart, which is a good six feet away. It clangs off the side, rattling the metal caging before falling to the floor with a *thwack*.

"Nice shot," I say, walking over, and he grins a little as he leans to grab it. I hold out my hands. "Let me try."

Without saying anything, he scoops up the bag and then, in one fluid motion, tosses it in my direction. I manage to catch it, but just barely. Without hesitating, I lift my arms, poised to shoot, but he shakes his head.

"Too close."

I take a few steps back, feeling nervous beneath his steady, gray-eyed gaze. This time, the bag goes sailing through the air, landing square in the center of the cart, and I turn back to him with a triumphant look.

He nods. "Not bad."

"I'm better with an actual basketball."

"Oh yeah?"

"Actually, no," I admit. "I'm kind of terrible. But I'm great with those mini ones."

"Pop-A-Shot?"

"Exactly," I say. "I'm insanely good at Pop-A-Shot."

"And not very modest," he points out, entirely straight-faced.

"Well," I say with a shrug, "it's hard to be modest when you're as good as I am."

He stretches out an arm, leaning against a shelf full of brightly packaged cookies. "Sounds like something to see," he says, not quite looking at me. He has this way of ducking his head when he's talking to you so that it's hard to tell what he's thinking. It's maddening and intriguing and confusing all at once. In Spanish, I used to ask him questions just to watch him turn around, his pale eyes skipping from my forehead to my desk, never exactly meeting my gaze, and I would try to guess whether he liked me or was afraid of me or something else entirely.

For months and months, that's all there was between us: questions about verb conjugations and past perfect tenses, *hola*s and *muchas gracias*es and *adios*es. We didn't have any friends in common; it was hard to know if we had anything in common at all. It was a big school, and this was the first time I'd come across him, sitting there in Señor Mandelbaum's third-period Spanish class. But right away I wanted more of him.

He didn't make it easy. There was something oddly cagey and way too direct about him all at the same time. He was mostly quiet and overly polite, but then he could also be honest to a startling degree. I'd once asked him if there was something in my eye, and he turned around, looked at me carefully, and then shrugged.

"Yeah," he said. "Eye goop."

But the thing about Griffin was that he was also sort of jaw-droppingly beautiful. He had messy brown hair and a square jaw and those gorgeous gray-blue eyes, and with his ridiculous height—he was a good foot taller than me, his legs always jammed against the bottom of his desk in class—he could've passed for a surfer or a skier, some kind of impossibly rugged and dashing figure from a movie.

Except, for some reason, he managed to ruin it by wearing the same outfit pretty much every single day: khaki pants and a light-blue button-down shirt, a strange uniform of sorts that made him look like a Boy Scout or a Bible salesman or someone who worked in the world's most boring office.

Still, it wasn't enough to keep the girls from staring at him during lunch, which was the only other time I ever saw him. He generally kept to himself, eating with his headphones in, his eyes focused on his phone, which made it hard to tell whether he was just really good at ignoring the attention or he simply never noticed it.

There was something magnetic about him. Whenever I saw him, I had the completely unfamiliar urge to take him by the shoulders, plunk him down in a chair, and make him open up to me. He was a mystery that—for reasons I didn't quite understand—I felt desperate to solve. But there was only so much you could learn about someone in stilted Spanish. I was anxious for more time with him. And I wanted it to be in English.

Now, Griffin's eyes drift past me to the checkout lines, and I can't tell if he's running late or getting bored. But something about seeing him here, out of context—away from the familiar backdrop of the high school—makes me momentarily brave.

"Have you ever been to Hal's?" I ask, before I can think better of it.

"That bar on McKinley?"

"It's an arcade too. Maybe we should . . ." I pause for a second, hoping he'll pick up the thread, but he doesn't. He only scuffs his flip-flop against the shiny linoleum floor, and the thought hangs there between us, awkward and unfinished.

I've never done this before, whatever it is I'm trying to do here. I've never attempted to make the first move. And now I can't help feeling a pang of regret about all the times *I've* been the one to hesitate in this situation: staring too long at a text about hanging out, clearing my throat after the suggestion of a movie, pausing at the more formal invitation to a school dance. I wish now that I could take them back, all those extra seconds. Because this—this horrifying pause, this awful silence—is brutal.

I point to the bag of candy, which is lying flat in the bottom of the cart, and then I try one last time. "Maybe we should see who would win a real game . . ."

For a second, it seems certain he's going to say no. His face slips into a kind of blankness, and he looks unaccountably tense, and I steel myself, preparing to get rejected right here in aisle 8. But then something seems to settle in him, and he blinks a few times, his features softening.

"Okay," he says finally. "How about tomorrow?"

That night as I brush my teeth, my little sister, Meg—eleven years old and my constant shadow—leans against the door of the bathroom we share.

"So," she says, batting her eyelashes in an overly dreamy sort of way. "Is it a date?"

I consider this for a moment, then spit into the sink.

"I don't think so," I tell her.

I'm a million miles away the next morning, thinking about the moment when Griffin will pull into the camp parking lot later, thinking about the dress I stashed in the staff bathroom so that I won't have to wear my grubby uniform again, thinking about the way my heart lifted when I spotted him yesterday—thinking about pretty much anything except for the game of freeze tag happening around me, where a couple dozen six- and seven-year-olds are running around the soccer field, stumbling and wobbling and tripping over themselves like miniature drunks—when someone lets out a sharp cry.

I snap back immediately, scanning the field until I find Noah, who is crouched on the ground, his knees tucked up beneath him, his hands over his ears, his head curled down so that only a mop of reddish hair is showing.

Beside him, a small girl named Sadie Smith is staring with wide eyes. "All I did was tag him," she says quickly, blinking up at me.

I give her a pat on the shoulder, trying to be reassuring. "It's fine," I tell her. "Go tag someone else."

But she remains there, her eyes fixed on Noah, who is rocking now. I turn around to see that they're all watching. It's impossible to tell who's been frozen and who's still free, because each and every one of them is standing stock-still.

Over near the school buildings, which the day camp borrows during the summer, I spot Grace, one of the junior counselors, carrying over the midday snack: a giant box of Popsicles, which leave everyone tie-dyed and sugar-happy but are always the highlight of the day.

"Snack time," I call out, and just like that, they're off, sprinting across the field to meet Grace, with more energy than they've shown during any of the games this morning.

Once we're alone, I sit down on the grass beside Noah, who lets out a soft moan but doesn't otherwise acknowledge me. It's been about a month now, and I've learned this is the best tactic. At first, when this kind of thing happened, I would try to talk to him, or reason with him, or soothe him in some way. Once, I even tried to take his hand, which turned out to be the worst possible thing I could've done. He wrenched it away from me, then promptly began to wail.

Now I peek under his arms, which are clasped around his knees, to where his face is hidden. His cheeks are pink from the heat, and his mouth is screwed up to one side, and there's a single tear leaking from his right eye, which breaks my heart a little.

"Hey, Noah," I say softly, and he stiffens.

I sit back again, picking a few blades of dry grass, then letting them scatter in the breeze from the nearby lake. In the distance, the other campers are running around with their Popsicles, their chins sticky and their shirts already stained. On the blacktop, the older kids are playing basketball, the sound of the ball steady as a drumbeat.

On the first day of camp, Mr. Hamill, the director—a middle-aged man who worked as a gym teacher for most of the year and was never without a whistle around his neck—had asked me to arrive an hour early. It was my third summer as a counselor, and I assumed I was getting a promotion. When I'd started working here a few years earlier, it was mostly just because I needed a way to earn some extra spending money. I'd loved going to camp as a kid, and it seemed a better alternative than bagging groceries or scooping ice cream or any of the other jobs that might consider hiring a fourteen-year-old whose only résumé item was babysitting.

But now, after a couple years of corralling kids and pressing on Band-Aids, leading wildly off-key songs and supervising glitter usage during craft time, I'd come to genuinely enjoy it. Still, everyone knew it was easier to work with the older kids, who tended to be more self-sufficient, less likely to burst into tears or wander off or forget to put on sunscreen. So I hoped that might be where I was headed this summer.

Instead, it turned out Mr. Hamill wanted to tell me about Noah.

"Listen, Annie," he said in a thick Chicago accent that wasn't often heard this far out in the suburbs. "We're gonna try something out this summer. And if it doesn't work, it doesn't work."

I nodded. "Okay . . ."

"It's a new camper," he continued, looking uncharacteristically nervous. "He's, uh, on the spectrum. You know. He has autism. So I just wanted to give you a heads up, since it might be a challenge. He's not all that verbal, for one thing, but I guess they're working on that. And he's pretty active. Apparently, they tried a special-needs camp last year, but it didn't keep him busy enough. It sounds like he has a lot of energy."

"So he'll be in my group?"

"Yeah, he's six, so he's one of yours. The idea is to be patient, but also get him involved as much as possible, you know? I figure we'll give it a try, as long as it's okay with you, and basically just see how it goes."

"Okay," I said brightly, because that's what I do. I smile, and I nod, and I give it my best shot. That's always how it's been. If my friends are fighting, I'm the one who tries to smooth it over. If someone is mad at me, I walk around with a pit in my stomach until we've managed to sort things out. If somebody asks me a favor, or gives me a challenge, or needs something from me, the answer is always yes.

And if the kids at camp aren't having fun, it feels like I'm failing.

Which is what makes Noah so tough. I've spoken to his mom enough over the last month to know that he just needs time. But sitting here on the warm grass, watching his shoulders shake— it's almost too much to bear. And worse than that is the feeling that no matter what I try, I just can't seem to reach him.

The thing is, I'm good with these kids. I know that Emerson is allergic to peanuts and to save a red Popsicle for Connell. I know that Sullivan will always want to play kickball when given the choice, and that Ellis likes to sit on my lap after lunch. Caroline keeps a stuffed rabbit in her backpack, and Will wears his lucky astronaut socks every day. Georgia sings under her breath when she's nervous, and Elisabeth lights up when you compliment her on her cartwheels.

There's a key to every lock, a trick that works for every kid.

Every kid except Noah.

We sit there for a long time. The other campers head into the gym for a game of dodgeball, led by one of the junior counselors, and the sun drifts higher in the flat, white sky. But still Noah remains hunched on the ground, curled into himself like a pill bug. Every once in a while I reach over and give his shoulder a pat, which makes him flinch.

Finally, just before pickup—almost as if he's been keeping track—he lifts his head.

"You okay?" I ask, but he doesn't say anything. His eyes are focused on the school building, where the other kids are lining up to go home.

When he still doesn't answer, I say, "I promise we'll play a different game tomorrow." I don't know if it was freeze tag that set him off, or if it was an unexpected hand on his back, or if it was just the sun and the grass and the day all around him. It could have been anything. It feels horrible not to know exactly what.

But still I keep talking, sounding desperate even to myself. "We'll try capture the flag," I promise, even though each day we attempt a new game, and each day it ends this same way. "Or red light, green light. Or follow the leader! I think you'd really like follow the leader . . ."

Noah doesn't say anything. He simply stands up, his face entirely blank, then brushes the grass off his knees and walks toward the parking lot.

It's not much, but I take it as a yes. And I follow him.

At the end of every day, there's the chaos of pickup time: a half hour of attempting to direct traffic and shepherd kids as mothers glare at the cars in front of them and nannies shout for their charges not to forget their lunch boxes and counselors do their best to make sure nobody gets hit by a slow-moving minivan.

Today, I'm in charge of keeping things running on time, which basically means standing in the middle of it all and hoping I don't get clipped by a side mirror. It's only 2:07, and already more than half the kids have been whisked away. The rest are sitting cross-legged under the trees in front of the entrance to the school, digging through their backpacks or trading woven bracelets or tossing things at the junior counselors.

We're right on schedule, but I still can't help glancing at my watch. Griffin is supposed to be picking me up at 2:30, and though everyone is usually gone by twenty after, that still leaves me only a few minutes to change. I've brought my favorite outfit, a pale-yellow sundress that's probably a bit much for a trip to an arcade. But there's no way I'll be wearing my sweaty camp clothes when I see him again. Not this time.

By 2:18, there are three kids left: a pair of eight-year-old identical twins who match right down to their orange sneakers, and Noah, who is sitting with his back to the parking lot, tapping intently on the trunk of a tree.

Most of the other counselors have taken off. There's only me and Alex Sanchez, a soon-to-be senior who likes to tease me about my freckles, which have been multiplying by the day, and who is generally a lot nicer than he needs to be, considering the fact that he's a whole year older than me and the star of the football team.

But that's the thing about summer: The regular hierarchies collapse like sand castles at this time of year. Everything shifts and settles and takes new shape.

It's a great equalizer, this season.

Soon, the twins' mother pulls up—full of apologies—and Alex heads off, with a sympathetic glance in my direction.

"See you tomorrow, Freckles," he says, trotting over to his car.

It's 2:22 and the parking lot is quiet. Noah is hunched over, still facing the tree, and through the thin cotton of his camp T-shirt I can see the knobs of his spine. The wind ruffles his red hair as he examines the fraying end of his shoelace.

Behind us, the door to the school opens and Mr. Hamill walks out with a pink Post-it note stuck to his finger. He hands it to me with a sheepish look, and I see that there's a phone number scrawled across it.

"So I tried his mom a few times," he says. "But there's no answer, and I have to leave for a dentist appointment." He points at his mouth and winces. "Broken crown."

My eyes travel over to the entrance to the parking lot, where Griffin's car will soon appear.

"I feel terrible about this," Mr. Hamill says with a sigh. "But his mom's not usually late, so I can't imagine she'll be long. Do you mind waiting with him?"

Noah shifts on the grass, swiveling to face us. When I glance down at him, our eyes meet briefly, and he holds my gaze for a split second before looking away again.

It's now 2:28.

"Of course," I say, because that's the kind of thing I always say. "I'm happy to."

By the time Griffin's car—something old and loud and blue—turns into the drive at 2:30 on the dot, I'm midway through dialing Noah's mother for the second time. I lower the phone and hang up, feeling panicked. This isn't how it was supposed to go. Noah is now walking in circles around the trunk of the tree, dragging his fingers across the rough bark as he spins, and I think again of the small duffel bag I tucked away, full of not just a change of clothes but also deodorant and perfume and a brush, all of which I could desperately use right about now.

But there's no time for any of that: Griffin is already walking toward me, a hand lifted awkwardly, his eyes pinging between me and Noah, who has stopped circling and is now simply staring.

"Hi," I say, and Griffin smiles. He's wearing the usual blue shirt and khakis, but his hair is freshly combed and still a little damp, and though it's approximately a thousand degrees out—the air so humid it has a weight to it—he still somehow manages to look improbably cool.

Which only makes me feel like more of a mess.

"Hi," he says.

"I'm really sorry," I begin, even before he's all the way across the parking lot. I gesture at Noah, then shrug helplessly. "His mom isn't here yet, so I have to wait with him, which means I can't—"

"That's okay," Griffin says. "I'll wait with you."

"You don't have to do that," I say automatically, and he raises his eyebrows.

"I know," he says stiffly. "But I want to. Otherwise I wouldn't have offered."

His words linger between us for a beat too long, until I finally say, "Okay then."

"Okay then," he says with a nod, already walking past me to where Noah stands underneath the tree. The two of them look at each other for a second, then both immediately avert their eyes. Griffin takes a step forward, and Noah takes a step back, like two dancers practicing a choreographed routine. There's a long pause, and I watch them, curious to see what will happen next. Finally, Griffin lifts his hand in a kind of half-wave.

"Hi," he says. "I'm Griffin."

Noah squints up at him, tilting his head. And then, to my surprise, he says it back: "Hi."

It's not that Noah doesn't *ever* talk. It's just that he rarely does so on cue. If you ask him a question, he tends to look away. If you say hello, he ignores you. If you try to include him in a game that requires singing or chanting or talking, he usually shuts down. When he does speak, it's mostly to himself.

So now, hearing him respond to a greeting like it's something that happens every day, my throat goes thick with unexpected emotion.

"What should we do while we wait?" Griffin asks, his eyes trained on the small, startled boy in front of him.

I hold my breath, waiting, as the silence seems to stretch on forever.

But just as I'm about to interrupt—to come to his rescue, to cut through the quiet, to help out by suggesting a game—Noah hops to his feet and says, "Basketball."

Griffin, it turns out, is better with a basketball than he was with a bag of candy. I stand at the edge of the blacktop with the phone pressed to my ear, listening to it ring for what feels like the thousandth time, as he sinks another effortless shot from the free throw line and Noah chases after the rebound.

"I'm feeling less confident about our Pop-A-Shot competition," I say, giving up on the call. I've left several messages now, and there's not much more to be done except to wait.

"I don't know," Griffin says without looking at me. "Someone told me you're insanely good."

"Who said that?"

The corners of his mouth turn up in a half-smile. "You."

"Oh." I flush. "Right."

Noah is attempting to dribble, which mostly consists of slapping at the ball with his open palms, and Griffin walks over, bending close to demonstrate how to soften his hand. I fold my arms across my chest, watching with interest. I keep waiting for Griffin to make a wrong move and set Noah off, the way I always manage to do when I touch his shoulder or speak too loudly or get too close. But he doesn't. He seems to know instinctively what not to do, and because of it, Noah has said more to him in the last twenty minutes than he's said to me all summer.

I'm admittedly a little jealous.

"Hey, Noah." I clap my hands, which makes him wince. "Pass it here."

He stops trying to dribble and glances over at me, his face impassive. Then he turns back to Griffin, handing him the ball.

"Thanks, dude." Griffin quicksteps around him and darts for the basket. There's something so fluid about him when he has the ball in his hands. He's long and lean, and all of his stiffness, all of his usual guardedness, seems to fall away.

"My turn," Noah says, and Griffin bounces it to him gently.

"You're good with him," I say, when he jogs over to stand with me. Around us, the schoolyard is quiet except for the sound of a distant lawn mower, and the afternoon sun is caught in the trees at the edge of the soccer field. "Do you have younger brothers or sisters?"

He shakes his head. "Only child."

"Well, that explains it."

"What?"

"Why you never talked to anyone in Spanish."

He glances sideways at me. "I talked."

"Yeah, when Señor Mandelbaum asked you a question."

On the court, Noah flings the ball up toward the basket, but it only makes it a couple feet in the air before falling to the asphalt with a heavy thud.

"You never talked, either," Griffin points out.

"Did too."

"Puedo ir al baño? Doesn't count."

"Hey," I say, laughing. "Is it my fault if I had to ir al baño?"

He raises an eyebrow. "Twice every class?"

"Señor Mandelbaum was seriously, seriously boring," I admit. "Most of the time I just ended up reading out in the hallway."

"En inglés?" Griffin asks, and I laugh.

"Si," I tell him. "En inglés."

We stand there in silence, watching Noah heave the ball at the basket again and again. As his arms get tired, each shot falls shorter, until he's basically throwing it straight up in the air, then dodging it as it comes back down again.

When the ball rolls my way, I scoop it up and take a shot myself, but it doesn't go much farther than Noah's attempts, barely grazing the bottom of the net.

"See?" I say, frowning. "This is why Pop-A-Shot is better."

I glance over at Griffin, who looks amused, and it occurs to me that whatever this is—this maybe-date, which was questionable even before it took such an odd detour—it should be going horribly wrong. With an empty playground for a backdrop and a six-year-old sidekick, how could it be anything else? This certainly wasn't how I'd imagined it, all those times I stared at the back of his head in Spanish class.

But for whatever reason, Griffin looks almost happy right now.

And I realize I am too.

"Let's play a game of caballo," he suggests, and Noah lets out a burst of unexpected laughter.

"Caballo," he shouts, pumping an arm in the air. "Caballo, caballo!"

"What's caballo?" I ask Griffin, who's already walking over to the basket, and when he turns around, he can't help laughing.

"It's horse," he says with a grin. "En español."

It's nearly four o'clock by the time I start worrying that this is more than just lateness and that something might be seriously wrong with Noah's mother.

The good news is that he doesn't seem to have noticed. Having finally grown tired of basketball, he's lying on his back in the grass, an arm shielding his eyes from the sun, his foot moving in time to some unknown rhythm.

"It's been two hours," I say to Griffin, who is sitting beside me in the shade, our backs against the brick wall of the school. Our shoulders are only a few inches apart, our knees almost touching, and I keep hoping that he'll scoot closer. But he doesn't.

"That's a long time," he says, gazing off in the direction of the empty soccer fields in the distance. "A lot can happen in two hours."

I tip my head back and close my eyes. That's exactly the thought I've been trying to avoid. Beside me, I can feel Griffin studying me in profile, and it's hard not to turn and face him. But I know that if I do, he'll look away again, those pale eyes of his like tropical fish, so quick to dart away.

"Maybe something happened to her," he says, and I look over at him sharply.

"Don't say that."

"Why not?"

"Because . . ." I say, before trailing off.

"Because it might be true," he finishes, and there's something too matter-of-fact in his tone, a bluntness that's unsettling. I can't decide if that's because what he's saying is true or because I'm rarely so honest myself.

I clear my throat. "I'm sure everything's fine."

"Based on what?" he asks, but there's no challenge to his words. There's not even any emotion behind them. He's simply asking.

"Because," I say, fumbling a little. "Because it has to be."

Griffin considers this. "That's not very logical."

"Who said anything about logic?" I say, just as my phone rings, jittering roughly across the pavement. I grab it, relieved to see the number I've been dialing all afternoon, and angle myself slightly away from Griffin.

As soon as I pick up, there's a flood of words, rushed and frantic and apologetic. "His sister broke her arm on the swings," Noah's mother says. "One minute she was pumping her legs and the next she was jumping off, and everything was so chaotic with the ambulance and the hospital and getting the cast, and I didn't have the number for the camp with me, and my husband is out of town on business, and—"

"It's fine," I say for what feels like the millionth time this afternoon. "We have him. He's totally fine."

"I'll be there in three minutes," she says, and then the call ends, and I let out a long, relieved breath.

"See?" I turn to Griffin, who I can tell has been listening. "Everything's fine."

"Well," he says with a shrug, "there were only ever two options. Either it was going to be fine or it wasn't."

A few minutes later, as we head over to the parking lot, I'm astonished to see Noah reach up and take Griffin's hand.

Without meaning to, I come to an abrupt halt.

I've never once seen Noah initiate contact with anyone before. And for that matter, I've never really seen Griffin do it, either.

But now he folds the younger boy's hand in his own as if they've known each other forever, as if this happens every day, as if it's not the most extraordinary thing in the world.

That night, my sister pokes her head into my room.

"So," she says, her eyes very bright, "was it a date?"

I think of Griffin in his blue button-down, the flicker of surprise on his face when Noah reached for his hand, the nearness of him as we sat against the brick wall of the school, the way the clouds passed overhead and the world had been quiet around us.

I think of the way we'd left things in the parking lot. By then, it was too late to head out to the arcade, and we decided to try again another day. As he walked back toward his car, though, I felt a rise of panic at the open-endedness of it all, and without thinking, I called out, "Tomorrow?"

He stopped.

"Mañana," he agreed with a smile that made me dizzy.

"*Annie.*" Meg's voice is full of impatience, and I realize she's still waiting for an answer.

"Yeah?"

"Was it?" she asks, and I shake my head.

"No," I say. "It was better."

In the morning, once everyone is assembled in the gymnasium, where we start our day, I ask the kids what they'd like to play first.

"Kickball!" says Nadim Sourgen.

"Red rover!" says Gigi Gabriele.

"Nothing!" says Tommy King.

There's some conferring—heads put together, hushed whispers, peals of laughter. Then, out of nowhere, Noah pipes up. "Caballo!"

This is followed by a surprised silence. The other kids look over at him as if they'd forgotten he was there.

"What's caballo?" asks Jake Down.

"It's Spanish," I say. "For horse."

"Like in riding?" asks Lucy Etherington.

"Like in basketball," I say, smiling at Noah, who has already hopped to his feet, his hands on his hips, ready to play. "Caballo it is."

This time, I'm not leaving it to chance. At the end of the day, even before we've trooped out to the parking lot for pickup, I leave Grace and another junior counselor to look after the kids and I hurry to the bathroom to change into my dress.

When I emerge from the cool of the building into the afternoon heat, all the campers turn to stare at me. They've only ever seen me in a messy ponytail and the same white T-shirt and green shorts. They've only ever seen me looking tired and sweaty and harried.

But now I'm wearing a yellow sundress that swishes when I walk, and I've let out my ponytail so that my dark hair falls to my shoulders. I've got on perfume and deodorant and even bit of makeup. And from the expressions on their faces, it's clear I look like an entirely different person.

"You smell good," says Tommy O'Callaghan, with a note of surprise.

"Like flowers," confirms Wells von Stroh.

"Thanks," I say, hoping Griffin might have a similar reaction.

All the parents are on time today, even Noah's mother, who

arrives with a rueful wave. His sister is in the back, and she lifts an arm to show off her bright pink cast. As I walk him over to the car, Noah keeps his usual distance, but when his mom rolls down the window to ask how his day was, he looks up at her.

"We played caballo," he says, climbing into the back seat.

"What's caballo?" I hear her ask as they pull away, and I'm still smiling at the disappearing car when I see Griffin across the parking lot.

The first thing I notice is that he's wearing a different button-down. I squint to make sure I'm seeing it right, but it's true. This one is the exact same style as the others, only it's checkered blue and white. It takes me a moment to realize he has on jeans, too; they're a little long, so he's cuffed them at the bottom, but they still drag on the ground, making soft scraping noises as he walks over.

"Wow," I say when he reaches me. He's not even bothering to hide the fact that he's staring at my dress, and this suddenly feels like an actual date. "You look really nice."

"Oh." His eyes snap up, then back down again. "Yeah, my mom—" He stops, then lets out a sheepish laugh. "My mom told me not to say that she helped me pick out this outfit. But I guess I just did."

I laugh, too. "I guess so."

"She also told me to tell you that you look nice."

"Your mom sounds like a smart lady," I say, watching his face go pink, and it's all so endearing: this guy who looks like he should be a total player, like he should know exactly what he's doing when it comes to dating, but is actually getting advice from his mother. His awkwardness is completely charming and entirely unexpected, but instead of putting me at ease, it makes me more nervous, as I realize just how much I like him.

"Ready to go?" I glance behind me at the remaining campers, who are staring at us, and the other counselors, who are grinning and wolf whistling. I know they'll have questions for me tomorrow. I only hope I'll know how to answer them by then.

At the car, Griffin opens my door, and I think *date!* But then he seems to go out of his way to make sure our arms don't accidentally touch as I climb in, and once again, I'm not so sure. When we're both buckled in, he fumbles with the keys for a second, and as we pull out of the parking lot he turns on the radio. I'm surprised to hear the measured voice of an NPR reporter giving a rundown of the day's news.

"I would've pegged you for classic rock," I tell him, and he automatically reaches for the knob, turning down the volume. "Or maybe just classical."

"I like the news," he admits after a long pause, so long that it's hard to tell if this is a response to my earlier comment or just an idle thought. "I like to know what's going on in the world."

"Smarty pants," I say, and he shrugs.

"I like facts. And statistics. There's something kind of soothing about them."

"About statistics? There's something kind of headachy about them for me."

"That's how I first got into basketball." He drums his fingers on the wheel, his eyes square to the road. I've spent so much time staring at the back of his head, or else trying to get him to meet my eye, that I've never had a chance to study him in profile—the gentle slope of his nose, the scar just below his right eye, the perfect cheekbones, and the way his hair falls over his ear. "The numbers."

"Definitely the most exciting part of the game," I say with mock enthusiasm, and I see him start to bob his head before he catches himself.

"You're joking," he says, and I nod.

"I am."

"Seriously, though," he goes on, "there's something really cool about all the stats, but it's more than that. It's a game of angles. I mean, think about it. If you're able to stand in one place and shoot the ball in the exact right way once, you should be able to stand there every single time and do the same thing, right? Technically speaking, you should be able to make the ball go in again every single time."

"Yeah, but that's not how it works," I say. "Because you're not a robot. You twitch, and it goes to the left. Or you raise your hand a little higher than the last time without realizing it. There are always a thousand different ways it could go wrong."

"Exactly," he said. "But here's the cool part: You can also adjust a bunch of various factors and still have it go in from the same spot, even while shooting it in a completely different way. So there are about a thousand different ways it could go right, too."

I look at him sideways. "Is this your way of talking a big game?"

"For Pop-A-Shot?" He shakes his head. "No, I'm sure you're gonna beat me."

"I have to admit, we used to have one in our basement, so I've had a lot of practice. But it's been a while."

"How come?"

"Oh," I say, blinking a few times as he eases the car onto another road. Ahead of us, the sun is slipping lower in the sky, and the buildings on either side of us have been replaced by a blur of trees. "We had to—we moved a few years ago. Out of a house and into an apartment. So . . . no more room for anything like that."

We're both quiet for a moment, and Griffin repositions his hands on the wheel. "It's not as good as real basketball anyway. The balls are too small."

"Maybe it's that your hands are too big."

"That too," he says. "But it messes up all the angles."

"So you're gonna blame your upcoming defeat on math?"

"Pretty much."

Just ahead, an ancient-looking wooden sign advertises Hal's Bar & Restaurant, and Griffin pulls into the gravel drive. There are only a couple other cars in the lot, and we park and walk over to the entrance together.

Inside, it's dark enough that it takes our eyes a few seconds to adjust. The bartender glances up, then away again. Nobody else even bothers. Hal's is a strange hybrid, part family restaurant and arcade, part hole-in-the-wall bar. On the weekends it's crawling with kids eager to redeem their tickets for dinky prizes. But during the week it has a seedier feel to it, dotted with regulars who sit silently hunched at the bar, drinking slowly and watching baseball on the boxy old TV in the corner.

We scoot past the bar and into the back room, which is filled with huge, blocky games like Pac-Man and skee ball and pinball, plus one of those giant tanks filled with stuffed animals and a useless metal claw. The place is quiet and dusty and entirely empty, which isn't particularly surprising for a Wednesday afternoon in the middle of the summer. Nobody would choose to spend a beautiful day inside a dimly lit arcade. Except, apparently, for us.

"Quarters," I say, marching over to the machine, and Griffin trails after me. I feed a few dollar bills into the slot, and the coins clink loudly as they fall into the metal drawer. Behind me, I can feel him waiting as I scoop them out, and my heart picks up speed. Something about the quietness of this place—which is meant to be full of people and lights and noise—makes it feel like we've stepped out of the real world.

"Hey," he says softly, and I spin around, my hands filled with coins.

"Yeah?"

In the dusty light from the window, his eyes look very, very blue, and the small scar below his right one is more pronounced.

"I just—" he begins, then stops.

I wait for him to continue. There's a Cubs game on in the next room, and the tinny sound of distant cheering rises and falls in the stillness. Griffin lifts an arm, and for a second I think he's reaching for my hand. But then we both look down, and I realize I'm still holding a pile of quarters. Instead, he takes a single coin, flipping it once with his thumb so that it lands perfectly in his palm.

"Tails," he says absently.

"What are the odds?" I joke, my voice a little wobbly, and Griffin gives me a funny look.

"Fifty-fifty," he says, as he walks over to the Pop-A-Shot machine, the moment slipping away all at once. This is how it always is with Griffin, like any progress you think you're making has a tendency to evaporate immediately afterward. Like no matter how much you think you're connecting, no matter how hard you try, it doesn't ever add up to anything. You're always stuck starting over again the next time.

I follow him over to the game, where two small hoops are arranged side by side, with a net that runs down toward the two players, so that each time you shoot, the balls come rolling back in your direction, an endless supply that only runs out when the timer ticks down and the buzzer sounds.

Griffin is already rolling up his sleeves. When he's ready, he grabs one of the balls, which is about two-thirds the size of a regular basketball, easy enough for him to palm. "These are pretty wimpy," he says as he studies it.

"You know who these would be great for?" I ask, grabbing another one. "Noah. Did you see how much trouble he was having yesterday? We played again this afternoon, and the regular ones are too heavy for him. But with these, I bet he could almost get it to the basket."

"And when he dribbles," Griffin says, bouncing the ball on the wooden floor a couple times, "he'd have a way better grip."

"Maybe we can win him one." I point at the glass case in the corner, which is filled with prizes. I usually don't even bother, since the amount of quarters it takes to win enough tickets to buy anything is about ten times what the thing actually costs. But, even from here, I can see a small green and white basketball half hidden by a stuffed elephant on the lowest shelf. "It's camp colors and everything."

Griffin turns back to the baskets. "Well, if you're as good a player as you are a talker, I'd say it's a definite possibility."

"The trick," I say, turning to face the hoop, "is to line yourself up just right."

"No," he says, as he feeds the quarters into the slot. "The trick is to get the ball in the basket."

The machine comes to life, all blinking lights and blaring jingles, and the timer on the scoreboard starts counting down from ten. I reach for the first ball, then stand poised and ready to shoot. Beside me, Griffin is doing the same, his face focused and ready.

And then the buzzer sounds, and I let the ball fly. It bounces off the rim, but before it's even landed back in the chute, I've launched the second one, which falls into the net with a satisfying swish, though I'm too busy to notice. I'm already shooting again, and then again, falling into a neat rhythm, the quick tempo pattern a kind of muscle memory, a callback to the hours spent playing in our basement, before my dad lost his job and we had to sell the games, before we moved to a smaller house, and then to a tiny apartment, before the fighting started, the late nights and the shouting and the name-calling, and my sister curled up in my bed with me, a pillow over her ears. Before all that—before we learned how to put on happy faces, before we understood that smiles were something you could hide behind, and words could be used as shields, when it was just the four of us in the basement, the concrete walls ringing out with the bright sounds of laughter and cheering.

Now, once again, I'm in constant motion, moving like a machine, steady and unseeing, and when it's over, even after the clocks have displayed their broken zeroes and the buzzer has long since sounded, I continue to shoot what's in front of me until all the balls are gone, and then I stand there, empty-handed and blinking.

"Whoa," Griffin says, staring at the scoreboard.

I haven't just beat him; I've demolished him. The score is 88 to 42.

"Whoa," he says again. "You were in some kind of crazy zone there."

"Yeah," I say, still not entirely sure I've come out of it, still not entirely sure I want to. "I guess I was."

We play all afternoon.

"Rematch," Griffin keeps calling, each time I beat him, and though my margin of victory gets slimmer each time, it also gets funnier and funnier.

"This is ridiculous," he says, laughing, after our eleventh round, where I beat him 76 to 62. He leans back on the pool table, shaking his head.

"And you thought I was just talking a big game," I say with a grin.

"You were," he points out. "But it turns out you have the skills to back it up."

I hoist myself onto the pool table beside him, letting my legs dangle. "Well, thanks for being such a good sport."

He looks surprised. "Yeah . . . it's kind of weird. I usually hate to lose."

"Tell me about it," I say, but he shakes his head.

"No, I mean it. I really, really hate to lose. I hate doing things I'm not good at, so if I love something, I get really into it, but if not, I can't be bothered. I'm usually either all in or all out."

"That doesn't sound like such a bad thing."

"It is," he says, scratching at the back of his neck. "Nobody likes a sore loser."

"You don't seem like a very sore loser to me."

"Yeah, well, that's the thing," he says, turning to look at me, really look at me, for the very first time, and there's something about catching his eye that feels like winning a prize. "With you, I don't seem to mind it as much."

The display case holds a ragtag assortment of dubious prizes: On the top shelf are baskets full of bouncy balls and candy, key chains and plastic rings, and below that are the bigger-ticket items, stuffed animals and inflatable bats, miniature footballs and gumball machines—everything wildly overpriced and a little bit dusty.

Griffin and I lean over the glass together, his shoulder brushing against mine in a way that makes my heart beat faster. I want him to notice, to lean into it, to turn and look at me again or to take my hand, to pull me close or kiss me—*anything*.

But he doesn't.

Instead, he rubs at the smudged glass with the sleeve of his shirt. In the column of light from the window, he looks impossibly handsome and incredibly far away.

We're both quiet for a long time, for too long, and I start to get edgy, searching for something to fill the silence, because that's what I always do. But I stop myself, deciding that it's his turn, which only makes me more anxious. Because suddenly it seems important, whatever he might say next. Suddenly, it feels like it has the power to tip this maybe-possibly-date in one direction or the other.

I stare down at an orange plastic frog as I wait, and it stares back up at me through the filmy glass. *Please let it be something meaningful,* I think. *Please let it be romantic.*

But after a moment, he frowns. "This stuff is such a rip-off," he says, and all the hope goes draining right out of me. He points at the basketball, which is tucked away toward the bottom. "In what world is that worth five hundred tickets?"

We pool our tickets together and I shuffle through the stack. After hours of playing, we still have only about a hundred and fifty between us.

"Maybe we could pay the difference," I suggest, but Griffin shakes his head.

"They make a lot more money when you have to play for it."

"Well, it's still really sweet of you," I tell him. "To think of Noah."

"It's not for Noah," he says, his eyes still on the case. "It's for me."

"Oh," I say, blinking at him. "Oh. I didn't—okay."

"Annie," he says, turning to face me, and I can see that he's smiling. "I'm only kidding."

I let out a laugh, relieved. "Sorry. It's just that you don't usually . . . I mean, you're always so . . . I guess I didn't . . ."

He tilts his head to one side. "Are you trying to say that I'm not very funny?"

"No," I say quickly, then pause and reconsider. "Well . . . yeah."

Griffin smiles. "It's okay. I'm really not."

"Well, you have lots of other good qualities," I say, watching as he rests both hands on the display case, rocking forward. "You're different."

Something flickers on his face, and there's a slight tensing of his jaw.

"In a good way," I say, hurrying on. "You're not like everyone else. You're nice. Not fake nice—actually nice. And you're not full of yourself, even though . . ."

He glances sideways at me, a question on his face.

I shake my head. "Never mind. All I'm trying to say is that it's refreshing, how you don't play games the way other guys do. You're honest. Maybe the most honest person I've ever met . . ."

"Annie."

"I'm serious," I continue, feeling oddly light-headed. I'm not prone to speeches like this, and I can't quite believe I'm saying all of it, but there's something about Griffin that makes me want to tell him everything I've been thinking. And so I do.

"And you were amazing with Noah yesterday. I've been trying to connect with him all summer, and I haven't been able to get through, and then you come along, and—"

"It's because I have Asperger's."

"—you're such a natural with him, and you two are bonding over—" I stop midsentence, not sure I've heard him correctly. "What?"

Griffin turns to face me, though he keeps his eyes on the floor. "I have Asperger's. Or . . . autism, I guess. I mean, that's what they're calling it now."

There's a long pause, and though I'm desperate to fill it, I'm having trouble figuring out how to respond. I need to choose my words carefully. I don't want to get this wrong. But, in the end, all I manage is a quiet, "Oh."

Immediately, I regret it. It hangs there between us, a punctuation mark arriving far too early in a conversation I'm hoping has only just begun.

"Yeah," he says, his face entirely blank.

"So . . ."

"So that's why I act the way I do, I guess." He shoves his hands into the pockets of his jeans. "I'm not always great with conversation. And sometimes I can be too honest." He shrugs. "It's why school can be hard, and why I don't have a lot of friends, and why I don't like to talk about it, and why . . ."

When he trails off, I bite my lip, waiting for him to continue. This is the most I've ever heard him speak at once, and the thought pops into my head swiftly and suddenly, like a puzzle piece snapping into place: *That's why.*

That's why he's so quiet in school. That's why he's so obsessed with numbers and facts. That's why he can never seem to tell when I'm joking. That's why he's always so guarded, so closed off. That's why it's so hard for him to look me in the eye.

Griffin takes a deep breath, and when he speaks again, it's like he's plucked the words straight from my head. "That's why," he says, dragging his eyes up to meet mine, "I don't really go on a lot of dates."

"So this is a date?" I ask, before I can think better of it, and Griffin looks doubly embarrassed now.

"No," he says, then shakes his head. "I don't know."

My face goes hot, and I scratch at my forehead. "Oh, yeah, I mean . . ."

"I didn't want to assume . . ."

"No, me neither . . ."

There's a brief pause as we both study our feet with great fascination, and then Griffin sighs. "I kind of wanted it to be."

I glance up at him. "Wanted it to be . . . ?"

"A date," he says, just as the bartender pokes his head into the room, glancing from Griffin to me and then back again with obvious suspicion.

"Everything okay back here?" he asks, and I'm not sure how to answer that.

Griffin nods. "Fine."

"We've had some issues with theft lately." He points at the display case, as if it's full of diamonds instead of jelly bracelets and yo-yos. "So if you want a prize, you need to come talk to me . . ."

"That's fine," I say, at the exact same time Griffin says, "We were just leaving."

"Okay," the bartender says, clearly pleased to hear this. "See you next time."

"Sure," Griffin says, but he doesn't sound convinced.

On the way back, the silence in the car is stifling, and I have a feeling there's an easy cure for it, if only I can find the right words or ask the right question.

But I'm too afraid of asking the wrong one.

One of Griffin's hands is on the wheel, the other is resting on the gearshift between us, and it's alarming how much I wish I could take it in mine right now. But I don't. I simply stare at the veins on the back of his hand, the ragged fingernail on his thumb, the knobs of his knuckles, the curve of his wrist.

This is usually my specialty. Some people are good at math, others are good at sports; I'm good at saying the right thing at the right time. I'm the one you want around when the room is still thick with anger after a fight, or when you need someone to smile sympathetically and listen to what's wrong. I can smooth over even the most awkward of silences, cheer you up when you're feeling down, lift the mood by sheer force of will. For better or worse, I'm a top-notch listener, a tireless ally, a relentless supporter.

But right now, I'm at a loss.

I want to say, *This doesn't change anything.*

I want to say, *It's not a big deal.*

I want to say, *It's going to be okay.*

But it does. And it is. And it might not be.

I clear my throat, not quite sure where to begin. "Listen, I'm sorry if I—"

But Griffin lurches forward in his seat and punches the button for the radio, turning the volume up high. The conversation is clearly over, and even though he's sitting in the exact same place he was earlier, the exact same distance from me, it's like I can feel him retreating, getting further and further away until it's almost hard to see him at all.

He drops me off at the school, where my car is the only one still left in the parking lot, sitting alone beneath a yellow cone of light. Griffin pulls up beside it, but he doesn't turn off his engine, and we sit there in the quiet car, neither of us speaking.

"I had a good time," I say eventually, and even in the blue light of the early dusk, I can see the corner of his mouth twitch. It's obvious he doesn't believe me. "Really," I say, pushing forward stubbornly. "It was a lot of fun."

He doesn't answer, only gives a grudging nod.

With a sigh, I open the door and step out, but once I've shut it again, I lean into the open window. "Seriously," I say. "Thank you."

This time, he lets out a grunt, as if I've said something preposterous, and I realize all at once that I'm not the one doing this wrong. He is.

He shifts the car into gear and starts to pull away, but I jog after him.

"Hey," I shout, hooking a hand around the open window, and he looks over at me, startled, then slams on the brakes. I bend down again, staring at him hard, and this time he looks back at me. But there's a challenge in his eyes. He's daring me to say the wrong thing, and I understand now that it was always going to be like this, no matter how I reacted. It's like he's been steeling himself for this moment for so long that it almost doesn't matter how it actually unfolded. He'd already made up his mind about how it would go. He'd already decided how I'd feel about it, before I even had a chance.

But, for once, I don't feel like acting the way someone else wants me to. I don't feel like going along with anything, or being agreeable, or putting on a happy face.

For once, I feel like being honest.

"I thought this was a date, too," I tell him, my cheeks already burning. "Or at least I wanted it to be."

"You don't have to—"

"Griffin," I say, so sharply that he looks over. His expression is hard to make out in the growing darkness. "I'm not just saying that. I'm not trying to be polite. I really like you, okay?"

It's true. I'm not saying it to make him feel better. Or because I feel bad for him, or even because he's so distractingly good looking. I'm saying it because it's a fact. And if I can spend so much time saying nice things when I don't really mean them, why shouldn't I be able to say them when I actually do?"

"I've liked you since the first day of Spanish," I continue, in spite of the fact that he's turned away again, making it hard to tell just how much of an idiot I sound like at the moment. "Te gustar."

He glances up at me with a frown. "Me gustas."

"Why, thank you." I beam at him, but his face remains impenetrable, and my smile slips. "Look, the point is, I had no idea you had Asperger's then, and I still couldn't stop thinking about you. So why would anything be different now?"

"It just is," he says quietly.

I shake my head. "Not for me."

"How could it not be?"

"Because I like you. *You.* The same *you* I've liked all year." I laugh. Something about all this honesty is making me giddy. Or maybe it's just Griffin. "How many times are you gonna make me say it?"

"It's not that easy," he says, but if he's expecting me to agree with him tonight, he's picked the wrong girl.

I grin at him, then give the hood of the car a tap, just before turning around to leave. "What if it is?"

As soon as I get into my car, my phone lights up with a text from my sister.

The glowing white letters read *Date: yes or no?*

I text her back: *Inconclusive.*

But then, a moment later, I change my mind and write, *Yes.*

The next day, I'm standing in the middle of the blacktop, a whirling blur of kids running circles around me. In the distance, the older campers are playing a well-coordinated game of kickball, and usually I'd be jealous of the order of it all, the calm sense of purpose to their activities. But today I can't help laughing at the younger kids—my rowdy, frantic, overexcited crew—who are ostensibly making chalk drawings, though only two of them are actually sitting on the pavement with a fat piece of chalk in hand. Elan Dwyer is drawing an elephant with wings, and Bridget DeBerge is tracing her foot. The others have started an impromptu game of tag, and they're sprinting around with obvious joy, red-faced and giggling and utterly delighted.

All of them except Noah, who has found a basketball.

I bend down beside him so that we're both surveying the hoop from the same angle. He's already panting from the heat, which is muggy and thick, and he smells the way all little kids do in the summer: like bug spray and sunscreen and sweat. He's holding the ball with both hands as he considers his next shot, his arms already sagging.

I think of the miniature basketball from yesterday with a pang.

"How's it going?" I ask, and he continues to squint at the basket as if he hasn't heard me. "You know," I say, pointing at the hoop, "the trick is to line yourself up just right."

"No it's not," comes a voice from behind me. "The trick is to get the ball in the basket."

I whirl around to find Griffin standing on the grass just beyond the pavement, wearing his usual outfit and holding the green and white basketball from the display case in one large palm.

"Hey," I say, looking from the ball up to him and then back at the ball again. "What are you doing here?"

He nods at Noah, who is staring at him, too. "I thought this might work better," he says, holding out the ball. Noah doesn't move; he just continues to watch Griffin for what feels like a very long time. But then some switch flips inside of him, and his face brightens, and he rushes over to grab the ball.

"What do you say?" I yell after him, as he tucks it under one arm and runs back toward the basket.

"You're welcome," Noah calls over his shoulder, and I laugh. "Close enough."

Griffin is still standing a few feet away, looking nervous and out of place. Amid the frenzy of high voices and peals of laughter and churning legs, he's like an oasis: calm and still and focused.

He clears his throat. "Do you think we could talk for a minute?"

"Sure," I say, looking behind me and catching Grace's eye. I make a motion toward the corner of the building and mouth, "Be right back." When she nods, I turn back to Griffin. "Come on," I say, and he follows me around the side of the brick wall, where it's shady and cool and the voices are muffled and distant.

We stand facing each other, and he steps forward so that he's very close to me. This time, I'm the first one to look away, glancing down reflexively, where I notice an apple juice stain on my camp shirt. I lift my chin again, forcing myself to meet his eyes, surprised when he doesn't waver.

"That was really, really nice of you," I say, trying to hold onto my thoughts beneath his clear gaze. "To go buy a ball for him."

There's a hint of a smile on Griffin's face. "I didn't buy it."

"What do you—" I stop, and my mouth falls open. "No way."

He nods. "I went back last night after I dropped you off."

"It must've taken so many hours."

"It did."

"And so many quarters."

"It did."

"Well, thank you," I say. "I mean, I have no idea how you managed to do that, given your Pop-A-Shot skills, but—"

"I need to tell you something," Griffin says, cutting me off. He looks instantly apologetic. "Sorry, I didn't mean to . . . Well, see? This is what I mean. This is why I don't have very many friends. I interrupt a lot. And I don't always notice other people as much as I should. I once left my grandma in a department store because I was so busy reading about mycology on my phone."

"What's mycology?"

"The study of fungi."

I squint at him. "What does that have to do with your grandma?"

"It doesn't," he says impatiently. "But I was so wrapped up in it that when I got up to leave, I totally forgot she'd come there with me."

"Oh."

"It's something I'm working on. But there's a lot that I'm working on, and I have been my whole life. I don't always listen. And I spend too much time talking about certain things—"

"Like mycology?"

"It's *fascinating*," he says, so emphatically that it's hard not to smile. "And I can't always tell if people are upset about something, so if you were, you'd have to tell me. Because I probably wouldn't ask. And I have trouble looking people in the eye—"

"Yeah," I say, with an encouraging smile. "But you're doing it."

"I know, but it's hard. It's like trying to hold in a sneeze or something." He looks away quickly, widening his eyes and then squeezing them shut before turning back to me again. "Not that I don't like your eyes, because I do. They're very pretty." He takes a short breath, rocking back and forth on his heels before hurrying on. "And I'm way too honest. Even though you said you like that, you don't realize—"

"Griffin."

"Yeah?"

"Is this what you wanted to tell me?"

He stares at me blankly.

"You said you needed to tell me something . . ."

"Oh yeah," he says, taking a quick step forward. "Just this."

It happens so fast there's not even time to be surprised; just like that, Griffin is kissing me, a kiss that's soft and tentative and much too quick. He pulls away again almost immediately, blinking at me. "I don't know if that was okay—"

Before he can finish, I grab his shirt and tug him toward me, and this time, I'm the one who kisses him. For a split second I feel him tense up, but just as quickly, he relaxes into it, and then—as if he's forgotten there's any reason to be uncertain, as if we've done this a million times before—his arms fold around me, and the space between us disappears, and the rest of it falls away. Suddenly, he's just a boy I really, really like, and I'm just a girl he's finally worked up the nerve to kiss. There are still about a thousand ways this could all go wrong. But there are a thousand different ways it could go right, too. And for the moment, none of the rest of it matters. It's just him and me. Me and him. The two of us.

Until it's not.

At the sound of high-pitched giggling, I force myself to pull away from Griffin. For a second, I stand there completely frozen, afraid to turn around. He blinks down at me a few times with a lazy smile, but then I see it register on his face, too, and he leans around me to look.

"Oops," he says with a sheepish grin, and I cover my face with my hands.

"Gross," says Nikko Heyward with obvious glee.

"Eww," agrees Jack Doyle.

"Disgusting," says Henry Sorenson.

Behind them, Noah is staring at us, too. The ball that Griffin brought him is tucked under his arm, and he holds it out hopefully.

"Caballo?" he says, and Griffin smiles.

"Vamos!" he says, rocking forward again. Then he claps his hands once and begins to jog back toward the basketball court, Noah and the rest of the kids skipping after him. "Vamos a jugar!"

I stand there, watching him: the way he stoops to give Noah a high five, the way he waits so patiently for the others to catch up, the way he looks back at me and smiles, sending a jolt of electricity right through me.

And I think, *That's why.*

Just as they get to the court—just as Noah sends the little ball sailing, and it clangs off the rim, and he jumps up and down as if he'd performed a game-winning dunk—Griffin turns around, again looking vaguely alarmed, then jogs back over to me.

"Almost forgot something," he says, reaching out a hand, and I take it.

THE MAP OF TINY PERFECT THINGS

LEV GROSSMAN

t was August 4th, and I guess it already had been for a while. To be totally honest I didn't even notice the change at first. My life was already serving up these big fat sweltery summer days anyway, one after the other, each one pretty much exactly the same as the one before it . . . probably a more powerfully alert and observant person would have picked up on the change sooner.

What can I say, it was summer. It was hot. Anyway, here's what was going on: Time had stopped.

Or it hadn't stopped, exactly, but it got stuck in a loop.

Please believe me when I say that this is not a metaphor. I'm not trying to tell you that I was really bored and it seemed like summer would never end or something like that. What I'm saying is, the summer after my freshman year of high school, the calendar got to August 4th and gave up: Literally every single day after that was also August 4th. I went to bed on the night of August 4th. I woke up, it was the morning of August 4th.

The chain had slipped off the wheel of the cosmos. The great iTunes of the heavens was set on Repeat One.

As supernatural predicaments go it wasn't even that original, given that this exact same thing happened to Bill Murray in *Groundhog Day*. In fact one of the first things I did was watch that movie about eight times, and while I appreciate its wry yet tender take on the emotional challenges of romantic love, let me tell you, as a practical guide to extricating yourself from a state of chronological stasis it leaves a lot to be desired.

And yes, I watched *Edge of Tomorrow* too. So if I ran into an Omega Mimic, believe me, I knew exactly what to do. But I never did.

If there was a major difference between my deal and *Groundhog Day*, it was probably that unlike Bill Murray I didn't really mind it all that much, at least at first. It wasn't freezing cold. I didn't have to go to work. I'm kind of a loner anyway, so I mostly took it as an opportunity to read a lot of books and play an ungodly amount of video games.

The only real downside was that nobody else knew what was happening, so I had nobody to talk to about it. Everybody around me thought they were living today for the first time ever. I had to put a lot of effort into pretending not to see things coming and acting surprised when they came.

And also it was boiling hot. Seriously, it was like all the air in the world had been sucked away and replaced by this hot, clear, viscous syrup. Most days I sweated through my shirt by the time I finished breakfast. This was in Lexington, Massachusetts, by the way, where I was already stuck in space as well as time, because my parents didn't want to pony up for the second session of summer camp, and my temp job at my mom's accounting firm wouldn't start till next week. So I was already killing time, even as it was.

Only now, when I killed time, it didn't stay dead. It rose from the grave and lived again. I was on zombie time.

Lexington is a suburb of Boston, and as such is composed of a lot of smooth gray asphalt, a lot of green lawns, a lot of pine trees, a bunch of faux-colonial McMansions, and some cute, decorous downtown shoppes. And some Historick Landmarks—Lexington played a memorable though tactically meaningless role in the Revolutionary War, so there's a lot of historical authenticity going on here, as is clearly indicated by a lot of helpful informational plaques.

After the first week or so I had a pretty solid routine going. In the morning I slept through my mom leaving for work; on her way she would drop my impressively but slightly disturbingly athletic little sister at soccer camp, leaving me completely alone. I had Honey Nut Cheerios for breakfast, which you'd think would get boring fast, but actually I found myself enjoying them more and more as time went by. There's a great deal of subtlety in your Honey Nut Cheerio. A lot of layers to uncover.

I learned when to make myself scarce. I found ways to absent myself from the house from 5:17 p.m. to 6:03 p.m., which is when my sister muffed the tricky fast bit in the third movement of Vivaldi's Violin Concerto in A Minor seventeen times straight. I generally skipped out after dinner while my parents—they got divorced a couple of years ago, but my dad was over for some reason, probably to talk about money—had a nastier-than-usual fight about whether or not my mom should take her car into the shop because the muffler rattled when you went over bumps.

It put things in perspective. Note to self: Do not waste entire life being angry about stupid things.

As for the rest of the day, my strategies for occupying myself for all eternity were mostly (a) going to the library, and (b) going to the pool.

Generally I chose option (a). The library was probably the place in Lexington where I felt the most at home, and that's not excluding my actual home, the one where I slept at night. It was quiet at the library. It was air-conditioned. It was calm. Books don't practice violin. Or fight about mufflers.

Plus they smell really good. This is why I'm not much of a supporter of the glorious e-book revolution. E-books don't smell like anything.

With an apparently infinite amount of time at my disposal, I could afford to think big, and I did: I decided to read through the entire fantasy and science fiction section, book by book, in alphabetical order. At the time, that was pretty much my definition of happiness. (That definition was about to change, in a big way, but let's not get ahead of ourselves.) At the point where this story starts it had been August 4th for I would say approximately a month, give or take, and I was up to *Flatland*, which is by a guy named, no kidding, Edwin Abbott Abbott.

Flatland was published in 1884, and it's about the adventures of a Square and a Sphere. The idea is that the Square is a flat, two-dimensional shape, and the Sphere is a round, three-dimensional shape, so when they meet the Sphere has to explain to this flat Square what the third dimension is. Like what it means to have height in addition to length and width. His whole life, the Square has lived on one plane and never looked up, and now he does for the first time and, needless to say, his flat little mind is pretty much blown.

Then the Sphere and the Square hit the road together and visit a one-dimensional world, where everybody is a near-infinitely thin Line, and then a zero-dimensional world, which is inhabited by a single infinitely small Point who sits there singing to himself forever. He has no idea anybody or anything else exists.

After that they try to figure out what the fourth dimension would be like, at which point my brain broke and I decided to go to the pool instead.

You might jump in at this point and say: Hey. Guy. (It's Mark.) Okay, Mark. If the same day is repeating over and over again, if every morning it just goes back to the beginning automatically, with everything exactly the way it was, then you could basically do whatever you want, am I right? I mean, sure, you could go to the library, but you could go to the library *naked* and it wouldn't even matter, because it would all be erased the next day like a shaken Etch A Sketch. You could, I don't know, rob a bank or hop a freight train or tell everybody what you really think of them. You could do *anything you wanted*.

Which was, yes, theoretically true. But honestly, in this heat, who has the energy? What I wanted was to sit on my ass somewhere air-conditioned and read books.

Plus, you know, there was always the super-slight chance that that one time it wouldn't work, that the spell would go away as suddenly and mysteriously as it had arrived, and I would wake up on August 5th and have to deal with the consequences of whatever crazy thing I just did.

I mean, for the time being I was living without consequences. But you can't hold back consequences forever.

Like I was saying, I went to the pool. This is important because it's where I met Margaret, and that's important because after I met her everything changed.

Our neighborhood pool is called Paint Rock Pool. It has a lap area and a kids' area and a waterslide that sometimes actually works and a whole lot of deck chairs where the parents lie around sunning themselves like beached walruses. (Or *walri*. Why not *walri*? These were the kinds of things I had time to think about.) The pool itself is made out of this incredibly rough old concrete that, I'm not kidding, will take your whole skin off if you fall on it.

Seriously. I grew up here and have fallen down on it several thousand times. That shit will flay you.

The whole place is sheltered by huge pine trees, and therefore is sprinkled with pine needles and a very fine dust of canary-yellow pine pollen, which if you think about it is pine trees having sex. I try not to think about it.

I noticed Margaret because she was out of place.

I mean, first I noticed her because she didn't look like anybody else. Most of the people who go to Paint Rock Pool are regulars from the neighborhood, but I'd never seen her before. She was tall, tall as me, five-foot-ten maybe, skinny and very pale, with a long neck and a small round face and lots of kinky black hair. She wasn't conventionally pretty, I guess, in the sense that you would never see anybody who looked like her on TV or in a movie. But you know how there's a certain kind of person—and it's different for everyone—but suddenly when you see them your eye just snags on them,

352 • LEV GROSSMAN

you get caught and you can't look away, and you're ten times more awake than you were a moment ago, and it's like you're a harp string and somebody just plucked you?

For me, Margaret was that kind of person.

And there was something else, too, even beyond that, which was that she was out of place.

Rule number one of the time loop was that everybody behaved exactly the same way every day unless I interacted with them and affected their behavior. Everybody made exactly the same choices and said and did exactly the same things. This went for inanimate objects too: Every ball bounced, every drop splashed, every coin flipped exactly the same. This probably breaks some fundamental law of quantum randomness, but hey, you can't argue with results.

So every time I showed up at the pool at, say, two o'clock, I could count on everybody being in exactly the same place, doing exactly the same thing, every time. It was reassuring in a way. No surprises. It actually made me feel kind of powerful: I literally knew the future. *I, god-emperor of the kingdom of August 4th, knew exactly what everybody was going to do before they did it!*

Which was why I would have noticed Margaret anyway, even if she hadn't been Margaret: She'd never been there before. She was a new element. Actually, the first time I saw her I couldn't quite believe it. I thought maybe something I'd done earlier that day had set off some kind of butterfly-wing chain of events that caused this person to come to the pool when she never had before, but I couldn't think what. I couldn't decide whether or not to say anything to her, and by the time I decided I should, she'd already left. She wasn't there the next day. Or the next.

After a while I let it go. I mean, I had my own life to live. Things to do. I had a lot of ice cream to eat and not get fat from. Also I had this idea that, with an infinite amount of time to play with, maybe I could find a cure for cancer, though after a few days on that I started to think maybe I didn't have sufficient resources to cure cancer, even given an infinity of time.

Also I'm not smart enough by a factor of like a hundred. Anyway I could always come back to that one.

But when Margaret came back a second time, I wasn't going to let her get away. By this time I'd seen the same day play out at the pool about twenty times, and it was getting a little monotonous. Heavy lies the head that wears the god-emperor's crown. I was ready for something unexpected. Talking to strange beautiful girls is not something I excel at particularly, but this seemed important.

Anyway, if I said something stupid she'd just forget about it tomorrow.

I watched her for a while first. One of the evergreen features of August 4th at Paint Rock Pool was that every day at 2:37 one of the kids playing catch with a tennis ball massively overthrew it, so that it was not only uncatchable but also cleared the fence at the back of the pool, at which point it was essentially unrecoverable, because beyond that fence was a perilously steep and rocky gully, and then beyond that was Route 128. Nothing that went over that fence ever came back.

But not today, because along came Margaret—just casually; I would even say she was *sauntering*—wearing a bikini top and denim shorts and a straw sun hat, and when the kid threw she reached up on her tiptoes—flashing her even paler shaved underarm—and snagged the ball out of the air with one long skinny arm. She didn't even look at it, just pulled it down, flipped it back into the pool, and kept walking.

It was almost like she knew what was coming too. The kid watched her go.

"Thank you," he said, in a weirdly accurate impression of Apu from *The Simpsons*. "Come again!"

I saw her lips move as she walked: She said it too—"Thank you, come again"—right along with him. It was like she was reading it off the same script. She plopped down on a deck chair and reclined it all the way back, then changed her mind and hiked it back up a notch. I went over and sat down on the deck chair next to hers. Because I'm smooth like that.

"Hi."

She turned her head, shading her eyes against the sun. Up close she was even prettier and more string-plucking than I'd thought, with a spray of freckles splashed across the bridge of her nose.

"Hi?" she said.

"Hi. I'm Mark."

"Okay."

Like she was granting me the point: Yes, fair enough, your name might well be Mark.

"Look, I don't know how to put this exactly," I said, "but would you happen to be trapped in a temporal anomaly? Like right now? Like there's something wrong with time?"

"I know what a temporal anomaly is."

Sunlight flashed off sapphire pool-water. People yelled.

"What I mean is—"

"I know what you mean. Yes, it's happening to me too. The thing with the repeating days. Day."

"Oh. Oh my God!" A massive wave of relief broke over me. I didn't see it coming. I fell back on my deck chair and closed my eyes for a second. I think I actually laughed. "Oh my God. Oh my God. Oh my God."

I think up until that moment I hadn't even understood how deeply freaked out I was, and how alone with that feeling I'd been. I mean, I was having a perfectly fine time, but I was also really starting to think that I was going to be stuck forever in August 4th and that no one but me would ever know it. No one would ever believe it. Now at least somebody else would know.

Though she didn't seem nearly as excited about it as I did. I would almost say she was a little blasé.

I bounced back up.

"I'm Mark," I said again, forgetting that I'd already said it.

"Margaret."

I actually shook her hand.

"It's crazy, right? I mean, at first I couldn't believe it. I mean can you seriously believe it?" I was babbling. "How messed up is this? Right? It's like magic or something! Like it seriously doesn't make any sense!"

I took a deep breath.

"Have you met anybody else who knows?"

"Nope."

"Do you have any idea why this is happening?"

"How would I know?"

"I don't know. I don't know! Sorry, just a little giddy here. I'm just so, so glad you're in this too. I mean not that I'm glad you're trapped in time or anything, but Jesus, I thought I was the only one! Sorry. It's going to take me a second." Deep breath. "So what have you been doing with yourself this whole time? Besides going to the pool?"

"Watching movies, mostly. And I'm teaching myself to drive. I figure it doesn't matter if I mess up the car because it'll just be fixed in the morning."

I found her hard to read. It was weird. Granted, I was hysterical, but she was the opposite. Strangely calm. It was almost like she'd been expecting me.

"Have you?" I said. "Messed up the car?"

"Yes, actually. And our mailbox. I still suck at reverse. My mom was pretty pissed off about it, but then the entire universe reset itself that night and she forgot, So. What about you?"

"Reading mostly."

I told her about my project at the library. And about the curing cancer thing.

"Wow, I didn't even think of that. I guess I've been thinking small."

"I didn't get very far with it."

"Still. Points for trying."

"Maybe I should scale it down and just go after athlete's foot or something."

"Or pinkeye maybe."

"Now you're talking."

We sat in silence for a minute. Here we were, the last boy and girl on earth, and I couldn't think of anything to say. I kept getting distracted by her long legs in those shorts. Her fingernails were plain, but she'd painted her toenails black.

"So you're new, right?" I said. "Did you just move here or something?"

"Couple of months ago. We're in that new development on Tidd Road, across the highway. Technically I think we're not even eligible to come here, but my dad fudged it. Look, I gotta go."

She stood up. I stood up. That was a thing I would learn about Margaret: Even with an infinity of time available, she always seemed to have to go.

"Can I have your number?" I said. "I mean, I know you don't know me, but I feel like we should probably, you know, stay in touch. Maybe try to figure this thing out. It might go away all by itself. But then again, maybe it won't."

She thought about that.

"Okay. Give me your number."

I did. She texted me back so I'd have hers. The text said *it's me*.

I didn't text Margaret for a few days. I got the impression that she liked her personal space, and that she wasn't necessarily overjoyed at the prospect of spending forever with a person of my undeniable dorkiness. I'm not one of your self-hating nerds or anything; I'm comfortable with my place in the social universe. But I get that I'm not everybody's idea of the perfect guy to spend an infinite amount of time with.

I lasted till four in the afternoon on day five A.M. (After Margaret).

Four o'clock was about when the repetitiveness of it all started to get to me. At the library, I watched the same old guy clump up to the circulation desk with his walker. I heard the same library flunky walk by with the same squeaky cart. The same woman with hay fever disputed a late fee while having a sneezing fit. The same four-year-old had an operatic meltdown and got dragged out of the building.

The problem was that it was all starting to seem less and less real—the endless repetition was kind of leaching the realness out of everything. Things were mattering less. It was fun to just do whatever I wanted all the time, with no responsibilities, but the thing was, the people around me were starting to seem slightly less like people with actual thoughts and feelings, which I knew they were, and slightly more like extremely lifelike robots.

So I texted Margaret. Margaret wasn't a robot. She was real, like me. An awake person in a world of sleepwalkers.

Hey! It's Mark. How's it going?

It was about five minutes before she got back to me; by then I'd gone back to reading *The Restaurant at the End of the Universe* by Douglas Adams.

Can't complain.

Getting dangerously bored here. You at the pool?

I was driving. Jumped the curb. Hit another mailbox.

Ow. Good thing time is busted.

Good thing.

I thought that brought things to a nice, rounded conclusion, and I wasn't expecting anything more, but after another minute I got the three burbling dots that meant she was typing again.

You at the library?

Yup.

I'll swing by. 10 mins.

Needless to say, this outcome greatly exceeded my expectations. I waited for her out on the front steps. She drove up in a silver VW station wagon with a scrape of orange paint on the passenger-side door.

I was so glad to see her I wanted to hug her. It took me by surprise again. It was just such a relief not to have to pretend anymore—that I didn't know what was coming next, that it hadn't all happened before, that I wasn't clinging to a sense that things mattered by my absolute fingernails. Probably falling in love is always a little like that: You discover that one other person who understands what no one else seems to, which is that the world is broken and can never, ever be fixed. You can stop pretending, at least for a little while. You can both admit it, if only to each other.

Or maybe it's not always like that. I don't know. I've only done it once. Margaret got out and sat down next to me.

"Hi."

"Hi," I said.

"So. Read any good books lately?"

"As it happens I have, but hang on. Wait. Watch this."

The collision happened every day, right here on this spot. I'd seen it at least five times. Guy staring at his phone versus other guy staring at his phone and walking his dog, a little dachshund. The leash catches the first guy right in the ankles and he has to windmill his arms and do a little hopping dance to keep from falling over, which gets him even more wrapped up in the leash. The dog goes nuts.

It went perfectly, the way it always did. Margaret snorted with laughter. It was the first time I'd seen her laugh.

"Does he ever actually fall over?"

"I've never seen it happen. Once I yelled at them—like, Watch out! Sausage dog! Incoming! And the guy looked at me like, Come on, of course I saw the guy with the dog. That would *never happen* in a *million years*. So now I just let them do it. Besides, I think the dog enjoys it."

We watched the traffic.

"Wanna drive around for a while?" she asked.

"I don't know." I played hard to get. Because I'm smooth like that. "You don't make it sound like the world's safest activity."

"What can I tell you? Life's full of surprises." Margaret was already walking to the car. "I mean, not our lives. But life generally."

We got into the station wagon. It smelled like Margaret, only more so. We cruised past the many olde-timey shops of Lexington Center.

"Anyway," she said, "if we die in a heap of hot screaming metal, we'll probably just be reincarnated in the morning."

"Probably. See, it's the *probably* part that worries me."

"Actually I've been thinking about that, and I'm pretty sure we'd come back. Other people do. I mean, think about how many people in the world die every day. If they didn't all come back, then all those people would turn up dead in the morning when the world reset. Or they'd be vanished or Raptured or something. Either way, somebody would have noticed by now. Ergo, they must get resurrected."

"And then die again. Jesus, people must be having to die over and over again. I wonder how many."

"One hundred fifty thousand," she said. "I looked it up. That's how many people die every day, on average."

I tried to picture them. A thousand people standing in a line, all marching off a cliff. And then a hundred fifty of those lines.

"God, imagine if you had a really painful death," I said. "Or even just a really shitty day, like you're sick and suffering. Or you get fired. Or somebody dumps you. You'd get dumped over and over again. That would be horrible. Seriously, we have to fix this."

She didn't seem interested in pursuing this line of inquiry. In fact, she went stone-faced when I said it, and it occurred to me for the first time to wonder whether August 4th might be not as simple a day for her as it was for me.

"Sorry, that was getting a little depressing," I said.

"Yeah," she said. "Probably lots of good things are happening over and over again, too."

"That's the spirit."

We'd reached the edge of town. It's not a big town. Margaret took an on-ramp onto Route 2.

"Where are we going?" I asked.

"Nowhere special."

It was, as always, a blazing hot afternoon, and the highway

was clogged with rush hour traffic.

"I used to listen to the radio," she said, "but I'm already sick of all the songs."

"I wonder how far this thing goes. Like, is it just Lexington that's in the time loop, or is it the entire planet that's stuck like this? Or is it the entire universe? Wouldn't it have to be the entire universe? Black holes and quasars and exoplanets, all resetting themselves every day, with us in the middle of it? And we're the only beings in the whole universe who know about it?"

"That's kinda egocentric, don't you think?" she said. "Probably there are a couple of aliens out there who know about it too."

"Probably."

"Actually I was thinking, if it is just a local thing, maybe if we went far enough we'd get outside the field or zone or whatever it is and time would go forward again."

"It's worth a try," I said. "Like, just get in the station wagon and floor it and see what happens."

"I was more thinking of getting on an airplane."

"Right."

Though to be honest at that moment I was enjoying just riding in Margaret's car so much that I wasn't sure I wanted time to start working again quite yet. I would've been happy to repeat these five minutes a few hundred times. She turned off the highway.

"I lied before. About where we're going. I want to show you something."

She turned into a sandy parking lot. Gravel crackled under the tires. I knew where we were: It was the parking lot for the Wachusett Reservoir. My dad took me here all the time when I was little and he was teaching me how to fish. It's stocked with zillions of pumpkinseed sunfish. Though once I passed puberty I developed empathy with the fish and refused to do it anymore.

Margaret checked her watch.

"Shit. Come on, we're going to miss it."

She actually took off running through the thin pine woods around the reservoir. She was fast—those long legs—and I didn't catch up with her till she stopped suddenly a few yards short of the brown sandy beach. She put a hand on my arm. It was the first time she ever touched me. I remember what she was wearing: a T-shirt, orange washed to a pale sherbet peach, with an old summer camp logo on it. Her fingers were unexpectedly cool.

"Look."

The water was glittering with beads of molten gold in the late afternoon. The air was still, though you could hear the drone of the highway in the background.

"I don't—"

"Wait. Here it comes."

It came. A hawk swooped down out of the air, a dense, danger-ous bundle of dark feathers. It hit the water hard, back-winged fran-tically for a second, spraying jeweled droplets everywhere, then beat furiously back into the sky with a flashing, wriggly pumpkin-seed sunfish twisting in its claws and was gone.

The hot, dusty afternoon was as still and empty as before. The whole thing had taken maybe twenty seconds. It was the kind of thing that reminded you that a day you'd already lived through fifty times could still surprise you. Margaret turned to me.

"Well?"

"*Well?* That was amazing!"

"Wasn't it?" Her smile could have stopped time all on its own. "I saw it just by chance the other day. I mean today, but you know. The other today."

"Thank you for showing it to me. It happens every time?"

"Exactly the same time. 4:22 and thirty seconds. I've watched it three times already."

"It almost makes being stuck in time worthwhile."

"Almost." Then she thought of something and her smile faded a little. "It almost does."

Margaret dropped me off at the library—I'd left my bike there—and that was that. I didn't ask her out or anything. I figured it was quite enough that she was trapped in time with me. It's not like we could avoid each other. We were like two castaways, except instead of being stranded on a desert island we were stranded in a day.

Because I am a person of uncommon strength of will, I didn't text her again till two days later.

> Found another one. Back stairs of library—the ones in the parking lot—11:37:12.

> Another what?

> One. Come.

She didn't answer, but I waited for her anyway, just in case. I didn't have anything better to do. And she came, the boatlike station wagon heeling into the parking lot at 11:30. She parked in the shade.

"What is it?" she said. "Like another hawk?"

"Keep your voice down, I don't want to screw it up."

"Screw what up?"

I pointed.

The rear entrance of the library had concrete stairs leading down to the parking lot. There was nothing particularly extraordinary about the stairs, but they had that mysterious Pythagorean quality that attracts fourteen-year-old skateboarders like a magnet attracts iron filings. They flocked to it like vultures to a carcass. They probably showed up the second the concrete was dry.

"That's the thing?" she said. "Skate rats are the thing?"

"Just watch."

Each kid took his or her turn going down the steps, one after the other, did his or her thing, then walked back up the wheelchair ramp and got back in line. It never stopped.

"Okay," I said. "So what do you notice about these skate rats?"

"What do you mean?" Margaret was visibly unintrigued.

"What do they all have in common?"

"That ironically, despite the fact that skateboarding defines their very identity, they all suck at it?"

"Exactly!" I said. "The iron law of skate rats the world over is that they never, ever land that one trick they're always trying to land. Now look."

A skateboarder rolled toward the top of the steps, knees bent, jumped, and his skateboard went clattering off at a random angle without him. Cue next skater. And the next. And the next.

I checked my watch. 11:35.

"Two more minutes," I said. "Sorry, I figured you'd be late. How's everything else?"

"Not bad."

"How's the driving?"

"Great. I need a new challenge. It's between juggling and electrical engineering."

"Gotta be practical. Juggling's the future."

"It's the sensible choice."

A skater went down, a potentially ugly fall, but she rolled out of it and came up fine. The next one chickened out before he even got to the top of the steps.

"Okay, two more." Miss. "One more." Miss. "Okay. Showtime!"

The next turn belonged to a round-faced, thick-bodied kid with a dark hair-helmet under his real helmet, whom we'd already seen muff a few tricks. His face was set and determined. He pushed off, found his balance, set his feet, crouched down, hit the steps, and jumped.

His board flipped once, then came down hard on the railing in a perfect grind. Seriously, it was like in a video game—this was like X Games–level shit. The kid grinded all the way down the rail, ten feet in one long second, arms out wide. The first time I saw it I figured that was it. He'd nailed the trick, that was enough; his name would live in song and story forever. But no, it wasn't enough. He had to go for all the glory: a full 360 flip out of the grind.

With an athleticism that seemed to have nothing to do with his pale, doughy physique, he popped off the rail and into the air, levitating while his board spun wildly along both axes. Then *wham!*— he stomped down on it, both feet. And he stuck it.

He stuck it! The board bowed so deeply it looked like it was going to snap, but he kept his feet, and as he straightened up . . .

his face! He couldn't believe it! He made the happiest face that it is anatomically possible for a human to make.

"Oh my God!" He held up both fists. *"Oh my fucking God!"*

The rats came pouring down the steps. They mobbed him. It was, and might quite possibly always be, the greatest moment of his life.

"Tell me that wasn't worth it," I said.

Margaret nodded solemnly. She was looking at me differently than she had before. She seemed to be seeing me, really paying attention to me, for the first time.

"It was worth it. You were right. It was a perfect thing."

"Like the hawk."

"Like the hawk. Come on, let's go get something expensive and bad for us for lunch."

We got the most brutally fattening thing we could find, which was bacon cheeseburgers—extra bacon, extra cheese. That was the day we came up with the idea for the map of tiny perfect things.

It's tough getting through daily life, finding stuff that doesn't suck to take pleasure in—and that's in normal life, where every twenty-four hours you get a whole fresh new day to work with. We were in a tougher situation, because we had to make do with the same day every single day, and that day was getting worn pretty thin.

So we got serious about it. The hawk and the skate rat were just the beginning. Our goal was to find every single moment of beauty, every tiny perfect thing, that this particular August 4th had to offer. There had to be more: Moments when, for just a few seconds, the dull coal of reality was compressed by random chance into a glittering diamond of awesomeness. If we were going to stay sane, we were going to have to find them all. We were going to have to mine August 4th for every bit of perfection it had.

"We have to be super-observant," Margaret said. "Stay in the moment. We can't just be alive, we have to be super-alive."

In addition to being super-alive we were going to be organized. We bought a snazzy fountain pen and a big foldy survey map of Lexington and spread it out on a table in the library. Margaret found the spot on the Wachusett Reservoir and wrote "HAWK" and "16:32:30" on it in snazzy purple ink. (Military time made it seem that much more official.) On the spot marking the rear steps of the library, I wrote "11:37:12" and "SKATE RAT."

We stepped back to admire our work. It was a start. We were a team: Mark and Margaret against the world.

"You realize that when the world resets in the morning the whole map's going to be erased," she said.

"We'll have to remember it. Draw it again from scratch every day."

"How do you think we should go looking for them? The perfect things?"

"I don't know," I said. "Just keep our eyes open, I guess."

"Live in the now."

"Just because it's a cliché doesn't mean it's not true."

"Maybe we can work in sectors," she said. "Like divide the town into a grid, then divide the squares of the grid between the two of us, then make sure we've observed each square at every moment in the twenty-four-hour cycle, so we don't miss anything."

"Or we could just walk around."

"That's good too."

"You know what this reminds me of?" I said. "That map in *Time Bandits*."

"Okay. I have no idea what that means."

"Oh my God! If the universe stopped just so I could make you watch *Time Bandits*, then I think it's all worth it."

Then I started trying to explain to her what it said in *Flatland* about the fourth dimension, but it turned out I was totally man-splaining, because not only had she already read *Flatland* but also, unlike me, she actually understood it. So she explained it to me.

"We're three-dimensional, right?"

"I'm with you so far."

"Now look at our shadows," she said. "Our shadows are flat. Two-dimensional. They're one dimension down from us, just like in a flat universe the shadow of a two-dimensional being would be a one-dimensional line. Shadows always have one fewer dimensions than the thing that cast them."

"Still with you. I think."

"So if you want to imagine the fourth dimension, just imagine something that would cast a three-dimensional shadow. We're like the shadows of four-dimensional beings."

"Oh wow." My flat little mind, like the Square's, was getting blown. "I thought the fourth dimension was supposed to be time or something."

"Yeah, that turned out to be a made-up idea. They've even worked out what a three-dimensional representation of a four-dimensional cube might look like. It's called a hypercube. Here, I'll draw one for you. Although with the caveat that my drawing will be merely two-dimensional."

I accepted this caveat. She drew it. It looked like this:

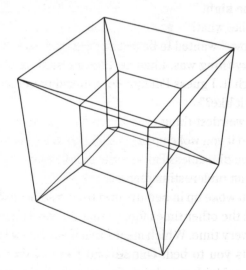

I stared at the drawing for a long time. It didn't look all that four-dimensional, though I guess how would I know?

"Do you think," I said, "that this whole time loop was somehow created by superior four-dimensional beings with the power to ma-nipulate the fabric of three-dimensional space-time itself? That they folded our entire universe into a loop as easily as we would make a Möbius strip out of a piece of paper?"

She pursed her lips. She took the idea more seriously than it probably deserved.

"I'd be a little disappointed if it was," she said finally. "You'd think they'd have something better to do."

She texted me two days later.

Corner of Heston and Grand, 7:27:55.

I got there at 7:20 the next morning, with coffee. She was already there.

"You're up early," I said.

"Didn't sleep. I wanted to see if anything weird happened in the middle of the night."

"Weird like what?"

"You know. I wanted to be awake when the world rolls back."

The crazy thing was, I had never even tried that. I had always slept through it. I guess I'm more of a morning person.

"What's it like?"

"It's the weirdest thing ever. Every day has to start exactly the same way, so if you woke up in your bed on August 4th—which I'm assuming you did, unless I'm severely underestimating you—"

"You're not underestimating me."

"So if you woke up in bed the first time, you have to wake up in your bed all the other times too, so that the day starts exactly the same way every time. Which means that if you're not in bed at midnight, it puts you to bed. One second I was sitting on the floor dicking around with my phone, the next the lights were off and I was under the covers. It's like there's some invisible cosmic nanny who grabs you and tucks you in."

"That really is the weirdest thing ever," I said.

"Plus, when you hit midnight, the date on your phone doesn't change."

"Right."

"I guess that part's not that weird."

"So what are we looking for here?"

"I don't want to spoil it," she said. "I think that should be part of the rules. You have to see it fresh."

Heston and Grand was a busy intersection, or busy enough that it had a stoplight. It was weird to see rush hour traffic—everybody heading off to work, so urgent and focused, mocha Frappuccino in the cup holder, to do all the stuff they'd already done yesterday, which would get undone again at midnight. To make all the money they would unknowingly give back overnight.

7:26.

"I don't know why I feel nervous," she said. "I mean, it pretty much automatically has to happen."

"It's going to happen. Whatever it is."

"Okay, watch for the break in traffic. Here we go."

Lights changed somewhere upstream, and the road emptied out. A lone black Prius turned off a side street and rolled up at the red light right in front of us.

"Is that it?"

"Yup. Look who's driving."

I squinted at it. The driver did look weirdly familiar.

"Wait. That's not . . . ?"

"I'm pretty sure it is."

"It's whatshisname, Harvey Dent from *The Dark Knight*!"

"No," she said patiently, "it's not Aaron Eckhart."

"Wait. I can get this." I snapped my fingers a couple of times. "It's that guy who gets his head cut off in *Game of Thrones*!"

"Yes!"

It was Sean Bean. Actual Sean Bean, the actor. Realizing he'd been spotted, he gave us his trademark rueful, lopsided grin and a half-wave. Then the light changed and he rolled on.

We watched him go.

"Weird to see him with his head back on," I said.

"I know. But so, what do you think?"

"I liked him better as the guy who threw up in *Ronin*."

"I mean what do you *think*? Is it mapworthy?"

"Oh, definitely. Let's map it."

We went back to her house to redraw the map and watch *Time Bandits*, which she still hadn't seen. Her parents weren't there; her mom had left for a business trip that morning, and her dad was always away at the same yoga retreat, forever.

But she was exhausted from having stayed up all night, and she fell asleep on the couch five minutes in, before the dwarfs even show up. Before the little boy even realizes that the world he lives in is magic.

It was like a big Easter egg hunt. Margaret got the next one, too: a little girl who made one of those enormous soap bubbles, the kind you make with two sticks and a loop of string, that always pop after like two seconds, only this one didn't. It was huge, approximately the same size as she was, and it drifted low over Lexington Green, undulating like a weird, translucent ghost amoeba, farther and farther, past where you could even believe it hadn't popped yet, before it finally crossed a sidewalk and met its end on a parked car.

I found another one two days later: a single cloud, alone in the sky, that for about a minute, seen from the corner of Hancock and Greene, looked exactly like a question mark. But I mean *exactly*. Like someone had typed it in the sky.

A full five days later she saw two cars pulled up next to each other at a light. License plates: 997 WON and DER 799. The next day I found a four-leaf clover in a field behind my old elementary school, but we disallowed it. Not moment-y enough somehow. Didn't count.

That night, though, about eight o'clock, I was biking the streets at random when I saw a woman walking by herself. Thirtyish, heavyset, dressed like a receptionist at a real estate agency. Somebody must have texted her, because she looked at her phone and stopped dead. For a terrible second she squatted down and covered her eyes with one hand, like the news had hit her in the stomach so hard she could barely stand.

But then she straightened up again, raised a fist in the air, and ran off into the night singing "Eye of the Tiger" at the top of her lungs. Good voice, too. I never found out what the text was, but it didn't matter.

That one was fragile: The first time I tried to show it to Margaret we ended up distracting the woman and she didn't even notice the text. The second time she got the text but apparently didn't want to sing "Eye of the Tiger" in front of us. In the end, we had to hide behind a hedge for Margaret to get the full effect.

We wrote them all down. CAT ON TIRE SWING (10:24:24). SCRABBLE (14:01:55)—some guy playing in the park made *quixotic* on a triple word score. LITTLE BOY SMILING (17:11:55)—he's just sitting there smiling about something; you kind of had to be there.

It wasn't all about the perfect things. We did other things, too, that had nothing to do with any of this stuff. We had contests: Who could come up with the most cash in one day without actually taking it out of the bank. (I could, by selling my mom's car on Craigslist while she was at work. Sorry, Mom!) Who could acquire the best new skill that we'd never tried before even once. (I won that one, too. I played "Auld Lang Syne" very badly on the saxophone; she spent the day trying and increasingly furiously failing to ride a unicycle.) Who could get on TV. (She won by talking her way into the local news station, posing as a summer intern, and then "accidentally" walking on set while they were live. They got so many e-mails from people who enjoyed her cameo that by the end of the day they'd offered her an actual internship. That was Margaret for you.)

I couldn't have cared less who won. With all apologies to the rest of humanity who were forced to repeat August 4th over and over again like so many lifelike animatronic automatons, being stuck in time with Margaret was better than any real time I'd ever had in my life. I was like the Square in *Flatland*: I had finally met a Sphere, and for the first time in my life I was looking up and seeing what a crazy, enormous, beautiful world I'd been living in without even knowing it.

And Margaret was enjoying it, too, I knew she was. But it was different for her, because as time passed—I mean, it didn't, but you know what I'm saying—I began to wonder if there was something else going on in her life, too, something she didn't talk about and that

I didn't know how to ask her about. You could see it in little things she did or didn't do. She checked her phone a lot. At odd moments her eyes went distant, and she got distracted. She always left a bit early. When I was with her, I was only ever thinking about her, but it wasn't like that for Margaret. Her world was more complicated than that.

We finally watched *Time Bandits*, anyway. It holds up pretty well, though I don't think she liked it as much as I did. Maybe you have to see it as a kid, the first time. But she liked Sean Connery.

"Apparently it said in the script, 'This character looks just like Sean Connery but a lot cheaper,'" I said. "And then Sean Connery read the script and called them up and said, 'Let's do it.'"

"That must have been a perfect moment. But I don't get why he comes back at the—"

"Stop! Nobody knows! It's one of the great mysteries of the universe! Forbidden knowledge. We shouldn't even be talking about it."

We were on the foam couch in her family's rec room, which had a thinly carpeted concrete floor and one glass wall that looked out at a big backyard.

I'd spent most of the previous hour inching imperceptibly sideways on the couch, nanometer by nanometer, and then subtly shifting my weight so that my shoulder rested against hers and we were sort of leaning against each other. It felt like some cool sparkly energy was flowing out of her and into me and lighting me up from the inside. I felt like I was glowing. Like *we* were glowing.

I don't think anybody in the history of cinema has ever enjoyed a movie as much as I enjoyed *Time Bandits* that night. Roger Ebert watching *Casablanca* could not have enjoyed it one-tenth as much.

"Margaret, can I ask you something?" I said.

"Of course."

"Do you ever miss your parents? I mean, I can hang out with mine pretty much whenever I want—and anyway, where my parents are concerned, a little of that goes a long way. But you hardly see yours at all. That's got to be hard."

She nodded, looking down at her lap.

"Yeah. That's kind of hard."

Her corkscrewy hair fell down over her face. It reminded me of double helices, of DNA, and I thought about how, somewhere inside them, there were tiny corkscrew-shaped molecules containing the magic formula for how to make corkscrewy hair. How to make Margaret.

"Do you want to go find them? I mean, we could probably track them down inside of twenty-four hours. Hit that yoga retreat."

"Forget it." She shook her head, not looking at me. "Forget it. We don't have to."

"I know we don't have to, I just thought . . ."

She still wasn't looking at me. I'd hit some kind of a nerve, a raw one that led off somewhere that I didn't quite understand. It hurt me a bit that she wouldn't or couldn't say where. But she didn't owe me any explanations.

"Sure. Okay. I just wish you'd gotten a better day, that's all. I don't know who it was that chose this day, but I question their taste in days."

She half smiled; literally, one half of her mouth smiled and the other didn't.

"Somebody has to have bad days," she said. "I mean statistically. Or the bell curve would get all messed up. I'm just doing my part here."

She took my hand—she picked it up off my lap in both of hers and sort of it squeezed it. I squeezed her hand back, trying to keep breathing normally while my heart blew up inside me a hundred times. Everything went still, and I almost think something might have happened—like that might have been the moment—except that I immediately blew it.

"Listen," I said, "I had an idea for something we could try."

"Does it involve unicycling? Because I'm telling you, I never want to see another of those one-wheeled devil-cycles in my life."

"I don't think so." I kept waiting for her to put my hand down, but she didn't. "You remember you had that idea once, where we travel as far as we can and see if we can get outside the zone where the time loop is happening? I mean, assuming it's limited to a zone?"

She didn't answer right away, just kept looking out at her

backyard, which was getting darker and darker in the summer twilight.

"Margaret? Are you okay?"

"No, right, I remember." She let go of my hand. "It's a good plan. We should do it. Where should we go?"

"I don't know. I don't think it matters that much. I figure we should just head straight to the airport and get on the longest flight we can find. Tokyo or Sydney or something. But you're sure you're okay?"

"Absolutely. Absolutely okay."

"We don't have to. It probably won't work. I just thought we should try everything."

"We absolutely should. Everything. Definitely. Let's not do it tomorrow, though."

"No problem.

"Day after, maybe."

"Whenever you're ready."

She nodded, three quick nods, as if she'd made up her mind. "The day after tomorrow."

We couldn't start out before midnight, because of the cosmic nanny effect, but we agreed that at the stroke of midnight we would both leap out of bed and she would immediately book us flights on Turkish Airlines to Tokyo, leaving Logan Airport at 3:50 a.m., which was the earliest flight to somewhere really far away that we could find. Margaret had to be the one to do it because she had a debit card, because she had a joint bank account with her parents, which I didn't. I promised I would hit her back if it worked.

Then I snuck out into the warm, grassy-smelling night to wait and be attacked by numberless mosquitoes. There was no moon; August 4th was a new moon. Margaret came rolling up with the lights off.

It felt close and intimate, being in her car with her in the middle of the night. In fact it was the most boyfriendy I'd ever felt with Margaret, and even though I was not in actual fact her boyfriend, it was a thrilling feeling. We didn't talk till we were cruising along the empty highway, surfing the rolling hills on the way into Boston, under the indifferent, insipid orange gaze of the sodium streetlights.

"If this works, my parents are going to think we ran away together," she said.

"I didn't even think about that. I left mine a note saying I caught the bus into Boston for the day."

"I'm just picturing my dad saying over and over that it's okay if I'm pregnant, he totally understands, he just wants to talk about it."

"The Tokyo thing's going to be the weirdest part. Like, where did that come from?"

"I'm going to say it was your idea," Margaret said. "You were tired of reading imported manga; you wanted to go straight to the source."

"It's cool that you're so supportive of my enthusiasms."

We were joking, but I knew—really knew right then—that I was in love with Margaret. I wasn't joking, I was completely serious. I would have run away to Tokyo with her anyway, like a shot, for no reason at all. But I told myself I wasn't going to say anything, I wasn't going to do anything about it, till the time thing was fixed. I didn't want her to feel like she was stuck with me. I wanted it to count.

Also, yeah, I was terrified. I had never been in love before. I had never wagered this much of my heart before. As badly as I wanted to win, I was even more scared of losing.

Gazing out the car window at the black trees against the light-pollution-gray sky, I thought about how much I would miss August 4th, our day, if this worked. Mark and Margaret Day. The pool, the library, the tiny perfect things. Maybe this was crazy. After all, I had time and I had love. I had it all, I had everything, and I was throwing it away, and for what? For real life? For getting old and dying like everybody else?

But yeah: everybody else. Everybody in the world who wasn't getting to live their lives. They were getting robbed of everything, every day. My parents, getting up day after day after day and doing the exact same things, over and over again. Having their stupid fight about the car. My sister practicing her Vivaldi and never getting any better. Did it matter, if they didn't know it? I wanted to think that maybe it didn't. But I knew that it did.

And I knew that, deep down, I'd had enough of living without consequences too. Low-stakes living, where nothing mattered and all your wounds healed over the next morning, no scars. I needed something more. I was ready to go back to real life. I was ready to go anywhere, if it was with Margaret.

And it would be good to see the moon again.

This late at night the airport was almost empty. We collected our tickets from the kiosks and wandered through security. No lines. 3:50 a.m. is the only time to fly. We had no luggage so we breezed through security and just sat at the gate and waited. Margaret didn't feel much like talking, but she rested her head on my shoulder. She was tired, she said. And she didn't like flying.

After a while I went off to find us some Diet Cokes. They called our flight. We shuffled down the jetway with a lot of other tired, disheveled-looking people.

We'd gotten seats together. Margaret seemed more and more out of it, sunk inside herself, staring at the seat back in front of her. She felt far away even though we were sitting right next to each other.

"Are you worried about flying?" I asked. "Because, you know, even if we crash we've still got the whole reincarnation thing going. And anyway, if a plane crashed on August 4th we would've heard about it by now."

"Don't jinx it."

"You know, in a way I hope this doesn't work, because if it does we're going to be out a ton of money. Did you book round-trip?"

I was babbling, like I did the day we met.

"I didn't even think about that," she said. "Though, on the bonus side, if it works we'll have saved the world."

"At least there's that."

I closed my eyes. My numberless mosquito bites itched. We hadn't had a lot of sleep. I liked the idea of falling asleep next to Margaret.

"Though, what if," I said, eyes still closed, "what if the world is going to end on August 5th? What if that's what's happening here? What if somebody made time start repeating exactly *because* the world was about to get hit by an asteroid or something, and that person had, in effect, saved the world by stopping time forever—albeit at a terrible cost—and if we break the time loop, then actually we'll be dooming the Earth to certain destruction?"

She didn't answer. It was a rhetorical question anyway. When I opened my eyes again some Turkish flight attendants were closing the doors. It took me a second to realize that Margaret wasn't in her seat anymore. I thought she must have gone to the bathroom, and I even got up to check on her, but I was immediately herded back to my seat by concerned Turkish Airlines employees.

After five minutes I had to admit it to myself: Margaret was no longer on the plane. She must have run out just as the door was closing.

My phone chimed.

I'm sorry Mark but I just can't I'm sorry

Can't what? Fly to Tokyo? Fly to Tokyo with me? Leave the time loop? *What?* I started texting her back, but a Turkish flight attendant told me to please turn off all phones and portable devices or switch them to airline mode. She said it again in Turkish, for emphasis. I shut down my phone.

We taxied to the runway and took off. It was a long flight to Tokyo—fourteen hours. I watched *Edge of Tomorrow* three times.

After all that, it didn't work. I waited in the gate area at Narita—which looks surprisingly similar to all other airports everywhere, except that everything's in Japanese and the vending machines are more futuristic—until it was midnight in Massachusetts and the cosmic nanny reached out from halfway around the world and put me to bed, back in my house.

When I woke up that morning, I texted Margaret, but she didn't text me back. She didn't text me back the next day, either. I called her, but she didn't answer.

I didn't know what to think, except that she didn't want the time loop to end and, whatever the reason was, it had nothing to do with me. My entire world was just the little bubble I shared with her, but her world was bigger than that. Maybe she had someone else, was all I could think of, because of course everything had to be about me. There was somebody else and she didn't want to leave them behind. To me our life together was a perfect thing, and I couldn't imagine wanting anything else. But she could.

It hurt. I'd had one glorious glimpse of the third dimension, and now I was banished back to flatness forever.

For the first time I wished I was one of the normal people, the zombies, who forgot everything every morning and just went about their business as if it was all fresh and new and for the first time. *Let me go,* I thought at the cosmic nanny. *Let me forget. Let me be one of them. I don't want to be one of us anymore. I want to be a robot.* But I couldn't forget.

I went back to my old routine, back to the library. I still had two more *Hitchhiker's Guide* books to go, and I was nowhere even near done with the A section—I still had Lloyd Alexander and Piers Anthony to go, and beyond them the great desert of Isaac Asimov stretched out into the distance. I spent all day there, except that I went outside at 11:37:12 to watch the skateboarder nail his combo.

In fact I got into the habit of checking in with a couple of our tiny perfect moments every day, which was easy because, obviously, we had a handy map of them. Sometimes I redrew it; sometimes I just went by memory. I watched the hawk score its fish. I waved to Sean Bean at the corner of Heston and Grand. I watched the little girl make her huge bubble. I always hoped I'd see Margaret at one of them, but I never did. I went anyway. It helped me feel sad, which is maybe part of the process of falling out of love, which it was obviously time for me to do. I was getting good at feeling sad.

Or maybe I was just wallowing in self-pity. It's a fine line.

I did catch a glimpse of Margaret once, by chance. I knew it would happen sooner or later; it was only a matter of time (or lack thereof). I was driving through the center, on my way to see the Scrabble game, when I spotted a silver VW station wagon turning a corner a block away. The classy and respectful thing to do would have been to let her go, because she obviously wanted nothing to do with me, but I didn't do the classy thing. I did the other thing. I floored it and made the corner in time to see her turning right on Concord Avenue. I floored it again. Follow that car.

I followed her out to Route 2 and along it as far as Emerson Hospital.

I'd never known Margaret to go to the hospital. She'd never talked about it. It freaked me out a bit. My insides went cold, and the closer we got, the colder they got. I couldn't believe what a stupid jealous bastard I'd been. Maybe Margaret was sick—maybe she'd been sick this whole time and just didn't want to tell me. She didn't want to burden me with it. Oh my God, maybe she had cancer! I should have stuck with trying to cure it! Maybe that was the whole point of this whole thing—Margaret has some rare disease, but then we work together, and because we have the repeating-days thing we have all the time we need, and finally we come up with a cure for it and save her and she falls in love with me . . .

But no; that wasn't this story. This was a different kind of story.

I waited till she was on her way in, then I parked and got out and followed her. Listen, I know I was being a prying asshole, it's just that I couldn't stop myself. *Please don't let her be sick,* I thought. *She doesn't have to talk to me, she can ignore me for the rest of eternity, she just has to not be sick.*

The lobby was hushed and businesslike. Margaret was nowhere to be seen. I read the signs next to the elevator: Radiology, Surgery, Birthing, Bone and Joint Center, Wound Care . . . After weeks of timelessness it was strange to be here, where so much of time's damage and destruction ends up. There's nowhere less timeless than a hospital.

I tried them all. I finally found her in Cancer.

I didn't speak to her, I just watched. She was sitting on a bench, knee to knee with a woman in a wheelchair who was way too young to look as old as she did. Bald and desperately thin, she was crumpled in a corner of the chair like an empty dress, her head drooping, half awake. Margaret was bent forward, speaking softly to her, though I couldn't tell if the woman was awake or not, with both her gray, thin hands in Margaret's young, vital ones.

It wasn't Margaret, it was her mother. She wasn't on a business trip. She was dying.

I drove home slowly. I knew I shouldn't have followed Margaret to the hospital, that I had no business intruding on her private tragedy, but at least now I understood. It made sense of everything: Why Margaret always had somewhere else to be. Why she was so distracted. Why she didn't want to escape the time loop. The time loop was the only reason her mother was still alive.

I still didn't understand why Margaret had kept it a secret, but that didn't really matter. This wasn't about me. I thought I was the hero of this story, or at least the second lead, but I was nowhere near it. I was just a bit player. I was singing in the chorus.

I didn't know what to do with myself, so I stopped in the center of town and bought a map and went home and filled it out. I looked over the tiny perfect things to see what was left. Too late for BOUNCY BALL (09:44:56). Too late for CONSTRUCTION SITE (10:10:34). Still time for REVOLVING DOOR (17:34:19). And good old SHOOTING STAR (21:17:01).

I realized it had been a while since I saw a new perfect thing. Somewhere along the way I'd stopped looking for them. I wasn't super-alive anymore. I'd stopped living in the now. I'd dropped back into the then.

But what was even the point? Suddenly it all seemed kind of silly. Perfect moments, what did they even mean? They were blind luck, that was all. Coincidences. Statistical anomalies. I did some Googling and it turned out somebody had actually bothered to do the math on this, a real actual Cambridge University mathematician named John Littlewood (1885–1977; thank you, Wikipedia). He proposed that if you define a miracle as something with a probability of one in a million, and if you're paying close attention to the world around you eight hours a day, every day, and little things happen around you at a rate of one per second, then you'd observe about thirty thousand things every day, which means about a million things a month. So, on average, you should witness one miracle every month (or every thirty-three-and-one-third days, if we're being strictly accurate). It's called Littlewood's law.

So there you have it, a miracle a month. They're not even that special. I stared at the map anyway, giving particular staring attention to the ones that Margaret had found, such is love. And I did love her. It made it better to understand why she couldn't possibly love me, not now, probably not ever, but I'm not going to pretend it didn't hurt.

The perfect moments were surprisingly evenly distributed. There were fewer of them in the nighttime, because nothing was happening and we weren't really looking anyway, but the rest of the day was evenly filled. There was only one bare patch in the schedule, right around dawn—a bald spot where statistically you would've expected a perfect moment, but we'd never found it.

The longer I stared at the map, the more it looked like there was a pattern in it. I played a game with myself: Pretend that the points on the map were stars in a constellation. What did it look like? Look, no one should ever have to apologize for doing stupid things when the person they love has walked out of their life and they have way too much time on their hands. And I had an eternity of time. I sketched in lines between them. Maybe I could make—what? Her name? Her face? Our initials intertwined in a beautiful romantic love knot?

Nope. When I'd connected all the dots they looked like this:

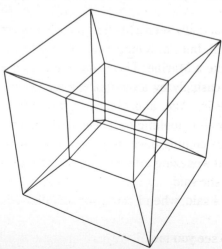

Except not quite. There was one dot missing, down in the lower left corner.

I stared at it, and a funny idea struck me: What if you could use the map not just to remember when and where perfect things happened, but to predict when and where they were *going* to happen? It was a stupid idea, a terrible idea, but I sketched it in with a ruler anyway. The missing dot was right on top of Blue Nun Hill, which I happened to know well because it made an excellent sledding hill in winter, which at this rate it would never be again. Something should really be happening there, and judging by the rest of the schedule, it should be happening right around dawn.

The sun rose at 5:39 a.m. on August 4th, I happened to know. I waited until time flipped at midnight, then I set my alarm for five, to wake up in time for the last tiny perfect thing of them all.

I drove over to Blue Nun Hill in the warm summer darkness. The streets were deserted, the streetlights still on, houses all full of sleeping people resting up so they'd be bright-eyed and bushy-tailed and ready to sleepwalk through another day. It was still full night, not even a hint of blue on the horizon yet. I parked at the bottom of the hill.

I wasn't the only one up. There was a silver station wagon parked there too.

I have never actually seen a Marine or any member of the armed forces take a hill, but I'm telling you, I'm pretty confident that I took that hill like a Marine. There was a big boulder at the top, dropped there casually by a passing glacier ten thousand years ago, during the Ice Age, and Margaret was sitting on it, knees drawn up to her chin, looking out at the darkened town.

She heard me coming because I was doing a lot of un-Marine-like gasping and wheezing after running all the way up the hill.

"Hi, Mark," she said.

"Margaret," I said, when I could sort of talk. "Hi. It's good. To see you."

"It's good to see you too."

"Is it all right if I join you?"

She patted the rock beside her. I boosted myself up. The hill faced east, and the horizon was now glowing a deep, intense azure. We didn't talk for a while, but it wasn't awkward. We were just getting ready to talk, that was all.

"I'm sorry I disappeared like that," she said.

"It's okay," I said. "You're allowed to disappear."

"No, I should explain."

"You don't have to."

"But I want to."

"Okay. But before you do, I have a confession to make."

I told her how I'd followed her to the hospital and spied on her with her mother. It sounded even worse when I said it out loud.

"Oh." She thought about it. "No, I get it. I probably would've done the same thing. Kind of creepy, though."

"I know. It felt that way even at the time, but I couldn't stop myself. Listen, I'm just really sorry. About your mom."

"It's okay."

But she choked on that last word, and her face crumpled, and she crushed her forehead into her knees. Her shoulders shook silently. I rubbed her back. I wished more than anything that I could spend all of my monthly one-in-a-million miracles at once, forever, to make her sadness go away. But things don't work like that.

"Margaret, I'm so sorry. I'm so sorry. I'm so sorry."

Birds were twittering joyfully now, tactlessly, all around us. She busily wiped away tears with the back of her wrist.

"There's something else I have to explain," she said. "The day before this whole thing started I went to see my mother at the hospital, and the doctors told me they were stopping treatment. There was no point—"

She squeaked that last word, and the sadness strangled her again, and she couldn't go on. I put my arm around her shoulders and she sobbed on my neck. I breathed in the smell of her hair. She felt so thin and precious, to have all that grief inside her. She'd had it this whole time, all by herself. I wished I could take it from her, but I knew I couldn't. It was her grief. Only she could carry it.

"When I went to bed that night, all I could think was that I wasn't ready." She swallowed. Her eyes were still red, but they were dry now, and her voice was steady. "I wasn't ready to let go. I'm only sixteen, I wasn't ready to not have a mom. I needed her so much.

"That night, when I went to bed, all I could think was that tomorrow cannot come. Time cannot go on. I am pulling the emergency brake of time. I even said it out loud: 'Tomorrow cannot come.'

"And when I woke up that morning, it was true. It was the same day again. Time had stopped for me. I don't know why; I guess it just didn't have the heart to keep going. Somebody somewhere decided that I needed more time with her. That's why I ran off that plane to Tokyo. I was afraid it would work, and I wasn't ready."

We were silent for a long time after that, while I thought about the love inside Margaret, how much of it there must have been that even time couldn't stand up to it. There were no fourth-dimensional beings. It was Margaret's heart, that was all. It was so strong it bent space-time around it.

"But I knew there was a catch. I always knew it. The catch was that if I fell in love, it would end. Time would roll forward again, like it always does, and it would take my mom along with it. I don't know how, but I knew that was always the deal. When I could fall in love with someone, that's how I would know it was time to say good-bye to her for real.

"I think that's why you're here. For me to fall in love with. That's why you got sucked into this. I knew it as soon as I saw you."

The sun was almost up, the sky was getting bright, and it was like I could feel a sun rising inside me, too, bright and warm, filling my whole self with love. Because Margaret did love me. And at the same time I was crying—the sadness didn't go away, not in the slightest. I was happy and sad, both at once. I thought about what time is, how we're being broken every second, we're losing moments all the time, leaking them away like a stuffed animal losing its stuffing, until one day they're all gone and we lose everything. Forever. And then, at the same time, we're gaining seconds, moment after moment. Every one is a gift, until at the end of our lives we're sitting on a rich hoard of moments. Rich beyond imagining. Time was both those things at once.

I took both Margaret's hands in mine.

"Is it time? Is this the last day?"

She nodded solemnly.

"It's the last one. The last August 4th. I mean, till next year anyway." Tears were streaming down her cheeks again, but she smiled through them. "I'm ready now. It's time."

The sun cracked the edge of the world and began to rise.

"You know what's funny though?" she said. "I keep waiting for the thing to happen. You know, the perfect thing, the last one. The way it's supposed to on the map. But maybe we missed it while we were talking."

"I don't think we missed it."

I kissed her. You can spend your life waiting and watching for perfect moments, but sometimes you have to make one happen.

After a few seconds, the best seconds of my life so far, Margaret pulled away.

"Hang on," she said. "I don't think that was it."

"It wasn't?"

"It wasn't perfect. I had a hair in my mouth."

She swept her hair to one side.

"Okay, kiss me again."

I did. And this time it was perfect.

ACKNOWLEDGMENTS

Thank you to every single reader who picked up my first anthology. It's challenging to find a modern audience for short stories, and I'm thrilled that so many people gave it a chance. I hope you enjoy this collection, too. I'm tremendously proud of it.

Thank you to Kate Testerman. For everything. Thank you to Sara Goodman for being so classy and for teaching me so much about this job. Thank you to Michelle Cashman, Alicia Clancy, Angie Giammarino, Anna Gorovoy, Olga Grlic, Brant Janeway, and Jessica Katz for the additional support and hard work. Thank you to Venetia Gosling, Kat McKenna, and Rachel Petty for rocking it in the UK. Thank you to Jim Tierney for another set of gorgeous illustrations. Thank you to the authors of my first anthology for their continued encouragement. And thank you, especially, to the authors in this anthology for being brilliant, hilarious, ambitious, and kindhearted: Brandy, Cassie, Francesca, Jen, Jon, Leigh, Lev, Libba, Nina, Tim, and Veronica. I have loved working with you all.

Thank you to my family. Always.

And thank you to Jarrod Perkins. Always + always x always.

Leigh Bardugo is the *New York Times* bestselling author of *Six of Crows* and the Grisha trilogy. She was born in Jerusalem, grew up in Los Angeles, and graduated from Yale University. These days, she lives and writes in Hollywood where she can occasionally be heard singing with her band. Visit her online at leighbardugo.com.

Francesca Lia Block is the Margaret A. Edwards Lifetime Achievement Award-winning and bestselling author of *Dangerous Angels: The Weetzie Bat Books* and over twenty-five other works of fiction, non-fiction, and collected short stories and poetry for adults and young adults. She lives in Los Angeles. Visit her online at francescaliablock.com.

Libba Bray is the *New York Times* bestselling author of the Gemma Doyle trilogy, the Michael L. Printz Award-winning *Going Bovine*, the *Los Angeles Times* Book Prize finalist *Beauty Queens*, and the Diviners series. A horror fan who rarely dated in high school (Where was the love, boys of Denton, Texas?), she now lives with her family in New York City. Visit her online at libbabray.com.

Cassandra Clare is the *New York Times* bestselling author of the Mortal Instruments series and Infernal Devices trilogy. She was born overseas and spent her early years traveling around the world with her family and several trunks of books. Cassandra lives in western Massachusetts with her husband, their cats, and these days, even more books. Visit her online at cassandraclare.com.

Brandy Colbert is the author of the critically acclaimed *Pointe*, and two forthcoming young adult novels. She lives and writes in Los Angeles. Visit her online at brandycolbert.com.

Tim Federle left Pittsburgh as a teenager to dance on Broadway before writing his first book for young readers, *Better Nate Than Ever*, followed by a sequel that won the Lambda Literary Award. Tim's YA debut novel, *The Great American Whatever*, was just released. Visit him online at timfederle.com.

Lev Grossman is the author of the *New York Times* bestselling Magicians trilogy. He lives in New York City. Visit him online at levgrossman.com.

Nina LaCour is the author of *Hold Still, The Disenchantments,* and *Everything Leads to You,* and the co-author (with David Levithan) of *You Know Me Well.* She lives in California with her wife and daughter. Visit her online at ninalacour.com.

Stephanie Perkins is the *New York Times* and international bestselling author of *Anna and the French Kiss, Lola and the Boy Next Door,* and *Isla and the Happily Ever After,* as well as the editor of *My True Love Gave to Me: Twelve Winter Romances.* She lives with her husband in Asheville, North Carolina. Visit her online at stephanieperkins.com.

Veronica Roth is the #1 *New York Times* bestselling author of *Divergent, Insurgent, Allegiant,* and *Four: A Divergent Collection.* Now a full-time writer, Ms. Roth and her husband live near Chicago. Visit her online at veronicarothbooks.com.

Jon Skovron is the author of *Struts & Frets, Misfit, Man Made Boy, This Broken Wondrous World,* and most recently, *Hope & Red,* the first book in the Empire of Storms series. He lives just outside Washington DC with his two sons and two cats. Visit him online at jonskovron.com.

Jennifer E. Smith is the author of six novels for young adults, including *Hello, Goodbye, and Everything in Between* and *The Statistical Probability of Love at First Sight.* She earned a master's degree in creative writing from the University of St. Andrews, and her work has been translated into thirty-one languages. Visit her online at jenniferesmith.com.

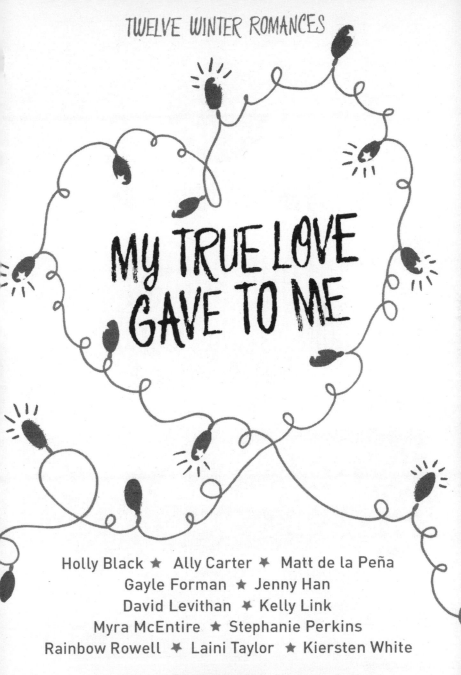

TWELVE WINTER ROMANCES

MY TRUE LOVE GAVE TO ME

Holly Black ★ Ally Carter ✳ Matt de la Peña
Gayle Forman ★ Jenny Han
David Levithan ✳ Kelly Link
Myra McEntire ★ Stephanie Perkins
Rainbow Rowell ✳ Laini Taylor ★ Kiersten White

Edited by STEPHANIE PERKINS